I0693992

THE PRESERVATION OF SPECIES

PART I

RULE OF EXTINCTION

PART II

STRUGGLE FOR EXISTENCE

PART III

BEASTS OF PREY

THE PRESERVATION OF SPECIES

Just before a comet decimated life on Earth, thousands of mysterious capsules delivered people to an orbiting starship, placing some in suspended animation, and depositing others in a menagerie filled with prehistoric specimens.

David, Sierra, and a small group of survivors escaped the mothership in a stolen shuttle, only to find Earth overrun by billions of bug-like monsters known as *gorgers*.

The group returned to the menagerie and rescued David's daughter from Randall, a treacherous murderer who was attempting to build a community he could rule. As they debated Randall's fate, an alien caretaker approached in the night ...

THE PRESERVATION OF SPECIES

PART III

BEASTS OF PREY

GEOFF JONES

For Sydney

BEASTS OF PREY

Man, biologically considered, and whatever else he may
be into the bargain, is simply the most formidable of all
the beasts of prey, and, indeed, the only one that preys
systematically on its own species.

– William James

TRANSFORMATION

Chapter One

David Williams stared into the absolute darkness of night. He and ten other people were gathered in the center of a strange little village in a fucked-up zoo aboard a massive alien spaceship.

Somewhere out there, one of the alien caretakers flew toward them. It had left the superstructure of the mothership and entered the island habitat, flying on a carriage roughly as big as a king-sized bed.

David picked up his son Barry and carried him closer to the big rock fire pit, where Barry's sister, Kim, sat aboard a hovering carriage they'd stolen from the aliens. Kona, their golden retriever, followed him.

Barry clung tightly around his neck. "What's going to happen? What do we do?"

The six-year-old never stopped asking questions.

"We're going to get some answers," Sierra said. She stood in the center of the group holding a huge silver pistol at her side, her arm cocked so its barrel pointed in the air. "We're going to make them tell us everything they know about the gorgers. Then they're going to help us take back Earth."

Kim, who was twelve, sat cross-legged up on the floating platform with an alien device in her lap. She was using it to search through the mothership's storage chamber for her mom, hoping to find her among all the people and animals kept in suspended animation. David struggled to hold out hope. There had only been a few thousand pods and people had been killing each other for them.

Priya sat beside Kim with a device of her own, her face bathed in light from images projected onto her retinas.

"The caretaker is crossing the beach," Priya said, monitoring the alien's approach. "It's headed straight for us."

A half-mile dirt path led through the pine forest to the beach, but the caretaker was undoubtedly flying over the treetops. It would reach the village in two minutes, maybe less.

"What do you think they want?" David asked.

"Maybe they're pissed at us because we captured their turncoat," Cameron said, gesturing toward Randall with a loose gun barrel.

Cameron sat cross-legged on a blanket with an array of firearms spread out before her, all in various states of disassembly. When Priya spotted the approaching alien on her device, Cameron had just finished taking apart the newly-discovered guns to inspect them and clean them. Now, the former Army officer was scrambling to put them back together.

Five people stood around her, waiting for weapons. Sierra and David had rescued three of them after they were accidentally sent back to Earth. The other two were women Randall had brought here, in his disgusting attempt to build a harem.

Randall lay unconscious in front of the village's two storage sheds, at the edge of the bonfire's glow, next to a guy who'd been helping him. Both were in suspended animation, lifeless but somehow still alive, thanks to devices the aliens had implanted in their necks. Vine ropes bound their wrists.

The group had been trying to figure out what to do with them when Priya spotted the alien. As a doctor, David hated the idea of sentencing someone to death, but Randall had killed people and his buddy was guilty of attempted murder. They'd also threatened Kim. It was a terrible situation all around. One of many.

Cameron clicked something into place and handed a pistol to Felicia, a quiet, guarded woman who'd been in the village since the beginning.

"Maybe it's just coming to watch," Felicia said. "All those bastards ever do is watch."

Until David had knocked one of the aliens out of the sky, they'd kept themselves hidden, floating overhead on their carriages, cloaked by an invisible bubble.

"It's flying over the forest," Priya said.

Kim leaned close and some of the lights from Priya's device shifted to the girl's face. She chewed her lip as she watched, then returned to her own device and tapped the flat panel on its lower half.

Sierra turned to the two new women. "You should sit down. It will probably try to stun you."

"Does it hurt?" asked Wanda, a tall redhead.

"No," Sierra said. "But you could get banged up if you collapse."

Wanda grabbed Harmony's wrist, which was covered in bracelets, and pulled her over to sit against the short rock wall of the fire pit.

"Getting it removed from your neck is what hurts," Barry said.

David and Sierra had cut the implants out of everyone's necks except for the two new women.

And Kim.

Kim still had a device in her neck.

"Kim, you have to get down from there," David said. "You could get stunned, too."

She gave him a look that reminded him of his wife. "I'm sitting down, and this carriage is padded. If I get stunned, Priya can wake me up." Even her tone sounded like Lindsey.

She was right. She was just as safe there as anywhere. They could hide in one of the village's huts, but those didn't even have doors. They could go outside the perimeter wall, but unless they took torches, they wouldn't be able to see a thing. Night was pitch black in the menagerie. It was best to sit tight and stay with the others. There was safety in numbers.

Barry squirmed in David's arms. "Toss more wood on the bonfire, Bud," David told him. "We need as much light as possible. I don't want any surprises." He put the boy down, hoping he would stay close as long as he had a job to do. A large stack of firewood curved around half the fire pit.

"Is it still just one of them?" Sierra asked. Her white motorcycle pants and matching leather jacket glowed yellow from the light of the flames.

"Yeah," Kim said. "It's about halfway now."

David's heart swelled with pride. Kim was learning the device quickly. She had a knack for technology.

Cameron snapped a piece of metal in place and handed a pistol to Reggie. "Don't point that at any of us."

Reggie nodded, then winced. His hand went to the back of his neck, where David had sliced out his implant.

Cameron had already begun to assemble the next gun, moving with cool precision. Kona shoved her nose in her face. She glanced up and locked eyes with David. "Quit staring at me, Ace, and get your damn dog out of the way."

David was still mourning his wife, but he'd developed a strong connection with Cameron. Everything about her captivated him, from her no-bullshit attitude to her lean, muscular body. She'd seen him at his worst, more than once, and she liked him anyway, judging from the kiss she'd given him a few days earlier.

"Kona, come," David ordered. The dog padded over, tail wagging.

"It's almost to the village," Priya said.

"Barry, get back over here." David wanted both of his kids close.

Barry tossed another branch onto the fire, which sent up a cascade of sparks, then walked over and wrapped his arms around David's thigh.

"Everyone stay calm when it gets here," Sierra said. "We've got this."

David took a deep breath. Sierra was right. The aliens' entire security system was built around the stunning devices. They'd never needed anything more. Prior to humans, none of the species they'd collected had been able to remove the devices.

"It just crossed the wall," Priya said. "It's over the fields."

David glanced into the dark, where a few acres of tilled dirt covered the lower half of the village.

Cameron popped to her feet, holding a small silver pistol. Reggie and Felicia stood behind her, both holding guns from Randall's cache.

"Check your targets," Cameron growled. "If anyone gets hit by friendly fire, I'll kill you."

"Dad!" Kim shouted.

He spun. Her carriage floated upward.

David stepped up onto the rock wall surrounding the fire pit and reached for her. The edge of the vehicle caught his armpits.

Priya shouted something and rolled off the back. She shrieked as she landed.

"Kim!" David's weight pulled against his arms as his feet left the ground. He clutched the side of the rising carriage like a swimmer at the edge of a pool.

"Priya, stop that sled," Sierra shouted.

Priya didn't answer.

"Dad, help," Kim said. "Should I jump?"

"Yes," he shouted. "No, wait. I don't know." He couldn't tell how high they were. His chin was hooked against the surface of the carriage and he couldn't see anything except the vague shape of his daughter, directly in front of him.

A high-pitched zipping noise blasted the area. It was the sound the alien machines made when they stunned people. Kim slumped forward.

"Kim! Kim, answer me."

His weight pulled against his armpits. Every muscle clenched as his acrophobia kicked in. Not knowing how far up they were made it even worse.

"David!" Cameron shouted.

"Drop," Reggie yelled. "Let go."

He couldn't let go. He couldn't abandon Kim. His arms, flat across the surface of the carriage, slipped toward the edge. Sweat slickened his palms.

"No, hang on," Cameron yelled. "You're too high."

David tensed, picturing the ground a hundred feet below.

He slipped further. He was going to fall and break his back and Kim would float away in the dark and he'd never see her again. He brought his knees up under the carriage, trying to brace them against the bottom of the hull, but that only made him slip further.

The wind tugged at his legs as they picked up speed. The ground had to be a thousand feet down.

His sweaty hands slid another inch across the surface of the carriage. His arms trembled, but there wasn't anything to hold onto. This was it. This was the end. He pictured blunt force trauma devastating his body as it slammed into the ground.

He slipped further, then his fingers caught in a groove where the padding ended and the metal frame of the carriage's hull began. Finally, something he could grip. He clenched with all his might.

"Kim?" he whispered. "Are you there?" She didn't answer.

The glint of the bonfire danced in the corner of David's eye, then disappeared as the carriage rose into the darkness.

Chapter Two

Sierra Preston turned in every direction, searching for the caretaker. "Where are you?" she shouted at the black sky. "Show yourself." She held the big pistol out in front of her with both hands.

Cameron snatched a burning log from the fire pit. "I'm going after David."

"Wait," Sierra said. "We have to stick together." Cameron was the closest thing to a soldier in the group. They needed her here.

"That's why I'm going after him." Cameron's voice trailed off as she disappeared into the fields.

Reggie and Felicia crowded Sierra, bumping into her. They held their guns at the ready.

"Priya, what happened?" Sierra shouted.

Still no answer.

Kevin, one of the original villagers, called out. "She's hurt. I think she hurt herself jumping off the carriage." Kevin was great at stating the obvious, but little else.

Sierra zeroed in on his voice and spotted Priya, crumpled by the fire pit, whimpering and holding her leg. Kevin crouched next to her, his arm in a sling from an earlier injury.

Several feet away, Wanda and Harmony lay slumped against one another, both stunned. Beyond them, Barry was shaking Kona, a lifeless mound in the dirt. The alien had stunned the dog, too.

Reggie and Felicia jerked their guns back and forth, peering into the dark. Felicia froze. "Sierra. Behind you."

She spun around.

An alien sled uncloaked four feet off the ground, right in front of the storage sheds.

Sierra pointed her revolver at the caretaker riding on top, unsure where to aim. The aliens were big brown blobs, like elephant seals, but without fins or faces. A cluster of spiny limbs protruded from folds and flaps at one end. "Bring back that other sled," Sierra demanded.

The sled produced a series of rumbles, translating her words to the alien's language. A moment later, similar rumbles fluttered from the folds of skin at the front of the creature.

The vehicle translated, using a robotic voice. *"Human specimens removed control implants. Humans are unsuitable for observation."*

"Yeah, fine." Sierra said. "Bring back our friends and we'll leave." She held the gun steady, stabilizing her wrist with her other hand. "We'll clear out of here. We're going back to Earth."

"Earth belongs to gorgers."

"The hell it does," Reggie muttered, close behind her.

"You told us the gorgers sent the comet. That's bullshit. They're animals. They don't have any technology. They're just big bugs." She spat this last word with contempt.

"Gorgers need no technology. Gorgers consume."

Sierra couldn't understand why the caretakers didn't just wipe out the gorgers. The two species seemed like enemies. The caretakers had sent pods that saved people, after all. "You could help us. You must have some way to fight them."

"Gorgers cannot be killed."

"Bullshit. We killed several already."

"Gorgers cannot be killed."

The conversation wasn't going anywhere. Sierra pulled back the hammer. "If you help us, we'll leave in peace. If not, I'll blow a hole in you."

"Do it," Felicia whispered.

Sierra nodded. The caretakers had sent the pods, but they'd also treated her and everyone else like prisoners, or worse, like specimens. They'd watched and done nothing when children were killed. They'd helped Randall murder Waldmire. Sierra's finger tightened.

A brief rumble came from the creature. *"Caretakers cannot be killed."*

"Yeah, you said the same thing about the gorgers."

"Human specimens must be returned to storage." The caretaker's spidery arms reached for the controls in the front of its sled and another high-pitched zipping sound blasted through the air.

"Try that all you want," Sierra said. "You can't stun us."

"Caretakers need assistance with human specimens."

A new voice muttered in the dark. "What the fuck?"

"That last message wasn't for us," Reggie said.

A hollow chill came over Sierra. *Randall.* The alien hadn't been trying to stun her, it had just un-stunned Randall and his buddy, Jerry. They were somewhere beyond the sled, hidden from view.

The creature touched the controls again and the sled started forward, accelerating. It was going to ram her.

She pulled the trigger. The gun jerked her hand, like something alive. Reggie and Felicia fired as well.

Yellow goo exploded from the folds at the front of the alien. It slumped, dragging its limbs across the controls. The nose of the sled dropped as it careened toward her.

Sierra dodged sideways, diving to the ground.

The sled just missed her. Its front corner caught in the dirt, causing it to arc in the other direction. The nose lifted back up and it started to climb, but it was too late. The alien crashed into the closest storage shed, crumpling the front opening.

"We got it," Felicia shouted.

Sierra could barely hear over the ringing in her ears. She spat dirt and pulled herself up on one elbow.

Back where the sled had been floating a moment earlier, Randall and Jerry crouched side-by-side.

Chapter Three

David's fingers clenched the shallow groove. He hung from the side of the carriage as it flew through the dark, his weight pulling on his arms, which were up at shoulder height. His shirt, a white button down he'd found in the supply shed, flapped in the wind as the vehicle soared through the air.

He caught sight of the bonfire again, a tiny spark back in the center of the village. He shuddered. It was a million miles away, and he was a million miles up.

The light vanished as a jagged black wall rose behind him.

He forced himself to breathe. He had to keep his senses. The surface of the carriage pressed against his chin. His arms trembled with exhaustion.

A jagged black wall *hadn't* risen up behind him. The carriage had simply passed over the forest canopy.

The pine trees growing around the village were at least two hundred feet tall. A fall from this height would kill him, even if he crashed through the branches. He had to get on top of the carriage before his arms gave out.

He swung his right leg, trying to bring it up, to take some weight off his arms.

His thigh barely rose ninety degrees before his old gunshot wound seized up. "Fuck."

He dropped his right leg and tried with his left.

Success.

His heel caught on the top of the carriage, and his shoe touched the short wall that wrapped around the front third, where the controls were. He stretched, hooking his heel against metal. Finally, he had leverage. He pulled himself up onto the flat surface.

Panting, he reached in the dark, found Kim, and scooped her into his arms. He felt her face, her neck, and her chest. She had no pulse and she wasn't breathing.

She seemed unhurt otherwise, but he couldn't be sure because he couldn't see anything. The goddamn menagerie had no stars or moon or any other light source at night.

He twisted Kim's head gently and spotted a red glow on the back of her neck, confirming what he already knew. She was stunned.

"Now what?" he whispered.

The aliens had to be flying him into the bowels of the ship. He would descend through the sea and exit the menagerie. There would be light in the alien sections, but he'd be alone. It took two people to operate the carriage and he had no way to revive his daughter. Without a co-pilot, he couldn't even turn around and fly back.

He flexed his fingers, still cramped from hanging on, and faced forward. Wind sapped the sweat from his skin and tugged his hair. He tried to focus, to come up with a plan.

He'd left Barry in the village. A caretaker was there. He had to get back.

Gunshots popped in the distance. "Shit." He had to get back *now*.

The wind ceased. David tensed in the still air. Why had they stopped moving? He flailed around with one hand, holding onto Kim with the other. His fingers smacked something smooth and curved. It had to be one of the alien devices Kim and Priya had been using. He stretched, feeling its surface. The device had closed, its two halves coming together to make a sphere.

The devices could revive Kim, but David didn't know how to operate them. He didn't even know how to turn them on. He had to get them back to Priya. She was the only one who knew how to work the goddamn things.

The carriage hadn't stopped. If they'd stopped, David would have felt his body jerk to the side and the stupid orange spheres would have rolled into him.

So why did the wind cease?

The only other explanation was that the carriage had become cloaked. But why? There was no need to hide in the dark.

Unless ... They were almost to the water.

The bubble that cloaked the carriages also created a semipermeable force-field that kept water out. If it had turned on, that meant he must be close to the sea. They would descend through the water to the portal that led into the guts of the alien ship.

He was running out of time.

Chapter Four

Sierra lay on the ground, her ears ringing from the revolver's blast and her hand tingling from the recoil. The acrid smell of gunpowder stung her nostrils.

Smoke rose from the alien sled. It had crashed into the doorframe of the supply shed, crumpling the side wall. The vehicle now leaned across the opening, nose-high.

"Holy shit," Felicia said, somewhere behind her.

Randall and Jerry staggered to their feet. Jerry swung his head back and forth, his mouth gaping like a koi. He seemed like a younger version of Randall, skinny, with baggy pants and a narrow face. Both of them were still bound at the wrists with vine ropes.

She had to stop them. These men had done terrible things and they would keep doing terrible things. They'd been sentenced to die and the group had been debating how to handle their executions. Sierra pushed herself to one knee. Pins and needles jabbed her fingers. She raised her gun.

Randall grabbed Jerry and pulled him toward the shed.

A gunshot went off behind her. Sierra flinched. The sound sent daggers through her already shrieking ears.

Jerry howled and fell, clutching his thigh.

"Got him," Reggie shouted.

Randall sprinted sideways, diving into the damaged shed with his arms in front of him. He landed out of sight, behind the crashed vehicle.

Jerry crawled after him, using his elbows and one knee, dragging his other leg in the dirt.

Felicia fired at him, but missed completely. Jerry crawled faster and disappeared behind the wreck.

Sierra got to her feet and stepped sideways, trying to get a clear shot into the opening.

Reggie grabbed her arm. "What if they got guns in there?"

"That's the shed with the food." She crept forward, with Reggie and Felicia on either side. The caretaker appeared dead, but they still had to stop Randall.

The front of the alien's sled had jammed into the shack's entrance on the right side, about halfway up. The back end dropped to the dirt at a thirty-degree angle with a wet smear of orange goop dripping down its surface. The caretaker's body had slid off and lay crumpled on the ground.

The shed's roof listed forward over the opening and a wisp of smoke rose from the wreck. The interior was an empty shadow. Something round flew out in an arc toward Sierra's head. She ducked as the object sailed past. It looked like a gourd.

A loud bang came from her right and a puff of dirt exploded in front of the shed. Felicia had fired, apparently flinching.

"Save your ammo," Sierra said. "They're trapped." Cameron would be furious about losing so many precious rounds.

The crash had crumpled the front of the shed, but the other three walls were still intact. Randall and Jerry couldn't escape unless they came back out the front. And judging from the blood on the ground, Jerry might not be going anywhere.

One of the caretaker's spindly limbs twitched and trembled.

"It ain't dead yet," Felicia said. "Should we put it out of its misery?"

"We can't spare the ammo," Sierra said, trying to channel Cameron. Hopefully she'd be back soon with David and Kim.

Felicia growled in disagreement but didn't fire.

Sierra leaned sideways and shouted toward the opening "Randall, come out of there, now."

"Fuck you," Randall shouted back. Another gourd flew from the dark opening.

She didn't bother to duck. The gourd passed two feet overhead.

The caretaker convulsed at the back of its sled. Something bulged against its sack-like body, like a fetus kicking its mother's belly from the womb. Orange fluid bubbled from the folds of skin where its limbs protruded from its body. The back end stretched and writhed. It stank of mildew and rotten fruit.

Sierra knew she ought to be watching the shed, but she couldn't tear her eyes away from the dying creature.

The caretaker's limbs shook and jittered, as if it was having a seizure.

"God-damn," shouted Randall, obviously watching the same thing from inside the shed.

"We should get out of here," Reggie said, moving back toward the bonfire.

The front of the alien swelled and burst, spraying gallons of orange gore up onto the wrecked vehicle. The fluid washed back down and sloshed across the dirt. It smelled dangerous and unhealthy, like the pesticide aisle at a gardening store.

Bile rose in Sierra's throat. She and Felicia backed away from the spreading puddle.

Pink limbs tore through the flaps and folds. The original limbs flopped aside. A writhing wet mass clawed its way out from the front of the caretaker, covered in slime. Multi-segmented limbs rose on either side.

"You gotta be fucking kidding," Reggie said, backing up further.

"*¿Qué carajo?*" Felicia said, staying at Sierra's side.

Sierra trembled, unable to make sense of what she was seeing. She wanted Priya or David or Cameron to come help figure this out. What the hell was happening?

Shoot first and ask questions later. The quote came to her in the voice of Rick Preston, the man she'd believed was her father. It wasn't one of his business idioms, though. It came from his love of old westerns.

She raised the revolver. It felt like it weighed a hundred pounds. Her hand shook. The pulsing mass was a good fifteen or twenty feet away.

Jerry appeared at the entrance to the shed, his eyes wide. Blood blackened one side of his jeans. He inched along the front wall. His lips pulled back in a tight grimace with each step.

The spindly legs protruding from the writhing mass bent in three or four places and stabbed the ground on both sides. It picked itself up and shook like a dog, spraying fluid everywhere. Its segmented tail flexed, rising and curving up over its body. The creature had the pink-wet shine of a newborn farm animal.

Recognition slowly dawned on Sierra.

Jerry gasped. He sped up, but his wounded leg crumpled under him and he fell against the front of the shed.

"It's a gorger," Sierra whispered.

"How?" Felicia asked. "How is that possible?"

The creature sprayed a burst of slime onto Jerry. He screamed and collapsed, his hands swiping at his body. His wails turned to shrieks as flesh came loose in his fingers.

Sierra shoved her confusion aside, overwhelmed by urgent fear. It was a gorger all right. The creature was smaller than the gorgers they'd seen on Earth, barely as big as Kona, but it vomited digestive acid just like the rest of them. She brought her other hand up to steady the revolver.

Jerry's eyes oozed down his face and a gaping hole opened where his nose had been. Teeth showed through the tatters of his lips. His screams faded to nothing. The creature leaned forward, sinking its mouth into his guts.

"*¿Que demonios?*" Felicia raised her gun and fired three times. All three shots missed, unless she was aiming for Jerry. The top of his skull exploded.

The gorger spun, facing her. Sierra felt a desperate urge to flee, but there wasn't anywhere it couldn't follow. The creature charged, its legs splashing through its slimy afterbirth.

Felicia fired again until her gun clicked empty. The gorger kept coming, now only five feet away.

Sierra braced herself and fired three times into the top of the monster's tube-like head, hitting it right where Cameron had killed one on Earth.

The gorger slumped to the ground. All ten legs reached out, clawing at the dirt. Its tail uncurled and lay flat behind it.

"Gorgers *can* be killed," Sierra said.

Movement at the shed caught her attention. The rear of the vehicle lifted from the ground, dripping tendrils of snotty slime. It tugged free from the doorway, leveling itself. No one sat at the controls. Some other alien had to be operating it remotely.

Randall knelt beside Jerry's body, doing something to his remains and hissing through his teeth.

Sierra raised the revolver and pulled the trigger. The gun clicked empty.

Randall heaved himself onto the sled right as its cloaking device turned on. The blurry haze lifted away, vanishing in the dark sky.

Chapter Five

David rolled one of the alien devices to the back of the carriage and kicked it off. He held his breath, listening. If they were still over the trees, he would hear the crash of breaking limbs. If he heard a splash, it meant they were over the water and he was out of time.

A muffled thud came a moment later. The beach? The path? There was no way to know. Were they still moving horizontally, or had they begun to descend? If he could feel the wind again, he might be able to tell.

He rose up on his knees, his vertigo amplified by the complete lack of light. He couldn't feel any movement. He couldn't trust his balance. He felt like he was about to fall over the side and tumble to his death. He wanted to lie down and plaster himself against the surface of the carriage.

Shoving aside his fears, he licked one finger and reached up, stretching, until he felt wind, which meant his hand was outside the force-field bubble.

They were still moving forward. He took slow, steady breaths, trying to calm himself.

The wind stopped. It was the signal he was waiting for. The carriage was descending.

He dropped to his butt and grabbed the second device. Careful not to bump Kim, he rolled it across the carriage and kicked it off.

Splooosh!

The sound confirmed what he expected. They were over water.

He reached under Kim's neck and behind her legs, picking her up. His injured thigh protested, but he pushed through the pain.

Walking on his knees, he crept to the back of the carriage until the cushy surface gave way to the harder edge, digging into his kneecaps.

This was his last chance. If he rode the carriage into the alien ship, he'd be trapped, alone, and unable to revive Kim. He had to get back to the others. He had to jump.

Fears roared through his mind. If he was too high, hitting water would be like hitting concrete. Hell, he might not still be over the water.

He froze. What if he waited until right when the carriage went below the surface? He could push off directly into the sea.

No, the force field might work differently when submerged, or the carriage might pull them down, like a sinking ship. He had to jump while he could.

David staggered to his feet and leaped into the inky blackness. The sickening sensation of falling yanked his stomach up his gullet. He held Kim tight against his chest and scissored his legs, trying to keep them beneath him.

They hit the water hard. Kim jerked upward. Her head knocked into his chin, snapping his jaw shut and lighting up his vision with stars.

Cold wetness smothered him. He flailed and kicked, clutching desperately to his daughter. If she sank to the bottom, he'd never find her.

The rising bubbles told him which way was up. Gripping Kim close, he swam, desperate for air, until finally he broke the surface and sucked in one breath after another, swishing his legs to stay above water.

He pulled Kim's face up next to his. Suspended animation meant she wasn't breathing, which probably meant she couldn't drown, but he still wanted to keep as much water out of her lungs as possible.

He'd done it. He'd gotten her off the carriage. Somewhere on the beach, or maybe on the path, lay the alien device that could wake her, assuming it had survived the fall. He gritted his teeth. There would be time to worry about that later. First, he had to get to shore.

David twisted his head around, seeing nothing but black. He sucked in a mouthful of water.

He had no idea which way to go. He couldn't see the goddamn island.

Chapter Six

The torch wasn't going to make it all the way to the beach. Only a few tiny flames still sputtered. Alice Cameron left the path and scoured the ground for dead branches. The gunshots behind her had stopped. It sounded as if Sierra and the others at the village had used up half their ammo. Cameron didn't even consider going back. Whatever had gone down was over by now. She and David might be the only people left.

The idea had a certain appeal. She was tired of worrying about everyone else. She and David could take a canoe to one of the other islands and forget about the rest of them. David was cute, smart, kind, and most of all, he seemed to actually care about her, unlike the guys she usually fell for.

She found a fallen pine tree wedged against two other trunks. The needles looked dead, but it was hard to tell in the dark. Cameron touched her torch to one of the larger clumps and blew on the embers. The needles burst into flame. Bracing her boot against the dead tree, she broke off the branch, snapping the dry wood easily.

She lifted it overhead and ran back onto the path.

The breeze produced from sprinting caused the fire to spread. She held the branch overhead like she was running to the Olympics or something. It lit the path better than the burning log had, brightening the underside of the canopy above.

Cameron's neck throbbed where David had cut out her implant, making it difficult to plan ahead. The aliens must have controlled Kim's carriage remotely, which was alarming, but not surprising.

She assumed it was flying to the sea, where the exits to the rest of the mothership were located, but for all she knew, it could have flown off to some other island. Maybe the aliens were feeding David and Kim to the dinosaurs.

Just ahead, the glowing tunnel of foliage came to an end. The blaze on her burning branch was dying down, but enough remained to last a few minutes longer. A little light went a long way when there wasn't any other light at all.

She left the dirt path for the sand of the beach. The big silver shuttle they'd used to fly to Earth and back was gone. Apparently the aliens had taken it away as well.

She saw no sign of David or Kim or the carriage. Breathing hard, she stopped at the shoreline, beside the big wooden raft they'd built to explore the islands.

"Fuck. Where did you go?" The thought of losing David hurt. She really cared for him. Maybe the aliens had carted him off to storage. If so, she might be able to find him eventually. She wondered if she should head back to the village and clean up whatever mess she found there.

Splashes came from the dark.

"Hello?" Cameron shouted. "David?"

"Help." The voice was weak and distant, but it sounded like him.

Cameron's torch barely cast enough light to see past the shoreline. She needed another branch to burn, but she didn't want to take the time to run back into the woods.

The raft.

Before they'd learned how to operate the alien vehicles, Cameron had been in the process of covering the big raft with all manner of spikes. They'd been planning to row it to neighboring islands to search for other survivors, and wanted some sort of protection against the local wildlife, which included all kinds of prehistoric creatures from Earth.

The raft itself was made of thick logs. It would take a hell of a blaze to burn them. But the spikes sticking off in every direction were much smaller.

Cameron placed the burning branch onto the main deck, propping it against a cluster of spikes on the stern. She broke off a couple of other spikes from one of the pontoons and placed them across the flames. They caught quickly.

She ran to the shore, watching and waiting. "David? Can you hear me?" The blaze behind her grew larger.

Finally, she spotted him.

He swam toward her holding Kim in his arms. She sloshed out and helped drag the girl to the beach.

"Is she—?" Cameron wasn't sure what to even ask. If his daughter was dead, it would kill him.

"She's stunned," David sputtered, gasping for breath. "I think she'll be okay." Cameron heard desperation in his voice. "Hold her legs up for me."

Cameron grabbed the girl's feet while he dropped to his knees, clutching her torso. "I don't understand," she said. "What are you doing?"

"Kim went under the surface. Her throat and lungs probably filled up." David held the girl's shoulders as water drained from her mouth.

The spikes on the raft blazed, brightening the beach.

"One of those devices should be somewhere nearby," he said, still breathing hard.

Cameron spotted the orange sphere at the edge of the firelight. "I see it. Do you know how to revive her?"

"No. We need Priya." He got to his feet, still holding his daughter's torso.

"I'll go grab it." She eased Kim's legs into his arms, feeling his warmth through his clothes, then turned away for the device.

"Wait," he said.

She turned back.

"Thank you for coming for me." It looked like he wanted to say more. She wanted him to say more. Instead, he took a deep breath and started across the sand, carrying his daughter back toward the village.

"Any time, Ace."

Chapter Seven

Everything hurt. Randall Pond's skin burned, stinking goop covered him, and his stomach wouldn't stop roiling.

The hovercar carried him through pitch black, then through a glowing chamber like the inside of some giant belly, and then back into darkness again.

What the fuck happened?

He'd had everything under control until Kim started mouthing off about her old man. The next thing he knew, Randall was on his back, hands tied, with an alien warden floating over him.

The hovercar carrying Randall lurched to a stop and his stomach lurched with it. Putrid fluids from the dead alien had soaked through his clothes and covered his burns, probably infecting him with all kinds of diseases.

He turned his head and puked. The vomit pooled around him, puddling into his hair.

That fucking alien had birthed something else, some kind of spider-crab-scorpion thing that spat burning acid all over Jerry, melting his goddamn face.

Some of the spit had landed on Randall, too, and he smelled like barbeque pork, which made his stomach churn even more.

He lay still, hoping he might start to feel better. He didn't.

Eventually, he rolled over and pulled himself to a sitting position. It wasn't quite pitch black here. Gray shapes loomed around him in the dim light, like in the inside of a warehouse.

Where the fuck was he? How the fuck was he supposed to get out of here? And how the fuck was he gonna pay back Dave and Sierra for what they'd done?

He squeezed his hands into fists and pulled them apart, tearing through the last of the vines. Excruciating pain burned his wrists, worse than everything except his armpit. When Jerry's face started melting, Randall had dipped his wrists in the acid, which had dissolved the vines they'd tied him with. He was free, but he'd paid a dear price for it. As his eyes adjusted to the dim light, he could see skinless red flesh on the heels of his palms.

He crawled to the edge of the hovercar. He was parked in a row of hovercars extending off into the dark. There were hovercars behind him, in front, and on both sides. It was a goddamn hovercar bonanza. Too bad he didn't know how to drive them. He lowered his legs over the side so he could hop down, then froze, gripping the edge as tightly as he could.

There wasn't any ground. Some other shapes floated beneath him. They looked like gigantic drops of frozen mercury, bulbous at one end, with a long skinny point at the other. A second layer floated below the closest one, and more layers below that, as far down as he could see.

Randall scooted back from the edge and examined his wounds. He touched his face, which was burned on one side, as well as part of his neck, and under his arm. The armpit was the worst. He must have had his hand up when that spider creature puked on Jerry. All of his pit hair was gone, and most of the skin. His shirt was in tatters.

"Mother fuck."

He looked around to see if he could spot anything else. An empty gray ceiling hung maybe thirty feet above him.

He couldn't go up and he couldn't go down, so he turned to the side.

The hovercars floating around him looked close enough to jump to. He picked a direction and got to his feet. He felt dizzy, which probably meant he was in even worse shape than he thought. "Great."

Randall's legs weren't injured, though. The one thing he could do was jump. He got a running start and leaped.

He sailed across the gap and nearly overshot his landing. The next hovercar dipped under his weight and tipped sideways, then righted itself.

Randall's armpit burned. He lifted his arm and it burned. He lowered it by his side and it burned. He yelled, letting out a long, guttural cry. "Where the hell am I? Where the hell are you fucking aliens?"

They didn't answer.

After three more jumps he realized the gravity was lower here. The aliens must have flown him to a different world. Maybe he'd blacked out along the way. He wished he could black out again.

The low gravity meant he could hop from one hovercar to the next without breaking a sweat. He continued forward, wondering if he would ever find anything different.

Chapter Eight

Both bones in Priya Rami's lower leg were fractured. Before modern medicine, a broken leg could be a death sentence. That had to be true now, too. What the hell was she supposed to do? She sat against the half-meter stone wall of the fire pit, her hands clenched around her thigh just above the knee, trying to keep it stabilized. As long as she held perfectly still, the pain stayed at a glowing crimson throb. The slightest movement sent electric knives into her shin. She was still in shock. The pain would grow much worse when the adrenaline wore off. She moaned. "Where's David?"

The commotion over by the sheds had stopped after a dozen gunshots. She'd heard enough to know that Sierra was still alive. Reggie and Felicia, too.

"Where's Daddy?" Barry cried. He sat a few meters away, beside Kona, who lay stunned. Barry's chin wrinkled, like he was about to start bawling for real.

She glared at him. She needed a doctor way more than he needed his daddy.

When she'd jumped from the carriage, she'd landed on the rock wall surrounding the fire pit. Terrified of falling into the coals, she'd shifted her weight, leaning sideways. Her foot had caught in the rocks and her shin had twisted. She'd felt the bones snap, like a branch in her hands. A tingling chill had raced up her leg, into her crotch, and up her spine. The pain followed.

"Where's David," she repeated, her words as thin as tissue.

Sierra appeared, standing over her and breathing hard. "Priya, you gotta come see this. The caretaker, it's a gorger." The words made no sense. Priya held both hands tight around her thigh, focused on keeping it stationary.

Reggie and Felicia stood on either side of Sierra, surrounding her like sentinels.

Sierra's gaze locked on Priya's shin. "Shit. How bad is it?"

"Bad," Priya said. Tears welled in her eyes.

Kevin joined them. He already knew about Priya's leg. He'd come to check on her right after she broke it, then disappeared, probably off hiding somewhere. "The two new women are out cold," he said. "They don't seem hurt."

"Can't we wake them up?" Felicia asked.

"No," Reggie said, pointing at Priya. "She let them take our devices."

His words felt like a punch in the gut. "Let them?"

Reggie took off his cap and rubbed his bald head. "You shouldn't have jumped off. You should have stayed on that thing. You could have flown it back here. Now we're stuck."

Priya's tears broke loose, rolling down her cheeks. Of course she should have stayed on the carriage. And she never should have sent those pods to Earth. Oh, and she never should have let Charlie get himself killed. *Should have, should have, should have.*

"I want Daddy," Barry said. He started to sob.

"If the carriage is gone, we can't fly out of here," Kevin said. "We're screwed. We're stuck here."

"Jesus, Kevin, keep your mouth shut sometimes," Felicia said.

"We aren't stuck here," Sierra said. "We can dive down with stone weights, just like Priya and I did before."

"I can't do that with a broken leg," Priya whispered. Fresh tears streamed down her face.

Reggie craned his neck to look across the fire pit. "Is that pod still over there?"

An empty pod had been sitting up by Randall's cabin, supposedly meant for Kim.

Priya's jaw dropped. Reggie meant to pack her away, to stick her in suspended animation, just as they'd done with a few injured people back on Earth.

"No," Kevin said. "The pod is gone."

The four of them towered over her. Priya wished someone would sit. She wished someone would put an arm around her. Normally, hugs made her uncomfortable, but right now, she desperately needed one.

"Where's Randall?" Kevin asked, looking toward the sheds.

"He took off in the carriage," Reggie said. "Jerry is dead, though. The gorger got him."

"Gorger?" Priya asked. Sierra had said something about a gorger, hadn't she? Ice twisted her guts. "What gorger?"

"There was a gorger inside the caretaker," Felicia said. "Like a parasite or something."

"I don't think it was a parasite," Sierra said. "It was more like a metamorphosis."

"What, like a bug?" Felicia asked. "What does that even mean?"

"It's bad, whatever it is," Kevin said.

Sierra exhaled. "It means we have only one enemy. That's what it means."

"Terrific," Felicia said.

Sierra looked around. "We'll split up. A few people can stay here to protect Priya and those two." She gestured at the unconscious women. "The rest of us will dive down in the water and find another sled and bring it back here. Hopefully with David and Kim."

"And Cameron," Kevin said. "What about Cameron? Where the hell is she?"

"Right here." Cameron's voice carried to them from somewhere in the dark.

Everyone turned toward the fields. Kevin shifted. His foot moved right next to Priya's leg.

"Watch out," she hissed.

"Daddy!" Barry ran to his father.

David brought Kim over and laid her next to Kona. Priya wanted him to look at her leg, but the expression on his face told her to wait.

Cameron carried one of the orange control devices. She placed it on the ground beside Priya. "Wake them up."

The device scared her. She didn't want to touch it. What if it no longer worked? What if she couldn't remember how to use it? She removed her hands from her thigh and reached for the sphere. Her leg didn't move, but the raw nerves in her broken bones screamed anyway. Her fingertips brushed the orange surface. "Push it closer," she whispered through clenched teeth.

David rolled the device right next to her and she placed both hands on it, keeping her body perfectly still from the hips down.

The control device split apart and the interface came alive. Priya remembered what to do, and it helped turn her mind away from her leg, if only a little.

After a few minutes of tapping, she found the correct interface. A zipping sound blasted through the night and Kim sputtered awake, coughing water. David swept her into his arms.

Sierra crouched next to Priya and put a hand on her shoulder. "You did good. Thank you."

Priya leaned into her, taking comfort from her touch.

The other two women sat up, as well as Kona. The dog scratched her ear with her hind leg.

"Hey, Kona," Kevin called. "Who's a good girl?"

The dog ran over, bumping Priya's foot as she passed.

"Gaaaahh!"

Clammy sweat slimed the back of her neck. *Faint*, she told herself. *Pass out. Please.* She didn't know where she was. She barely knew who she was. The only thing she knew was that there wasn't any pain worse than this.

When David started building a splint around her leg, she learned she was wrong.

Terribly wrong.

Chapter Nine

After jumping from one hovercar to another for at least ten minutes, Randall finally came to something new. A bunch of round clusters floated in front of him, arranged in a grid pattern just like the hovercars. They looked like enormous metal grapes.

The easiest thing would be to turn and keep jumping across hovercars in some other direction, but that felt like a waste of time. The stupid bubble-things were different, and right now, anything different was good.

He tried to figure out how to get over there. His wrists hurt and his armpit was killing him. His stomach felt even queasier than when he'd first arrived.

Each cluster contained eight giant pink bubbles connected by a bunch of branching rods and poles. The bubbles themselves were as big as a hovercar. He thought he could make the jump onto the branches connecting them. Identical clusters floated side-by-side as far as he could see in both directions, and rows and rows of them floated below.

Some sort of shapeless structure hung on the ceiling above one of the bubble clusters to Randall's right, like a giant wad of gum or something. He hadn't seen anything on the ceiling until now. It was different, and again, different was good, because everything else here was exactly the fucking same.

He jumped across six hovercars to the right until he was as close as he could get to the clump on the ceiling, but he still couldn't make any sense of it.

Randall backed up, took two strides, and jumped to the closest cluster of spheres. He crossed the distance easily, but his knee knocked into one of the bubbles, which made him miss his landing.

He flailed with both hands, an instinctive reaching motion that brought excruciating pain to his armpit. *"Gaaaahh!"* He caught one of the branches as he dropped, swinging beneath the bubble cluster. It felt like the flesh separated under his arm.

Tears formed in his eyes. Goddamn it, he was actually crying.

The bubble cluster bobbed under his weight, then drifted back up to its original position. Randall hissed and swung his legs. This got the bubble cluster swaying again, but the movement actually helped. After three swings, he caught one of the branches with his feet. Hanging horizontally took away the stretch from his armpit, dampening the pain. Slightly.

He crawled his way along the bottom of the structure until he found a spot where he could pull himself up in the middle. He climbed up on a crossbeam that connected the bubbles. Once he was on his own two feet again, he wiped his eyes and stood there for a long time. He shifted his arm out and back in, trying to find a position that didn't feel like it was being sliced off. He couldn't. He waited for his stomach to settle. It didn't. If anything, it had gotten worse.

The surface of the closest bubble felt smooth and cold. The stupid things didn't make any sense. Hopping over here had been a mistake. At least on the hovercars, he could jump from place to place. Now he was stuck.

Randall leaned back and shouted upward, "What the fuck am I supposed to do now?"

The clumpy thing on the ceiling was directly above. From here, it looked like a hole.

Randall stepped up on another branch and climbed. As he worked his way higher, the tugging in his stomach grew stronger. He crawled on top of the highest bubble, where he felt light on his feet, as if he weighed nothing at all.

Puffy bulges surrounded the hole above him, which made it look like an old worn-out anus. The opening was eight or ten feet wide and pitch black inside.

He rose on his tip-toes, which made him actually float for a second. The gravity was even lower here, maybe because he was higher up, or maybe it had something to do with the hole.

"Are you really going to do this?" Randall asked himself. There was no way to know where that hole led. It might feed him into an incinerator.

The only answer came from his armpit. *Jump, motherfucker.*

Randall bent down and pushed straight up.

His leap propelled him even faster than he expected. As he flew, the tug in his stomach grew stronger.

Randall plunged upward into a wet, sticky darkness.

Chapter Ten

Reggie Darnell stuck a branch into the husk left behind by the alien caretaker and lifted it so he could peer inside. He lowered his torch with his other hand to light up the interior. A web of connective tissues and membranes stretched across the cavity, but that was all. It really was little more than a shed-off skin. He pulled out the stick and the leathery sheath collapsed, blowing fetid air into his face.

He stood straight, waving away the smell. Another scream came from the direction of the bonfire, where David was tending to Priya. She'd sent half the village to Earth. People had died. She damn near deserved what she was going through.

The thought made Reggie ashamed of himself, but that was nothing new these days.

"What did this thing look like before, when it was normal?" Harmony asked. The frizzy-haired woman was following him around like a puppy.

"They're just a big lump," Reggie said. He nudged the caretaker's floppy limbs with his branch. "All these arms and feelers stick out from one end, but there's no real face." He paused, waiting for another round of screams to pass.

Somehow, David's kids were sleeping through the noise. They lay side-by-side on the blanket Cameron had been using to clean the guns, with Kona curled up between them.

"But they can talk and operate machines?" Harmony sounded unconvinced.

"That's right."

"How does this one contain that other one?"

Reggie shrugged. He walked to the body of the gorger, a few feet away.

Harmony followed him. "Maybe it's like a caterpillar that skips the cocoon stage," She said. "The adult transforms inside it."

Wanda stood looking down at the creature. She had stunning red hair and a perfect V-shaped jaw line. Both of the women Randall had brought to the village looked like supermodels. Sick motherfucker.

The gorger didn't have much of a face either, just a gaping hole at the end of a worm-like tube. Dozens of mandibles surrounded the mouth, along with two fierce-looking pincers.

"*Shhhi-iii-itt!*" Priya shouted. Everyone froze for a moment and looked toward the bonfire.

"And these things are all over Earth?" Harmony asked, pointing. Her bracelets jangled together, rattling like a full tray of silverware.

"Yeah," Reggie said. "Except most are bigger." The gorger lying in front of him was roughly the size of David's dog.

"But these ones can't talk or operate machines?" Wanda asked.

"Didn't seem like it," Reggie said. "They mostly just eat. And they don't like bright light."

"*Aaaaggghhh,*" Priya screamed. "Fuck you."

Reggie closed his eyes and breathed deeply. His sense of right and wrong was utterly fucked up these days. Priya didn't deserve that kind of pain. She'd made a mistake. She hadn't killed anyone on purpose.

The gorger's tail lay unfurled on the ground, ending with a clump of finger-like protrusions. Its legs, each thick as a broomstick, looked like oversized crab legs, except they were black and shiny.

"I don't get it," Harmony said. "How does it go from being smart enough to operate machines to something that's just a bug? Is there anything like it in nature?"

Reggie pointed down. "Obviously, there's something like it in nature."

She crossed her arms, silencing her stupid bracelets.

Felicia walked over with a blanket from one of the cabins. She made her way around the puddle of alien gore to Jerry's half-melted body, still slumped against the front wall of the shed. She unfolded the blanket and placed it over him.

"Thank you," Reggie said, taking off his cap and rubbing his scalp. The sight of blood made him woozy. The fact that he'd shot Jerry made him feel something else, something he didn't quite understand. A weird mix of satisfaction and self-loathing.

"*De nada,*" Felica said. She ducked into the undamaged shed.

"So what made this thing come out of that other thing?" Wanda asked.

"It happened when Sierra shot it," Reggie said.

Sierra reminded him of his son, which gave him an even more uncomfortable mix of feelings. Admiration and regret. Love and despair. Hope and hate. Juggling those emotions left him empty, like he wasn't himself anymore.

"Yeah, but what makes them change normally?" Harmony asked.

Reggie shrugged. "No idea."

"Arrrghh, god-dammit," Priya snarled. Her voice sounded throaty, like she was possessed by the devil.

Kevin stepped out of the shed that had been damaged, holding a reed basket filled with vegetables. He glanced off toward Priya as he walked, which caused him to stumble on Jerry's blanket-covered corpse and crash into Wanda, almost knocking her down.

"Hey," she snapped. "Look where you're going."

"You watch out," Kevin said. "I have a broken arm, you know." He carried the basket over to one of the worktables.

"Come on," Harmony said. She took Wanda by the elbow and steered her away. "That idiot will be the death of us."

Kevin glared as they walked off.

Felicia emerged from the intact shed, holding an eight-foot spear.

"You going hunting?" Reggie asked.

"Cameron won't give me any more ammo. She said I used too much." She twisted the spear in her hands. "It's probably for the best. I think every shot missed."

"Does Cameron have a plan?" Reggie didn't have any ideas himself. The forward-looking part of his brain had died on Earth. Now he functioned best when someone gave him instructions. It helped him to not think.

"She says we need to get out of here. Says it isn't safe."

Reggie snorted. "No place is safe."

"Yeah, well, she thinks we need to get all the pods out of storage before the aliens close down this big zoo."

He looked off into the dark. "I say leave them in storage. At least there, they aren't hurting. Or hurting anyone else."

"Damn. I thought I was bitter. How'd you get to be so cheerful?"

From what Reggie had heard, Felicia had been through hell before getting in a pod. He didn't want to compare notes with her. He didn't like thinking about the past any more than he cared to think about the future. "Just tired, I guess. That's all."

Chapter Eleven

Two Days Before Impact

Reggie watched the news of the capsules on television for twenty minutes with his nineteen-year-old son Chase before the boy jumped up and went for the door. "I'm going to go find one, Pops."

Reggie smiled. He didn't have much in these last few days, but at least he had his son. When the Ender was first discovered, Chase had returned home from his freshman year at the university in Champaign. It broke Reggie's heart that Chase would never get his degree, but the world was coming to an end. There wasn't much point to college anymore.

Reggie turned and faced the boy. "Don't go getting your hopes up too high now." He pointed at the television. "Most of those pods are already taken."

"Gotta do as we can, Pops."

"Okay, okay. You be safe out there, hear me?"

Chase tilted his head. "Yeah, yeah. I'll watch out for the cows." So many fences were down across central Iowa lately that herds of cows wandered everywhere.

"Just stay clear of trouble," Reggie said.

"What trouble? Nobody's around."

The community had dried up weeks ago, and only one house in ten was still occupied. Chase went out the door and Reggie turned back to the television, enjoying the daydream that his son might find a capsule somewhere out here in the middle of nowhere.

Less than five minutes passed before Chase ran back in, grabbed him by the wrist, and tugged him from his seat. "You're not gonna believe it, Pops."

"What? What is it?"

Chase smiled, lighting up the room. He pointed at the television screen. "One of those."

"Here?"

"It's in Jasmine's yard."

Reggie rolled out of his recliner and followed his son through the front door, where the muggy Iowa morning smothered him. Chase led him up the desolate street, past more abandoned houses than he could count. Reggie's loafers became wet and heavy with dew from the tall grass.

"What did Jasmine say?" Reggie asked.

Jasmine was one of the few neighbors who'd stuck around after the comet showed up.

"She isn't there," Chase said.

When the round white object came into view, Reggie skidded to a stop, almost falling on his ass. His heart stuttered triple-time, like he was having a heart attack. Wouldn't that beat it all if his ticker conked out right at their moment of salvation?

Vincent Smith, who lived two blocks in the opposite direction, stood with his arms crossed about ten feet from the capsule. "Look at this god-damned thing, Reggie. Just look at it."

Reggie took off his cap and rubbed his head, bald as a baby's butt ever since he'd hit thirty. Chase's full afro showed no signs of thinning, thanks to his mother's genes. God rest her soul.

"It's real, Pops." Chase beamed. "It's ours."

"It's Jasmine's," Vince said.

He was right. The capsule sat in the center of Jasmine's front yard. "Where is she? Does she know?"

Vince held up his cell phone. "She's coming. I caught her halfway to work. I told her we'd wait for her."

"What do we do?" Chase asked. "All we have to do is touch it, right? Let's do this."

Reggie held up his hand and crept closer. "I think so." He kept his voice low, as if the capsule was sleeping and he didn't want to wake it.

From what he'd seen on the news, if you touched a capsule, it opened. And if you climbed in, it closed and flew away, simple as that. Reggie looked at the Ender hanging in the sky to the north, a second sun promising an ugly end to everything.

On the news, people were killing each other for the capsules. Here, out in the middle of nowhere, they had it all to themselves. Nobody came around anymore. The neighborhood was all but abandoned.

Tires screeched somewhere close by. Vince, Chase, and Reggie all turned.

"That's got to be her," Chase said.

Reggie's heartbeat picked up again. They were going to do this. They were really going to do it. That capsule would take them away from here. His heart couldn't decide if it should be exhilarated or terrified. It just bounced back and forth between both of them.

A sparkling silver Oldsmobile rounded the corner and stopped. Two people got out, a man in his fifties and a woman with blue hair who looked even older. Both were white.

"That ain't Jasmine." Vince's voice turned sour.

"You two need to let me do the talking," Reggie said.

The man looked them over. "Morning," he said, without bothering to put a "good" in front of it.

"Can we help you?" Vince asked, ignoring Reggie's instructions.

"I'm Commissioner Hamilton," the man said, as if that explained everything.

"Commissioner of what?" Vince asked.

Hamilton looked down his nose at him. "Commissioner of the county you're standing in."

Vince scowled. "What the fuck are you doing out here?" Vince was famous for his love of profanity.

"Do you wanna go in the capsule with us?" Chase asked, also ignoring Reggie's instructions. "There's plenty of room."

Commissioner Hamilton didn't answer. He waited for the wrinkly woman to walk around the car. She carried a leather satchel that was too small to be a suitcase and too large to be a purse.

"What do *they* want?" asked the woman.

"Nothing to worry about, dear." Hamilton walked over, with the woman waddling behind him.

Reggie couldn't decide if she was his wife or his mother.

They stopped a good ten feet away and Hamilton wagged his finger at the capsule. "That spaceship is county property. We're here to claim it."

"The fuck you are," Vince said.

Hamilton's woman put her hand to her cheek.

Reggie looked down. "Jesus, Vince, I told you to let me do the talking."

Hamilton hitched his suit pants over his belly. "County ordinance eleven dot sixteen dot seven-seven."

"I don't know about any ordinance," Reggie said. "But this here is Jasmine Simm's yard, and we're going to wait until she gets home." He was pretty sure the county didn't have any ordinances about strange white capsules falling from the sky.

Hamilton glared at the small rose-colored house. It sorta seemed like he was looking down his nose at it, too. "When is this Jasmine girl coming back?"

"She's a woman, not a girl," Chase said.

"Any fucking minute," Vince said.

"We can't wait," the woman said. "We need to get a move on." She stepped toward the capsule, holding her handbag out in front of her. "And I don't much care for the company here."

Vince started forward. "Now, stop right there."

Reggie held up both hands. "Everybody calm down. Commissioner Hamilton, let me tell you what I've seen on the news."

He'd seen seven or eight people get into capsules. He thought ten could fit, if everyone squeezed in tight. He just needed a chance to talk it through.

The woman kept walking. "We don't need that *person* to tell us anything." She reached for the capsule with one hand.

Just before her fingers made contact, Chase grabbed her elbow and yanked her back. She tumbled off balance and fell on top of him.

"Ack," she quacked, sounding for all the world like a duck. "Uck, uck, aaack."

"Holy shit," Vince shouted. He stood looking at them with his mouth hanging open.

"You take your hands off her, boy," Hamilton said, even though Chase had already scrambled out from under the woman.

Hamilton pulled her to her feet.

Reggie moved to help, but she flinched away from him. "Listen, please," Reggie said. "There's room in that capsule for all of us. That's what I'm trying to say." He kept his tone cool and collected, hoping to de-escalate the situation.

"That boy just assaulted my wife," Hamilton spat, ending the mystery of their relationship. He wagged his finger at Reggie, then wagged it over at Vince, then to Chase, and finally brought it back to Reggie again. "You keep away from us. All of you."

Reggie took off his cap and wrung it like a washcloth. Chase had bought it for him after getting accepted at the University of Illinois. It had a big orange "I" on it, with the word "Dad" embroidered beneath. Reggie had wept when he saw that goddamn hat. "I'm telling you, there's room for all of us. As soon as Jasmine gets home, we can all get in."

Tires rolled on the asphalt behind him, right on cue.

Commissioner Hamilton glanced at the street and smiled, which made his cheeks puff up red.

"It ain't her, Pops," Chase said, also smiling. "It's the sheriff. He's here to help."

"Now you come right over here," Reggie said, reaching for his son. "You don't know what he's here for."

"We have to give him a chance," Chase said. "Gotta do as we can."

Chapter Twelve

Kim Williams waited for the screaming to stop, then waited a few minutes more. Dad had told her to get some sleep, probably because he didn't want any distractions while he helped Priya. Kim cracked an eyelid. Barry lay beside her with one arm over Kona, whose back leg kicked occasionally. Kim couldn't sleep right now. No way.

She needed to use the device to keep looking for Mom. She knew it was a long shot, but she had to try. Mom would have tried. And she had to find Tyrell, too. He'd saved her from the croc-dinosaur Randall brought into the village. He'd cut off its head with its own pod, but he'd been trapped inside when it happened. She owed him her life.

After several minutes without any screams, Kim decided that Dad must have finished setting Priya's leg. Unless maybe she'd died. The thought shriveled her heart. She liked Priya. She kinda even wanted to be like her. Priya had figured out so much of the alien technology.

Moving slowly, Kim sat up.

Dad, Sierra, and Cameron sat next to Priya by the big fire pit. Kim walked over and put her hand on Dad's shoulder.

"Hey, Sweetie. You can't sleep?"

Kim faked a yawn. "I got a little rest." That phrase always seemed to satisfy him and Mom.

Priya lay with her head near the short rock wall, her eyes closed and beads of sweat on her forehead. She was alive. They would have covered her with a sheet or something if she had died. A brace surrounded her leg, like the braces she'd seen on pictures of polio kids in history class, except this brace was wooden and tied together with vine ropes.

The orange device sat near Priya's head, folded up into a ball. Kim walked over and sat next to it, but didn't touch it. "Can I look for Mom?"

"It isn't safe," Cameron said. "Priya accidentally sent everyone to Earth with that thing."

Kim pressed her lips together. She wanted Dad to decide, not Cameron. "I won't do anything. I'll just look."

"Let's wait until Priya wakes up," Dad said. "You two can look together."

"When will that be?" she asked.

"Not for a while," Dad said. "She needs rest. When daylight returns, I want to see if we can find some willow trees. The bark has a chemical that works like aspirin. It'll help with the pain, and it'll help when I take out your implant."

Kim shivered. She hated getting shots, and having her neck sliced open sounded a lot worse. Besides, getting stunned wasn't that bad, as long as there was someone around to wake you.

Cameron shook her head. "There's no time for that. We need to get out of here."

Sierra squinted. "The village?"

"No, we need to leave the whole ship," Cameron said. "We need to get back to Earth."

"Priya can't go anywhere," Dad said. "She can't walk."

"Can't we wait a day?" Sierra asked. "We'll set guards. It's the middle of the night. No one's gotten any sleep."

"We have to leave," Cameron said. "You just started a war."

"What do you mean?" Kim asked.

Cameron pointed at Sierra. "She killed one of the aliens. They're not going to just let us stay here."

"What can they do?" Dad asked. "So far, they haven't been able to do anything but stun us, and we're safe from that now."

"Speak for yourself," Wanda said, walking over with Harmony by her side.

Kim patted the device next to Priya, careful to use only one hand, so it wouldn't turn on. "If they stun anyone, we can use this to revive them, just like before."

Harmony put her fists on her hips, which made her bracelets slide down against her sides. "They took our flying thing. We can't leave. Maybe we should just stay in this place."

"This place isn't a place," Cameron said. "It's an alien ship."

"You gotta understand, that's a little hard to believe," Harmony said.

"You gotta understand, I'm not bullshitting you," Cameron snapped.

"Cameron is right," Sierra said. "We aren't safe here."

"Cameron is always right," Cameron said.

"Why isn't it safe?" Wanda asked.

Sierra got to her feet. "We're at their mercy. They could flush us into space, or simply drain all the oxygen." She huffed. "They could turn into gorgers and eat us, or a hundred other scenarios we can't even imagine."

Kevin wandered over. "We don't know that they'll do any of that," he said. "But we do know if we go to Earth, a million of those things will try to eat us." He pointed over at the dead gorger.

Cameron rolled her eyes. "Kevin the coward doesn't get a vote."

Kim swallowed. She'd never heard an adult call someone a coward right to his face.

"Just because I don't want to die, doesn't make me a coward."

"No, being a coward makes you a coward."

"Knock it off, Cameron," Sierra said.

Kim smiled. Sierra was like Mom. She didn't put up with nonsense from anyone.

Harmony raised her hands, which made her bracelets crash to her elbows. "What if some of us want to stay?"

"Works for me," Cameron said.

Sierra shook her head. "No. We aren't leaving anyone behind." This also sounded like Mom.

"I'm not debating any longer," Cameron said. "Wake Priya. We need a shuttle. The one on the beach is gone."

"I can do it," Kim said. "Let her sleep. I won't mess anything up, I promise." If she did it for them, maybe they'd let her search for Mom. She looked at Dad.

He seemed uncertain. "You're sure?"

"Yes. I won't send anyone to Earth or do anything else."

He nodded. "Okay. You have to get us a carriage, though. We can't get into a shuttle without a carriage because the entrance is a hundred feet up, and we need a carriage docked inside to fly it, anyway."

Kim didn't understand what that meant, exactly, but it didn't matter for now. She touched the device with both hands, turning it on, trying not to look as eager as she felt. Trying to look adult.

The orange sphere split around the equator and the top half rotated until only a sliver touched the bottom half. The bottom rotated and lifted as well, like it was standing on its tip-toes. The top half projected tiny spotlights into her eyes, which made it look like holograms floated in front of her.

"Get two carriages," Sierra said. "We need to take food with us."

"Wait," Cameron said. "I want to watch." She came around and sat next to Kim.

Kim shielded the lights from her eyes. She didn't like the idea of being monitored, especially by Cameron. She wanted to be trusted. "I promise I won't do anything else."

"It isn't that," Cameron said. "More people need to know how to use this thing."

"Why is that?" Dad asked. He looked like he already knew the answer.

Cameron nodded at Priya. "She's out for the count. If something happens to Kim, we don't have anyone else who can use these things."

And there it was. Cameron wanted to learn how to use the device in case Kim died. This whole discussion sucked. Kim tried not to think about it. She had to keep going before the adults all changed their minds. She lowered her hand and the projections jumped back to her eyes.

Cameron leaned in close and a few lights shifted over to her. "How do you interface with it?"

Kim pointed to the bottom half of the device, which normally looked like a smooth, empty metal surface. But when the device was on, the lights projecting into her eyes made it look like it had buttons on it. "These controls are like navigation on a map. See those round things? Those are the shuttles."

"Why do they have so many shuttles?" Cameron asked. There were thousands.

Kim shrugged. She touched the controls that shifted her view up, to the top of the hangar. "This is where they keep the carriages." There were only a few dozen. She selected two, which required four fingers, stretched almost all the way across the surface.

"How do you tell them where to go?" Cameron asked.

"You have to navigate back here, and then touch the ground to give them a destination." This was the part she wasn't completely sure about, because she hadn't done it before. But if Randall had been able to do it, it couldn't be that difficult. She scrolled and scrolled, until finally the map changed from the ordered geometric lines of the alien ship to the irregular shapes of the islands.

Cameron whistled through her teeth. "There are at least a hundred islands in this place."

Kim moved down to an island on the lower left and zoomed in on the village. Ghosted boxes showed locations where the carriages could be sent. They seemed to be on a grid, and the closest spots she could choose were either up near Randall's cabin and the dead croc-monster, or down in the fields. She selected the spots in the fields. "There. The dotted lines show the path they'll take."

Cameron pointed, her finger intersecting the holograms. "What are all those other lines?" Dozens of other lines led into the village.

"I don't know," Kim said. "They aren't anything I did. They were already there."

"They look like pods," Cameron said.

She was right. Each dotted line ended at a ghosted oval.

"Are they sending us pods?" Felicia asked.

Kim shielded her eyes with her hands. Felicia and Reggie had joined the group. Now everyone was crowded around except Barry and Kona.

"I don't know." Kim said. "It won't let me select them."

"I bet they're empty," Felicia said. "They're going to try to put us back in storage."

"They can't think we're dumb enough to get in them," Reggie said.

Felicia snorted. "We got in them before."

"There's like forty of 'em," Cameron said, looking up. "There's only eleven of us."

"Let me try something," Kim said, tapping.

"What are you doing, Sweetie?" Dad asked.

"I'm following the lines back to storage. All the pods in storage are organized by whatever's inside them. We can tell what's in them by looking at the pods next to where they came from." And once she navigated to storage, she might be able to spend some time searching for Mom and Tyrell.

"Where is storage?" Cameron asked.

"Below the hangar area." Kim pointed at the holographic map, where pods floated in a three-dimensional grid.

"There are even more of those than the shuttles," Cameron said.

She was right, and it was one reason looking for Mom was so difficult. Kim followed the dotted lines to their origins. A bunch of ghosted ovals showed where the pods had come from.

She touched the first pod in the row that looked solid, *without* a dotted line leading away from it. An image popped into her eyes, showing a two-legged dinosaur curled up, like it was asleep.

"Oh, shit." Cameron said. "Dinosaurs."

"What the hell did you do?" Kevin asked.

"I didn't do anything," Kim said. Her voice came out high and whiny. She hated it, but she couldn't help it.

"Back off," Dad said.

"I was watching," Cameron said. "She didn't do anything."

"I don't understand," Wanda said. "What's going on?"

"There's at least forty dinosaurs coming this way," Cameron said.

What kind of dinosaurs?" Sierra asked.

Cameron rose to her feet. "Looks like Tyrannosaurus."

Kim's heart sped up. "I think it's Allosaurus." Barry had taught her that Tyrannosaurus had two fingers and Allosaurus had three. He'd been a total know-it-all about it.

"What the hell difference does it make?" Reggie snapped.

"It doesn't." Kim shielded the lights from her eyes and looked at her father.

He looked scared. "I'm going to wake up Barry." He stood and left the group.

Kim wanted to ask him to hurry right back, but she didn't want to sound like a little kid. She wanted to be brave. She hated feeling so frightened.

"Alright," Sierra said. "We need to get on those sleds the second they arrive. Everyone get ready."

"There's a problem," Kim said, shaking her head. "The pods with the dinosaurs will get here first."

Chapter Thirteen

Two Days Before Impact

A shark's grin stretched across Commissioner Hamilton's face. Reggie wanted to punch that smile so badly he could taste it. He might even pop out some of those evil little teeth.

"You can't take this from us," Chase said, gesturing at the pod. "We'll share it with you, but you can't take it all for yourself."

"Sheriff Dart will decide what's going to happen." Commissioner Hamilton's mouth closed, hiding those wicked teeth.

Chase believed the police were the good guys. It was their job to keep the peace. To serve and protect. Sometimes, it was true, thank Jesus. But not always.

"That motherfucker ain't gonna decide nothing good," Vince said, shifting away from the others.

Reggie counted to himself. If Jasmine ever made it home, they'd have seven people. There was plenty of room in the capsule. Everybody just needed to settle down.

"Howdy, Commissioner," Sheriff Dart said as he slammed the door on his squad car. He tipped his hat at Mrs. Hamilton. "Ma'am." Dart looked just like his name, skinny, pointed, and dangerous.

"Sheriff, can I speak with you?" Reggie asked, trying to take hold of the situation.

Sheriff Dart glared at him. It might have been a sneer, or maybe it was just how Dart's nose met up with the lines alongside his cheeks. "You'll get your turn," Dart said. He walked over to Commissioner Hamilton and the two of them spoke quietly.

Chase tugged on Reggie's sleeve. "Pops?" The incredulity of that one syllable struck him like a sledgehammer.

A third car rolled up behind the police car, boxing it in.

"Jasmine," Vince said. "'Bout fucking time."

Reggie nudged Chase toward Jasmine's car. "Run over there and catch her up. Tell her what's going on here." He wanted his son out of the way so he could talk to Dart alone, nice and calm.

Chase's eyes held his, and he smiled, as if he knew his Pops was going to take care of everything. That look made Reggie feel eight feet tall and damn near invincible.

Sheriff Dart, the commissioner, and his wife all started toward the capsule.

"Hold on," Reggie called out, moving toward them.

They kept walking.

"Now hold on," Reggie repeated, raising his voice.

Sheriff Dart stopped and turned. His face looked sallow under the glow of the comet.

Reggie would only get one shot at this. He had to get it right. "Jasmine just got here." He gestured toward the street. "This is her property, but she will welcome all of us into that capsule. I promise."

Dart seemed to sneer again. *It's just his face,* Reggie told himself. *Just his face.*

"Commissioner Hamilton has authority here," Dart said. "You'd best understand that."

Reggie took another step closer. Dart's left hand came up, stopping him. His right went to the butt of his gun.

"There are seven of us," Reggie said. "We'll all fit, easily. It doesn't have to be like this."

Mrs. Hamilton pulled her bag up against her chest.

Commissioner Hamilton turned to look back at Reggie, squinting. "We don't know who you are. We don't know anything about you and we don't have time to run a background check. You go find your own capsule."

Reggie kept his arms at his sides, trying not to look threatening. "I can vouch for everyone here. We're good people. Chase is going to college in Champaign. Vince works over at the clinic, cleaning up after people." He saved the best for last. "And Jasmine works in Des

Moines, where she takes care of orphaned babies. You can't find better people." Hamilton and Dart had to see it. "Please." That last word seemed like begging, and it made him feel small, but he said it anyway. This was their only chance.

Hamilton leaned over Sheriff Dart's shoulder. "I don't care. The simple truth is, you are not going to get in that capsule with us."

And there it was. They wouldn't share a life raft with Black people.

"We need to leave before more of them come," Mrs. Hamilton said.

There was only one option left. Reggie would tackle Sheriff Dart. He'd probably get shot, but maybe he could knock him down and hold him at bay. Vince and Jasmine could disarm him. Reggie would take a bullet if it meant Chase might live.

He set his feet.

Sheriff Dart drew his gun and raised it. But he didn't aim at Reggie, he aimed past him.

In the corner of his eye, Reggie saw Chase, running toward the sheriff.

Dart fired.

Mrs. Hamilton screamed.

Vince shouted, "Motherfucker."

Dart aimed down and pulled the trigger again. The world turned red. Dart was shooting Chase on the ground.

Reggie charged, blind with rage. Dart tried to bring the gun up, but it was too late. Reggie's hands closed around his neck and he kept charging, driving him backwards. They crashed into Commissioner Hamilton and Reggie kept pushing.

Mrs. Hamilton screamed again.

Sheriff Dart fired twice more. If he hit anything, Reggie couldn't tell and didn't care. His fingers tightened around Dart's throat and he dug with his thumbs. He clenched. His mind focused only on squeezing. Something crunched beneath his thumb.

"Reggie!" Jasmine shouted. She tugged his shoulders. "Reggie, stop!"

He clenched harder, digging, squeezing. Both thumbs sank to the first knuckle. Blood pooled around them. Something else popped beneath his hands. It felt good. He wanted more popping, nothing but popping, forever and ever.

A blanket of numbness fell across everything. Jasmine pulled his hands from Dart's throat. There was a wet red hole where Reggie's thumbs had been.

Chase.

He turned toward his son but Jasmine stopped him. "No. Shug, don't you look that way."

Reggie felt something draining, as if his very soul was oozing from his body, dripping down his legs and out through his feet. He whispered, "Chase?"

Jasmine ushered him in the other direction, toward the capsule. The top half floated in the air now, just like on TV. Vince had his hand on it.

"Chase?"

He wanted to look back. Maybe Jasmine was wrong. Maybe his son was okay. Maybe he'd just been knocked out. Maybe he needed first aid.

Mrs. Hamilton held her bag in front of her face like a shield and backed away.

Jasmine helped Reggie into the capsule. "Don't you mind them, now," she said. "Just climb in."

Reggie did as instructed, too numb to do anything else. The inside of the capsule curved like a big bowl. He spilled down to the middle and looked back. Maybe Chase would climb in after him.

Jasmine blocked his view. Vince climbed in next to her.

The top half of the capsule began to lower silently.

"What about them?" Vince asked, pointing at the commissioner and his wife. "There's room."

Jasmine looked at Reggie. He would realize later that she'd given him the chance to weigh in, but at the time, he didn't even know where he was.

"Come on," Jasmine waved, making the decision for him. "Get in. There's room for the both of you."

Commissioner Hamilton looked at his wife.

"Hurry now," Jasmine said. "It's closing."

Mrs. Hamilton squeezed her bag against her chest and shook her head.

The pod sealed shut, bringing a darkness down on Reggie that never went away.

Chapter Fourteen

Reggie's time was up, and he knew it. More than three dozen pods with dinosaurs in them floated toward the island. When two dinosaurs rampaged through the village, they'd killed nine people, including his buddy Vince, who'd been devoured while trying to squeeze through a narrow opening in the wall. There was no way to survive against three dozen.

Jasmine's fate might be even worse. She'd been packed in a pod after getting injured in Washington, D.C. If Reggie and the other ten people here were killed, she would spend the rest of eternity in suspended animation.

He shook his head. *Those goddamn pods.*

"Where are the sleds?" Sierra demanded. "How long until they get here?"

Kim tapped something on the device. "They haven't reached the islands yet."

"Ten minutes at least," Priya added. Sierra had woken her as soon as they realized what was about to happen.

"This place sucks," Wanda said.

Reggie couldn't argue with that. "We should try for the canyon," he said. "Climb up to the plateau."

"I can't climb," Priya whispered.

"Maybe we could rig some ropes to pull you up."

"Okay," Sierra said. "We'll take the device with us. We'll need it to call the sleds up there."

"Wait," Priya said, holding up her hand. "The pods aren't just coming to the village. Some of them are landing in the canyon and three or four of them are going to the plateau."

"So much for that," Reggie said. His time was definitely up.

"The beach?" Sierra offered. "We could take the raft."

"The raft burned up," Cameron said.

David walked over with Barry in his arms and Kona beside him. The boy dug his face against his father's chest, still trying to sleep. Reggie remembered holding Chase that way, feeling his hair against his chin, smelling his breath. He missed it so much.

Kona leaned into Reggie, as if she sensed his pain. He patted the golden retriever. It was a nice gesture on the dog's part, but it wasn't enough. Not by a long shot.

"How much ammo do we have?" David asked.

Cameron shook her head. "Enough for two or three dinosaurs. And that's only if we get lucky."

For a long moment, no one said anything. The fire sputtered and popped. Kona flinched.

Fire, Reggie thought. *Animals don't like fire.* They could use it to hold the dinosaurs at bay.

He started to open his mouth, then stopped, clamping it shut. If he just sat quietly, it would all be over soon. No more pain.

"There has to be something we can do," Sierra said. "We can't give up."

She reminded him of Chase so much it hurt. He couldn't just sit and do nothing. He had to try. For Sierra. A vague idea took shape in his mind. He leaned over the rock wall of the fire pit and grabbed two burning logs. He placed them on the ground outside the pit and reached for more.

"What are you doing?" Felicia asked.

"A firewall." Reggie tossed another pair of logs next to the first two and grabbed more. "We can build a big ring of fire around us. Come on. Help me."

Kevin stared, his mouth hanging open.

"We have maybe five minutes," Priya said.

"That will never work," Felicia said. "Those flames wouldn't stop a rabbit."

"It's just the start," Reggie said. "We have tons of firewood." A three-foot tall pile of branches sat on the other side of the fire pit. "Throw the rest of that wood in the fire. All of it. Get it lit."

Several of the others ran over and started tossing logs onto the fire. Felicia and Cameron stayed and helped Reggie. They had half the circle laid out now, curving nearly twenty feet around Priya.

"Three minutes," Priya said. "They're almost here."

Felicia placed a couple of burning branches onto the circle, then looked at him. "We should hide in the cabins. This isn't going to work."

The ring of fire looked like something used to summon witches in a horror movie, not a wall of flames.

"It's just the foundation," Reggie said. "Keep going." The ends of the circle were almost connected.

Across the fire pit, the others had thrown half the firewood onto the flames, nearly smothering them, but they would catch. They had to. They sat on a foot of glowing coals.

"Kevin, come with me," Reggie said.

Kevin was doing half the work of everyone else. Hell, even Barry was throwing more wood on the fire.

Reggie led Kevin past the sheds to the work area, where sixteen wooden racks sat by much smaller campfires. Each rack was basically a big easel, used for smoking meat.

With Kevin's help, Reggie dragged two of them to the ring of fire. He laid a rack over the burning logs. The boxy frame allowed air to circulate and provided something they could lean other logs against.

Kevin dragged the second frame into place. "Keep it more to the outside," Reggie instructed. "Don't crowd it inward or we'll cook ourselves." They started back for more racks.

"Shit, they're here," Kevin said.

A pod as big as a house passed overhead, its white surface glowing orange from the bonfire, which had finally begun to blaze. The flames inside the fire pit were fifteen feet tall.

"Kids, get in the circle," David said. The three of them moved into the ring of fire.

Sierra, Felicia, Wanda, and Harmony continued feeding wood onto the bonfire on one side, while the rest fished out burning branches on the other side and stacked them against the wooden frames in the circle.

Reggie and Kevin pulled three more racks over to the ring and ran back for more.

The pods touched down, the closest blocking the side entrance to the village. Two others landed in the fields, right at the edge of the firelight. One came down on the far side of the storage sheds. Dozens of others landed out of sight in the dark.

"There's no more time," Kevin said.

"We have to hide in the cabins," Wanda said.

Kevin pointed at the closest shed, crumpled from the crash. "Those dinosaurs will rip the cabins to pieces."

"You got any better suggestions?" Wanda asked.

Hissing came from every direction as the pods opened.

"That's it," Sierra said. "Everyone into the circle."

Most of the firewood had been thrown on the bonfire. Reggie hoped it was enough. It had to be. He dragged the last two smoking racks into place.

"Keep that wood coming," Reggie said.

The wall of the fire pit formed one edge of their circle. The people standing closest reached in, grabbed burning logs, and passed them down the line to the others in an odd perversion of a bucket brigade.

A roar came from the pod in front of the village's side exit.

Kona barked. David crouched next to her, one arm around her neck. He clamped his hand over her mouth, holding it shut.

"I can't do this," Wanda cried. "I can't."

A cacophony of roars answered from other pods.

Harmony reached into the fire and apparently grabbed a hot branch, because she jerked her arm back with a yelp. Her bracelets clattered.

"Goddamn it," Felicia hissed. "You'll draw them to us."

Cameron snatched Harmony's arm and yanked off the bracelets.

"Hey," she shrieked, rubbing her wrist.

Cameron tossed the bracelets into the bonfire and reached for her other arm.

"I got it," Harmony said. She stripped off the rest and threw them in.

A brown dinosaur climbed from the pod near the village wall. It was smaller than a Tyrannosaurus, but it was still plenty big. It had longer arms, with three sharp claws on each one. Bony ridges above its eyes gave it an angry expression. It marched around its pod, keeping its nose low to the ground.

"I bet it smells the shitters," Kevin said. Three outhouses stood just outside the wall in that direction.

"Keep the wood coming," Reggie said.

All of the smoking racks had caught fire except for the last two. The wall of flames was five feet tall around most of the twenty-foot circle.

"Where are those carriages?" David demanded. Sweat dripped from his forehead. They were all sweating. Heat hit them from every side.

Noise exploded from somewhere beyond the fire pit, growls and screams and crunches and some sort of heaving.

Felicia froze. "What's that?"

"They're fighting over the carcass," Reggie said.

The decapitated croc-dinosaur was up that way, beyond the light of the flames. A spark of hope grew. All that dead meat would distract the dinosaurs. It sounded like a feeding frenzy up there.

An Allosaurus came up from the fields, straight toward them. Everyone froze.

"It's coming," Kevin gasped. "It's going to get us."

Reggie tried to swallow. He could barely breathe. The Allosaurus stepped closer.

"Get ready to run," Sierra whispered.

Wanda whispered back, "Where?"

Sierra didn't respond, but the answer was obvious. They would scatter in every direction and maybe some of them would make it. There were only a few spots where the flames were low enough to jump through. Reggie picked out one close to him.

The dinosaur's scales shimmered in the firelight. The bottom of its head glowed against the black sky.

Kona growled. David huddled over her, clamping her muzzle with both hands.

The roars up by the carcass grew louder and something up there sounded like it was screaming.

The Allosaurus coming toward them walked alongside the ring of fire without looking down. Its tail swung back and forth as it passed, sending an eddy of wind through the flames.

"Oh my God," Wanda breathed. "Oh my God."

"Shhh-shhh-shhhhh." Sierra patted the woman's back.

"Hey," Cameron said quietly.

Reggie realized she was talking to him. He met her gaze and held it.

"Nice job," Cameron said. "You saved us all."

Reggie nodded, allowing himself a moment of happiness, such as it was. His plan had worked. He pulled down his hat and wiped his head.

"The carriages are here, Priya whispered. "They just landed."

"Where?" Kevin craned his neck, peering through the flames. "I don't see them."

"They're in the fields. About halfway down."

"Bring them closer," Harmony said.

"It doesn't work that way," Priya said. "We have to get to them."

Chapter Fifteen

Randall floated through some kind of stinging jelly. His skin was on fire, and not just his injured armpit and his wrists, but everywhere, even through his clothes. He held his breath, certain that if he opened his mouth and the goop got in, it would kill him. He kept his eyes closed and crossed his arms over his chest, drawing both knees up to his elbows.

He felt like he was falling, but the last thing he remembered was flying upward, through the opening in the ceiling. He desperately wanted to know where he was, where he was going, how fast, how far, but he couldn't dare open his eyes.

The hot sting crept into the tip of his cock.

Fuck. It was over. He was through. He tensed every muscle in his body, opened his mouth, and screamed. When all the air was out, the jelly pressed in, flames in his lungs. He waited for the end to come.

It didn't.

The pain continued, but it grew dull, like the tingle he got when his arm fell asleep, except covering his entire body. He still couldn't make himself open his eyes. Maybe this was death. Maybe hell was floating in stinging goo for all eternity.

At some point, he bumped into a wall, or maybe the ceiling or the floor. There was no way to know. Still squeezing his eyes shut, he picked a direction and followed the wall, pulling with his arms while he kicked. He swam forever. Minutes? Hours? Nothing changed. He never ran out of air, and it didn't even seem like he was growing tired. He wasn't breathing, but his mouth was open, and he could feel the goop, heavy in his lungs.

Finally, he noticed a dull glow ahead, bright enough to detect through his eyelids. Randall swam toward it, kicking along the wall, reaching out.

His fingers sank through something different at the bright spot, a new kind of goop, thicker than the crap he was swimming in. Randall wanted to open his eyes to look, but he couldn't make himself. He just couldn't. His arm sank to the elbow.

Was this the exit? Maybe it was the same opening he'd entered through. If he pushed forward, maybe he would fall through the ceiling and end up right back where he started.

Anything was better than the stinging jelly. Randall shoved his other hand forward and kicked with his feet. Out in front of him, his fingers broke into open air. His face touched the wall and the glow grew bright against his eyelids. He kicked and kicked as the membrane tightened around his head, then his chest.

Air cooled his arms, then his head. The stinging pain grew sharper, blazing now, inside and out. The moment Randall's mouth emerged, he puked and coughed, spewing jelly from his lungs. The pain grew hot.

As he passed through the membrane, gravity took hold of him, pulling him at a right angle, making him dizzy.

When his legs came through, he dropped and lay curled up with his eyes closed. The pain slowly subsided to a dull throb. He barely had the strength to move. His muscles felt like they'd been stretched too far.

As goop drained from his ears, sounds reached him. Not just any sounds, but the rumbles of wardens.

Finally, someone to give him some goddamn help.

Randall lay with his forehead against the floor and forced his eyes open. They burned, but not as much as he feared.

He turned his head, just a little. It was all he could manage.

The floor sloped up and away to a raised platform maybe ten feet higher than where he lay, with two huge wardens up there, twice as big as the other ones he'd seen. The platform was in the center of the room and the floor sloped back down from it in every direction.

He pushed himself up. A giant dome covered the room, but the walls weren't walls, they were windows, and they kept changing, expanding and shrinking. The windows looked out onto meaningless machinery.

One of the wardens slithered down the slope toward him, moving like some pale white thing beneath a rotten log.

There was nowhere to run, nothing he could use as a weapon, and Randall barely had the strength for either. He grunted and pushed himself up to sit against the wall. The warden stopped in front of him. It was as tall as he was, and three times as long. The whole blobby thing was as big as one of the giant prehistoric rhinos. Its feelers reached out and touched him.

The warden let out a rumbling burst of rotten air.

A translation came from a loudspeaker somewhere. *"Specimens must remain in habitats or storage."*

"You brought me here," Randall blurted, though it was only half true, if that. The hovercar had brought him part way and he'd come the rest of the way on his own. It dawned on him that they hadn't meant to bring him anywhere. The hovercar had simply returned to its parking spot. They probably didn't even know he was on it.

The alien rumbled for a bit without any translations. The other alien up on the center platform rumbled back, probably arguing about whether to stun him or just kill him outright.

"Don't you know who I am? I'm Randall. I'm the specimen that helps you." He pushed himself to his feet.

"Assistance is not required. Caretakers are responsible for specimens. Overseers are responsible for the carrier."

"What the fuck is the carrier?"

"The starship carrying the specimens is the carrier."

Randall froze. "Wait. We're on a ship?"

The warden didn't respond.

"Look, I'm the only one who can help you with the humans. Those wardens– the *caretakers*– they don't know what the fuck they're doing." They'd sure proven that time and again. "One of your caretakers got torn apart by some kind of bug monster. What the hell was that?"

"The caretaker received physical trauma, which triggered spontaneous metamorphosis into adulthood."

"Adulthood? That bug thing was an adult?" The alien in front of him was twice as large. "When are you going to become an adult?"

"Implants prevent maturation until replacements are bred."

"Implants, huh?"

He wondered if he could cause enough physical trauma to trigger the transformation. Of course, that would be suicidal. He didn't want to be trapped in this dome room with something that would vomit on him and try to eat him.

He needed to get these fuckers on his side, at least for now.

"I'm guessing your buddy didn't want that to happen? *That's* why you need my help. Those other humans will keep causing physical trauma if they ain't stopped."

The alien up on the platform warbled again and a map of the island replaced half of the dome ceiling. It looked exactly like the map he'd seen with the orange ball device, except this one was displayed on a goddamn jumbotron.

"Assistance with the human specimens is not required. Predatory theropods have been released on island seventy-five."

"What the fuck does that mean?"

The map showed red dots moving around in the village. The overseer must have selected one of the dots, because a big floating hologram of a dinosaur popped out, filling the room right above Randall. He held up one hand, blocking his eyes, and the dinosaur vanished.

"This whole room is a device," he muttered. The dome projected images into his eyes, just like that orange ball thing.

He noticed something else when he raised his hand. Most of the pain had dissipated. He touched his armpit through the tatters of his shirt. The skin there felt smooth, like an old scar.

From the look of the map, Dave and Sierra were fucked, which was great, but that also meant Randall had to find another angle if he was going to convince these aliens they needed him.

The alien in front of him blurted out more farty noises. *"Human specimen must leave overseer station."*

"Fine. How do I get back to the islands?" He'd call it a draw and get out of here. From the looks of the map, he would need to find a new island, since the one with the village was crawling with dinosaurs.

"Return through the brood chamber. A harvester will collect you."

The map was replaced by an image of the parking garage with all the hovercars and those giant clusters of bubbles. A silver and yellow drone floated nearby, just like the one that had visited him several times in the village.

"Will that harvester take me to the islands?"

"Caretakers have determined that all human specimens must return to storage."

They wanted to torpor his ass and put him in a pod. Fuck that. He needed to get out of here before the harvester showed up.

The room was a giant dome, maybe a hundred feet tall. Starting about eight feet up, the whole thing was honeycombed with little holes that projected into his eyes. The raised platform in the center of the room, where the other warden remained, was about thirty feet across. He couldn't see any way out of the place other than the little sphincter in the wall next to him. If the harvester came after him, there was nowhere to go. Randall tensed.

Then he relaxed.

The opening on the wall wasn't big enough for a harvester drone to fit through.

He took a few tentative steps around the warden. It was huge, but it didn't appear to have any way to hurt him, unless maybe it tried to slither on top of him and squish him.

"You ain't got no hovercars in this place," Randall blurted. "You can't torpor me, can you?"

"Human specimen must return through the brood chamber."

Randall smiled. He wasn't going anywhere. He wandered around the room. The overseer followed him, slithering along like a van-sized slug, repeating its demand for him to leave every few seconds.

He felt powerful. He was facing off against the biggest damn aliens he'd ever seen, and they couldn't do a thing to him.

When he'd completed the full circle, he stopped, realizing something a bit less appealing. They couldn't force him to leave, but at the same time, he was trapped here.

He was in another goddamn prison cell.

Chapter Sixteen

Sierra crowded toward the center of the ring, her cheeks hot from the flames surrounding her. We're getting out of here," she said. Looking down at Priya, she added, "All of us."

Priya gave her a thin smile.

"Reggie, can you and David carry Priya to the sled?" Sierra asked. They both nodded.

She looked at Cameron. "And you have to help David fly. Can you take the device?"

Priya tapped both sides of the device and it folded back into a sphere. Cameron picked it up.

Sierra leaned close. "Don't drop that," she said quietly. Her life depended on it.

Cameron winked. "Not a chance."

David knelt in front of Barry and Kim. "You guys stay right with me."

"And Kona," Kim said.

He nodded. "And Kona."

A roar came from beyond the light of the bonfire. A half-dozen roars answered it, most from the direction of the decapitated carcass.

"Kevin, Wanda, Felicia, Harmony, you're with me on the second sled," Sierra said.

Wanda wagged her finger. "Why do they get to go first? I want to go first." Her voice rose. "You're letting the *dog* go first." The poor woman was shaking, like she was freezing, which was impossible because they were all getting rotisseried by the flames surrounding them.

Sierra put her hands on Wanda's shoulders. "It's okay. You're going to make it. I promise."

"Why can't we all go together?" Harmony asked. "In the same car?"

Sierra shook her head. "We'd overload it. And we need room for food. Everyone who can, grab some food off the worktables. There's nothing to eat on Earth."

"Who's going to fly the second carriage?" Felicia asked, her tone wary.

"Priya," Sierra said. "Once she's on the first carriage, she's going to operate the second carriage with the device."

Priya gave her a thumbs-up. Reggie and David bent on either side of her and lifted, pulling her arms over their shoulders.

"Keep her leg off the ground," David said.

"Yes, please," Priya said.

There weren't any dinosaurs within sight of the flames. Hopefully, they were all up by the carcass. It sure sounded like they were.

Sierra crouched by the wall of fire and grabbed the end of a branch. She used it to sweep open a gap in the flames. Cameron hopped through before she'd finished.

Felicia knelt on the other side of the gap and helped widen the opening. David and Reggie sidled through next, holding Priya off the ground between them.

"Stay right with me," David said. Kim, Barry, and Kona followed. Kim held her brother's hand on one side and the dog's leash on the other.

David looked back. "Give us thirty seconds. We'll be slow and she needs time to set up the device."

Sierra nodded, but he'd already turned away. She and Felicia used their branches to shove most of the fire back into place. The wall of flames was growing shorter. They wouldn't be safe here for long.

Another series of roars came from around them, including several that sounded far off in the woods.

"I can't do this," Wanda said, swinging her head back and forth.

"Look at me." Sierra got right up in her face. "If we stick together, we'll get through this."

"Twenty seconds," Felicia said.

Wanda's head stopped jerking and her mouth clenched in an ugly grimace.

"I promise," Sierra said. "You're going to be okay."

The sounds of grunting and crashing came from up near the carcass.

"It's awful dark," Kevin said. He rose up on his tiptoes to look over the flames. "What if we can't find it? Should we take some torches?"

"No," Sierra said. "That might draw their attention. We don't want them to see us."

"Ten seconds," Felicia said.

Sierra counted down seven more seconds, then decided that was enough. "Let's go." She kicked a burning log, opening a passage through the flames. The others stared at her, uncertainty on their faces. Sierra took off. The best way to get them moving was to show them the way. Nobody would want to be left behind.

The air outside the ring of fire tasted gloriously cool and smelled like nothing, a huge improvement over the suffocating wood smoke. Sierra glanced back. Felicia followed a few feet behind.

Harmony, Wanda, and Kevin remained inside the circle of flames, like maybe they were waiting to see if Sierra got eaten.

Shit. Come on.

She waved for them to follow and kept going, weaving between the tables where they'd piled all the food. She grabbed a cloth bag of tubers and a chunk of dried meat. Felicia took a second bag and picked up a spear.

As she ran around the last table, Sierra glanced back again. Kevin and Harmony hopped through the flames, then finally Wanda.

Yes.

They were going to get through this. Sierra grabbed the binoculars from the last table, then ran to the path in the center of the fields, just barely lit by the bonfire.

Something flashed up ahead, then rose into the sky. It was Priya, aboard the first sled, turning on her device. *Yes. We've got this.* Sierra sped up.

The second sled came into view, right in front of the perimeter wall. It grew brighter and brighter as she ran, which didn't make any sense.

Daylight. Chills shot through her. High above, the blue ceiling-sky turned on, bringing the pale light of daytime.

Felicia ran next to her, breathing hard. *"Mierda."*

Sierra picked up her pace and glanced over her shoulder. Wanda, Harmony, and Kevin were still sixty feet back.

A dinosaur lay in the field on one side, just off the path. Sierra had run right past it. Blood covered its face and a four-foot rib bone sat beside it, stripped of meat.

Her heart skipped. She ran faster, only a few seconds from the sled.

The dinosaur was half the size of a Tyrannosaurus, which somehow made it more threatening. It spotted her and rose on both legs in a quick, smooth motion. It hadn't spotted the others yet.

Sierra and Felicia reached the sled at the same time. If Priya didn't fly them away soon, the dinosaur would come and pluck them right off.

For a moment, she considered running past the sled. She could flee into the woods, but then what? There were dinosaurs all over the island. She had to trust Priya.

She climbed aboard next to Felicia, turning around.

Harmony, Wanda, and Kevin were at least forty feet behind.

The Allosaurus was three easy steps from them.

"Run," Sierra shouted. "Keep coming."

Two steps. The Allosaurus opened its jaws. It had them.

Wanda poured on the speed, her long legs swinging in long strides. She began to pass Kevin. Sierra held her breath. If she could keep that pace, she might make it. If the three of them split apart, they might throw off the dinosaur enough to escape it.

Kevin body-checked Wanda, slamming into her with his shoulder.

Wanda crashed into Harmony, arms flailing. They tumbled in the dirt and the dinosaur pounced, jabbing, biting, stabbing with its head.

Sierra turned away. Shock threatened to overwhelm her.

Kevin reached the sled, climbed on, and shoved past her.

"Mother fuck," Felicia growled.

Sierra looked back. She couldn't help herself. She convulsed, her gorge threatening to blow. She'd told Wanda she would be okay. She'd promised.

Dinosaurs wandered all over the village. At least a dozen clustered up by Randall's cabin, at the remains of the carcass. Two wandered through the trees on the left, where people had camped in the open air. Another one came in through the side entrance, squeezing past the pod that had landed there. It trotted straight toward them. Sierra tensed, ready to bolt, but she felt so numb she wasn't sure she could.

The sled lifted from the ground.

"Thank God," Kevin said.

"Thank Priya," Felicia countered.

They ascended into the air and flew toward the beach. Within seconds, the forest canopy blocked their view of the village. A gray column of smoke rose from their dwindling fire ring. Out ahead, the other sled floated over the turquoise sea.

"*Pendejo,*" Felicia said, holding her spear toward Kevin. "You killed them."

He shook his head and scooted away, leaving behind an armload of smoked meat he'd brought.

Sierra coughed out a choking sob. He could have used the meat as a diversion.

"I didn't do anything," Kevin said, cradling his injured arm against his chest. "We barely knew those people."

The other sled flickered and disappeared, cloaking so it could descend through the water. Sierra wondered if Priya would need to cloak their sled, or if it would happen automatically. She almost didn't care. She felt hollow, empty.

"I didn't do anything," Kevin said again. "I didn't kill anyone. The dinosaur killed them. Not me."

"I saw you," Felicia said. The tip of her spear trembled, a foot from his chest.

"All I did was give her a push."

Felicia's mouth fell open and she shook her head.

Kevin scooted farther away from her, which brought him even closer to Sierra. "If I hadn't done that, I'd be dead now. I had no choice. You'd have done the same thing."

The sled left the forest and flew over the beach. Two dugout canoes lay below them, and the blackened remains of the big raft that had first brought Sierra here. She breathed deeply, bellows stoking a fire.

"What are we going to do about this?" Felicia asked.

Sierra didn't answer. Instead, she turned and shoved Kevin, as hard as she could. A line passed through his body as he fell off the sled. They were cloaked after all.

He screamed as he fell, then shrieked when he hit the beach. It sounded like he'd re-broken his arm, and maybe something else.

“Holy shit,” Felicia said.

Sierra tilted her head. “All I did was give him a push.”

Chapter Seventeen

Randall walked the perimeter of the room three more times before the big overseer finally slithered up to hang out with the other one. There wasn't much to see here, just a round room with a dome on top and a sloped floor leading up to the platform in the center. The aliens tapped away at a bunch of waist-high consoles ringing the platform, which seemed to change the images projected on the walls.

The images themselves were boring as shit. Most of the time, they showed nonsensical machinery. Pipes. Gears. Wires. Randall couldn't make heads or tails of it. Every so often, the images showed something more like a computer screen, with graphs and charts that made even less sense.

Boredom gave him the courage to walk up to the central platform. The slope rose about fifteen degrees, but in the low gravity, it felt like nothing. The second overseer was slightly smaller than the one that had confronted him and had a deformed limb hanging against the side of its body.

Neither alien paid him any mind. They just kept tapping away. Every so often, one would slither to a different console and tap on it instead. When the smaller one moved, the gimpy limb flopped against its hide.

The images on the dome were a hell of a lot sharper from up on the platform. It felt like looking through the walls, like he had x-ray vision, except it couldn't be x-ray vision, because what he saw on the other side kept changing. It was just those goddamn lights putting images in his eyes.

"Can you show a movie on this thing?"

The aliens didn't answer. They just tap, tap, tapped.

"What about Dave? You said the wardens sent dinosaurs to take care of Dave. Can you show that?"

This question got an answer. *"Caretakers are responsible for the specimens."*

"Yeah, yeah, but your caretakers suck. Show me the village. Prove how responsible they really are."

Both overseers moved to one side of the platform, where they tapped the console. The view from the closest part of the dome was replaced by an image of another alien, in a much smaller room. It looked like the same place he'd seen Sierra arguing with them back when they'd asked for his help. He'd sure helped all right. He'd blown out the brains of her geezer friend. Holy fuck, that asshole had pissed him off.

The alien in the small room buzzed and rumbled for a bit. The aliens on the platform rumbled back. It almost sounded like an argument.

After a few minutes, the alien on the wall disappeared and something amazing happened.

The entire dome projected one image, and it was from up in the air, above the islands. It felt like the room was flying. Randall spun around. The view had to be coming from a harvester floating out over the water.

The world shifted as the drone broke into a dive. Randall leaned back on the closest console, his legs wobbly from the sense of falling. He recognized the plateau in the middle of the island and even spotted a cluster of brown shapes that had to be them giant rhinos.

The view descended further, right down to the village. It really was full of dinosaurs now. They'd stripped the giant crocodile thing down to its bones. He saw no sign of Dave or Sierra, but how could they possibly be alive with that many dinosaurs running around?

Randall crossed his arms. That was supposed to be *his* village.

The view swung away from the buildings and the drone shot down the path to the beach. Randall leaned forward, grinning. This felt like rocketing through a tunnel, with the trees flying by on both sides and the branches whizzing past overhead.

The opening at the end of the trail came into view, blocked by the ass-end of another dinosaur. It clomped out onto the sand right before the drone caught up to it.

Someone crawled across the beach.

Randall held his breath, but as the drone flew closer, he saw that it wasn't Dave or Sierra, or even that bitch Cameron. It was the asshole with the broken arm who was always telling people shit they already knew. Kyle or Kenny or something like that. He was right out in the middle of the beach, with a bloody ten-foot-long track in the sand behind him.

The dinosaur marched closer. Randall licked his lips.

The asshole crawled toward the water as fast as he could, but he didn't stand a chance. The dinosaur tore into him like a hawk on a mouse. It stomped on his legs, bent, and pulled his arm right out of the sling. Randall snorted.

The guy on the beach wailed. Blood fountained onto the sand. The dinosaur bent down and came back up with most of his chest in its mouth. The wailing stopped.

"Human specimens are no longer causing problems," rumbled the larger overseer.

Randall wasn't so sure. Just because that guy was gone didn't mean the others were, too.

The images disappeared, replaced by the same boring bullshit that had been up there earlier, and it was all side-by-side again, instead of that glorious view that surrounded them.

"Bring it back," Randall said. "Show me more of the islands."

"Caretakers monitor the preserve. Overseers monitor the carrier."

"All right, you want to show me the carrier? Show me some parts I can understand. What the hell was that slimy crap I swam through to get here?" He gestured at the sphincter on the wall. "What did it do to me?"

"Biomolecular nanites perform cellular and genetic repairs."

More goddam fancy words. "Yeah, it healed me. I figured that part out. What the hell do you use it for?" He was pretty sure they didn't keep a pool of medical goop next to their command dome just in case an injured bastard like him came along.

Instead of answering, the alien with the floppy arm tapped something on the screen, and a new image covered a quarter of the dome. Hundreds of blobby aliens floated in the same pink goo Randall had swum through. Maybe thousands of them.

The aliens drifted around, sorta like sea creatures on a nature show. One floated by with a familiar orange object out in front of it. Randall pointed. "There. That's the device the wardens gave me." Tiny lights shone onto the alien's front end as it manipulated the device with its spidery limbs.

Randall glanced over at the sphincter. "Are those things in there right now?" He'd had his eyes closed the whole time, but he didn't remember bumping into anything.

"The brood chamber remains barren until gorgers are harvested," rumbled the bigger overseer.

Randall wasn't positive, but that sounded like an annoying way to say, "it's empty."

"Are there more of those orange devices somewhere?" Some of the lower walls round the room looked like panels that might open. For all he knew, one might hold a drawer full of them.

"Yes."

"Well, can I borrow one? I could use it to help you with the human specimens." If he got one of those devices again, he might be able to figure out some shit, like how to get back to the islands without getting torpored.

The hologram disappeared and the larger alien blurted a short sound. *"No."*

Randall got the distinct impression the big one didn't like him. It reminded him of his Aunt Marge, a hulking woman who had taken care of him when he was little and his mother was strung out. Aunt Marge hadn't much liked him either.

He started another circuit of the room. He could be patient. Lockup had taught him that much. At some point, however, he would need food and water. He wondered what he would have to do to get these fuckers to feed him.

Chapter Eighteen

Kim hunched down, arms crossed, gripping her elbows tight, as the carriage dove to the bottom of the sea. The light grew dim and she could almost feel the weight of all that water.

A violet glow suddenly surrounded them. Kim wanted to ask what was happening, but she also wanted them to think she was brave, so she pressed her lips together.

The glow vanished and they dropped through the ceiling of a vast chamber, almost as dark as the bottom of the sea. Butterflies flitted in her stomach. Kona whimpered.

"I feel funny," Kim said, worried she might barf.

"It's the low gravity," Dad said. "You get used to it."

Kim rose up on her knees for a better view. Dad and Cameron sat at the front of the carriage, manipulating the controls on the short wall that wrapped around the front third of the vehicle. As they descended, they wove between giant floating spheres that reminded Kim of the solar system mock-up hanging from the ceiling at the science museum, but way bigger.

"What are those things?" she asked. Some of the spheres were as big as her house.

Priya answered without bothering to sit up. "Sierra told me one of them was filled with the same rocks that are scattered around the islands."

"Rocks?" Reggie looked back at her. "What about the rest?"

"No idea," Priya answered.

"Where do we go now?" Cameron asked.

"All the way to the bottom," Priya said. "I sent the other carriage there. It should be right behind us."

Kim leaned over the side as they flew to the bottom of the slope, where it ended at the base of a featureless wall. The slope and the wall didn't connect, though. Instead, a horizontal floor extended into a dark opening that ran the length of the wall. "Where are all the aliens?" she whispered.

Priya sat up and pointed into the dark tunnel. "They hang out in little round pits about a kilometer that way. But there aren't many of them." The carriage settled to a stop. "Keep us moving," Priya said. "You can't select something while it's moving. If we're stopped, they might be able to select us and send us off somewhere."

"Let's go in a slow circle," Dad said to Cameron.

Just as they started moving again, Kona broke free from Barry's grasp and leaped off the carriage. She flew ten feet through the air. When she landed, she leaned forward, nose low, and puked.

Barry jumped down after her. "Kona!"

"Barry, get back in here." Dad used his serious tone.

The carriage circled right next to him, moving slowly.

Barry froze. "I can't see you." He was only five feet away.

"Crap. We're still cloaked." Priya reached for the device. Kim leaned close and watched as she uncloaked them. Chemical smells flooded in, like a swimming pool that had just been treated, along with a whiff of dog vomit.

"Watch this." Barry crouched down and jumped toward the carriage, flying through the air.

"Careful," Priya hissed, shielding her leg. Barry landed next to her, a stupid little smile on his face.

While Priya was distracted, Kim pulled the device onto her lap. She wanted to try out the low gravity too, but this wasn't playtime. Barry was too young to understand. She could sense from everyone's mood that they weren't safe here. Mom called it "reading the room."

Kona wobbled backwards for a moment, then she seemed to get her bearings. She took a few steps and pranced in a circle, like a deer.

"Kona, come," Dad called, using the same tone he'd used with Barry.

She wagged her tail and jumped into the carriage. Kim blocked her from crashing into Priya's leg.

"Hey," came a voice. It sounded like Sierra. "We're over here."

Thank God. The others had made it. Kim looked around, but she couldn't see them. *Of course.* They were cloaked. Kim found Sierra's carriage using the device and uncloaked it.

The other carriage floated just above the ground about thirty feet away. Sierra and Felicia were the only ones onboard. Kevin, Wanda, and Harmony were missing.

"What happened?" Dad said. "Should we go back?" He muttered an instruction to Cameron and their carriage slid toward Sierra's.

Priya nudged Kim. "Send them back and forth," she instructed. "Keep them moving." Kim selected Sierra's carriage and chose a spot just a few yards away.

"Where are the others?" Reggie asked. He glared at Priya. "Did you fly their carriage away too early?"

"No," Sierra said. "That isn't what happened. It was Kevin. It was all Kevin."

As soon as Sierra's carriage came to a stop, Kim sent it back where it started.

"Are they okay?" Barry asked, which was stupid, because obviously they weren't.

"They're dead," Sierra said. "All three of them."

Dad pulled Barry into a hug. Kim wanted a hug too, but Priya's leg was in the way. Then Dad let go of Barry so he could keep their carriage moving. They circled the other carriage slowly, like a shark, while it slid back and forth, like a door at the grocery store.

"Son of a bitch," Cameron said.

Reggie took off his hat and looked down, his eyes closed. Seeing him do that made Kim need a hug even more.

"Let's just fly to a shuttle and get out of here," Sierra said.

"Hold on," Dad said. "I've been thinking about that. We can't just leave."

"You said we could," Felicia said. "You told us they don't have any air traffic control, because dinosaurs can't hijack their ships." Her tone mocked Dad's voice, and Kim wanted her to shut up before Dad snapped at her.

He kept his cool. "It isn't that. We have to get everyone out of storage. If we just leave them here, the caretakers might kill them, or fly away with them, or who knows what."

Mom. He was looking out for Mom. Kim grinned, feeling light, and not just from the low gravity. She pulled the device closer. She should be looking for Mom right now, while the grown-ups argued. She waited for the other carriage to reach its destination, sent it back again, then navigated toward the storage chamber, which was below everything else.

"Leave them," Reggie muttered, putting his hat back on.

"You don't mean that," Sierra said.

"You better believe it." Reggie scowled. "People are terrible. Why in the world do you want more of them?"

Sierra's carriage slowed down as it approached its destination. Kim scrolled back, selected it, then got it moving again. She sent it farther away, hoping no one would notice, to buy herself a little more time.

"I'll tell you why," Sierra said. "First, we need help if we're going to fight the gorgers. They outnumber us a million to one. Second, if you were in storage, you'd want someone to come get you. And third, if we actually survive, we're going to need a bigger gene pool to keep going. No offense, but none of you are really my type."

"Humanity may be over anyway," Priya said.

"What are you talking about?" Dad asked.

"None of the women who have been here for months ever got their periods, remember? And nobody has gotten pregnant."

"It's the implants," Sierra said. "The neck implants must prevent it somehow."

"We don't know that for sure," Dad said.

Kim wished they would stop talking about sex. She tried to focus on the device. She'd returned to the storage section, which was huge, way bigger than the sloped room they were in. Countless oval objects floated in front of her, in a three-dimensional grid.

"I'm not going to sit here and debate this," Sierra said. "If we can't leave them here, let's just send them all to Earth."

Kim froze. They'd need the device for that.

"I don't know how," Priya said. "I only know how to select them one at a time, and there are thousands."

Kim thought there must be some way to do it. Priya was right about one thing, though. There were way too many pods. She still hadn't found her way back to the section of storage that contained humans. She tapped a pod to get a sense of scale. It held a dinosaur that looked like a Brontosaurus. Way too big. She scrolled across the grid and tapped a smaller one, which held a bird. She pressed her lips together, resisting the urge to groan.

"Where would we send them?" Felicia asked. "The gorgers are everywhere."

"Greenland was safe," Sierra said.

Cameron turned around and looked at her. "There weren't any gorgers in Greenland because there was nothing but snow and ice for two hundred miles. If we sent everyone there, they'd freeze. And if they didn't freeze, they'd starve."

"What if we send the pods down, but leave them closed?" Sierra asked. She sounded desperate.

Priya shook her head. "I don't know how to do that either."

Kim exhaled. There were so many things she needed to figure out, after she found Mom. And Tyrell, too. She'd almost forgotten about him.

"So what do we do?" Felicia asked.

"We'll scout the entire planet until we find a place that's safe," Sierra said.

"The whole planet is overrun by gorgers," Reggie said, still sounding angry.

"We don't know that," Sierra said.

"What difference does it make?" Dad asked. "We can't go scouting because we can't leave the pods here with the aliens. And we can't send the pods away because we don't have a place to send them."

For a long moment, no one said anything.

Kim kept scrolling, growing impatient. Every few seconds she had to zoom back out to keep the other carriage moving.

"Here's another idea," Sierra said. "We kill all the aliens."

Cameron responded with enthusiasm. "Fuck, yeah." Normally, Kim didn't like the F-word, but coming from Cameron, it sounded sorta cool.

"If we kill all the aliens, who will fly the ship?" Felicia asked.

"It should be safe," Priya said. "I think. It will almost certainly hold its orbit." Priya was close enough that Kim heard her swallow, like she really wasn't sure. "Everything here is automated."

"There's eight of us," Felicia said. "How the hell are we going to take out a whole ship?"

"There are only four caretakers on board," Sierra said. "Right, Priya?"

"That's all I could ever find," Priya said. "But you already killed one. They're down to three now."

"What about Randall?" Cameron asked.

"We need to find him and kill him, too," Sierra said.

"I'm good with that," Cameron said.

Kim wanted to agree, but she kept it to herself. Dad wouldn't like to hear her talk about killing someone, even if it was Randall. She chewed on a fingernail, growing frustrated. She still hadn't been able to find the pods with people. Mom and Tyrell would be stuck in storage.

Except Tyrell wasn't in one of the people pods.

He'd been trapped in the pod that brought the croc-monster. And Randall had chosen the croc-monster. That lazy turd never would have gone very deep looking for stuff.

She zoomed back out and searched the outer edge of the grid for pods a little smaller than the one with the Brontosaurus.

Sierra and Dad and the others were talking about how to kill the aliens. Kim tuned them out. It sounded like Sierra wanted to ask a bunch of questions first, but Dad thought it was dangerous.

She tapped a pod that looked like the right size. Dinosaur. She was warm. She scrolled along the row, skipping a bunch of smaller pods, then tapped the next big one she came to. Crocodile. Kim leaned forward. She was getting warmer, but this was a regular-shaped crocodile. The one that attacked the village had been half-dinosaur. She scrolled more and tapped another. *Ugh.* It contained some kind of giant pterodactyl thing with a neck like a giraffe.

"It sounds like we've got a plan," Sierra said.

Crap, they were wrapping up. Kim zoomed out. The other carriage was slowing to a stop again. The moment it did, she sent it to a new spot, then went back to searching through storage.

A minute or two later, Felicia climbed onto the carriage next to her and helped Reggie lift Priya from her seat.

"I need the device, Kim," Priya said, grunting as they picked her up.

"One sec," Kim muttered, stalling. She tapped a pod in the next section and saw a weird deformed elephant. Her shoulders fell. Cold. She found another group of pods that looked the right size. She tapped one and gasped. It contained a croc-monster exactly like the one that attacked the village. She'd found it. She tapped pod after pod. There had to be hundreds of them, all the same size, all in a row.

"Kim, now," Dad said. He was using the tone.

Kim got to her feet and picked up the device, which was easy to carry in low gravity. She hopped down, which was also easy, and kind of fun. She carried the device to the other carriage and handed it up to Priya, who had settled in near the front.

"Hey," she whispered, pointing at the screen. "One of these giant crocodile pods should have a guy inside. You gotta find him. He can help us."

Priya narrowed her eyes. She looked tired, annoyed, and uncertain.

"Please," Kim said. She didn't wait for an answer or an argument. Instead, she turned and jumped all the way back to the other carriage, crossing her fingers as she flew.

Chapter Nineteen

"Is there food?" Randall had already asked the question a dozen times, but the overseers only ignored him. He was hungry and thirsty and bored as hell. He stood at the edge of the platform in the center of the room. The 3D video dome, which had to be the best goddamn movie theater ever, showed nothing but boring-ass pipes and dials and machinery.

One of the overseers made a wet farting sound. Randall waited for a translation, but none came. Instead, he was hit by the worst taco-shit smell ever. He winced. Had that big fucker actually farted?

A three-foot wide column of water streamed down from the top of the dome, landing right in the center of the platform.

Randall dashed up between the aliens and reached out with both hands, cupping the water. He took a sip. The stench was worse up here, but the water tasted fresh. He tilted his head back and stepped forward, allowing it to pour straight into his mouth.

His foot landed in a thick pile of alien feces.

The alien hadn't just farted, it had taken a shit, right out its back end, over a grate in the platform. The water spilling from the ceiling washed it down a drain in the floor.

After Randall drank his fill, he lifted his foot and managed to rinse most of the sludge from his boot before the waterfall shut off. At least now he had access to water, though it was dependent on the aliens' shit schedule. He also now knew where he should do his own business.

"Is there food?"

Still no answer.

He was trapped and didn't have any options. If he tried to hurt these two fuckers, they'd turn into scorpion monsters and spit acid on him. If he swam back through that stinging shit, the harvester drone waiting on the other side would pack him away. And if he just sat here, he would starve.

The only good news was that he wasn't hurting any longer. That stinging shit really had healed him.

The alien with the gimp arm growing out of its head produced a rumble from the front end. The translation came a second later. *"Randall."*

The dome flicked to life. It showed a pair of hovercars floating through some dark chamber. Sitting on top were Dave, Cameron, Sierra, and the whole fucking bunch of them.

Randall laughed. "We don't need you, Randall. We can take care of everything, all by ourselves. We can send some dinosaurs to eat them, except we won't call them dinosaurs, we'll call them therpopods or some goddamn thing, just to show how fucking smart we think we are."

"Specimens must return to the preserve," rumbled the larger alien. The big turd really did remind him of Aunt Marge.

He held up his hands. "So stun them. Send one of your drones and stun them." Christ, did he have to spell out everything for them?

"Human specimens removed implants."

"How?" If he could somehow figure that out, he could swim back through the stinging shit and have full reign of the place.

The alien didn't answer.

"Well, call in the army. Send in some guards or soldiers or something and shoot them."

Marge rumbled a response. *"The carrier has no armaments."*

"What do you do when you get attacked?"

"The carrier does not get attacked."

The hovercars had flown out of camera range and the image shifted to one of those small circular rooms, where three aliens sat on hovercars parked nose-in along the walls.

A gunshot sounded. Orange slime oozed from a hole in one of the caretakers. The other two buzzed like a wasp nest. One of them disengaged its hovercar from the wall and floated backwards.

Felicia dropped into view, landing on the one that had been shot. She drove a spear into its back.

Sierra jumped down to the center of the pit, holding Joe's big Smith & Wesson revolver.

Randall watched with fascination. Those two broads were fucking up the aliens quite effectively.

Felicia's pike squelched through the body of the first alien. Orange goop geysered from the wound. The creature's limbs stretched out, reaching. Several new limbs, pink and wet, broke through the folds at the front of its body. Felicia wrestled her spear deeper and jerked it from side to side.

The alien was trying to transform, but she was killing the creature inside before it could even get out.

Sierra darted to the alien floating away from the wall and pressed the barrel of her revolver against its body. "Stop moving or I'll blow a hole in you."

"Caretakers cannot be killed."

She gestured backwards with her head. "Your buddy just proved otherwise."

Randall chuckled. He hated Sierra, but he had to give her credit. She was kicking ass.

"Human specimens must be placed in storage." A high-pitched zip punctuated its sentence. They were trying to stun her.

Randall grinned. She really had removed her implant.

"Wrong. We're going back to Earth, and you're going to help us."

Randall turned and gaped at the aliens on the platform. They hadn't told him going back to Earth was an option.

"Earth belongs to gorgers."

"Not anymore," Sierra said. "Get your gorgers off Earth and we'll let you live."

The caretaker didn't respond. She pressed the barrel deeper into its flank.

"Earth belongs to gorgers."

She braced her legs and pulled the trigger. Orange gore sprayed the curved wall on the other side of the creature and Sierra flew backwards across the room, knocked off her feet in the low gravity. The alien convulsed.

"This one's turning," she said as she picked herself up.

Felicia shoved her pike into the side of the second creature. Fluttery screeches came from inside the alien's body. She tucked the pike under her arm and shoved deeper.

Her spear must have broken through something, because it plunged forward two feet, pinning the thing inside.

Sierra moved to the last alien.

"You better tell him to answer her questions," Randall said, eager to see what else he might learn.

Flopsy slithered closer, his arm flopping against his head. *Randall must assist.*

Randall pictured the bumblebee drone on the other side of the goo chamber, where it was waiting to put him in storage. One of those drones had used a cattle prod to snap through ropes back in the village. He licked his lips, wondering if it could snap through Sierra.

"I know how to stop her. Tell your buddy to keep her talking."

"Randall must assist," Flopsy repeated.

"I'll tell you," he said, licking his lips again. "But only in exchange for food."

Chapter Twenty

Priya kept her carriage moving in an octagonal course about fifty meters out from the pit. The moment the carriage reached one destination, she sent it to the next. As far as she could tell, it wasn't possible to select a moving carriage, which meant as long as she didn't sit still, the aliens couldn't send her anywhere else.

The gunshots told her that Sierra's negotiations were underway. Hopefully, she was asking the right questions, without being too cocky. Priya wished she could be down there with her to make sure.

She scrolled through the pods in storage Kim had told her about while she flew to each location. It helped distract her from the throbbing ache in her leg.

The creatures were definitely some sort of prehistoric reptile, but Priya wasn't sure which species. Whatever they were, they looked nasty.

David and Cameron passed her, circling in the opposite direction. David gave a small nod. His carriage moved more smoothly, drifting in close to the pit to monitor the others, then swooping back out to watch for trouble.

Kim made eye contact.

Priya shook her head. *No luck so far.*

With Reggie standing guard at the rim of the pit, two carriages circling nearby, Felicia down in the pit helping out, and the implants gone from most of their necks, they had the upper hand. Even with a broken leg, Priya felt hopeful. Maybe not as confident as Sierra, but hopeful nevertheless.

She tapped another pod. Giant prehistoric reptile. Another pod. Giant prehistoric reptile. She wondered if Kim was wrong. Another pod.

This one contained a young Black man and the decapitated head of a giant prehistoric reptile.

"Bingo."

Her carriage stopped at its next destination. She held her breath and navigated the interface back to her location in the hangar as quickly as possible, hoping the aliens weren't watching. Hoping they wouldn't send her off somewhere else. She selected her carriage and sent it to its next point. It turned forty-five degrees and lurched forward.

She navigated back to storage and found Kim's buddy again.

If Kim said he could be trusted, maybe he could help. She selected his pod and then a spot near the edge of the pit, not too far from Reggie. A dotted line appeared. Kim's friend was on his way.

Chapter Twenty-One

Sierra pulled back the hammer on her revolver and stepped close to the alien on the sled. Two down, one to go. This was the last caretaker on the ship.

The creature's limbs retracted into the folds on its front end. Up close, the alien smelled like mildew and raw chicken.

"Let's try this again. Answer my questions, or I'll blast a hole in you."

"Caretakers cannot be harmed. Severe physical trauma will initiate metamorphosis."

"Yeah, I know. You've got one seriously fucked up life-cycle. Why is that? Why do you turn into mindless bugs?"

"Gorgers enjoy a lifetime of gratification without responsibilities or obligations."

She snorted. Put like that, it didn't sound so bad. Except it came at Earth's expense. She had to figure out how to get them off the planet. "Gorgers were on Earth before, right? Millions of years ago."

"Yes."

"But they didn't stay. We've never found a gorger fossil. How do they leave?"

"Harvesters collect gorgers after consumption is complete."

"Now we're getting somewhere," Felicia said, standing behind her.

Sierra nodded. "What's a harvester?"

The caretaker's limbs stretched for the controls on the wall in front of it.

Sierra pressed the gun deeper into its hide. "Don't try anything."

"Observe."

The spidery fingers tapped several controls and the wall came alive. Dozens of lights projected three-dimensional images into Sierra's eyes. The effect prevented her from seeing anything around her. She raised her hand, shielding her face. "You guys got my back?"

"Don't worry," Felicia said.

"Definitely," Reggie said, still up on the rim of the pit.

She lowered her arm and allowed the lights into her eyes. She kept the revolver pressed into the alien's side.

A holographic image floated in front of her, showing a barren moonlit landscape. "Is that Earth," Sierra asked.

"Yes. Sixty-six million years ago."

The camera panned down to show bloated gorgers littering the ground.

"There are Gorgers lying everywhere," Sierra explained for Reggie and Felicia's benefit. "Are they dead?"

"Gravid," the alien responded.

"What the hell does that mean?" Reggie asked.

"Pregnant," Felicia said.

Knobby bulges protruded along the gorgers' tails, which were swollen to twice their normal size. A silver and yellow machine flew into view. Metal arms telescoped from the front of the machine and wormed their way under the closest gorger.

"There's a big robot drone picking up the gorgers," Sierra narrated. "So that's a harvester? Why isn't the gorger moving?"

"Gravid gorgers enter torpor."

Torpor was their word for hibernation, or suspended animation, or whatever.

The drone carried the gorger to a giant sphere hovering nearby. A hole spiraled open on the sphere and the drone placed the gorger inside. In the distance, a cluster of spheres hung beneath the tail end of a shuttle.

"They're loading them up in these big round carriers to fly them off Earth," Sierra said. She assumed that the spheres had also brought them to Earth in the first place.

"Where do they take them?" Felicia asked.

The images switched to show hundreds of gorgers floating in a vast, pink sea. Many of them were clearly dead. Maybe all of them. Their bodies were in tatters, especially their tails. Oblong shapes the size of human skulls floated among the corpses.

"What is that, storage?" Sierra asked.

"Eggs gestate in the brood chamber."

"What happens to the gorgers?"

"Reconstituted tissues are used to nourish the subsequent generation."

The projection ended.

Sierra tensed, imagining a room nearby filled with pregnant gorgers. "Are those eggs on the ship right now?" She took a breath and relaxed her trigger finger. She didn't want to kill this bastard while it was being so forthcoming.

"The brood chamber remains barren until gorgers are harvested."

She nodded. She was definitely getting somewhere. "Okay. Send your harvesters to Earth and load them up." She dug the gun barrel back into the caretaker's flank for emphasis. "Do that and we'll let you live."

"Gorgers cannot be harvested until they enter torpor."

Sierra exhaled. "When will that happen?"

"Gorgers enter torpor after two hundred years of consumption and copulation."

"Fuck that," Felicia said. "Kill that goddamn thing and let's get out of here."

"Hold on," Sierra said. "Why does it take so long?" Maybe there was some way to speed things up.

"Nanogenetics prolong gorger lifespan to extend consumption and copulation."

Reggie snorted from the rim of the bunker. "Feeding and breeding. These fuckers bioengineered themselves so they can spend centuries doing nothing but feeding and breeding."

"What about you?" Sierra asked the caretaker. "When do you turn into a gorger?" She twisted the gun. "I mean, if I don't shoot you."

"Implants prevent metamorphosis through hormone manipulation."

She huffed. The aliens had implants, too. "Wait, do implants control human reproduction?"

"Yes."

Finally, some good news. The human race wasn't doomed.

"We need to get out of here," Felicia said. "Kill that fucking thing."

Sierra held up her hand. There had to be more. Something they could use. "How did you capture the dinosaurs and rhinos and all those other specimens? They couldn't have gotten into pods the way humans did."

"Harvesters implant sleeping specimens before placing them into storage containers."

"That's it. Make the harvesters implant sleeping gorgers."

"Gorgers sleep in cracks, crevasses, and tunnels where harvesters cannot reach."

Convenient. Of course they did. They couldn't stand the sunlight. Sierra wasn't sure she should trust these answers, but every one of them seemed plausible. "What about humans?" she asked. "Harvesters didn't implant sleeping humans. You just sent the pods and we got in them. What's up with that?"

"Storage containers triggered torpor. Implants were added to human specimens later."

"That isn't what I'm asking. Why did you send pods to Earth without any harvesters to do the harvesting?"

For a long moment, she thought the alien wouldn't answer. Maybe it didn't understand the question. Or maybe it was hiding something.

"Let's go," Felicia called out.

The alien finally rumbled again. *"Electromagnetic communication signals were detected from Earth after the comet was launched."*

"You mean like television and radio?" She relaxed her grip on the gun. It was still pointed at the caretaker, just not pressing into its hide. This was the missing piece, the connection between species she'd been searching for. "You realized humans were different from anything you'd ever collected before. But you'd already sent the comet, right?"

"Correct. Harvesters could not reach Earth in time, but we believed human specimens would enter storage containers voluntarily."

Sierra lowered her gun. "You saw we were intelligent, sentient. You wanted to save us. How many other sentient species have you encountered?"

"None."

"We can learn from each other. We can help each other. Isn't that why you saved us?"

Again, the alien waited to respond. Sierra gave it time to work through what she'd said, to come to terms with it. If she could make peace with the aliens, maybe they could agree on a compromise that would allow humanity to return to Earth.

Finally, the rumbles came again. *"Communication signals showed human specimens enshrouding Earth's land mass more successfully than any species ever encountered."*

She stepped back, scrunching her nose. "I don't understand. Why was that important?"

"Specimens are tested in the preserve for compatibility before barren worlds are seeded. Human specimens showed potential to propagate faster and more extensively than any other specimens."

It was almost too much to comprehend. "Wait. You're seeding other worlds with life from Earth? Why?"

"Future consumption."

"Mother fucker," Reggie said.

"It isn't a zoo," Sierra said. "It's a nursery."

"Shoot that piece of shit," Felicia said.

Sierra nodded. Her finger tightened, then she remembered one last question. "Where is Randall?"

The alien rumbled a reply, but the noise wasn't translated.

"Something's coming." Reggie called out.

"What?" Felicia shouted. "What is it?"

"Where's Randall?" Sierra asked again.

"It's some kind of robot," Reggie said. "Get out of there, both of you."

Sierra stepped away, braced her back against the wall, and pulled the trigger, blasting a fist-sized hole in the caretaker.

She looked up and recognized the shape descending toward the pit. She'd seen one just like it on the holographic projection a few minutes earlier. A harvester.

Chapter Twenty-Two

The last gunshot rang out right after Priya sent her carriage to another destination. She scrolled through the projected map, willing the carriage to move faster, but she was at least thirty seconds from her next stop.

"Priya, get over here," Reggie shouted.

"I can't," she muttered to herself. "It doesn't work that way."

A three-meter long alien drone floated silently down toward the bunker, just like the one that had picked up Sierra's stunned body the last time they were here. It was shaped like a robot version of a caretaker, with an oblong body and a bunch of mechanized arms protruding from the front end.

Priya turned back to the device, her fingers hovering over the control panel. The moment her carriage came to a stop, its icon solidified on the map. She tapped it with two fingers and then tapped a spot right next to the pit. The icon ghosted again. Her carriage spun and lurched straight toward Reggie. Priya hissed as the movement jostled her leg.

"On my way," she shouted. She would only be another minute. Until then, all she could do was watch.

Reggie pulled Felicia out of the pit with one hand, lifting her easily in the low gravity.

The drone floated in from a thirty-degree angle, about five meters above them and descending rapidly. David and Cameron were nowhere to be seen, probably staying clear so that Kim wouldn't get stunned.

"Look out," Felicia shouted, pulling Reggie back from the bunker. Foamy vomit shot up from below, like an ocean wave crashing against a breakwater.

A gorger. Felicia hadn't speared the last gorger.

Reggie and Felicia circled the rim, looking down. Sierra was still in there, but Priya couldn't see her. *Has she been hit by the acid?*

"Goddamn it, Priya, get over here," Reggie shouted.

"Yelling at me won't make it go any faster," she muttered.

Sierra jumped up on the opposite side of the pit and pulled herself out. She looked okay. Reggie and Felicia ran toward her.

The drone flew across the bunker, closing on her, blasting that zipping noise that triggered the neck implants.

"Nice try," Sierra yelled, cocky as ever.

Reggie and Felicia caught up to her, grabbed her, and pulled her back toward Priya.

The drone slowed and turned to follow, but its momentum carried it in the wrong direction for several meters.

Priya's carriage came to a stop beside the pit, a quarter of the way around from them. She grabbed the wooden brace around her leg and shifted it to the side so they wouldn't bump it when they climbed aboard. She tried to move it carefully, but shards of pain erupted below her knee.

The drone circled around, closing on them.

"Look out," Priya shouted.

Felicia turned and raised her pike. A dozen mechanical arms reached for Sierra, as if programmed to target her specifically. Felicia thrust with the stick, shoving the drone up and away.

"Get us out of here," Sierra shouted as she ran toward the carriage.

"Hurry," Priya called. "What did you learn?"

"Nothing helpful," Sierra said. "We're on our own. Just get us to a shuttle. We're leaving."

Kim's friend. Priya sucked in a breath of air. She'd forgotten all about him, and he wasn't even here yet. "We have to wait," she said.

"We can't wait," Reggie yelled.

The drone swooped back across the pit. Felicia raised the spear and tried to shove it again, but the end got caught in a crevice between all the different arms. The drone spun, yanking Felicia off her feet. She fell on her side at the edge of the bunker.

Reggie was right. They couldn't wait. Priya leaned into the device. Thousands of shuttles floated a hundred meters above them. She zoomed in and found the one directly over the observation bunker, careful not to touch it yet. She had the carriage selected and ready to go the moment the other three were aboard.

David and Cameron would have to pick up Kim's friend once he got here.

The drone bobbed out over the pit, taking the spear with it.

Sierra ran back and yanked Felicia to her feet.

The carriage dipped as Reggie climbed on. He waved the others closer. "Come on, come on."

Priya held her fingers over the control panel, ready to fly them away. They would accelerate quickly, but not instantaneously. Felicia and Sierra were almost there, and the drone was right behind them. Priya waited one more second, then tapped the destination to get going.

The carriage moved forward and rose.

Felicia climbed on. Reggie shoved her toward the front, dangerously close to Priya's leg.

Sierra ran, her lips pulled back in a grimace. The drone reached for her. She jumped. Her upper body landed on the back of the carriage. Reggie and Felicia grabbed her hands.

Yes! Priya had timed it perfectly.

An arm extended from the drone with a metal finger as big as an ice pick on the end. It stretched, touching Sierra's back right between her shoulder blades.

Bright light exploded with a thunderous boom, like a transformer blowing. Sierra flew backwards through the air. Reggie and Felicia tumbled forward, slamming Priya's brace. She screamed as pain ripped through her calf.

"Shit," Reggie shouted.

Priya blinked, unable to see anything but a bright afterglow and swirling sparks of agony.

Wind flicked her hair as the carriage picked up speed.

"Go back, go back," Felicia spat.

"I can't," Priya said, squinting away tears.

Sierra lay near the edge of the pit, smoke wafting up from her body.

"You have to," Reggie said. "The others can't help her. David and Cameron have to fly. Kim can't do anything 'cause she'd get stunned. It's up to us."

"It doesn't work that way," Priya growled. "I can't send us back until we reach the next stop."

"Somebody has to help her," Reggie said.

"Someone will," Priya said. "Where's David?"

The carriage continued to rise toward the shuttle overhead.

"He's coming," Felicia said. She waved him closer.

The other carriage swooped up next to them. David and Cameron matched Priya's ascent.

"Meet us in the shuttle directly above the bunker," Priya shouted. "Kim, I found your buddy. He's on his way."

Kim squeezed both fists in front of her, smiling.

Below, the drone circled toward Sierra's body.

"What the hell happened?" David shouted. "Is she alive?"

"She is," Priya said, desperately hoping it was true. "You have to keep that thing away from her. Go."

David and Cameron peeled off.

Above, the metallic belly of the shuttle grew larger. Below, the drone slowed as it closed on Sierra, still lying motionless beside the pit.

The pod with Kim's friend floated in from the other direction. Priya had done everything she could. The stranger would have to save Sierra, assuming she was even still alive.

Chapter Twenty-Three

The top half of the pod lifted, revealing a circle of dim light. Tyrell Carpenter rolled onto his hands and feet, doing his best to ignore the gash in his leg. Adrenaline coursed through him. He was ready to run, ready to fight, and ready to rip off Randall's head if he got the chance.

As the gap widened, that seemed unlikely. He wasn't in the village. Empty darkness surrounded him in every direction except one, where light rose from a round pit in a metal floor.

"Tyrell! Tyrell, we need you!"

He scrambled forward at the sound of Kim's voice. *She was alive.* As soon as the gap widened enough, he squeezed through and dropped to the ground, keeping his weight on his good leg. His stomach lurched. Something felt wrong.

A woman's body lay near the edge of the pit, some fifty feet away, wearing white motorcycle pants and a matching leather jacket.

He steadied himself against the side of the pod. "Where am I? What's happening?" He felt woozy, like he'd had too much to drink. He stank of blood from the croc-dinosaur, and his clothes were sticky with it. He wished he had his firearm.

"That's Sierra." Kim's voice came from somewhere above. "You have to help her."

He shouted into the darkness. "Where are you?"

Some sort of flying car dropped down between him and the pit. Several people sat on top. Tyrell couldn't make them all out in the dim light, but one of them was Kim.

"Please!" she shouted.

He stepped forward and stumbled, but not from his injured leg. It felt like he might float away. He tried to stop, and toppled onto his hands and knees. "What the hell?"

A drone followed Kim's flying car, just like the one that had hauled Mitchell's body away, right outside Randall's cabin. The drone swung in a wide arc toward the pit.

No, it moved toward the woman's body. Someone named Sierra.

The drone reached for her with those creepy octopus arms. An oversized hypodermic needle stretched toward her neck.

The flying car swooped down. "Oh, no you don't," shouted a white guy sitting up front. The car bumped the top of the drone, knocking it away.

Tyrell wasn't sure what was going on, but Kim clearly wanted him to help the woman on the ground. He got to his knees and pushed forward. He flew three feet and stumbled onto his face. *Gravity.* The gravity was lower here. Where the hell was he?

The drone took off after Kim and the others. They'd lured it away from the woman.

Moving slowly, Tyrell staggered forward. His head swam and his stomach threatened to revolt.

"Go get her," Kim shouted. *"Please."*

Kim and the drone flew off into the dark chamber, which extended forever in every direction. Tyrell lumbered over to Sierra.

She didn't have a pulse, but her skin, which was a shade lighter than his own, felt warm. Branching brown lines ran along her arms and crept up the sides of her throat, like a henna tattoo, except thick, like scar tissue. He eased his arms under her knees and neck. The smell of woodsmoke permeated her motorcycle leathers.

He lifted her in one easy motion. She was fit, maybe a hundred and thirty pounds, but in the low gravity she was light as a pillow. Now what the hell was he supposed to do?

He spotted a sliver glint twenty feet away. A gun. He started toward it. If nothing else, he could shoot that damn drone.

Something moved at the rim of the pit. A long, sharp finger came over the edge. Then another, and another.

Tyrell took a slow step back.

A gaping mouth appeared, surrounded by teeth. Those weren't fingers, they were legs. A monster pulled itself over the rim, a demon clawing its way out of hell.

"What the fuck?"

Tyrell stumbled back, almost falling, but managed to catch himself without dropping Sierra. He turned and strode clumsily to the capsule that had brought him here, then stopped. Two inches of blood pooled inside, not to mention that croc-dinosaur's nasty head. He couldn't put this poor woman in there.

The monster skittered across the ground toward him. It looked like a mouth on legs, with a big writhing tail that curved up in the air behind it. Tyrell's skin crawled. He flinched and twisted. His mind didn't know how to respond to something so horrifying.

He placed Sierra on the ground beside the pod, then turned back and stomped toward the creature. The gun was too far away, but he could still kick this thing's ass.

Squeezing his hands into fists, he took three wide steps, arcing so that he came at the monster from the side. Using his good leg, he punted it as hard as he could. His boot connected with the creature's body right where the legs attached. It went flying into the pit with a squeal.

Tyrell shuddered and let out an embarrassing squeal of his own.

The stench of the thing hit him, a mix of chemicals, sour milk, and beer vomit.

"Tyrell!"

The flying car floated down near the pod, hovering five feet off the ground. Kim sat right on the edge. Two other adults sat near the front, and a little boy.

"Put her onboard, quick," the man said.

Kim beamed, waving him closer. "Come on, hurry."

Tyrell grabbed Sierra and placed her up on the flying car next to Kim.

Kona was on there too. She made a *woo-woo* sound that filled Tyrell with joy.

Kim patted a spot on the other side. "Climb on.

He held up a finger. "One second."

He turned and ran back for the firearm. If it belonged to Sierra, he'd give it to her when she woke up. If not, it was his.

He ran in long, loping strides, finally getting the hang of low-gravity movement, and only limping slightly. He watched the pit, in case that mouth-monster climbed out again.

"Look out," shouted the man on the flying car.

Tyrell ducked and turned, but the man wasn't shouting at him, he was warning his passengers. The silver and yellow drone was back. It descended toward them, right above Tyrell's pod, which had begun to close. Kim's car accelerated away. The drone flew after it, making that same zipping sound Randall had used to knock out Mitchell.

Tyrell bounded toward the gun. It was a .44 magnum Smith & Wesson. "Now we're talking." The cylinder held three rounds.

He spun around. Kim and the flying car were nowhere to be seen.

"Kim? Where'd you go?" His shoulders dropped. "Kim?"

A rustling sound came from the pit. The mouth-monster was still alive. Or maybe there were more of them down there.

He turned around slowly. His eyes adjusted, and he spotted Kim's flying car, a quarter mile away. Was he supposed to follow them? It seemed like his only option.

He took off in a loping gait toward Kim, hoping it was the right thing to do and wondering where the hell he was.

One other thought bubbled up out of the blue, surprising him. He wanted to make sure that Sierra woman was okay.

Chapter Twenty-Four

"Kim, does she have a pulse?" David shouted without looking back. He wanted to check for himself, but he had to focus on flying. He couldn't understand how Sierra had been knocked out. She didn't have an implant. He also had to figure out how to get back to Tyrell without leading that drone right to him.

Kim didn't answer.

BWWWWAAAAP! The harvester tried to zap them again. It sounded like it was right behind them. At least it was chasing them and not Tyrell.

"Bank right, ninety degrees, then climb," David said.

Cameron followed his instructions, matching his movements on the controls, but she was slow. He had to repeat his own movements until they aligned with hers. The carriage spiraled upward.

"Can you feel a pulse?" he asked again.

"No, Daddy," Barry cried. "I can't feel it."

David jerked around. Barry had his hand on Kim's neck, not Sierra's. The drone had zapped her. Kona was out, too. He told himself to breathe. It was okay. She could be revived, just like before. Hell, they could revive her with this very carriage once they had a chance to stop and remember which controls to use.

One of Sierra's legs hung off the back of the carriage and Kim wasn't very far from the edge herself. "We've got to get them up between us," David said. "So they don't slide off."

"Full stop?" Cameron asked.

He nodded. "Good idea. Hang on, Bud, we're going to slam to a stop. Three, two, one."

Together, he and Cameron brought the carriage to a standstill in perfect sync. Arms and legs slid forward, bunching up against David's back.

"Pull their legs up here," Cameron said. She dragged Kim's feet into the space between the two of them.

David twisted and grabbed one of Sierra's ankles. Barry helped him maneuver her legs into place. It was as secure as they were going to get. "Hold onto me, Barry."

Kona lay unconscious behind Cameron. He had to hope the dog would stay in place.

"Daddy, it's coming."

The drone closed on them. One of its arms snaked over the back of the carriage, reaching for Barry.

David spun back to the controls. "Go, go, go."

They shot forward. The legs wedged between him and Cameron shifted from the acceleration, but neither body slid out of place.

"Where's Tyrell?" He was risking all their lives for a guy he'd never met. But Kim trusted him, and he'd saved Sierra. Or at least he'd tried. David still didn't know if Sierra was even alive.

They raced along, a hundred feet above the floor. The grid of shuttles hung another two hundred feet above them.

"I see him," Cameron said, leaning over the side. "He's following us."

"Call the route," David said.

"Wide turn to the left," she said. "Make sure that drone stays out behind us."

David touched the controls and they entered the turn, banking to help keep everyone in place. "Barry, feel Sierra's mouth and see if she's breathing."

"Down ten feet," Cameron said.

David still couldn't see Tyrell, but Cameron had better vision than anyone he'd ever met. He trusted her.

"I can't feel it," Barry said. "She has lines on her skin."

David didn't know what that meant, but if she wasn't breathing, they needed to start CPR. "Bud, I want you to push on her chest, right between her boobs, as hard as you can."

"Daddy."

"Do it now," David said. "You'll be a hero. Push, wait, push again." He didn't look back. He had to trust him, too. "Push, wait, push again. Push, wait, push again."

He spotted Tyrell about a hundred yards off to the side, running their way. David pointed. "There he is. Tighten the turn."

"No," Cameron said. "We have to circle wide and come up behind him. If we fly straight at him, we'll lead the drone right to him."

"Okay. Good call." He glanced over his shoulder. Barry was giving Sierra chest compressions. "That's it, Bud. Keep going. Push, wait, push again."

Tyrell turned, running toward them.

"Other way!" Cameron shouted. "Run away. We'll come up behind you."

Without slowing, Tyrell swung away from them, leaning into the turn as he ran.

David glanced back again to see which side of the carriage had more room. Barry continued the chest compressions. Hopefully, he was circulating enough blood through Sierra's brain to keep her going.

"Come up on his left," David said.

Ahead, Tyrell kept running, barely visible in the gloom.

"Down three feet," Cameron said.

They moved in sync, and the carriage shot along, only a foot off the floor.

"Keep running," David shouted.

Tyrell kept going. He even sped up a little.

The front corner of the carriage passed him, close enough that Cameron could have reached out and touched his head.

"Jump on," David shouted. A moment later, the back end plunged under his weight. If they dropped low enough, they might scrape the floor, and if the carriage took damage, they were screwed. He started to instruct Cameron to climb, but he didn't have to. They both hit the controls instinctively.

"What the hell is going on?" Tyrell asked, panting. "Where are we?"

"Later," David barked. "Do you know CPR?"

"Kinda," he grunted.

"Take over for Barry. We have to get her breathing again."

"What about Kim? Is she okay?"

"She's fine for now." He looked back. "Please. Try to help Sierra."

Tyrell nodded, moved into position, and started chest compressions.

"Oh, shit," Cameron whispered.

David spun forward. A wall of silver and yellow drones rolled toward them. Dozens, approaching from the right. He blinked, trying to moisten his eyes, dry from the constant wind. The observation pit was somewhere behind them. They had to meet Priya in the shuttle directly above it. "Tight circle left," he said. "Bank into it."

The turn pressed him into his seat, even in the low gravity. As they swung around, the pit came into view, a glowing dot in the distance.

"Steady climb." They rose toward the silver ceiling of floating shuttles.

The sound of deep breathing came from behind. Tyrell was giving Sierra rescue breaths.

"Look out," Cameron shouted.

A drone dropped in front of them.

"Down. Right," David shouted.

They dropped and spiraled. The arm of the drone buzzed as they passed it. The hair on David's neck tingled, as if he'd just walked under a high voltage line.

A moment later, the drone produced the zipping sound, attempting to stun them. David tensed, wondering if it had been close enough to zap Tyrell.

"I think I got a breath," Tyrell said.

David exhaled. He was still with them, and maybe Sierra too. "Level out," he instructed.

Their trajectory flattened and a swarm of drones swept toward them, now coming from their left. Sweat dripped down David's back.

He picked out the shuttle that was directly over the pit, then counted back from there. "Six shuttles. We need to fly into the sixth one from here. Help me keep track."

The drones surged up like a tsunami from the left.

"We aren't going to make it," Cameron hissed.

She was right. The drones were climbing fast, and they were flying straight toward them.

"We have to get up between the shuttles." He gestured with his chin. "Slip right."

The cloud of drones continued to rise toward them.

They shifted sideways until the gap between two rows of shuttles was directly above them.

"Climb."

They angled the carriage into the gap, which felt huge, far wider than it needed to be.

"Wings," David blurted, suddenly remembering. Long canard-like wings protruded from the shuttles near the front, too thin to see in the dim light, especially at this speed. The wings would decapitate them. "Higher."

The carriage pitched up sixty degrees and they rose right over the nearest wing, just missing it.

"Level off." They shot forward, straight down the empty space between the lowest rows of shuttles and the ones above them.

THONK

David flinched. "What was that?"

"One of the drones crashed," Tyrell said.

THONK CRUNCH THONK

David leaned over the side of the carriage. He could no longer see the observation bunker. "How far are we?"

Cameron looked over her side. "I can't tell."

He tried to visualize their route. The entrance into a shuttle was through a tunnel that ran down its long, tubular tail. The shuttles were all parked with their tails pointing toward them, thank God, but the target they were aiming for was tiny. They needed to be lined up ahead of time, and there was only one way to do that. "We have to get back beneath the shuttles."

"Say the word," Cameron said.

David waited until a wing passed beneath them. "Down, now." His butt lifted from the surface of the carriage as the nose dropped. Another zipping sound came from behind.

"Still with us?" Cameron asked.

"Yeah," Tyrell said. "Barely."

They leveled off as they dropped below the lowest row of shuttles. The third one passed by overhead, or maybe the fourth. David had lost count. "Which shuttle is that?" He still couldn't see the pit. It had to be directly ahead, hidden from view by the nose of the carriage.

Barry reached forward, pointing alongside his head. "That one is number four." As they swept under the shuttle, he moved his finger. "That one is three."

David glanced back. The closest drone was thirty or forty feet behind them.

"Here comes number two," Barry said.

The long tubular tail of the next shuttle came into view above them, with its circular opening right at the end. They passed beneath it. He and Cameron shifted sideways a few feet, centering their flight path.

He still couldn't see the pit below. He had to trust Barry. "We fly into the next one. Straight in. No slowing down."

Cameron glanced over, uncertainty on her face. David nodded. It was their only chance.

The belly of the shuttle above slid past. The tail of the next one came into view. Their target. David didn't bother to give Cameron instructions. They both knew where they were going. They moved in sync.

The carriage rose as they passed under the nose of the last shuttle.

David closed his mind to everything except flying. He had to trust that Barry's count was correct. He had to trust that the drones weren't too close. He touched the controls, bringing the carriage up until the opening in the tail was dead ahead.

He and Cameron both ducked as they passed inside. The sound of the wind changed from a steady hiss to a tight whoosh. They were in.

Priya's carriage floated out in front of them, right in the center of the spherical cabin.

"Now," Felicia shouted.

Priya's face glowed from the lights on her device. She moved her carriage into the docking arm, which caused the pastel panels all around the cabin to brighten. At the same time, the opening in the tail behind them spiraled shut, closing before the drones could enter.

"Slow, slow, slow," David said to Cameron. "Full stop." One of the unconscious bodies pressed against his back. The moment they stopped, he turned around.

Barry held Kim's hand. He looked small. David squeezed him. "You did great, Bud."

Tyrell sat with Sierra's head in his lap. "She's breathing."

Priya tapped at her device, then looked up. "We're on our way."

"Okay," Tyrell said, speaking loudly. "I've been pretty damn patient. I've done everything you people asked. Somebody tell me what the hell is going on. Where are we? What was that thing back in the pit? Who are you people? And where's Randall?"

"Here's another question," Sierra said, looking up at him. "Who are you?"

Chapter Twenty-Five

Flopsy and Marge rumbled at each other for a long time after the dome's projection disappeared. None of it was translated, but they seemed pissed. Randall couldn't understand why. The aliens had only lost three of their own and they'd hit Sierra with a gazillion watts of electricity. His suggestion worked.

While they talked, he tried to process everything he'd learned.

These fuckers turned into bugs that were feasting on the remains of Earth, and when they were done, the bumblebee drones would bring them back here, to that room full of goop where their eggs would hatch and the next generation would start all over again.

Meanwhile, they collected animals from Earth so they could drop them on a random planet somewhere, and then do the same damn thing there. Humans had apparently been a last-minute discovery. They'd gotten all excited about how quickly people covered the planet.

Sierra's panties were in a bunch over the fact that this whole process took hundreds of years, but as far as Randall was concerned, that was the silver lining. None of it mattered. He'd be dead long before the gorgers were brought back onboard. They could spend the next hundred years picking the bones clean on Earth for all he cared.

At least *they* had food. Randall was fit to starve. "Hey."

Flopsy and Marge ignored him.

"Hey!"

They kept rumbling at each other.

He walked up and smacked the closest console with his palm. "Hey, turd-face, listen up."

Both overseers stopped rumbling.

"You agreed to feed me if I helped. I did my part, and it worked."

Flopsy rumbled and shifted back a few feet. *"Use the feeding tube."*

On the inside of the console, a tiny door opened at crotch-height and a black nozzle slid out.

Randall glared. "You gotta be shitting me."

Flopsy reached for the controls.

"Wait." Randall's hunger won out over his pride. He got on his knees and placed his lips over the end of the nozzle.

Warm mush shot into his mouth. It tasted like smashed-up vegetables with grit mixed in. He closed his eyes and sucked it down.

When the flow finally ended, he pulled away, his stomach cramping. "What the hell was in that?" He held up a finger before they could answer. "No. Don't tell me."

Marge rumbled something, but it clearly wasn't directed at him because it wasn't translated. Flopsy rumbled a response.

Randall threw up his hands and walked down from the central platform, hoping he wouldn't get the runs from whatever he'd just swallowed. He certainly wasn't hungry any more. He might never be hungry again after sucking down that shit.

Behind him, Flopsy broke away from Marge and humped down the slope, moving like a zoo walrus looking for its fish treat. His floppy arm smacked the side of his head as he shuffled. He stopped at the curved outer wall, on the opposite side of the room from the sphincter Randall had arrived through. A small panel opened in front of him.

Randall walked over. "What's going on?"

Flopsy didn't answer. Instead, he extended two of his bony little finger-arms and tapped some holes behind the panel. A hatch the size of a freight elevator slid open, allowing a gust of wind into the room. It didn't exactly smell fresh, but it was better than the musky stench coming from Flopsy.

Randall stuck his head through the opening. The other side looked like that big hangar where the hovercars had been parked. He couldn't see the floor. It was too dark out there and too far down.

"You can't leave me here with Marge." Randall leaned close. "She hates me." A rumble came from a speaker somewhere, translating Randall's words.

Flopsy tapped the panel again.

"Seriously. Where are you going? What's wrong?"

"Seventeen harvesters are damaged, one shuttle is gone, and the preserve is no longer controlled."

"What do you mean a shuttle is gone?" Randall's hackles rose.

"Human specimens removed a shuttle from the carrier."

He couldn't believe it. "You didn't zap them? Sweet Christ on a Kawasaki. You should'a sent *all* the drones after them, like I said." He wanted to rip off Flopsy's gimp arm and beat him with it. It had taken him forever to convince them to send more than one harvester after Sierra and the others, and even then, they'd only sent a handful.

"Harvesters are precious. Harvesters must be protected."

"Yeah, you fucking told me. How did they get the shuttle out of your carrier? Why didn't you close the airlocks or turn on a tractor beam or, I don't know, shut off the goddamn power?"

Flopsy's rumbling reply sounded just as angry. *"Not possible."*

"You let them get away." These fuckers simply weren't prepared for human beings. All of their technology was built around picking up dinosaurs and mammoths and monkeys that couldn't even think about fighting back.

"Gorgers will consume them."

Randall wasn't so sure about that. "Okay, fine. What's the problem with the preserve?"

"The preserve requires a caretaker. Human specimens killed the caretakers."

"Yeah, I saw that on the big screen. Go get some more."

"There are no more caretakers."

Randall stared at the blobby fucker, barely able to process what he was hearing. "Ain't you got backups?"

"Only one caretaker was needed. Human specimens killed all three reserve caretakers."

"Where's the rest of your people?"

"Earth."

"No. Not the gorgers. Where are the rest like you?"

"There are none until the next breeding cycle."

"And that isn't for a hundred fucking years," Randall said, growing excited as the opportunity before him took shape. "Are you seriously telling me that you and Marge are the only two aliens left on this entire goddamn ship?"

"*Yes.*"

"Holy shit." He was two heartbeats away from being completely in charge. Once he learned how everything worked, he could kill these two fuckers and have the run of the place.

"So you're going to be caretaker while Marge stays up here to be overseer."

"*Yes.*"

"Good for you."

"*No. Caretaker is a low position.*"

He laughed. That explained the arguing earlier. They'd been fighting about who had to take the shit job. Marge had won. Of course she had. The biggest asshole always won.

"All them human specimens are still in storage, right?" A few days back, he'd brought eight people into the village. Two of them had turned out to be decent choices. Those were shitty odds, but there were thousands to pick from. He could find more.

"*Yes.*"

"Okay, listen. Here's a solution. I'll be caretaker."

Marge rumbled loudly from the center of the room. "*You failed to care for a single island.*"

Randall clenched his jaw. "I wasn't a caretaker. I was a specimen. I was trying to manage things from the inside. Put me in one of them control rooms where I can actually be in control."

"*Specimens belong in the preserve,*" Marge said. "*There is no precedent for using a specimen as a caretaker.*"

Randall chuffed. "Yeah, well, you didn't have no precedent for specimens that could fly your ships around and kill your buddies, did you? Things changed when you started collecting humans. You got in over your head, and if you ain't smart enough to see that, you're just as stupid as you are ugly."

Marge rumbled, but whatever she said wasn't translated.

A hovercar floated up and stopped right outside the hatch, waiting for Flopsy to shuffle aboard. Randall took the initiative. He stepped onto the hovercar first.

"*A specimen cannot be caretaker,*" Flopsy said.

"I ain't moving." Randall crossed his arms. "You just have to trust me. Send me down to that caretaker station and tell me what to do." If the controls worked like they did on that orange device, he might even be able to figure them out on his own.

Flopsy reached for the panel on the wall with two limbs.

Randall smiled. He was going to be in charge of everything on the islands.

The hatch closed.

He sat down and waited for the hovercar to carry him away.

It didn't move.

"I'm ready," Randall shouted.

The back side of the hatch was blank, without even a panel or button he could use to open it, just a big rectangular square in the middle of a big empty wall. Randall walked over and knocked. No answer.

The ceiling was maybe thirty feet up, and it was too dark to see walls in any other direction. Randall leaned over the side, but still couldn't see the floor. He poked at the controls at the front of the hovercar for a while. Nothing happened. They were going to just leave him here.

"Ha ha. You're fucking hilarious."

He sat down and waited.

Chapter Twenty-Six

Sierra lay flat on her back, taking long, slow breaths. She was on a carriage inside a shuttle and she was in pain. Beyond that, she didn't know much else. It felt like fire ants were stinging her. She reached across her chest and touched her arm. Rigid blisters covered her skin. Based on the stinging, they probably covered her neck, the top of her chest, and most of her back.

"What about Kim?" asked a man hunched over her. His voice sounded desperate. "You have to do something about Kim."

"It's okay, it's okay," David said. "She's stunned." He nodded to Cameron and counted to three. The zipping sound echoed around the shuttle's cabin.

A steady thumping came from nearby. Sierra turned her head. Kona's tail slapped the surface of the sled, over and over again.

"Where are we?" Kim asked. She drew in a breath. "Tyrell!"

"Ah, thank God," said the man, apparently Tyrell.

"Is everyone else okay?" Sierra asked, still flat on her back. "Did everyone make it?"

David crouched beside her. "Yes. We're all here. What happened? Where does it hurt?"

"Everywhere."

He pulled her shirt away from her shoulders. "Those are Lichtenberg scars. You get them when capillaries burst from electrical shock."

"Is there permanent damage?" she asked. "My organs? My mind?"

"Hopefully not, but I ... I can't know for sure. Right now we can only treat the symptoms."

"I have something that can help with the pain," Tyrell said.

David looked up at him and his mouth dropped open. Sierra expected him to ask about whatever he had that might help. She desperately *needed* him to ask.

Instead, David stood and stepped back, pointing. "You're the guy from TV. You shot those people on the golf course."

Tyrell rose as well. David took a step closer, like he was about to shove him off the sled. Cameron appeared at his side. The three of them faced off above Sierra while she lay on her back, looking up at them.

"That isn't what happened," Tyrell said, balling his hands into fists. His cargo pants were torn and bloody on one leg.

"Dad, stop," Kim cried. "He saved my life. And Kona. He didn't shoot anyone."

"I *did* shoot someone," Tyrell said. "I shot the guy who butchered all those people you saw lying on the golf course. He also killed my squad. His sons were about to kill me, too."

Sierra pushed herself up on one elbow. The effort sent shards of glass through her temples. At least it was dim inside the shuttle. The pastel lights dotting the curved interior were about as bright as she could handle.

"That isn't what it looked like on TV," David said.

"I saw it, too," Reggie said. He stood on the other sled, maybe a yard away.

Tyrell's lips pulled back from his teeth. "That video came from the sons. You only got their side of it."

Sierra staggered to her feet between David and Tyrell, forcing them to step back. Her head throbbed. Spiraling scars covered her arms.

"How do we know you aren't making that up?" Reggie asked.

Felicia stood next to him on the other sled, which was docked at the shuttle's front wall. Priya and Barry sat behind them. Everyone was here. They should be celebrating, not fighting. Everyone had made it and the caretakers were all dead.

"Please," Kim cried. "You have to believe me. He's a good guy."

Tyrell's face melted at her words. He seemed genuinely touched.

Sierra turned slowly, looking at everyone. "Come on. Are you going to believe what you saw on TV, or Kim?" She glared at Reggie. "I trust her judgment. If she's vouching for him, that's good enough." She stopped turning when she faced David.

Everyone was silent for a long moment. David nodded.

Kim's face brightened. Reggie looked down.

"Thank you," Tyrell said quietly. "I promise, I'm here to help."

"I hope so," Sierra said. "If you try anything funny, Priya will stun you."

The corners of his eyes twitched with the hint of a smile.

"Now, unless anyone objects, I'd like to lie down and pass out."

Tyrell looked past her, to the other carriage. "Wait. Where are Wanda and Harmony?"

"They're dead," Sierra said. She squeezed her eyes shut. The memory of the Allosaurus ripping them apart flooded back.

"Christ. I thought I saved them."

"You did," Kim said, sounding sad. "This happened later."

Sierra collapsed to her knees, then dropped back on her butt and lay down.

David turned to Tyrell. "You have something that can help with the pain? I'm a doctor."

"Morphine." Tyrell pulled a small first aid kit from a pouch on his pants. He and David sat down on either side of her.

David took the pouch. A moment later Sierra felt the bite of a needle in her arm.

"Wait, hasn't that expired?" Cameron asked. "It's been more than a hundred years."

Tyrell flinched. "What?"

"If it's expired, it should be inert," David said. "It won't help, but it won't hurt either."

"You know, I could use some explanations here," Tyrell said. "I have got a shit-ton of questions."

The poor guy had a point. "What do you want to know?" Sierra asked.

"What happened to Randall? Where is he?"

"He's somewhere back on the ship," Sierra said. A light buzz tickled her eyes.

Felicia waved her hand. "Let him rot up there."

"No," Sierra said. "The people in stor'ge."

"You slurred your words," David said. "I think the morphine is still good."

"Is there more?" Priya asked. She sounded miles away.

"A little," Tyrell said.

Cameron crouched beside him. "What other supplies have you got?"

"Not much." He ticked off a list. "Some papers, glow sticks, zip ties, a flint, and a whistle."

Sierra listened intently, but none of the items seemed useful, and it was increasingly difficult to concentrate.

"Let's have a look at your calf," David said.

Tyrell pulled apart the shreds of his pants leg. "What does she mean by storage?" he asked.

"There are thousands of people in suspended animation," David said. "They're fine for now."

"Don't be so sure," Tyrell said. "If Randall gets hold of them, he'll kill them. He's a goddamn monster."

"I t'ink I like t'is guy," Sierra said. The burning in her skin had ceased and her eyelids weighed a hundred pounds. She let them fall shut and listened as Tyrell asked more questions, but she could barely make out the words, and soon she couldn't hear anything at all.

DEVOLUTION

Chapter Twenty-Seven

Cameron matched David's movements as the shuttle entered Earth's atmosphere. They'd actually done it. She'd come a long way since that fateful ride down Mona Kea. They'd killed all the caretakers and escaped the mothership. Now they just needed to find a place to colonize.

Everyone agreed to start the search in North America. It was home. They flew west across the Atlantic, directly into the sun. The projections from the front wall kept the light dim enough to look at without hurting their eyes.

"Where should we try first?" David asked.

Cameron smiled. She'd found a partner, and he was far better than any man she'd ever been with, even Charlie. She pointed at a hook of land reaching toward them, jutting out beneath a layer of cirrus clouds. "Is that Cape Cod?"

"I worked there one summer," Felicia said. "It doesn't look right."

They descended beneath the cloud deck and the sun vanished. Below, a thin stretch of barren land curved into the sea. Rocky piles dotted the ground like ant hills.

"A hundred and fifty years have passed," Priya said. "Never mind the fact that Earth was clobbered by the Ender. It's bound to have changed."

"Do we have to wait until night to know if there are gorgers around?" Tyrell asked. He sat in the other carriage with Sierra, who was still out from the morphine, and Reggie, who seemed to be keeping a close eye on him.

As they descended, the rocky mounds covering the cape became recognizable. They weren't ant hills, they were the remains of buildings and, in some places, whole towns.

"The gorgers seem to tolerate anything short of direct sunlight," Priya said. "With this cloud cover, if they're down there, we should see them."

"I already do," Cameron said. She told herself not to get discouraged. It was a big planet.

As the shuttle passed over land, the scope of the devastation became blatant. Nothing remained standing and gorgers crawled on the rubble everywhere. They scurried in and out of cracks like ants. They mobbed the forests, which now lay in jumbled piles. Cameron's skin crawled. She'd rather face dinosaurs than nasty-ass bugs.

"What are they doing?" Tyrell asked.

"They eat anything organic," Priya said. "They vomit stomach acids on their food to soften it up."

"We knew we would see this," David said. "Let's keep looking."

As they flew south along the eastern seaboard, the outlook only grew worse.

In New York, some of the rubble piles were a hundred feet tall and the gorgers were so thick it was impossible to make out individuals.

They passed over a stretch of interstate running through what had once been New Jersey. Cars were lined up for miles in both directions, eight lanes across. Gorgers streamed between them, climbing in and out through broken windows.

"Why are they getting in the cars?" Barry asked.

"There are people in them," Kim said.

"What? We should help them."

"They aren't alive," Kim said. "They died when the Ender hit."

"Oh."

"How is there anything left?" Cameron asked. "Wouldn't they have rotted away by now?"

"They were probably charred to a crisp," David said. "I'm guessing the moisture was broiled out of them when the Ender hit, like a hot dog cooked in the microwave too long."

"Yum," Felicia said.

They flew into the suburbs, where gorgers crawled over collapsed houses like maggots on meat. The creatures puked on wooden siding, framing, and furniture, then slurped up the runny remains.

"I didn't realize there would be this many," Tyrell said.

"The caretakers told Sierra there are billions," Priya said.

"Let's try someplace different," Cameron said, disgusted by the sight of all those wriggling legs.

"Yes, please," Kim said.

"What are you thinking?" David asked.

"Let's try the middle of nowhere," Cameron said. It felt nice to have her opinion valued. "Somewhere in the Great Plains. That's where Priya and I found our pod."

They climbed above the cloud deck and flew west, accelerating to keep up with the setting sun.

"How did Wanda and Harmony die?" Tyrell asked quietly.

"A guy named Kevin shoved them into a dinosaur," Felicia said.

"A gutless coward named Kevin," Cameron corrected.

"Jesus," Tyrell said. "Why?"

"He did it to save himself," Felicia said. "He sacrificed them so he could get away."

"Where is the son of a bitch?" Tyrell asked.

"Sierra threw him off the back of the carriage," Felicia answered.

"Fuckin' A," Cameron said. This was the first time she'd heard what actually happened.

Beside her, David tensed. "That's murder," he said.

"She took action," Cameron said. "Nobody took action with Randall or Joe or Thad and look what happened. Sierra did what had to be done."

He shook his head. "She killed him without a trial or a discussion or anything. How is that any different from what they did?"

"Are you serious?" Cameron asked. "Thad drowned children. Joe tried to shoot your daughter."

"Jesus Christ," Tyrell said.

"That's right," Felicia said. "Randall shot Morrie in cold blood. And Waldmire. Do you really think Sierra is the same as them?"

David looked around. "I don't think she's the same as them, but you can't just decide to execute someone. That isn't okay."

"Why not?" Cameron asked.

"Because you might get it wrong." He pointed at Tyrell. "A few hours ago we were ready to execute this guy."

Tyrell leaned away, holding a neutral expression.

"I was there when Kevin killed those people," Felicia said. "I saw what happened. Kevin deserved exactly what he got."

"It's not about Kevin," Reggie said, his voice low. "It's about Sierra. When you kill someone, it changes you. Trust me."

"Is Sierra bad?" Barry asked.

"It isn't that simple," David said.

"I think it is," Cameron said. "We pussy-footed around with Randall, and now he's free."

"Things ain't like they used to be," Felicia said. "The old rules don't apply anymore."

"If we don't have rules, we don't have anything," David said.

"We have trust," Felicia said. She jabbed a finger toward Sierra, still lying unconscious on the other carriage. "Everything she's done has been for the benefit of this group. Not for herself. That's the difference. There isn't anyone I'd trust with my life more than her."

Tyrell whispered, "Damn."

"She's right, Ace," Cameron said.

David looked at her, but didn't say anything.

"Why don't we wait and see what she has to say after she wakes up," Tyrell said. "She deserves a chance to explain herself. I know that from experience."

No one else spoke, which suited Cameron just fine. There wasn't anything else to say on the matter.

The sky cleared somewhere beyond the Mississippi River, revealing a brown desolation that extended all the way to the Rockies. Towns dotted the terrain, connected to one another by the broken remains of highways, with vast empty stretches between them.

"It's all dried out," Felicia said. "We aren't going to be able to grow anything down there."

"Irrigation is a problem we can solve," Cameron said. "Millions of gorgers isn't."

She wondered if they could establish a base of operations in the middle of nowhere and go out scavenging in the carriages. The idea appealed to her. The thought of settling down in one spot like some sort of homesteader felt constraining.

"What's that off to the left?" Reggie asked.

A dark smudge covered a square mile of land just south of a small town.

"Let's have a look," David said.

The shuttle turned and descended toward a blackened swath that looked like a lava plain, covered with jagged waves and troughs. A dozen corrugated metal buildings were scattered around the dark smear, all in various states of ruin.

"I see gorgers," Kim said. "In the shadows."

Cameron spotted movement in the shadow of a building that looked like a silo. She turned her focus back to the lava field. "Did this come from some sort of volcanic eruption?"

Her question was directed at Priya, but Tyrell provided the answer. "That isn't lava. This was a feedlot."

"What's that mean?" Barry asked.

"Cattle," David said. "Those were cows. The Ender melted them together."

Now that she knew what she was looking at, Cameron was able to make out hooved legs, heads, and ribs jutting from the mass. In the shadow of the silo, a row of gorgers had buried their faces in the edge of the charred pile.

"Thank God we can't smell it," Felicia said.

"As nasty as that is, the numbers here seem low," Tyrell said. "There can't be more than a hundred gorgers. We should keep looking in this vicinity."

They climbed back up several thousand feet and flew north until they spotted open terrain without anything man-made nearby. Jagged cracks crisscrossed the dried and desiccated ground.

"This could work," Tyrell said. "It looks perfect."

Cameron glanced over her shoulder and gave him the stink eye. "It looks dead, is how it looks."

They brought the shuttle down on a small hill that felt a lot like the one where Charlie had parked his truck when they found their pod, except now everything was brown instead of green.

When they undocked the carriage from the central stalk, the front wall went dark and a weight fell across Cameron's shoulders, like when the dentist draped a lead vest over her for x-rays.

Kona whimpered.

"Oof," Tyrell said. "Is that normal?"

"Welcome back to Earth gravity," Priya said.

Behind them, the hatch at the end of the tail spiraled open and late-day light spilled in.

They crammed into one carriage and flew back to the tail, stopping shy of the end. They left Kona, whimpering, on the other carriage with Sierra, still out cold.

Cameron and the others all hopped down into the cylindrical tunnel, except for Priya, whose hopping days might well be over.

The opening at the end of the tail was a hundred feet up, giving them a view for miles. David kept his distance from the drop off, gripping both kids by their wrists. The air smelled of dead leaves, which was odd. There wasn't a single leaf in sight, not even a blade of grass.

"What do you think?" Tyrell asked, looking back and forth at the others.

"It looks delightful," Reggie said with a dry tone.

Gaping cracks covered the plains, like the bottom of a lake that had dried up. It looked like it hadn't rained in a decade.

Kim held binoculars to her face, gazing off into the distance. "I don't see any gorgers. That's something."

"There aren't any gorgers 'cause the sun's still out," Felicia said. "Give it another hour."

"Still, if there aren't any nearby, it should be reasonably safe," Tyrell said. "How far could they travel at night?"

No one answered. Probably because no one knew.

Cameron studied the jagged cracks below, some of which looked big enough to fall into. She squinted. Something moved down there. "Kim, let me have those binoculars."

She lifted the strap from her neck and handed them over.

Directly below the end of the shuttle's tail, the dark crack appeared to be filled with hairy, wriggling worms. Disgust and dread crept up Cameron's spine. She scanned along the crevasse until she found a wider spot. They weren't worms, they were gorger legs. The nasty fuckers were wedged in there like roaches, deep enough to keep out of the sun.

"Gorgers," she said, lowering the binoculars before her legs got too unsteady. "Hundreds, waiting to come out as soon as it gets dark."

"I guess we keep looking," Tyrell said.

She gave him another stink eye, but he didn't notice. His unbounded optimism was a bit much. Cameron was starting to wonder if there was any place left on Earth that wasn't infested.

Chapter Twenty-Eight

David knew he was missing something. He just didn't know what. But he needed to figure it out quickly, before despair overwhelmed him and everyone else. Hearing that life on Earth had been wiped out and the planet was overrun by alien creatures was one thing. Actually seeing the devastation was almost too much to bear. It left him disturbed and dismayed, right to his core. Judging from the dark mood in the shuttle, he wasn't the only one.

He wished he could talk it through with Sierra. She always had ideas, especially crazy ideas no one else would have thought of. It frustrated him that she never took the time to stop and think things through and it frustrated him even more that she usually got it right. Possibly even with Kevin.

"Should we keep heading west?" Cameron asked.

The shadows of dusk stretched across the ground like grasping fingers. Or gorger legs.

David didn't answer. The shuttle might be fast enough to keep pace with the sun, but the thought of chasing daylight around a dead world felt dismal and exhausting.

"What if we look for survivors?" Kim asked. "Instead of a place to settle."

"There aren't any survivors," Reggie said. "No one survived this."

"Don't say that," Kim said.

"Humanity is pretty resilient," Tyrell said. "People must have survived somewhere."

"Exactly," Kim said. "And if we find them, we'll find a safe place."

"We certainly aren't going to find them here," Felicia said. "It's almost too dark to see anything."

"Lights," David said, snapping his fingers. That's what he'd been missing. He remembered flying over Minneapolis in his Cessna at night, marveling at the lights below. "Night is the perfect opportunity. If anyone survived, lights will be the easiest way to spot them. We should look for artificial lights, campfires, anything. There has to be a fortified encampment somewhere. They could even be using floodlights to keep the gorgers at bay."

"I like it," Tyrell said.

They flew back to the east at an altitude of roughly ten thousand feet. Based on what they'd seen earlier, David didn't expect to find anyone along the eastern seaboard, but he wanted to be thorough, to rule out every possibility.

It was fully dark below by the time they spotted Lake Ontario. They swung south and followed the coast, keeping just below the clouds. By the time they reached Florida, everyone but him and Cameron had fallen asleep.

"Are you going to put Sierra on trial when she wakes up?" Cameron asked. She looked like a ghost. The glowing pastel panels that dotted the shuttle's interior barely lit up the chamber, and very little light came from the front projection.

"It isn't like that," he said, trying to figure out how to change her mind without sounding like an ass.

"I would have done the same thing, you know," Cameron said.

"Yeah, well, I trust you, and I trust Sierra," David said. "But I don't trust everyone. If we're going to bring the rest of the people down from storage, we're going to need some sort of rules. If everyone makes their own decisions about life and death whenever they want, things are going to be much worse for all of us."

They broke out from the clouds over the Caribbean. David was able to make out Cuba, Hispaniola, and Puerto Rico below. All of the islands were just as dark as the eastern seaboard had been.

"I see your point," Cameron said finally.

He waited for her to say more, but she didn't. He decided to leave it at that.

When they reached South America, they zigzagged back and forth as they continued south, crisscrossing what should have been the Amazon Rainforest, though it was too dark to tell what was actually below them.

David reached out and took Cameron's hand. She squeezed his fingers, her eyes twinkling in the starlight.

Twice, they spotted lights, but both times turned out to be stars reflected from the surface of lakes.

"I see something," Cameron said as they made another U-turn at the Andes. "Thirty degrees to the right."

They shifted their flight path and after a few seconds, David saw it too. Orange light glowed a hundred miles ahead, deep in the heart of the continent.

The sight woke him up like a shot of espresso. He smiled. If they somehow found coffee, they'd be able to accomplish anything, and if coffee was growing anywhere, it had to be here.

He imagined what they would say to the people down there. They would have so many questions. What would they think of an alien spacecraft descending from the sky? Would they even be able to communicate? Felicia was fluent in Spanish, but what if they found people who spoke Portuguese? After a hundred and fifty years of isolation, they might have developed an entirely new language.

As they drew closer, they saw that the orange glow came from more than one source. David squinted. "Are those campfires?" he whispered.

"I don't think so," Cameron said. Judging from her tone, she'd already figured out what they were, and it wasn't good.

They descended to five hundred feet and flew over a glowing hellscape.

The flames appeared to be the remains of a forest fire, probably sparked by lightning. A few charred tree trunks remained standing, but most lay across the ground like matchsticks. Gorgers wandered all over, glowing orange in the firelight.

"Those things really are everywhere," David said.

Cameron took his hand again but didn't say anything. She wasn't the sort to give pep talks.

They spotted two more forest fires before reaching Cape Horn, both smaller than the first one.

"Let's keep going," Cameron said. "I've never been to the south pole."

The Antarctic snow glowed blue under the night sky. They didn't see any settlements or research stations, though neither of them knew exactly where to look.

"No gorgers down here, I bet," she said. "Nothing for them to eat."

"Nothing for us to eat either," David said.

"We could set up a base here, then go north to scavenge every few days."

"Scavenge for what?" he asked. "We can't bring all those people from storage to live on an icecap. What would we do for shelter?"

"I'm talking about just the nine of us," she said.

He didn't respond. His heart ached at the thought of Kim and Barry growing up on a dead world, watching the rest of the group die off from one cause or another over the years.

"Let's try Africa," he said after they'd wandered over Antarctica for an hour. They had to climb to the stratosphere to figure out which direction to go. He rubbed his eyes and told himself to be patient. They just had to keep looking.

At some point, after they'd descended back to a reasonable altitude and crossed the Cape of Good Hope, Cameron shook him awake.

"Wh— what happened?" he asked, though he knew the answer. He'd fallen asleep at the controls.

"You dozed off."

"Where are we?"

"Middle of Africa. Wake up Priya. It's her turn to take a shift."

He wanted to argue that he could last a little longer, but his eyelids told him otherwise. "What are we even doing?" he asked. "Are we wasting our time?"

"We'll find someplace," Cameron said.

He gave her a grim smile. "You aren't a very good liar."

Chapter Twenty-Nine

They had to return to the mothership. Priya was certain of it. No place on Earth was safe, especially not for her, not with a broken leg.

The shuttle came to a stop over New Guinea. The sun was high overhead now, but the rest of the group was still asleep. Priya rotated the control device so its lights projected into her eyes. She selected a new destination somewhere in the center of Australia, then rotated the device away so she could focus on the images projected by the shuttle's front wall.

"Where are we?" Tyrell's voice startled her, though it was barely a whisper. He crawled over and sat next to her, moving carefully to avoid bumping her leg. Kim had been correct. Tyrell was a good guy.

"That's Australia," she answered, raising her chin toward the front. The ground ahead of them was broken and jagged, perfect real estate for gorgers.

"What else have you seen?" he asked.

She wondered how much detail he wanted and decided an overview would suffice. "The gorgers have really done a number on the planet. They're everywhere. Europe looked as bad as the eastern United States. Maybe worse. It had a similar patchwork of cities and forests."

"Were any of the forests still standing?"

"Some, though most of the trees were dead. In northwestern Russia, the forests were dense enough for gorgers to wander around in broad daylight. Eastern Asia is a pyroclastic wasteland. It didn't look as if anything will grow there for a century."

She didn't bother to mention India, where her parents had been when the Ender hit. Seeing the ruins of Jaipur had brought tears and she didn't want to start crying again, especially in front of this man she barely knew.

"Any signs of survivors? Barricades? Fortifications? Did David see any lights in the dark?"

She shook her head. "No one survived the Ender."

Tyrell offered her a piece of jerky from one of the canvas bags in the back of the carriage. She took it eagerly. She'd been hungry for the past two hours, but hadn't wanted to crawl over the others to get it. The shuttle came to a stop along the eastern shore of a shallow sea that now covered the Australian interior.

"What about here?" Tyrell asked.

Priya took in the view. "Well, for starters, there's no fresh water for several hundred kilometers. Next, there isn't any soil. It's all rock and sand. We couldn't grow anything here. And third, there are gorgers."

"Are you sure?"

She glared at him, then rotated the control device back toward her face. She used two fingers to zoom in and selected an arroyo to the east. The shuttle flew to the new location in less than a minute.

Dozens of gorgers clung to the underside of a shaded rock wall, like roosting bats.

"I'm sure," Priya said. She selected a new destination and they started moving again.

"What about islands?" he asked.

"Well, I've only sampled a hundred or so, but none of them looked good. The smaller Pacific islands are gone. Medium-sized ones were scraped bare by the firestorm when the Ender hit. The larger ones are covered with gorgers."

"Even if an island is covered with gorgers, that's a finite number," he said. "We can deal with them."

"How?" she asked. "There are nine of us. Two are children and one is crippled." She held both hands out over her leg for emphasis.

"We'll have everyone in storage to help us."

"Again, how? You'd have to bring them down someplace safe enough, in broad daylight, explain to everyone what's going on, and convince them all to take up arms against the gorgers, never mind the fact that most of them won't be armed, and we'd need to secure the island before night fell."

Tyrell scowled. "There are lots of islands. Somewhere, there has to be one without gorgers on it."

Priya took another bite of jerky. "We're heading to Tasmania next. The Australian mainland may have shielded it from the brunt of the Ender's blast. And it's fairly remote." She shrugged. "Maybe the gorgers missed it."

"You don't sound optimistic," Tyrell said.

She swallowed the jerky, impressed he could read her so easily. She wasn't good at that sort of thing. "The gorgers won. Even if there are ten thousand people in storage, we can't fight off billions of gorgers, never mind the fact that we somehow have to produce enough food to survive."

"So we're done for?"

"I say we take our chances on the mothership. The islands up there are a perfect habitat for us."

"Is there enough room for everyone in storage?"

She shrugged. "I don't know. Maybe not."

The ship passed above the ruins of Melbourne and then rocketed out over the ocean.

"How is Sierra doing?" he asked.

"David gave her another half-dose of morphine before he went to sleep. He seems to think she'll be okay." Priya wished she could take another half-dose of her own to quiet the throbbing in her leg.

As they approached Tasmania, late-day sunlight streamed in from the right. The shuttle's path followed an inlet between two low ridges to the ruins of a small city.

"There have to be things down there we can use," Tyrell said as they passed over the rubble. "Even something as simple as a metal tool."

"It's infested with gorgers," Priya said. She pictured gorgers wriggling through collapsed buildings, eating the charred remains of the people who had died in them.

"How can you tell?" he asked.

"The dead zone," she said. "See how the trees around the city are nothing but jagged black stubs? There aren't even any weeds. When you get out in the countryside, you sometimes get a smattering of green here and there, but when you're close to a city, none."

The detritus of civilization passed by below. Crumbling piles of bricks memorialized the remains of houses. Lines of metal husks that had once been cars gave shape to stretches of roadway. The metal skeletons of industrial buildings showed where people had gone each day to build things, fix things, sell things, or whatever they did to earn a living.

Priya pointed to a large house in the suburbs. "Everything organic is picked over. If you look closely at the ruins, you can see there isn't any wood. The framing is gone. The furniture is gone. It's just bricks, metal, and concrete."

The shuttle continued out into the countryside south of the city and stopped at the location Priya had selected. She spotted a farmhouse a kilometer away and sent the shuttle to it. Bits of wood framing jutted from the rubble.

"See how that one still has some wood?"

"Yeah," Tyrell said. "Does that mean it's safe here? If the gorgers are all back in the city, maybe this is far enough away."

She shook her head, wondering where his optimism came from. "We're less than fifty kilometers from the city. That's an easy march, once the sun is down."

"We don't know how many gorgers are in that city," he said. "Maybe the dead zone you pointed out was created years ago. Maybe there aren't many left here. We could handle a few dozen. Maybe even a few hundred. If we bring everyone down from storage, there will be thousands of us."

He'd taken on a single gorger in the mothership. Priya tilted her head. He really didn't understand what they were up against.

"Let's go see if you're right," she said. She touched a spot on the map and sent the shuttle back toward the city. The view swung a hundred and eighty degrees. As the sun dropped, shadows from the ridgeline to the west stretched toward the ruins. Above, stars began to twinkle in the sky. It was the perfect time to spot gorgers, dark enough for them to come out, but still light enough to see.

The shadows reached the outskirts of the city as the shuttle came to a stop. Right on cue, gorgers streamed out, so thick they looked like sludge. They poured from the ruins in the thousands, fanning out like ants. Tendrils moved in every direction. They lined up at the edge of the shadow, moving with it, until finally, the sun dropped behind the plateau and they swarmed south across the barren plains.

"You still think we can handle them?" Priya asked.

Tyrell didn't answer.

Chapter Thirty

Reggie had to be dreaming, because his son was alive. Chase had made it into the pod with him and now they were returning to Earth. He couldn't square the fact that Chase hadn't been in the village with him all those months, but he ignored the discrepancy. Chase was alive. That was all that mattered.

In the dream, Chase piloted the shuttle, and he'd found a spot where they could bring everyone down from storage. Reggie grinned with pride. His son was a hero.

They landed in the center of a university quad. Chase and Reggie walked through the shuttle's tail onto bright green grass. Dormitories surrounded them, untouched by the Ender. The tail should have been a hundred feet in the air, but somehow they were able to walk straight out onto solid ground. Another discrepancy. Another indication this was a dream. Reggie ignored it.

Hundreds of pods landed around them. "Come on, Pops," Chase said. "Let's pick out a room before all the good ones are taken." He was suddenly younger, maybe nine years old.

Sierra, David, and Jasmine stood beneath a grand sycamore tree, waving them on. They wore the plastic toothless smiles of dolls.

Chase ran toward a towering marble building. Wide stairs led to double doors set behind a row of columns, with "Hamilton Hall" carved on a stone edifice at the top.

"Wait," Reggie called out.

He needed to tell him that dorm was already full, that they should pick another one. For some reason, the words wouldn't come.

Chase bounded up the stairs, taking three at a time.

Reggie tried to run after him, but his feet wouldn't move. He stretched out his hands, reaching.

Sheriff Dart stepped out from the door and shot Chase at the top of the stairs.

Reggie snapped awake, shaking and hissing between his teeth.

"Bad dream?" Felicia asked. She sat on the carriage next to him.

"I guess," he said, trying to sound like it was nothing. He was dripping with sweat.

She handed him a piece of fruit. He took it to be polite. He didn't think he could keep it down.

David and Cameron sat at the controls in the other carriage. Low sunlight beamed into Reggie's eyes from the front wall. They were flying over an ocean somewhere.

He turned away to check on Sierra, who lay near the back of the carriage. He desperately needed something to focus on, to help him stop thinking about Chase, sprawled across marble steps with blood pouring down beneath him.

Dark scars curled up and down Sierra's neck and arms like the fronds of a dead fern. She twisted in her sleep. A curl of hair fell across her face. Reggie moved it aside, careful not to wake her. *You should have let me kill Kevin*, he thought. He wished he could have taken that burden from her.

"Priya is right, we should go back to the mothership," Felicia said, addressing the rest of the group, all in the other carriage. "It's safe there."

"It's a prison," Cameron said. "It could fall out of the sky at any time, or fly across the galaxy to who-knows-where."

"There isn't room on the islands for everyone in storage," David said.

"We don't know that for sure," Priya said. "We only visited a handful."

They all sounded angry, like they'd been arguing for a while. Reggie wished he could go back to his dream and tell Chase to choose a different dormitory.

"There are lots of islands on Earth we haven't tried yet," Tyrell said. "We need to keep looking."

"Earth is a wasteland," Priya said. "We cannot survive here."

"You don't know that," David said. "We've barely scratched the surface."

"I say we give up on the people in storage and just focus on the nine of us," Cameron said.

Reggie nodded, though no one was looking at him. Sheriff Dart was in those pods. Not the real Sheriff Dart, of course, but people just like him.

"How would that be any easier?" Kim asked.

"We can land the shuttle where it's bright out and use a carriage to go scavenging," Cameron said. "We return to the shuttle before it gets dark. Whenever clouds show up, we fly somewhere sunny."

Kim tilted her head. "What would we eat?"

Cameron shrugged. "We could try fishing. We could make runs up to the mothership. Hell, we could bring down a pod with an animal every few days and cook it."

"I like it," Reggie said. He tried to keep his voice low and neutral. He didn't want them to know how frightened he was of the people in the pods. They'd think he was crazy.

"Cameron, that might be fine for a few weeks," David said. "But we can't go on like that for years."

"Sure we can."

"We can't just leave everyone in storage," Tyrell said.

"You don't know what you're saying," Reggie said. His words came out angry. He couldn't help it.

"What do you mean?" Tyrell asked.

"You don't know what kind of people are in those pods."

"And you do?"

They were all looking at him. Reggie didn't care. "Yes. I've seen it. We all have. People who murder children in the name of God. People who tie you up in the name of justice. People who ruin everything." His voice trembled so much he didn't even sound like himself. He didn't feel like himself.

"You can't write off humanity because of a couple of bad apples," Felicia said.

"Bad apples?" Reggie was breathing hard now. "Randall tried to fill the village with women so he could have his way with them. I would think that you of all people might take issue with that."

"Easy," David said.

Reggie wanted to grab David and shake him. "You really think it's smart to bring more people here?" His heartbeat thumped in his ears. "After Joe tied you up for days? After he pointed his gun at your girl's face?"

"Please stop," Kim said.

"I'm trying to keep you safe," Reggie said, yelling now. "You don't know—"

"She asked you to stop." The voice came from behind Reggie, like a ghost. It was Sierra.

He chomped his mouth shut. His lower lip trembled. He wished he knew how to make them understand. He wished he could make them see what he saw.

"Thank you," Kim whispered.

Tyrell hopped over from the other carriage and kneeled beside Sierra. "How're you feeling?"

"Pretty shitty," she said. "I've been listening to you all argue for the past ten minutes."

Reggie hung his head in shame. It sounded like something Chase would have said.

"What've we learned?" Sierra asked. "What've you seen?"

"We circled the planet," Priya said. "It's a wasteland. Gorgers are everywhere. There's nowhere safe."

"We don't know that," Tyrell said, keeping his tone low. "There are a million islands out there."

Sierra got to her feet. She looked shaky. Reggie started to steady her, but she waved him off. "Where are we headed now?" she asked.

"That's the question of the hour," Cameron said.

Anywhere but a university, Reggie thought, though he knew that was nonsense. The universities were all gone, just like his son.

We're over the Pacific," David said. "Heading east."

"How about food and water?"

"Half the food is gone and more than half of the water," Felicia said. "We could also use a bio break."

"Yeah, we need to empty the piss jug," Cameron said.

David turned around in his seat and stared at Sierra. A grim quiet fell over the shuttle.

"What is it?" Sierra asked.

"You murdered Kevin."

For a long time, no one said anything. Reggie could feel the group unraveling.

Sierra worked her jaw. Her lips tightened and loosened. She was building her defense, just like Chase used to do when Reggie caught him misbehaving.

Finally, she took a deep breath and spoke. "You're right. I shouldn't have done that. Not by myself. I should have waited. We should have decided what to do as a group."

Reggie couldn't believe his ears.

Felicia looked back and forth between David and Sierra. "Kevin deserved it," she said.

Sierra shrugged. "Yeah, he did. But if we're gonna rebuild society, we have to do things the right way."

David nodded and turned back around, facing forward.

Just like that, Sierra had defused the situation. Something loosened inside Reggie's chest. She never stopped surprising him.

"Enough with the talky-talk-talk," Cameron said. "What are we going to do right now?"

"We've been cooped up in here too long," Sierra said. "Let's find someplace sunny where we can get out and walk around, even if it isn't a good place to settle."

"Where?" David asked.

"Fly up high," Tyrell said. "Let's look for someplace green. If there's plant life, that has to mean there's fewer gorgers around."

"Not necessarily," Priya said.

Tyrell scowled at her.

"But it's worth a try," Priya added.

David and Cameron exchanged a glance. A moment later, the view turned skyward.

"After we've gotten some fresh air, I say we return to the mothership," Sierra said. "We can gather more food in the menagerie and we can see if anything changed up there since we left."

Most of the group nodded.

"We need to deal with Randall," Cameron said.

Sierra held up a hand. "Okay. One thing at a time. Let's just get some fresh air."

Reggie took a deep breath. His heart rate felt calm. Sierra hadn't just defused the situation, she'd come up with a plan for the group, and it was exactly what they needed. She really was the key to everything.

He just had to find a way to convince her to leave everyone else in storage.

Chapter Thirty-One

Tyrell's stomach lurched as the flying car lifted from the beach on a small island in the middle of Puget Sound. He hadn't felt any motion sickness in the shuttle, but then again, he hadn't felt any motion in the shuttle.

"Get back at the first hint of cloud cover," David called out. He and his kids walked around in the bright sunlight while Reggie and Cameron poked through a small pile of debris at the shoreline.

Tyrell gave them a thumbs-up without looking back, keeping his eyes on the horizon.

The island sat halfway between Vancouver and Seattle. On the mainland, massive piles of rubble marked the locations of cities, undoubtedly hiding millions of gorgers. On this little island, though, everything had been flattened, either by the initial firestorm or the tsunamis that followed. Dead trees lay jumbled everywhere and only the foundations of buildings remained. There simply wasn't any place for gorgers to escape the sun.

The important thing was the vegetation. When they'd flown up to the stratosphere to search for a place to land, the Pacific Northwest had stood out because of its greenery.

"This could work," Tyrell said. "Look at all the plants."

Sprigs of green burst between the log piles and scattered bricks.

"Yes, we could make a delicious grass salad," Priya said. She kept her face buried in her orange split-ball device.

The flying car lurched to a stop. Tyrell gripped the front console as his stomach lurched with it. The ever-present smell of char and rot didn't help. He tried not to let his queasiness show. Sierra, Priya, and Felicia all seemed immune to the unnatural motion.

"Keep following the shoreline," Sierra said. "Let's scout the perimeter before we go inland." Except for the curling scars on her arms and neck, which looked more pronounced in the sunlight, she wasn't showing any aftereffects from being electrocuted.

Priya tapped the device, programming a new destination. They rotated abruptly and jerked forward. "Evidently, they still get a decent amount of rainfall here," she said.

"It's hot, too," Felicia said. "I thought Seattle wasn't this warm."

"I think the climate shifted," Priya said. "Honestly, I bet Earth's orbit might have shifted, and maybe even the tilt of its axis."

"More plant life means more food for gorgers," Felicia said. She sounded glum.

"Good," Tyrell said. "That'll keep them on the mainland."

"We still don't know if they can swim," Felicia said.

Tyrell waved his hand. "They look like big bugs. There's no way they can swim."

"Plenty of bugs can swim," Priya said. She seemed to enjoy challenging him.

He narrowed his eyes. "Even ones that weigh eighty pounds?"

She twisted her mouth sideways but didn't respond. She didn't like being challenged back quite so much.

The flying car moved in a straight line across the northern end of the island. A string of other islands lay just offshore.

"There's room for expansion," Tyrell said. "We clear out this island, settle in, and then we can pick another one when we need more territory. It doesn't matter how many gorgers are on the mainland."

"Everything here is flattened," Sierra said. "Hopefully there won't be many to clear out."

Felicia made an exaggerated sniffing noise. "Ugh. What is that smell?"

Tyrell inhaled through his nostrils and regretted it.

"Rotten fish?" Priya offered. She wrinkled her nose.

Tyrell's stomach roiled. "I'd take rotten fish over whatever that is."

The flying car came to a stop. Sierra pointed further down the beach, where a mound the size of a bus lay at the shoreline. Priya sent them closer, stopping a few yards from the end of the shape, the bloated carcass of a whale.

"It's moving," Tyrell said. "Why is it moving?"

The skin bulged and undulated.

Felicia grimaced. "It looks like a caretaker, just before the gorger comes out."

Tyrell had heard descriptions of the caretakers, but he hadn't seen one. From what he'd heard, he hadn't missed out on much.

"That's a humpback," Priya said.

Sierra leaned sideways. "Take us out over the water so we can get a better look."

They shot out, then stopped abruptly just offshore from the carcass. A gaping hole in the whale's stomach opened toward them, with raw white edges.

"Lower," Sierra said.

They plunged until they were two feet above the surface, directly across from the opening in the whale's belly. Several gorgers jostled one another in the cavity. They'd torn into the whale so they could eat it from the inside out, sheltered from the sun.

"Well, that's disgusting," Felicia said.

Tyrell wanted to agree, but he kept his mouth closed, clenching his throat. His stomach was right on the precipice.

One of the gorgers puffed its neck and puked onto the inside of the whale's carcass. It grabbed a hunk of gooey blubber with its mouth and ripped it free.

Tyrell passed the point of no return. He threw himself to the opposite side of the carriage and blew chunks into the water. Bits of half-digested jerky floated in the bile below. The sight of it made him heave again.

Sierra rubbed his back. "You okay?"

"Sure," he muttered, wishing she hadn't seen him like this. He spat into the water.

Something moved below. Tyrell pushed up slowly.

Gorgers clustered on the sandy bottom, maybe ten feet down. One of them sucked a piece of vomit into its mouth.

"Priya, get us higher," Tyrell said.

The flying car lurched up a few yards, then stopped again. All three women joined him to look over the side. Gorgers covered the seabed.

Apparently, a few feet of water provided just enough shade from the sun.

"So much for settling on an island," Priya said.

Sierra looked pissed. "Shit."

Tyrell grasped for a counter argument. The gorgers hadn't been swimming, they'd been crawling on the bottom. Maybe they couldn't cross deep water. There wasn't any way to know for sure, though, and an island would be undefended from every direction. "We can keep searching," he offered. "We'll find something." He gave Sierra the best smile he could manage.

"We don't have time to keep looking," she said. "We need food. And Randall is still up there. For all we know, he could have killed everyone in storage by now. Priya, get us back to the shuttle."

The flying car rose and cut straight across the island. Tyrell held his breath as they passed over the whale carcass.

Sierra sat back, a discouraged frown on her face.

"Hey, that whale was a good sign," he said, trying to cheer her up. "It means there's still life in the sea."

"He's right about that," Priya said.

Sierra's face softened, but only slightly.

"That means we could try to fish," Tyrell said. "We could take these flying cars out over the ocean."

"I want to learn how to fly this thing," Felicia said. Priya offered her the control device. "No, I mean really fly it, like David and Cameron."

"You should," Sierra said. "The more people who can fly, the better."

"What's the difference?" Tyrell asked.

"All I'm doing is sending us from point to point," Priya said. "It moves from one spot to the next on its own. When David and Cameron fly, they're actually piloting."

Tyrell nodded, wondering if his stomach would have an easier time with pilots at the controls. When he'd first jumped aboard the carriage back in the mothership, he hadn't gotten airsick, but that might have been because he'd been amped with adrenaline.

The middle of the island stank of rotten vegetation, a marked improvement over rotten humpback whale. Empty roads crossed the ground, leading nowhere. As the carriage rose over the highest point, the shuttle came into view on the opposite shore, gleaming silver in the distance.

David threw a stick for Kona on a wide empty beach. It landed right at the shoreline and she raced after it.

"We can't count on fishing," Sierra said. "Not for several thousand people. We need crops."

"Where are we going to find crops?" Tyrell asked. He hadn't seen edible plants anywhere on Earth.

"There are all kinds of fruit trees in the menagerie we could try to transplant," she said. "Also, they must have some kind of seed bank. They have animals in storage. There must be plants, too."

Priya looked up from her device. "The spheres?"

Sierra nodded.

"Huh?" Tyrell gave her a curious look. They'd told him a lot, but he didn't remember anything about spheres.

"I found a giant container filled with landscaping rocks in the mothership," Sierra said. "There were hundreds of other containers, in all different sizes. The plants on the islands had to come from somewhere, and gorgers eat plant matter as much as animal matter. More, actually. It stands to reason they have seeds, or saplings, or something."

Out ahead of them, Kona grabbed the stick and ran back. Kim and Barry swung larger sticks at each other like swords. Reggie and Cameron stood nearby, watching.

Kona dropped the stick at David's feet. Tyrell felt a twinge of jealousy. He missed his dogs.

David picked up Kona's stick and pretended to throw it, faking her out. As soon as she took off, he turned and threw it in the opposite direction. Just like before, it landed right at the shoreline.

Tyrell's heart stopped. The stick landed in the shadow of the shuttle, which stretched out over the water.

"Kona, *no!*" he shouted, but they were too far away to be heard.

Realizing she'd been duped, Kona skidded to a stop and reversed course, heading toward the stick.

Something rippled just offshore.

"No!" Tyrell shouted again.

They were still a quarter mile away. Gorgers would spring from the water and swarm the dog. She was halfway to the stick, and all Tyrell could do was watch.

The whistle.

He slapped at his pocket, snatched out the plastic whistle, and blew with all his might.

Kona stopped right at the edge of the shadow and looked back. Three gorgers rose from the water behind her.

Tyrell inhaled and blew again, even louder.

"Kona, come!" he shouted.

He was closer now and she heard him. Kona dug her paws in the sand and ran back in his direction as a spray of acid landed right where she'd been standing. She spotted the gorgers behind her and started barking, but kept her distance.

The flying car jerked to a stop near David. Felicia hopped down, picked up a fist-sized rock, and nailed one of the gorgers. It squealed and retreated into the shallows. The other two stood watching, keeping in the shade from the shuttle.

"They're in the water," Sierra said as everyone gathered around. "That rules out islands."

David clipped Kona's leash onto her collar. He looked pale. "Thank you, Tyrell."

Tyrell scratched Kona's neck vigorously on both sides. "I couldn't let anything happen to my best girl."

"We should go back to the mothership," Felicia said. "It's the only place we can be safe."

"I agree," Priya said. "We have complete control up there. We can stun anything that gives us trouble."

David nodded slowly. "I'm starting to agree, too."

"We can't stay there," Sierra said. "We can't give up on Earth. This is our home. We can't leave all of humanity stranded on an alien spaceship."

"Where can we go?" Kim asked.

Sierra sighed. "I don't know. We have to keep looking."

"What about food and water?" Reggie asked.

"What about Randall?" Cameron asked.

Sierra held up a hand. "We should deal with Randall. As long as he's up there, the people in storage are in danger, and honestly the whole ship is at risk."

"How are we going to deal with him, exactly?" Tyrell asked.

"We already held a trial," David said, his face grim. "As a group. We agreed on a sentence."

"Let's go carry it out," Cameron said.

David nodded. He didn't look happy about it, but he wasn't arguing.

"How do we find him?" Tyrell asked.

"If he's still got his implant, I can find him with this," Priya said, patting her device.

Tyrell reached for the back of his neck. "Can I get mine taken out before we go up there? Randall knows how to stun people."

David nodded. "That's a good idea. Kim, too."

Kim's eyebrows arched toward each other. "How bad does it hurt?"

"A lot," Barry said.

David glowered at the boy. "That isn't helpful." He turned to Kim. "There's some analgesic gel in Tyrell's first aid kit, which will help, but we should try to find some ice, too."

Tyrell reached out to her. "It'll be okay, Kim. We can do this."

She gave him a weak smile and squeezed his hand.

"Sounds like a plan," Sierra said. "We remove Kim and Tyrell's implants so we can return to the mothership. Then we deal with Randall, replenish our supplies, and continue our search."

Priya looked like she wanted to protest, but before she could say anything else, Sierra held up her hand. "It doesn't hurt to keep looking," she said.

One by one, the others all nodded. Priya offered a half-hearted shrug.

Tyrell smiled. A day earlier, Sierra had been accused of murder and barely able to remain conscious. Now she was calling the shots.

He'd never met such a remarkable woman.

Chapter Thirty-Two

Reggie wandered across the snowy mountain peak while David prepared to operate on Tyrell and Kim. The sight of blood made his stomach want to crawl up his throat and the sight of David taking care of his children made his heart whither. It wasn't fair.

They'd landed the shuttle on a flat summit in a coastal range two hundred miles north of Vancouver. Landed was the wrong word, though, since the shuttle never actually touched the ground. It hovered four feet above the snowpack.

The cold suited Reggie. It matched how he felt inside. He stuck his hands in his pockets and stared down at a valley to the northeast, which looked fairly green, like the area around Seattle, but without the ruins of a city. The faint line of a small river ran up the middle.

Sierra approached him, crunching the snow. "Reggie, I need your help. You've always been a rock for me. I need to know I can count on you."

He drew in a frigid breath. "Listen to me, please. Let's call it good. Don't bring anyone else out of storage. They'll only cause more pain and suffering. Haven't we had enough of that?"

She looked up at him. A pair of binoculars hung from her neck. "What about Jasmine? Weren't the two of you close?"

"We were neighbors. That's all." He'd come to terms with the idea that Jasmine would spend the rest of eternity inside a pod. "She's at peace now."

"If we just leave her there, she might as well be dead."

Reggie said nothing.

Back below the shuttle, Tyrell stood and pressed ice against his neck, while David and Felicia moved on to Kim, who lay on one of the carriages. Reggie shuddered, even though he couldn't see any blood from this far off.

"You really want to just stick with the nine of us?" Sierra asked.

"Yes," Reggie said. "We'll look after each other, take care of each other. No more killing. No more hurting." Anything to stop the hurting.

She opened her mouth to say something, but Reggie held up a finger. "You remind me of my son. He was just going off to college when the Ender showed up. I don't talk about him, 'cause it hurts too much, but when I look at you, I think of him. You have the same gumption he had." Reggie's throat tightened.

She held his gaze. "I'm honored to hear that. I hope I can do justice to his memory."

"You can't," Reggie spat. She stepped back as if he'd smacked her, and though it shamed him, he liked seeing it. "You killed someone. Chase never would have killed anybody. It changes you. It breaks your soul." His voice cracked. "Trust me. I know this."

She stood quietly for a long time. "Chase was lucky to have you for a dad."

Icy tears rolled down Reggie's cheeks.

"I'm sorry I never knew him," Sierra said. "But I gotta believe he would disagree with you. He wouldn't want us to give up. He wouldn't want us to die alone."

Reggie shook with a quiet sob. He shouldn't have told her about Chase. He didn't want to talk about him. Something had broken inside him that would never heal.

Sierra pointed at Barry, off playing in the snow with Kona. "If it's just the nine of us, even if we manage to take care of each other, someday we'll all be dead, except Barry and his sister. They'll never have friends. They'll never have a first kiss. They'll never feel love for a child. They'll never feel love *from* a child, like you got from Chase. One of them will die first, and then the other will die alone, and that will be the end of us."

Reggie watched the boy run across the ice pack, tossing snowballs to Kona. His heart hurt so much.

"Do you want that for Barry?" Sierra asked. "Would you have wanted that for Chase?"

"No," Reggie said, his voice low.

"Some people *are* terrible," Sierra said. "You're absolutely right about that. Joe, Thad, Randall. They were awful. But that's only three people."

"It wasn't just them," Reggie said. "Don't forget about the people who followed them, who did whatever they told them to do."

Sierra nodded. "I know. We can't let that happen again. But you have to admit that there are good people, too, like our group here. Hell, even Cameron, most of the time."

Reggie's mouth curled up on one side. He couldn't help it. She really did sound like Chase.

The wind howled. Over at the carriage, Kim howled too. David must have gotten the implant out of her neck.

Reggie wanted to believe Sierra. He wanted to think that people were worth saving, for Chase's sake, more than anything. His soul ached for it. He wished he could talk to Chase about it, to hear what the boy thought. He swallowed. "What if you're wrong? What if we bring people out of storage and they do more of the same shit?" He wasn't sure he could bear it.

"I won't put up with it," Sierra said. "I'll do what has to be done. I don't want to. I don't like it, but I will."

"If you do that, it will destroy you," Reggie said. He could still feel Sheriff Dart's windpipe crunching under his thumbs.

"I won't let it," Sierra said. "You want to know how?"

He waited.

"I'll have good people like you helping me. Isn't that what Chase would have wanted?"

Her words shamed him. He stood for a long while and then nodded, fresh tears flowing. "Okay," he said.

She put her arm around him. "Come on. Let's just do as we can."

Reggie sobbed, but the tight pain loosened a little. "Chase used to say that," he whispered.

Sierra was strong. Stronger than him, for sure. Maybe she really could do what had to be done, without losing herself. Maybe it was because she was a woman. All of the awful things that had happened since the Ender had been caused by men. Hell, that was mostly true before the Ender.

"Will you give me a chance?" Sierra asked. "Please?"

He nodded.

She flashed him a smile. "That's all I'm asking. Come on, let's get everyone together. I want to discuss that valley down there."

Reggie took another look at the distant meadow. "I thought we were heading back to the mothership?"

"We will, but there's still daylight. We should check it out while we're here." She tilted her head. "It looks fairly green and there aren't many ruins in the area. That valley could be exactly what we've been searching for."

Reggie took a deep breath and allowed himself to hope. "Okay."

Chapter Thirty-Three

David forced himself to focus on his flying as the carriage shot out over the meadow. Wind whipped his hair and he felt every motion through the seat of his pants, unlike in the shuttle, where artificial gravity prevented him from feeling any movement. Despite all the sensations, his mind kept drifting off in three different directions.

First, his thoughts went to Kim and Barry, back in the shuttle, which they'd parked out in the open beside a crumbling two-lane highway. After the close call with Kona on the beach, they'd agreed that everyone who remained behind should stay in the shuttle, even with the bright sunlight. For the umpteenth time, he told himself his kids were safe. The entrance through the tail was a hundred feet off the ground. No gorgers could get in and Felicia and Priya were both armed, just in case. Still, it hurt to leave them behind, especially after Barry threw a tantrum about it.

"Right five degrees," he said, wanting to keep the carriage over the road. Cameron mimicked his movements perfectly, adding a bit of bank, the way he'd taught her. The controls allowed for all sorts of unnatural movements, but he made a point of flying the carriage like an airplane, which helped keep Reggie, Sierra, and Tyrell comfortable. Especially Tyrell, who was apparently prone to motion sickness. He sat in the very back, petting Kona.

The second thing occupying his thoughts was his uncertainty about their future. He hated not having a plan. The valley seemed promising, but his hopes had been dashed before, repeatedly. He couldn't decide if he thought the menagerie really would be safer. Everything there was artificial, but at least they could use the neck devices to control the dinosaurs and the other creatures. Sierra had made a good point, though. The ship could fall out of orbit or just fly away without warning.

"Something up ahead," Cameron said. "Let's check it out."

They touched the controls in unison, slowing down as they floated toward a pile of rubble set back from the road.

"Looks like an old farmhouse," Reggie said.

A corrugated roof lay scattered among chunks of brick and concrete, easily big enough to shelter a dozen gorgers. David and Cameron circled once, then returned to the two-lane road, much of which was overgrown with grass.

In several spots, the road had collapsed into the river that ran alongside it. Branches and logs littered the banks. Gorgers seemed to eat anything organic, so the presence of that much dead wood lying around had to be a good sign.

"I don't see any cracks in the ground, like in Nebraska," Cameron said. "And there aren't many trees to provide shade." She nudged him with an elbow. "Only one town for miles. This could be it."

The meadow extended four or five hundred miles from north to south and was at least two hundred miles wide, with high mountain ranges bordering the east and west. Dead trees dotted the slopes, but they were too sparse to provide shade for gorgers to move around. As far as they could tell, there was virtually no cover out in the open valley.

Cameron gave him one of her mysterious glances, which wasn't quite a smile, but looked like she was hiding some wicked secret.

She was the third thing distracting him.

They made an awesome team. They'd been through hell together and come out stronger. The attraction he felt for her was almost electrical, but they hadn't had a single moment alone for days. He wanted to talk with her, to connect with her. He wanted to hold her and kiss her. He wanted it so much it felt like a need.

"Why weren't there more towns up here?" Reggie asked. "It's beautiful."

"It used to be a lot colder," Sierra said. "Priya thinks the climate shifted after the Ender hit."

"I'll say this much," Reggie said. "It feels more like Earth than any other place we've been. It might actually work."

"Listen to you," Tyrell said. "All sunny and optimistic, for a change."

"It'll all come down to the town," David said.

They'd flown over the small town in the shuttle and were now flying back to get a better look from the carriage. The tallest buildings were only three or four stories. A few were still standing, while in the rest of the world, the cities had been reduced to rubble. David guessed that the mountain range to the west had shielded the area from the worst of the Ender's firestorm.

The land surrounding the town had appeared brown and barren for a mile in every direction, with tendrils that stretched further. Priya called it a dead zone. From the shuttle, it had looked like a splash of filth.

Out here, though, a few miles south, the meadow looked relatively normal.

"I wonder if we could drink that river water," Tyrell said. "I mean, if we boiled it first."

"What would we boil it in?" David asked.

"There has to be something we can use in town," Tyrell said.

Cameron gave David another glance, but this one looked hopeful, not salacious. He smiled. Hopeful was just as sexy.

The intact buildings might actually contain something useful, but they could also be crawling with gorgers.

"How much daylight do we have left?" Sierra asked.

David glanced at the sun, which was still a good distance from the mountains to the west. "Three or four hours, at least. This far north, the days will be pretty long in the summer, which works to our advantage."

"Yeah, but they'll be that much shorter in the winter," Cameron said. "Maybe we could set up here and then go back and forth to the southern hemisphere every six months."

"Do we have enough fuel for that?" Tyrell asked.

David laughed. "We don't have any idea."

"Are you kidding?"

He glanced back at him. "Nope. We really don't know. It could be that the carriage recharges when it docks in the shuttle and the shuttle does the same thing in the mothership. Or we could just drop out of the sky at any moment." It was one more uncertainty he just had to accept.

"You guys said everything is automated, though, right," Tyrell said. "We wouldn't just drop out of the sky, would we? This thing would land first, don't you think?"

"I don't know," David said. "We'll find out, won't we?"

Tyrell looked warily at the ground racing by thirty feet below. "Terrific."

"It's another reason to get everyone out of storage," Sierra said. "The more people we have studying this equipment, the faster we'll figure it out.

"In the meantime, we need to find some rope," Tyrell said.

"Why's that?" David asked.

"If these flying cars ever run out of power, and we're inside the shuttle when it happens, we won't be able to get down. The exit is a hundred feet up."

"Terrific," David said, echoing Tyrell. The reverse was true as well. They needed a way to climb back into the shuttle if they ever got stranded outside.

Cameron nodded forward with her chin. "Our town has a name."

They approached a fancy sign on a decorative brick monument. The raised letters were faded and weathered, but still legible.

"Home sweet home," Reggie said.

Kona barked.

"What do you think, girl?" Tyrell asked. "You like it?"

The ruins of a gas station lay a quarter mile past the sign, on the outskirts of town.

"I wonder if there's any gas left in the storage tanks," Tyrell said.

"It can't still be good," Reggie said. "Gasoline will barely last a year, much less a hundred."

"Besides," Cameron added. "Where are you going to find a car that still runs?"

"I'm not thinking about fuel," Tyrell said. "I'm thinking about fire. Even if the gas has degraded, it might still be flammable. We could use it on the gorgers."

Cameron gave David a sly look. "I'm starting to like this guy."

They slowed as they approached the gas station. All of the windows were gone and the lowest third of the building's walls had been eaten away, leaving only skeletal steel beams supporting the remains, as if the whole structure was built on stilts.

Kona growled and barked again.

"Gorgers," Cameron said. "Dead ahead."

The awning that had once sheltered the gas pumps had fallen over, becoming a wall that jutted into the air at an angle. Two gorgers crawled in its shadow, feeding on a thicket of dead juniper bushes that bordered the parking lot.

"We should search that building," Sierra said.

David turned halfway around in his seat. "There are two gorgers right there in plain sight."

"We knew we would encounter them," she said. "We have to figure this out."

"She's right," Cameron said. "This place looks like a pretty good trial run."

He lifted his hands from the controls. "I'm not going any closer until we have a plan. I'm sick of winging it."

"I hear you," Tyrell said. "And I've got some ideas."

Chapter Thirty-Four

Tyrell crept across the broken asphalt holding a ten-foot spear. Sierra followed close behind, also armed with a pike. They both carried guns, but they were determined to take out the gorgers at the gas station without expending any ammo. Tyrell thought they could pull it off. This group had their shit together.

The gorgers feeding on the charred juniper bushes noticed Tyrell and crawled to the edge of the shadow, as close as they could get without exposing themselves to direct sunlight. They didn't have eyes, at least not that he recognized, but somehow they'd sensed his approach.

Tyrell squeezed the homemade spear in his hands. They'd flown to the river and collected several stout sticks. After breaking off any side branches, Tyrell had asked David and Cameron to fly along just above the remains of the road. He and Sierra and Reggie had held the branches against the concrete, rotating them until the ends were worn down to sharp points.

"Don't get too close," Sierra said, a few yards behind him.

"How far do they spit?" he asked.

"Ten feet, at least, and they can come out in the sunlight a little if they want. They aren't vampires. They don't burst into flames when the sun hits them."

Tyrell stopped twenty feet from the awning's shadow.

Apart from a few wispy clouds, the sky was a deep glorious blue. The sun crept toward the snow-covered mountains to the west, where they'd stopped for the surgery, but they still had hours of daylight.

The salve David had applied to his neck was wearing off. Fortunately, surging adrenaline kept the pain manageable.

He crouched down and waited for Sierra to catch up, which gave him a view through the bottom of the gas station. The gorgers had eaten the paneling from the lower third of the walls, making the whole building look like the inside of a public restroom, where the stalls didn't extend all the way to the floor.

The inside of the building appeared empty, except for scattered debris. The gas station had once been divided between a shopping area in the front and a storeroom in the back. Now it looked like a decrepit barn, ready to blow over in the next strong storm.

All the gas pumps were gone, leaving only a raised concrete platform and the roof that had sheltered them, which now leaned at a sixty-degree angle, blocking the sun. The gorgers sidestepped back and forth beside the fallen awning, keeping right at the edge of the shadow.

Sierra moved up next to him.

"Those things are nasty," Tyrell said. "Big, too." His mouth felt dry. He hadn't had any water in hours.

They were twice the size of the one he'd punted on the mothership. Their backs were three feet above the ground and their tails curled up twice that high. Coarse bristles covered one of them, like on a big horsefly.

"Those are just teenagers," Sierra said, without any hint of fear. This woman had some steel in her.

Tyrell shifted right, where the asphalt was less ragged. He didn't want to stumble if he had to move quickly.

The two gorgers jostled past each other, testing the sunlight every so often. A pouch of skin pulsed under the neck of the one covered with bristles.

Sierra grabbed his bicep and pulled. "Step back. It's about to blow chunks."

The gorger spewed an arc of yellow liquid across the parking lot. Smoke rose from the asphalt where the globs landed.

"Lovely," Tyrell said, cringing. He realized something else, too. "They aren't like other animals."

"What do you mean?"

"Any other animal would be fleeing from us. We're bigger than they are."

"Maybe it's because they've never encountered humans before. They don't see us as a threat."

Tyrell shook his head. "They aren't just ignoring us. They're trying to come after us."

"They're hungry?"

He pointed at the wall of dead shrubbery. "There's plenty of food right there. They either see us as a better option, or they want us dead. Or both."

Sierra grunted. "Fine. We'll use that to our advantage."

The next part of Tyrell's plan was about to unfold. The flying car floated slowly over the building, approaching the gorgers from behind.

"Hey, ugly!" Tyrell called, tapping the ground with his spear.

Both gorgers danced at the edge of the shadow. The hairy one ventured a foot into the sunlight before retreating. The other one spat acid in their direction, but not nearly as far.

Tyrell gripped his spear and checked in every direction. Open space surrounded them. The sky remained cloudless. This was going to work.

The flying car stopped twenty feet above the gorgers, just as Tyrell had instructed. Reggie and David appeared at the back end, where they'd placed a four-foot chunk of concrete.

"Whenever you're ready," Tyrell shouted, his gaze fixed on the creatures.

David and Reggie moved to either side of the slab and heaved it from the back of the flying car.

The concrete plummeted, crushing one gorger and pinning several legs of the other. Slimy liquid burst from the mouth of the crushed creature. Sierra jumped sideways to avoid the spray, pressing against Tyrell.

He steadied her, made sure she was okay, then darted forward.

The gorger with the pinned legs screeched, clawing at the ground with the legs on its other side, straining to pull itself free. Tyrell circled in and drove his spear into the center of its body. Sierra was supposed to spear the other one, but it was clearly dead, so she impaled the same one, further down its back.

Two legs reached out, claws scratching at the asphalt, then grew still.

Tyrell pumped his fist. Sierra held up her hand for a high five. He grabbed her in a hug and spun her around.

She smiled. Her eyes sparkled in the afternoon sun.

David and Cameron brought the flying car down next to them, stopping a foot above the ground. Kona jumped off and sniffed the gorgers.

"Nice work," Cameron said.

"You guys were spot-on," Tyrell said. "We can do this. If we hit one building at a time, we can work our way through the whole town."

Sierra withdrew her spear and nudged the dead gorger. "I wonder if these things are edible."

Tyrell grimaced. "It spits acid. How can it be safe to eat?"

"The legs might be safe," David said, raising an eyebrow. "You know, like crab legs."

"Or the tail, maybe?" Reggie offered.

The creature's body was little more than a muscular tube, with its legs connected somewhere underneath. The front ended in a fanged mouth and the tail curved back over it, like a scorpion, but with floppy protrusions at the end, instead of a stinger.

"Ehhh, maybe not," Sierra said. "I think that's their reproductive system. When they get pregnant, the tail swells with eggs."

"Mmmm, caviar," Cameron said with a shudder.

"We should bring down a dinosaur or something from storage and feed it one as a test," Sierra said.

Tyrell chuckled. "Now that's something I'd like to watch." He turned toward the gas station. "Come on, let's see if there's anything in here we can use."

"Be quick about it," David said. "We still need to scout the town."

Tyrell walked into the front half of the building, which was little more than a skeletal frame. The glass windows and doors were missing, and most of the paneling had been eaten by the gorgers. Wire racks that once held junk food lay empty on the floor.

Sierra followed him in and stepped behind a counter covered with mold. A rusty cash register sat on top. "Aha!" She bent beneath the register and emerged with an aluminum baseball bat.

"Nice," Tyrell said. He stepped over a broken display rack and made his way toward the stockroom, hoping he might find a metal mop bucket they could use to boil water.

A good chunk of the HVAC system had fallen through the rotted roof, filling the short hallway to the back. Rather than climb over all that jagged metal, Tyrell turned to the frame of what had once been a beverage cooler. It opened in the back as well as the front, so that it could be stocked from behind, but all the glass was long gone, as were the shelves inside.

Tyrell bent down to peek below the walls, checking again to make sure there weren't any gorgers in the back half of the building. A steel claw hammer lay on the floor in the middle of the storeroom. The rubber grip was missing, but otherwise, it looked good as new. Tyrell walked through the cooler and bent to pick it up.

A gorger leaped onto him from high up on the wall.

He crashed backwards, landing on hard concrete. A bolt of pain shot through his head and another through his neck, where his implant had been cut out. The gorger's claws stabbed at his sides, his legs, his chest. He tried to shout for help, but only managed a hiss.

The creature's mouth stretched down toward his face. A million dagger-like mouthparts flexed wide, along with two sharp pincers as big as hedge shears. He grabbed its neck, trying to keep the fangs away, but it pressed forward with the strength of a bear.

The talons at the ends of its legs dug into his skin. Tyrell shrieked as a claw tore through the bandage on his calf.

When Sierra shouted his name, he knew he was dead. Her voice came from too far away. She would never get to him in time.

The mouth came closer, rows of jagged teeth trying to seize his face. Tyrell turned his head, pushing at the neck, losing ground inch by inch.

The gorger suddenly jerked sideways, sliding off him.

Kona gripped one of the creature's legs in her mouth. She pulled backwards across the broken floor and shook her head furiously. The leg broke.

Kona pounced, grabbing another leg.

Tyrell crawled through the remains of the cooler, scrambling across bits of broken glass, until he reached the front half of the building.

In the storeroom, the gorger's mouth twisted toward the dog. The pouch hanging underneath swelled. Tyrell realized he'd been throttling its throat, preventing it from puking on him. Now that his hands were off its neck, it was about to vomit acid all over the dog.

Sierra appeared and brought the baseball bat down like John Henry pounding a railroad spike. Gore flew from the creature's caved-in head. Kona yelped and darted away.

Sierra raised the bat and pounded the gorger again and again. One of its legs broke. Its back split open. She kept hitting it until it was a limp, broken pile with orange goo puddling beneath it.

Tyrell pulled himself to his feet, breathing hard. "Thank you." His leg throbbed and stars danced in his vision. He touched the back of his neck where David had operated on him and felt fresh blood.

"Don't thank me, thank Kona."

Tyrell went to the dog and ended up collapsing on his ass. She faced the dead gorger, sniffing and giving a low growl. He found a burned spot on her ear where a drop of acid must have splashed her, and a second one on her neck, but she seemed oblivious to the injuries. "Good girl, good girl." As she licked his face, tears started to flow. That had been close. Too close.

Cameron entered the storeroom, her Beretta drawn, and returned a moment later with the hammer. "Is this what you wanted?"

She extended it to him, and when he took it, she didn't let go. Instead, she pulled him to his feet. The room spun.

"Let's get back to the carriage," David said.

"Sounds good to me," Tyrell said. His words came out weak and thin. "Are we still gonna scout the town?"

Sierra moved beside him and pulled his arm over her shoulder. "Easy there, big guy. Your leg is bleeding." She turned to David. "He needs to be patched up."

Tyrell wanted to object, to put on a strong face, but between the pain in his leg and the way the room kept spinning, he decided against it.

Chapter Thirty-Five

Cameron felt a sense of serenity sitting in the carriage as it floated motionless a hundred feet above the ruins of the gas station. On Hawai'i, the feeling was called *"maluhia,"* but she'd never felt it there, thanks to the Army's strict regimen and the demons from her past. She felt it now, though. *Maluhia.* A gentle breeze cooled her skin.

They'd visited every continent and she'd seen enough to know that this stretch of western Canada was truly unique. Before the Ender, it had been too remote to warrant much commercial development. After the impact, the mountain ranges on both sides of the valley seem to have provided some protection from the firestorm. They could search for years without finding a better spot.

Other than a few small pockets here and there, the ruins of Fraser were the only place in the area that gorgers could shelter from the sun. If the infestation in town was small enough, this valley would be the perfect place to settle.

David, who had been patching up Tyrell, crawled forward and took his seat next to her. His sleeves were rolled up, and the late-day orange sky made him look tan. Cameron glanced over her shoulder. Tyrell lay between Sierra and Reggie with fresh bandages around his leg. Kona snuggled up next to him.

"How is he?" Cameron asked.

"I haven't sutured anyone in ten years," David said. "It isn't pretty, but he'll be okay. I think he's dehydrated from loss of blood. Do you have any water left?"

She pulled out her empty plastic bottle and shook it.

"I puked earlier, too," Tyrell muttered from the back.

David frowned. "Okay, he's definitely dehydrated. Let's get a quick look at this town and get back for some water."

They'd filled their bottles with snow when they stopped on the mountaintop, but the rest of their supply was back in the shuttle.

"We should drop him off, first," Cameron said, a plan starting to form.

"The town is right there." David gestured at the ruins a half mile in front of them. "We can make a quick pass."

"We need to wait until dusk," Cameron said. "That's when we'll know how many gorgers there are. If we fly over now, they'll all be hiding inside."

He raised his eyebrow. She wondered if he guessed what she had in mind. She hoped so. She wished she could just fly off with him. They could spend the rest of their lives exploring what was left of Earth, just the two of them.

"I'm fine," Tyrell said.

Cameron scowled, willing him to keep his mouth shut.

"How long until dark?" Sierra asked.

"Close to an hour," Cameron said. After the thirty-second nightfall they experienced in the menagerie, sunset on Earth seemed to take forever, especially this far north. Shadows from the western ridgeline crawled across the valley at a snail's pace.

"All right. That's enough time to get back and he needs water," David said. "Slow one-eighty." They turned the carriage around and started south.

The valley stretched out before them, as far as they could see.

"Plenty of space," Sierra said. "If there aren't too many gorgers in town, we can bring the pods down right away."

"What about Randall?" David asked. "If we get everyone out of storage, can we just leave him up there to rot?"

Cameron frowned. "We still need things from the ship and we can't leave him with access to that technology."

"We agreed on his sentence," Sierra said. "It's too dangerous to let him live."

Cameron was glad to hear Sierra holding strong on this point.

David looked back and held up a hand. "I'm not debating that. I just don't want to take my kids anywhere near him."

"Fair enough," Sierra said. "Once we get everyone safely down, we can send up a posse. The kids won't have to go."

"I'd like to volunteer for that team," Tyrell said.

"I'd like to lead the team," Cameron said.

The shuttle sat right where they'd left it. Cameron and David slid the carriage into the hole at the end and settled in the center of the tail. Kona hopped down.

Felicia held a finger to her lips. "Kim and Barry are asleep."

Cameron's heartbeat picked up. Her plan was actually going to work.

Sierra and Reggie helped Tyrell climb down from the carriage.

David started to rise. Cameron grabbed his arm and held him in place. "We need to get up there before it gets too dark, or we won't be able to see anything."

He narrowed his eyes and gave her a small nod, then turned to Felicia. "Is Kim okay? Any issues with her neck?"

"She's fine," Felicia said. "Priya gave her another lesson on how to use her little device."

Priya offered a small wave from her seat against the curved wall.

"We won't be long," Cameron said. "Save us some jerky."

"Make sure Tyrell drinks plenty of water," David said. "And keep an eye on the kids."

Cameron smiled. He was such a mom.

Sierra looked like she suspected something. Cameron didn't care. She knew what she wanted and she was going to get it. David called out the instructions and they slipped out through the tunnel. Once they got moving, the breeze felt electric.

They retraced their steps north, following the road. An orange glow covered the valley as the sun approached the western mountains.

"How many gorgers is too many?" David asked. "How many do you think we could actually deal with?"

She shrugged. "A few hundred. Maybe a thousand? We're going to have our work cut out for us. Dropping concrete blocks on them will take forever."

"We can do it," he said. His confidence sent a charge through her. "And we don't have to clear out every last one before we bring the pods down from storage. "There will be people who can help us. People who can defend the others. Plus, they'll have things we can use. Tyrell's first aid kit was a godsend."

"Good point," Cameron said. "There will undoubtedly be more guns."

"Yeah. It all depends on what kind of people got into those pods, doesn't it?"

She wondered if he was thinking about his wife. She sure hoped not.

They flew over the gas station, their hands moving in sync. "We need some scientists who can reverse-engineer this technology," David said. "Another dozen Priyas would be great."

She chuckled. "You know, farmers and construction workers would help, too."

"Amish," he said. "We need a pod full of Amish people. They'd know how to work the land and build things without technology."

She touched his forearm. "One problem. Do you think the Amish were allowed to use the pods?"

He laughed. The sound warmed her. "Good question."

They passed over the outskirts of town, where streets lined with gutted homes branched off from the main drag.

"Let's get higher," he said. "I don't want to bump into anything."

"I thought you were scared of heights?"

He looked over, holding her gaze. "You know, I'm getting better."

She matched his moves and the carriage climbed. The air felt crisp, but she wasn't cold. As they rose, a gibbous moon appeared over the mountain range to the east.

When Fraser's tiny downtown was a hundred feet below them, they stopped, floating in the open void. The first few stars twinkled above.

Cameron crawled to the back of the carriage where she could look straight down without the front console in the way.

David crawled up next to her. "A month ago, this would have been terrifying. Now, it's kinda thrilling."

She turned on her side and held his gaze.

He looked at the town for a moment, then back up at her. He swallowed, making his Adam's apple dance.

She leaned close and kissed him, her lips tugging at his, the stubble on his chin pressing into her skin. Blood pulsed in her ears. She moved her hand to the back of his head, hungry, pulling him tight.

After a moment, she paused and lay back on the carriage, pulling him onto her, pulling his mouth back onto hers. The swell in his crotch pressed against her pants. She reached down and fumbled open his zipper, freeing him.

David kept kissing, biting at her lips, tickling her tongue.

She shoved her own pants down, out of the way, and suddenly he was in her, faster than she expected, but she was ready.

They both moaned at the same time. She needed this so much.

She pulled off his shirt and opened her own so she could feel his chest against hers.

The carriage rocked against his thrusting. He slowed down for her, waiting, but he didn't have to wait long.

"Go," she whispered in his ear, wrapping her arms around his back, and he thrust harder and faster until they both climaxed, a hundred feet in the air.

Afterwards, he lay on her for a while, still inside her, as the moon rose higher in the sky. She loved the feel of his body against hers, inside and out. It felt right.

"I needed that," she said when he finally lifted away.

"Yeah, me too," he said.

She pulled him close beside her and savored the warm tingle running up her spine, the sense of connection, the feeling of release.

A gentle breeze whistled past.

Maluhia.

Another noise floated up from below, faint at first, but growing. It sounded like bugs.

Claws and talons clacked and scraped. Lots of claws and talons.

The sun had slipped behind the range to the west.

Cameron rolled over and looked down, the night breeze cool on her bare ass. Shadows covered the ruined buildings of Fraser.

"Shit."

Gorgers flowed from every opening in every building, until the rubble was furry with them. She shuddered. "That's more than a couple of hundred."

David stared silently for a while. "I count a hundred on one building. Multiply that times, what, two thousand buildings? That's more than two hundred thousand. And that's just the ones we can see. It would take years to kill that many."

Chapter Thirty-Six

The early light of dawn spilled into the shuttle's tail. Tyrell walked to the circular opening at the end, past the others, who all sat together, trying to figure out what to do. As far as he was concerned, it was too early for a debate, and he was pretty sure he could guess the outcome. Sierra would get her way. That woman knew how to get what she wanted.

He felt much better after a decent night's sleep, despite the bad news about Fraser. Easing himself down, he sat with his legs dangling over the hundred-foot drop. A trail of flattened grass meandered through the dewy meadow below. At least one gorger had wandered by during the night.

They could handle one, but not two hundred thousand. They were back to the drawing board, and Priya was pushing hard for settling on the island zoo inside the mothership. Tyrell wasn't ready to give up on Earth, especially after they'd found this valley. The fresh air, the mountain view, and the gurgling river were all too perfect.

"If we go back to the menagerie, we'll have complete control over everything," Priya argued behind him. "We can stun all the dinosaurs and put them in storage."

"We can't stay there," Sierra said. "We have no idea how long it will remain in orbit. Besides, we proved yesterday we can handle the gorgers if we work together."

"You proved you can handle two of them," Felicia said. "Three was almost one too many."

Tyrell frowned. She had a point.

He opened the satchel he'd received from Major General Dodge as he lay dying on the golf course. Tyrell had already thumbed through the papers, but he hadn't studied them closely. Dodge and his team had been instructed to collect a pod. Maybe the Air Force had some other information about the pods they could use. He angled the papers so the morning light fell across them.

The title on the first page read, "ORDERS TO COMMANDEER A DEVICE OF ALIEN ORIGIN." The president's signature ran across the bottom. Most of the page was filled with military acronyms and phrases like *by any means necessary.*

"We have to make this work," Sierra said. "What if we brought the pods down in the middle of the valley, away from town? We could organize groups to stand watch each night. We could arm them all with spears."

"You need to trust me on this," Cameron said. "That would work with a few gorgers, but not the numbers we saw. If they decided to come for us, everyone would die."

Tyrell glanced back to see Sierra's reaction. She nodded. She knew how to get what she wanted, but she also knew when to listen to the people around her.

He licked his fingertips and thumbed through the next five pages, which were filled with astronomical readings about the pods and their trajectory. He would show them to Priya later. She might get a kick out of them.

"Maybe we should look for another location," David said. "We haven't tried South America in the daytime. Or even much of Africa."

"I'm not ready to give up on this valley," Sierra said, her voice rising. "We've circled the planet and we haven't seen any place that's even come close. Plants are growing here, water is plentiful, and the meadow is wide open. There isn't any place for gorgers to hide."

"Except the town," David said.

"Yes, except the town. But in a way, that's a perfect set-up. When it's sunny, they're concentrated in the ruins of those buildings. Maybe we can build a wall around it or something."

Tyrell turned back to his papers. The next nine pages were dossiers about his team.

He was surprised to find info about himself. He'd been under the impression they'd called him up at the last second, but they had detailed notes, including his final Air Force evaluation before all the new recruits had been sent home.

"Even if we took care of the town, what's to stop more gorgers from coming in over the mountains?" Felicia asked. "Or up from the south?"

"It's too far," Sierra said. "There's too much open terrain to cross in one night. They'd be caught in the sun when morning came."

"What about a three-day storm?" Felicia asked. "That would provide plenty of cloud cover."

"Wouldn't that also explain how they got to Fraser in the first place?" Kim asked.

"I don't think so," Sierra said. "The harvesters brought them to Earth in those giant sphere containers. They seeded them all over the planet."

"You don't know for sure," Priya said. "Some of them could have migrated here."

"You're right," Sierra said. "I don't know for sure. The only thing I know for sure is that we can't give up. Look, if they come over the mountains, we'll fight them off." She snorted. "I don't think gorgers have meteorologists in their ranks. If a storm were to blow in, they wouldn't know how long the cloud cover would last. It makes sense that they wouldn't venture too far from shelter."

While they debated, Tyrell read about his high school grades, which were decent, his three speeding tickets, his construction jobs, his bank balance, and his vital statistics. They even had a paragraph about all the dogs he'd rescued and the abandoned ranch where he'd taken them. The word "trespassing" appeared twice, which ticked him off.

"What if we built a fort or something in the meadow?" Kim asked.

"Those things are like spiders," Reggie said. "They can climb over anything."

Tyrell flipped to the last page, which he hadn't looked at before. The overblown title read, "CHEYENNE MOUNTAIN COMPLEX ENDER SURVIVAL CONTINGENCY CODES." Tyrell perked up. He'd joined the Air Force hoping to somehow secure a spot inside the Cheyenne Mountain bunker.

"TOP SECRET" was stamped across the page in big red letters. Two codes were listed below the title.

```
Blast Door Admittance Code (verbal): B018Y2C4Q8
SPACE FORCE VHF Radio Code (verbal): B018Y2C800
```

Those codes were worthless. There wouldn't be anyone to hear them. A hundred and fifty years had passed since the Ender hit. Even if they had enough supplies, they couldn't have remained underground that long. Human beings couldn't live their whole lives in a cave, much less six generations. And if they'd tried to come outside after the dust settled, the gorgers would have wiped them out.

He glanced at the bottom half of the page and sat up straight.

```
POST-IMPACT EMERGENCY ACCESS INSTRUCTIONS
            SUMMIT HATCH ENTRANCE
            (38.7451, -104.8621)
STEP 1: Remove Steel Hatch Cover
STEP 2: Dial Hatch Code - 1499677014
STEP 3: Rotate Access Hatch Counter-Clockwise
STEP 4: Airlock ALPHA - Dial Reverse Code
STEP 5: Rotate Airlock Hatch Clockwise
STEP 6: Airlock BETA - Dial Original Code
STEP 7: Rotate Airlock Hatch Clockwise
```

"Ha-ha," Tyrell said. "I'm finally gonna get in that damn bunker." He stood, rising carefully on his injured leg. "Who's up for a little trip?"

Everyone looked over.

"I have codes that will get us into Cheyenne Mountain."

The others continued to stare.

He held up the papers. "It's a military bunker near Colorado Springs, under a half mile of granite. It was built to withstand a thirty-megaton bomb. It's got to be gorger-proof, and there has to be something in there we can use. Maybe even weapons."

He walked over to show them.

Reggie took the paper and studied it. "This is the underground military bunker where all those politicians went."

"Yeah," Tyrell said. "I enlisted in the Air Force when the Ender showed up, because they ran support ops for the place. It was their facility before the Space Force took it over. I thought I might be able to get inside somehow. They had food enough in there for decades, and all kinds of other stuff."

"The food won't be any good after a hundred and fifty years," Priya said.

"Munitions might still be good," Tyrell said. "Weapons."

David's eyebrow rose. Even Reggie looked hopeful.

"What kind of weapons?" Barry asked. "Do they have flamethrowers?"

Tyrell grinned at the idea of lighting up gorgers with a flamethrower.

"Dibs on a rocket propelled grenade launcher," Cameron said.

"It's yours," Tyrell said.

"Are there still people there?" Kim asked, standing on her tiptoes to look at the page.

"After a hundred and fifty years?" David shook his head. "No way."

"They could have survived," Sierra said. "People are resilient. And if they were armed, they could scavenge the surrounding area."

"If they ventured outside, they were toast," Cameron said. "The gorgers would have killed them."

Sierra didn't back down. "We've survived against the gorgers with only nine people."

"We've survived two days, and that's only because we have an alien aircraft," Priya said.

Sierra shrugged. "Regardless, we should check it out. If there are weapons we can use, it's worth the trip."

"How do you know we can find this place?" Felicia asked.

"The complex is easy to find," Tyrell said. "It's built in a massive mountain on the south end of the city. There's a road leading right to it, then a big tunnel that takes you to the blast door." He held up the papers. "This says 'Summit Hatch Entrance.' I don't know where that is, but we do have flying cars. I bet we can find it."

"We can make Colorado in less than two hours in the shuttle," David said.

"It's another delay," Cameron said. "We need to deal with Randall."

"If we find more weapons, that will help us deal with Randall," Sierra countered.

Cameron tilted her head, then offered a shrug.

Tyrell smiled. Sierra really did know how to get what she wanted.

"Let's go check it out," Sierra said. Everyone nodded.

Tyrell chuckled. He was finally going to get into that damn bunker.

Chapter Thirty-Seven

Stuck on the hovercar floating outside the dome room and miles above the floor, Randall's only way to keep track of time was to count how often he had to take a piss over the side. He'd slept for a while between his second and third pisses. He felt fairly confident they would eventually let him back in, because they'd have killed him already if they wanted him dead. Hell, he'd even taught them how. They could just send a harvester drone to electrocute his ass while he slept. But they hadn't, so it was just a matter of waiting. The hatch finally opened sometime after piss number four.

Marge's unpleasant girth filled the opening. *"Overseers will discuss allowing a human specimen to serve as caretaker."*

Randall gave her a smug smile. He was getting a job interview.

She turned and slithered back toward the consoles in the middle of the room, where Flopsy waited. Randall followed. The hatch closed behind him when he stepped through. He was parched, but he didn't mention it. He didn't want to come off as needy.

He walked up to the platform, passing Marge, who wasn't ever gonna win any races. "Where am I supposed to work, if I get to be caretaker?" he asked. The sooner he got it all down, the sooner he could take over.

"Caretakers work in observation bunkers."

The observation bunker would be perfect. He would get away from these two and could observe people from afar. He could build up a group that would follow his lead. Good people, like Jerry and Gale. More importantly, he could weed out the troublemakers, like Jordan and Dean. He could send harvesters to collect them and drop them somewhere with a bunch of dinosaurs.

He wouldn't need to live with his people until he was ready, but he didn't have to be a silent observer. He could communicate with them. He could send them deer and other animals to cook, and order them to send back a portion. Randall grinned. *Offerings.* They would send him offerings. He wouldn't just be a caretaker, he'd be God.

He adjusted his junk. Food wasn't the only kind of offering he would demand.

He could do it, too. All the tools would be right there at his disposal. Hell, once he learned how to fly the hovercars, he could float above them, invisible in the sky, *exactly* like God. Nobody would fuck with him, not even Dave.

Randall froze.

"Hey, Flopsy. What the hell happened to Dave and Sierra?"

The last thing he needed was for them to surprise him while he was in a bunker, like they'd done with the caretakers.

"Human specimens flew to Earth. Gorgers consumed them."

"Did you see it happen?"

"No."

"Did you shut down their ship?"

"Not possible."

Randall shook his head. "Why the hell don't you have some way to blow up their ship and be done with it?"

"Why would we have mechanisms to destroy our equipment?"

Randall looked up at the ceiling of the dome and sighed. It wasn't like a wooly rhino had ever stolen their shit and gone for a joy ride. "Okay look, can you find their shuttle?" He needed to be sure they were gone.

Flopsy tapped the console and the dome turned into that magnificent movie theater again. This time it showed a view of Earth from a satellite or something. The view zoomed in, showing a silver shape flying over mountains. A shuttle.

Randall chuffed. "Gorgers consumed them, huh?"

Flopsy didn't respond. The little gimpy arm hanging off the side of his head twitched.

Marge lumbered over and rumbled. *"Ten billion gorgers occupy Earth. No place is safe for human specimens."*

"In that case, they'll probably try to come back here," Randall said. "Can you lock the goddamn doors?"

Flopsy rumbled. *"Airlocks are automated."*

"Of course. Sweet candied Christ." Randall sighed. "Can you take control of their ship?"

"Harvesters are used to control shuttles."

"Fine, send some fucking harvesters. Take control of their shuttle, or better yet, zap them all, the way you zapped Sierra. Those bastards will kill as many gorgers as they can, and then they'll come up here and kill you."

"Seventeen harvesters were damaged inside the carrier. Harvesters must not be damaged."

Randall rolled his eyes. "Ain't this the sort of thing harvesters are made for? Dealing with specimens?"

"Specimen collection is secondary. The primary function of a harvester is to collect gravid gorgers."

"Ain't you got like a million harvesters?" Randall asked. "Christ, how many do you need?"

"Gorgers must be collected quickly once gestation begins. Egg viability outside the brood chamber is less than ten percent."

Randall crossed his arms. "If you don't take care of those assholes, none of that will matter. They will come up here and wreck everything. That's what they do. They killed all your caretakers, or did you forget?"

They'd sure as hell wrecked everything for Randall. They'd gotten Crystal killed, and then, when he'd finally started to figure shit out in the village, they'd come and wrecked everything again.

Flopsy and Marge rumbled at each other.

Randall forced himself to be patient. If they decided they could spare some harvesters, great. If not, he would start his caretaker training. Once he got access to those control devices, he would send down every last harvester to kill those bastards for once and for all. And he would find a way to finish off Flopsy and Marge, too.

After that, nobody would fuck with him.

Chapter Thirty-Eight

Reggie felt like he was flying. He *was* flying, of course, inside the shuttle as it raced south over the Rockies, but the panorama made it feel like he was personally soaring through the air. He wished Chase could see it. The boy had loved roller coasters and VR rides.

From this altitude, at this speed, and without any cities below, it was almost possible to imagine Earth wasn't devastated. It was almost possible to feel hope.

Out in the distance, smoke rose from beyond a jagged wall of rock. As the shuttle grew close, a vast crater came into view, so large its far side was barely visible on the horizon. Reggie winced. So much for imagining that Earth wasn't devastated.

"Is that where the Ender hit?" Barry asked.

"The Ender hit in the South Pacific," Priya said. "That has to be the Yellowstone Caldera. It's like a volcano. The comet's impact must have set it off."

"Let's get a little higher," David said.

He and Cameron sat side-by-side at the front of the docked carriage. It was obvious what the two of them had gotten up to last night, at least to the adults in the group. Reggie didn't care. What difference did it make?

They crossed over to the southern edge of the crater. Below, all of the trees had been stripped from the mountains. They weren't just knocked down, they were gone.

They'll grow back someday, Reggie thought. In fact, they'd probably grow back faster if there weren't people around to screw things up.

He squeezed a fist. He had to stop thinking that way. He had to trust Sierra. He'd grown more and more confident that she was the key to everything. Chase's mom had often said the world would be a better place if they'd put women in charge of everything. He'd always laughed it off, but now he wondered if she'd been on to something. Men seemed to care about power and authority, at all costs. Women didn't worry about that shit. They just took care of things. Chase's mom sure as hell had, before the cancer got her.

He relaxed his fist. Maybe things would be different with a woman in charge. He wrapped his heart around the idea. It was all he had.

David pointed left, and a moment later, the shuttle banked toward the east. The Great Plains came into view. Iowa was out there, some seven hundred miles away. Had Chase's body burned when the Ender hit, or had it laid there until the gorgers arrived? Had they come along and puked on his charred corpse to soften it up?

"Reggie." Felicia took his hand and uncurled his fingers. They had squeezed into a fist again. None of the others were looking at him, but there was plenty of worry on Felicia's face.

"Sorry," he whispered. "Just tired. Zoned off a little."

She narrowed her eyes. She saw right through him, he was certain. People didn't squeeze their hands into fists when they zoned off. She didn't comment, though. Instead, she gestured out the front, where skeletal frames of skyscrapers jutted from the ground like fingers reaching up from a grave. "That's Denver," she said. "I lived in a suburb on the southeast side." Ugly ruins passed by below.

"I'm okay," he whispered.

Felicia patted him on the back.

Women were the key. He had to put his faith in that.

"Colorado Springs is dead ahead," David said as they rocketed past Denver.

Tyrell moved up into the space between him and Cameron, pointing to the right. "See how the mountains sorta come to an end there? Cheyenne Mountain is that last big one."

"Got it," David said. "Let's scope out the city first. If anyone in the bunker survived, there might be signs of life outside. Everyone keep your eyes peeled."

It was a waste of time. Colorado Springs was just as dead as Denver. Reggie watched silently as they passed back and forth over the ruins. Finally, David and Cameron exchanged a glance and they banked to the west, toward the giant granite peak.

Tyrell rose, pointing. "There's the front entrance."

A hole gaped in the side of the mountain, looking down over the rubble of Colorado Springs. The opening was three stories tall, bigger than Reggie expected. "There's no door," he said. "Does that mean the gorgers got in already?"

"No," Tyrell said. "That tunnel curves in and then exits back out to the south. It's always open. They designed it that way."

"Why?" Barry asked.

"The blast door is on the side wall of the tunnel, further in the mountain. If a bomb went off nearby, the blast would pass through the tunnel and out the other end. The force wouldn't hit the door directly."

"Hey, what are those paths?" Felicia asked. A crumbling road led from the tunnel, but dirt trails fanned out from both sides of the road.

"Maybe the people inside have been coming out," Kim said. "Maybe they go down for supplies in the daytime and then go back inside before it gets dark."

"Why aren't they outside right now?" Barry asked. "It's sunny."

"Let's get a closer look," Sierra said.

David and Cameron put the shuttle down on the roadway just outside the tunnel. They undocked the carriage from the central stalk and floated out the tail, with Sierra, Tyrell, and Reggie onboard.

Outside, the air felt heavy and smelled of smoke. Everything was eerily quiet, without the sounds of birds or the rumble of cars in the distance. It didn't feel like Earth.

They floated ten feet above the roadway, straight toward the opening.

As they drew close, a scratching sound came from the tunnel.

"Trouble's coming," Cameron said.

Reggie squinted as they floated into the mountain, trying to let his eyes adjust. The first gorgers were twenty yards in. A pair stood on the road, back to back, with their tails stretched out behind them. The little finger-like knobs on their tails intertwined, and they kept shifting position. "What the hell are they doing?" he asked.

The gorgers turned at the sound of his voice, but their tails remained connected.

"I think they might be mating," Sierra said.

The knobs on their tails danced back and forth with wet, sticky squelching noises.

Cameron shivered. "Lovely."

As they went deeper into the mountain, the tunnel curved slowly to the left. More and more gorgers crowded the road below. At least half of them were connected at their tails. Several trysts involved more than two gorgers. Smaller specimens clung to the tunnel's rocky walls and ceiling.

"Full stop," David said.

"Is that the blast door?" Reggie asked.

Ahead on the right, an enormous concrete rectangle butted up against the tunnel wall. It was the only surface that wasn't covered with gorgers.

"Yeah," Tyrell said. "That's it. Still closed up tight."

"The design of this place screwed them," Cameron said. "If anyone survived inside, they couldn't ever leave, because this outer tunnel is gorger central."

"Reverse," David said. "Now."

On the ceiling, several gorgers crept closer. One released its grip and dropped, just missing the front of the carriage. It landed on a pair copulating below and broke them apart.

"Let's get out of here," Sierra said. "We aren't getting in this way."

Back inside the shuttle, they told the others what they'd seen.

"Does that mean we have to bail?" Kim asked.

"No way," Tyrell said, flashing her a smile. "It could be a good sign. It means the facility is still secure. We need to try the secret entrance."

David and Cameron piloted the shuttle up along the two-thousand-foot granite slope to the mountain's peak.

"If it's a secret, how do we find it?" Barry asked.

Tyrell shrugged. "It may take some hunting."

"Maybe not," Reggie said.

Directly ahead, the corner of a concrete structure protruded from the mountain. A ten-foot tall metal cylinder rose from the structure, with a small platform at the top, giving it the appearance of a tall, skinny mushroom.

"That isn't a very good secret," Kim said.

"It looks like the slope has been worn away around it," David said. "That was probably all buried once. I think the platform at the top used to be at ground level."

Tyrell nodded. "A hundred and fifty years ago, that little platform was probably hidden in the woods, maybe inside a little maintenance building or something."

They brought the shuttle down on the mountain's peak, a few hundred yards away.

Cameron got to her feet. "Sierra, Tyrell, Reggie, you're with me. Priya, can you send us over in a carriage?"

"I got a better idea," David said. "Kim, do you think you can help me fly?"

She beamed, nodding eagerly.

Each little moment between David and his kids picked at the scab of grief in Reggie's heart. He tried to ignore the hurt and be happy for them, but it wasn't easy.

"I'd like a flying lesson, too." Felicia said.

"Ok," David said. "That'll give us something to do while they're inside."

Reggie crawled onto the spare carriage with the others. Cameron handed him a gun. A few moments later, they floated slowly out the shuttle's tail. He pulled his hat low to shield his eyes from the bright sun. Below the carriage, a gravelly scree covered the mountaintop. Further down the slope, the rocks were as big as semi-trailers. There might be hundreds of gorgers sheltering beneath them.

It took Kim three tries, but she and David eventually brought the carriage next to the platform, like a dingy pulling up to a dock.

Cameron stepped across first, then Sierra and Tyrell climbed over. Reggie went last. There wasn't room for anyone else on the platform. The metal cylinder in the middle looked like an elevated manhole cover, rusted solid.

"Where do we enter the codes?" Sierra asked.

"Beneath that cover," Tyrell said. "It's protected from the elements."

A ticking sound came from somewhere nearby.

"Look." Kim pointed. A dark bird with a pale yellow breast tapped something in its beak against a stone on the slope below. It was the first living creature they'd seen on the planet, other than gorgers.

"That's a good omen," Reggie said, and he meant it. Life on Earth would continue. Maybe it was a message from Chase.

Sierra pounded the hatch with the hammer they'd found in the gas station, knocking off thick flakes of rust.

When she finally exposed a gap, Reggie and Tyrell slipped their fingers in. They pulled back the metal cover with a nails-on-chalkboard screech. The bird flew away. Ten metal dials lay in a row underneath, each one the size of the wheels on Chase's skateboards.

Reggie put his hands on his hips. "That's just an old-school lock. I expected something more high-tech."

Tyrell winked at him. "Anything high-tech wouldn't survive an electromagnetic pulse, would it?"

Sierra tried to turn one of the dials, but it wouldn't budge. She tapped it with the hammer and it rotated one digit.

Tyrell pulled out his papers and read off the code while Sierra knocked each dial into the correct position.

David and Kim floated in the carriage a few feet away, watching.

When the combination was set, Reggie grabbed a handle on the inner hatch and pulled, producing another horrible squeal. The door lifted and then came to a rest in the upright position, like a toilet lid.

"Well, if anyone's in here, they must have heard that," Sierra said.

"Nobody could live underground this long," Reggie said. "They'd go mad."

"Maybe they found another way out," Sierra said. "Maybe they found some way to make things work underground." She stood and looked at each of them. "If we don't hold on to some kind of hope, what's the point?"

Tears welled in Reggie's eyes. She really was like Chase. He wanted to believe her, more than anything.

"Tyrell, you had the code, you get the honor," Cameron said. "Keep your weapon ready."

He looked down into the dark hole. "You really think someone could be in there?"

"No, but we didn't think anyone was inside that gas station, did we?"

He gave her a guilty smile and disappeared into the opening, climbing down a ladder attached to the metal tube.

Maybe they would find someone inside, someone who could help them start over. They could all work together and build a new world, with a new way of doing things. Hell, if anyone was in there, they'd have to be stronger and smarter than the people who had come before. Reggie took in a deep breath of mountain air.

No one on the platform spoke. The world was silent except for the wind haunting the scraggly rocks.

A moment later, Tyrell reappeared at the top of the opening. "I found someone, alright, but she doesn't look so good. Come see."

Chapter Thirty-Nine

Cameron dropped off the ladder into a small room. The dried and withered corpse of a woman sat against the side wall. She'd been dead for a very long time, and judging from the hole in the back of her skull and the M1911 clutched in her skeletal fingers, she'd taken her own life. She wore a decayed jumpsuit so thin it looked like tissue, with "Michelle" stitched in cursive across a patch on her chest. The bones of her hand crumbled as Cameron picked up the pistol. She checked the chamber and the magazine. Empty.

The room itself was little more than a cinder-block box, with the ladder on one wall and a dark opening across from it that led down into the mountain. A security camera above the opening aimed at the ladder, but the little red light on the bottom was dead.

Sierra, the last one to climb down, crouched next to the body. "She's got a purse." Sierra lifted the corpse's other arm and removed a leather bag that looked like it would fall apart in a strong breeze.

"Anything useful?" Cameron asked. She peered into the opening on the opposite wall, which fed into a downward-sloping hallway. She could only see a few yards in.

"Nothing too exciting," Sierra said, rifling through the bag. "Wallet, pens, loose change, cellphone, sunglasses, and some papers." She held up a round plastic shell. "Need a make-up mirror?"

"You never know what we can use," Cameron said. "I'll run it up to the others." She took the bag from Sierra and tucked it under her arm. The straps were too brittle to hang over her shoulder.

At the top of the ladder, she handed the bag to David. "Add this to our collection."

David glanced inside, pulled out a pair of aviator sunglasses, and stuck them on his face. "What do you think?"

"They'd look better on me." She snatched them and hung them on the front of her shirt.

He raised his eyebrow. "You're going into the dark. You don't need sunglasses."

"I will when I come back out." She tapped the side of her temple.

He nodded and smiled, which gave her a glow, right in the center of her chest. This was her guy.

"What do you think?" he asked.

Cameron shrugged. "There were people living here for at least a little while. Hopefully they left something behind we can use."

Kim rifled through the woman's purse and pulled out a plastic bottle of hand lotion. She shook it, producing a dry rattle.

"Save that," Cameron said. "We can use the bottle."

Kim nodded.

Cameron turned back to David. "We may be gone for hours. Leave this hatch open. I want fresh air circulating in there as much as possible. If we aren't back by dusk, close the hatch and sit tight in the shuttle until morning. Open it back up for us as soon as the sun hits it."

He nodded. "What if you don't come out then?"

"We will. Don't you leave." She dropped back down the ladder before he could respond.

In the vestibule below, everyone had gathered around the entrance to the hallway.

Tyrell held up six plastic light sticks.

"Just use one," Cameron said. "We'll need the rest when we get down there."

He snapped the light stick and shook it.

Sierra frowned at the sickly green-yellow glow. "That isn't nearly bright enough. We need torches."

"The hallway is too tight," Cameron said. "We'd burn up all our air."

"Then we should use more glow sticks," Sierra said. The edge in her tone suggested that maybe Miss Sierra wasn't a fan of the dark.

In the past, Cameron might have mocked her for it, but she was trying to be nicer these days.

"Your eyes will adjust," she said. She grabbed the light stick and started into the tunnel, taking point. "Tyrell, bring up the rear. Everyone keep your guns holstered. If there's a rat or something in here, I don't want you freaking out and shooting me in the back."

"What about gorgers?" Sierra asked. "They like the dark. This is the perfect place for them."

"There shouldn't be any in here," Cameron said. "The place was sealed up tight. That's the whole point of this facility."

"I hope you're right," Sierra said.

The hall sloped down nearly twenty degrees. The floor was concrete, but the walls and ceiling were bare rock. A pair of heavy-gauge wires ran along one side, bolted in place near the ceiling every ten yards or so. Cameron gave them a tug. "We should cut a few hundred feet of this and take it with us on the way back. We can use it to get in and out of the shuttle."

"We should get some for inside the shuttle, too," Tyrell said. "For the carriage that's docked."

Cameron nodded. Tyrell had his head on straight, at least as much as anyone could in this fucked-up world. Inside the shuttle, one carriage had to be docked in the center of the chamber, some eighty feet up. If anyone wanted to walk around on the shuttle's floor or back in the tail, they had to use the second carriage as an elevator. A rope ladder would make it easier to use the piss jar, or simply take a break from the crowd.

The light from the room behind them shrunk to a dot as they descended.

Ten minutes in, they had to climb over a waist-high mound of rubble that had fallen from the ceiling.

"Do you think this place is stable?" Reggie asked.

His question made the ceiling feel somehow lower. "It was built to survive a nuclear blast," Cameron said, trying to convince herself as much as him. "If anything more was gonna come down, it would have come down already."

The light from the glow stick was more than adequate once their eyes adjusted.

Fifteen minutes in, after they had gone more than a thousand feet, they came to a massive steel door with "Airlock ALPHA" stenciled near the top and an oversized combination lock built into the center, much like the one in the hatch outside.

The door opened more easily than the exterior hatch, but it still required a few minutes of hammering to knock the rust loose.

Reggie snorted. "I can't believe that code is just the original code in reverse."

"Think about it," Cameron said. "Anyone possessing the code would need to destroy the papers so they wouldn't fall into the wrong hands." She tucked the hammer into her belt. "Reversing the original code adds a layer of security without the need to memorize a second set of numbers."

The air on the other side of the door felt ten degrees cooler.

"So far, so good," Sierra said.

"Something's bothering me," Tyrell said. "Why was that woman up there? I mean, I assume she didn't go out the hatch because of gorgers, but why did she stay up there?"

"Maybe something in the bunker drove her up there," Reggie said.

"Maybe Miss Melissa was exiled," Cameron said.

"Mrs. Melissa," Sierra said. "There was a wedding ring on her finger."

The hallway continued its downward slope after the airlock, but it also made a series of ninety-degree turns every two hundred feet or so, spiraling deeper into the mountain. After another half hour, Airlock BETA emerged from the darkness ahead of them.

"I wonder if Melissa locked these doors behind her, or if the people inside locked them to keep her out," Tyrell said.

"If we find anyone down here, we can ask them," Cameron said.

"Now you think people might be in here?" Sierra asked. "What changed your mind?"

"I was joking," Cameron said. "They couldn't have had enough food to last a hundred and fifty years.

They entered the code on the lock and opened the door. The other side smelled like old soil and decay. Tyrell's light stick seemed downright bright now, though the green glow only extended a few yards ahead of them.

Cameron shivered at the thought of living underground from birth to death. And maybe also from the temperature, which felt like it had dropped below sixty degrees.

"How deep are we?" Reggie asked. "How far have we gone?"

"Priya could tell you if she were here," Sierra said." She would have counted our steps and then used the angle of the slope to calculate our depth."

Tyrell chuckled.

After another half hour of walking, they came to a third door. A bronze plaque was mounted where the locks had been on the others.

CHEYENNE MOUNTAIN - AIR FORCE STATION AMERICA'S FORTRESS — JANUARY 20th, 1965

Restricted Area. Entry is unlawful without permission of the Installation Commander. All security instructions must be obeyed immediately else the use of deadly force is authorized.

A metal bar ran from the handle to a latch assembly mounted on the tunnel wall, like something in a barn, but there was no sign of a lock.

Cameron glanced back at Sierra. "You still think there might be survivors in here?"

She shrugged. "I hope there are."

"Well, let's find out if you're right." She twisted the handle. The latch bar lifted out of place.

Chapter Forty

Priya sat in the end of the shuttle's tail, enjoying the breeze and the mountain view, which extended for miles. Kona lay next to her, tracking David's carriage like she might watch a squirrel crossing from tree to tree in her backyard.

David was teaching Kim and Felicia how to fly, though Kim already knew most of the controls. Barry rode along with them, probably happy for a change of scenery. The carriage dipped down between Cheyenne Mountain's peak and a barren ridge to the west.

"You were supposed to keep close," Priya muttered. David had promised he wouldn't go far, in case the others came back or Priya needed help.

At least she was safe from gorgers. They undoubtedly filled the rocky crevices below her, but there wasn't a cloud in the sky and the shuttle's tail was a good thirty meters above the ground.

She pulled open the bag Cameron had found in the bunker and rooted around, wondering if there might be a bottle of aspirin or ibuprofen inside. There was always a tiny chance it could have retained some degree of potency.

Her broken leg was singing again. Only a dose and a half of Tyrell's morphine remained, and everyone had agreed to hang onto it in case someone got hurt worse.

Priya's fingers closed on the shape she was searching for. "Bingo." She pulled out a bottle of acetaminophen and shook it, rattling at least thirty tablets inside.

Kona looked up.

"What do you think, girl? Should I take the whole bottle?" If each pill retained only one percent of its initial potency, taking thirty would be less than a full dose. Even that would be better than nothing.

She twisted off the cap, then paused.

Of course, if she was wrong, and the drug was somehow still viable, she would overdose and die of liver failure after five days of incessant vomiting. "Nuts."

Kona tilted her head.

Priya decided to take two pills every two hours and see if she noticed any decrease in the pain in her leg. She swallowed them dry and rooted around in the purse again, pulling out a makeup mirror. The edges were blotched with oxidation, but the center remained functional.

One look at her reflection was enough. She needed a haircut, a bath, a facial, an eyebrow waxing, and at least a week's worth of sleep. She snapped the mirror shut and set it aside.

Next, she found a mostly-full pack of tissue, which she stuffed into her pants pocket. It would be a luxury to wipe her butt with something other than leaves for a change. Most of the rest of the items in the bag seemed worthless. She found a collection of keys, some pens that had long since dried out, a phone charger, and a knot of rubber bands that crumbled when she tried to pull them apart.

At the very bottom, she felt something hard and rectangular. At first, she thought it was an address book, also useless, but when she flipped it open, she gasped.

The Journal of Michelle Dodge

Day 1

I'll never see Robert again. The boys will never see their father again. General Thomas came by late this morning and told me Robert was on a secret mission and won't return to the bunker. He wouldn't even tell me what that mission is. Coward.

Of course, I'm the bigger coward.

I didn't tell Patrick or Michael. I just couldn't. Not tonight. I managed to keep it together until they were asleep.

God it hurts.

I love you Robert.

"Hey, David," Priya shouted. The others should know about the journal. It would almost certainly contain information about what had happened inside the bunker. But the carriage was too far away, out of earshot. As she watched, it dipped out of sight again.

Priya scratched Kona's belly and flipped to the last entry, something she would never do with an actual book.

Day 1527

I love you Robert.

I love you Michael.

I love you Patrick.

Fifteen hundred days. Four years and four months.

The entry before that one described reaching the exit and climbing out. Michelle had been amazed to find that the world was still there, and then horrified by the fact that it was overrun with gorgers, which she referred to as "giant snake crabs."

Priya stopped to consider the woman's terminology for a moment. She understood the desire to call the gorgers "crabs." Both had ten legs, after all. But the snake component didn't resonate. Gorger bodies were tube-like, true, but the proportions were nothing like a snake's body and they didn't have any other reptilian features.

She turned back to the front of the journal and started reading from the beginning. The woman wrote about how much she missed her husband, how difficult it was not knowing what happened to him, and how her boys, Patrick and Michael, were excited to explore the maze-like complex. Shit got real a day later when they closed the blast door.

She scanned ahead and found the moment of impact.

It hit. God in heaven, the Ender actually hit. We could hear it, even this deep. A steady roar, like standing near a waterfall. General Thomas told us that was the shockwave.

Patrick and Michael both came to me, and we held each other tight. Michael acted like he was doing it for my sake, but he was shaking. We were all terrified.

Not everyone believed it was real. A few dozen people were laughing about it. Senator Palmer went up and clapped General Thomas on the back, telling him the sound effects were a nice touch. General Thomas did not look amused. He nodded to one of the Guardians nearby, and they marched Palmer away from him.

It looked like Palmer took it personally, I'm happy to report. What an idiot. You don't go smacking generals on the back. Even I know that much.

She read on, skimming past endless descriptions of the food, the process for getting laundry washed, and other mundane details. A few days later, a small group of people started protesting, urging the general to open the blast door so they could go back outside.

Priya shook her head. The lay person's inability to understand basic physics never ceased to astound her. It wouldn't have been safe to go out on the planet's surface for years.

She kept reading. Eventually, the general came to visit Michelle and explained that her husband had been sent on a mission to get into one of the pods.

"What do you think, Kona? Did Robert make it? Is he up there in storage?"

Kona offered no opinion.

Michelle's sons were excited at first. They thought their father would return to rescue them someday, but as the weeks passed, they started getting pissy and eventually one of them stopped talking to her. The soap opera bored Priya. This woman had died more than a hundred years ago. The details of her life were irrelevant.

Even worse, she wouldn't stop writing about the food, and most of the comments were whiny complaints. "Try eating dried dinosaur for every meal," she said. That woman was lucky to have canned vegetables and freeze-dried fruit. Priya skimmed forward, then stopped herself when a word caught her eye.

Mycoprotein

"Of course." If they were growing fungal mycoprotein, they could produce a virtually endless supply of food.

She looked over at Kona. "You know, there might actually be people alive in there."

Kona thumped the curved floor of the shuttle twice with her tail and produced a small whine.

Priya cupped her hands around her mouth and shouted, "Hey David, get over here!" She really wanted to share what she'd learned, but the other carriage floated even farther away than before. It jerked back and forth in the distance like a child's remote-controlled car.

She scowled. David was supposed to come back periodically to check in, but when he was flying, he tended to forget about everyone else.

The heat of the sun tingled Priya's arms. She turned back to the journal, skimming ahead.

Three years after the Ender hit, the bunker's second in command left on a scouting mission and never returned. Then General Thomas died unexpectedly from an aneurysm. His third in command apparently suffered from bouts of dementia but had just enough sense to keep it hidden.

"Oh boy," Priya whispered. It was easy to see where this was going. The general had been making decisions for the good of the group. Smart decisions. The same sorts of decisions she would have made. But no one liked them.

Day 1107

Senator Palmer held a meeting and demanded that the Air Force turn over control to a democratically elected council. He kept saying, "This is still America," which brought cheers, even from the Airmen and the Guardians.

The Lieutenant General who recently took charge agreed that it was time. He didn't even debate it. Sarah told me he spends his days in his room arguing about basketball with a plastic Ficus.

Palmer promised that if he was elected, we would have a feast. He said General Thomas had been hoarding a supply of beef stew, keeping it just for himself and his men.

Priya flipped the page. Senator Palmer won the election handily and everyone got beef stew. She grimaced. Priya suspected it wasn't beef in that stew. It was General Thomas.
She scanned the next several entries. Things only got worse.

Day 1228

Sarah stopped by today and told me I needed to get with the program. I asked her what she was talking about and she said "keeping the human race going." She asked if I had any preferences in men.

I told her I was still mourning Robert. She said I ought to move on, if I knew what was good for me.

I guess I've been ignoring it, but nearly three hundred women are pregnant right now, including seven girls barely in their teens. It makes me sick.

I know people are having sex a lot. Patrick has been bragging about it, which I can barely handle. Christ, he's only fourteen.

I asked Sarah if she knew where Lori or Fran were. I haven't seen either of them in more than a week. She gave me a funny look and told me I shouldn't worry so much.

Then she said Senator Palmer is giving out more food from the stores so people can enjoy themselves, and that everyone should try to have some fun. "There are so many things we can't do. We should at least indulge in the things we can."

I kept my thoughts to myself because I didn't want to seem old-fashioned but I guess I still want more from life than just pigging out and sleeping around.

A hollow pit formed in Priya's stomach. "They were feeding and breeding, just like the gorgers," she whispered. These people turned into monsters in only three years. If their descendants were still alive, what would they be like?

She'd read enough. She reached for the control device and sent the spare carriage out of the shuttle and over to the hatch leading into the complex. It would be waiting for Sierra and the others in case they came out in a hurry.

She wished David would come back. He could go inside and warn the others that if anyone was alive in there, they might be dangerous.

A cloud passed in front of the sun. Priya glanced up. The skies had been clear the last time she checked.

Kona barked.

The cloud descended straight down. Priya squinted. Something wasn't right. Her heart thumped.

It wasn't a cloud.

A formation of harvesters dove toward David's carriage.

"*David!*" she screamed, as loudly as she could, but the others were still way too far to hear her.

Chapter Forty-One

Sierra held her breath as Cameron pulled the massive door. A high-pitched groan came from the hinges. Cameron jerked back after the door had moved only a few inches.

An instant later, Sierra knew why. She winced. "Smells like a septic tank." She noticed something else. "Tyrell, give me that light stick."

He handed it over and she shoved it into her pocket. The hallway grew dark.

But not completely dark.

A thin line of light glowed at the edge of the doorway.

"Holy shit, the power is still on," Tyrell said.

"How is that possible?" Reggie asked. "Is it nuclear?"

Tyrell shook his head. "They didn't have nukes here. They had massive stores of diesel, though. Like, ponds full of it." He helped Cameron pull the handle.

The door opened onto a mesh metal platform that overlooked an expansive flat surface. A rocky ceiling hung overhead, too smooth to be natural.

"That's a rooftop," Reggie said, looking down. The flat surface below them came to an end about five feet shy of the cavern wall, leaving a narrow gap that ran the length of the building.

Sierra stepped out onto the platform. It reminded her of a fire escape, right down to the ladder off to one side, except the whole thing protruded over a building, instead of from a building.

The only lights in the cavern, which came from somewhere down in the gap, cast blade-like shadows up the rocky walls.

The building extended farther than she could see straight ahead and off to both sides. Just like in the mothership, it was too damn dark here. She leaned over the metal railing. The ground was three stories down, but the building's roof was only a few feet below her.

A heaving thrum filled the chamber and the temperature felt like a cool Los Angeles morning.

"How can they still have power?" Reggie whispered.

Tyrell shrugged. "This place was built to last."

Reggie stepped forward and gripped the metal railing. "Yeah, but fuel doesn't last that long. It degrades."

"They must have had chemical stabilizers or preservatives," Cameron said. "Or maybe some way to process raw crude."

"Maybe it *is* degrading," Sierra said. "Maybe that's why the lights are so dim." She told herself not to get her hopes up too high, but it really seemed like there might be people alive here.

The ladder ran down the wall from the side of the platform to the cavern floor, with a skeletal metal frame around it.

Cameron went first, followed by Reggie, Sierra, and finally Tyrell. The climb down reminded Sierra of the canyon in the menagerie where so many things had gone wrong. Her heart was galloping in her chest by the time she stepped off onto the gravelly cavern floor. They were in a narrow alleyway between the rock wall and a tall, windowless building. A dark forest of enormous steel springs held the building three feet off the ground.

"What's with the springs?" she asked.

"Shock absorbers," Tyrell said. "This place was designed to withstand World War Three."

"This ladder is our evacuation point," Cameron said quietly. "If we run into gorgers, get back here." She started forward with the gray rock wall on her left and the even darker building on her right. They walked single file. The gap between the cavern wall and the building wasn't quite big enough for two people to walk abreast.

Sierra listened for gorgers as she crept along behind Reggie, but it was difficult to hear anything over the crunch of their shoes on the gravel, not to mention the close-in thumping of her heart. Tyrell brought up the rear.

Like the ceiling, the cavern wall was too straight to be natural. Tatters of white plastic covered the rock in places. A line of cable ran along the wall about fifteen feet up, with dim bulbs hanging from it. At least half of them were dead.

After walking a hundred and fifty feet or so, Cameron stopped, holding up her hand. "The building ends up ahead."

Sierra squinted. She couldn't see it, but she trusted Cameron. The woman had better eyes than anyone she'd ever met.

They crept forward. The crunch of gravel under their shoes seemed deafening.

Sierra bent for another look at the springs, then froze. Motion caught the corner of her eye. She dropped to a crouch. Her hand went to the revolver on her hip. "I saw something," she whispered. "There."

Something moved between the springs. Tyrell slid up next to her, his gun drawn. "Holy shit."

Sierra put her hand on his back, peering past him, her heart fluttering.

A small child, maybe seven or eight years old, huddled in the shadows beneath the building. She was bald, with huge blue eyes.

They'd found someone. Sierra couldn't believe it. They'd actually found someone.

"It's okay, sweetie," Tyrell said. "We won't hurt you."

The child grimaced and shuffled back.

Sierra slid past Tyrell and held the light stick out toward the girl. She retreated into the shadows, probably because she was naked, Sierra realized, feeling embarrassed and awkward. She placed the light stick on the ground and inched forward. "What's your name? I'm Sierra."

The child didn't answer. Her eyes danced back and forth as she moved sideways, keeping behind one of the three-foot tall springs.

"It's okay, we're here to help." Sierra put her hand on one of the coils for balance and leaned under the lip of the building. It felt like a crawlspace, dark and musty.

The child tilted her head, as if studying her. This girl had to have lived her whole life without ever meeting anyone new.

Hope and excitement filled Sierra. There were people here. People they could help. People who could help them. Humanity wasn't dead.

Sierra reached for the girl, her palm open. "Come on, sweetie, you can show us around."

The girl lifted a tool in both hands. At first Sierra thought it was a giant pair of pliers. Red plastic covered the handles. "Oh, can I see that?"

"Is there anyone else?" Reggie asked. "Where are her parents?"

The girl flinched at the sound of his voice. Sierra glared at him.

When she turned back to the girl, she saw that the tool wasn't a pair of pliers. It was some sort of heavy-gauge bolt cutter. The blades opened like a hungry mouth, reaching.

Sierra pulled her hand back, but she wasn't fast enough. Something caught her pinky.

The crunching pain was unlike anything she'd ever experienced. She shrieked, sucking air. She pulled her hand away as the pain exploded, desperately hoping it wasn't as bad as it felt.

It was worse.

Two of her fingers were gone.

Chapter Forty-Two

David kneeled on the carriage behind Kim and Felicia, who both sat cross-legged at the front. He was proud of them. Kim already knew most of the controls and Felicia was a natural. They dipped down and wove between two ridges.

Beside him, Barry threw his hands over his head like he was on a roller coaster. "Whee!"

David put an arm around the boy, happy to see him having fun, but also concerned he might tumble off and fall to the jagged rocks below. Kim and Felicia were tucked inside the short wall that wrapped around the front third of the carriage. In the back, though, there wasn't anything but a broad flat platform, with a foamy surface that went almost all the way to the edges.

He hoped things were going well inside the mountain. He wasn't sure how he felt about the previous night, alone on the carriage with Cameron. Part of him felt regret, that he'd moved too quickly. At the same time, he couldn't wait to see her again.

"This is fun," Felicia said. "Can we go faster?"

"Just a little," David said. He pointed to the controls that changed their speed. "Be smooth and gentle. We don't have seatbelts, you know."

His concern about falling off was perfectly reasonable. They were a hundred feet above rocky terrain, after all. Surprisingly, however, he wasn't gripped by the paralyzing fear of heights he used to feel. He wished he could tell Lindsey.

The thought gave him pause. His mind hadn't gone to Cameron. They didn't share the history that he had with Lindsey. Cameron hadn't been there with him when he broke out in cold sweats at the top of Willis Tower on a vacation in Chicago. He sighed. He missed Lindsey so much.

"What's that flashing?" Barry asked.

David scanned the console, but didn't see anything. "Where?"

Barry pointed to the top of Cheyenne Mountain. A bright pinpoint of light blinked off and on at the end of the shuttle's tail.

"That must be Priya. She's signaling us."

"What does she want?"

Guilt washed over him. He'd promised to check in and completely forgotten. How much time had passed? He looked around. The sun was still hot and bright.

A shimmer of silver and yellow floated directly above, growing larger. For the briefest instant, David didn't know what he was seeing. Then the shapes separated just enough and he identified them.

Harvesters.

Six or eight drones descended straight toward them.

"Full speed, now," he ordered.

He'd taught Kim and Felicia the importance of an immediate response, because every control had to be performed simultaneously by both pilots. The carriage shot forward.

Barry tumbled backwards. "Daddy!"

David sucked in a huge gasp of air. Barry came to a stop on the opposite corner of the carriage, at the edge. The baseball bat rolled straight back, catching in the narrow groove where the foamy surface ended and the outer metal frame began.

The harvesters dipped down right where the carriage had been only seconds earlier, then rose back up in pursuit maybe thirty feet behind. They flew along like a pod of dolphins, moving in sync, slipping around each other, never quite touching.

"What's happening?" Felicia asked.

"Harvesters are after us," David said. "Keep going."

"You should fly," Kim said. She sounded scared. "You're better."

"You can do it," he said as he reached back and clutched Barry's ankle. "Circle and climb. A hundred and eighty degrees."

They had to get to the shuttle, and to do that, they had to get out of this ravine. There wasn't time to change pilots.

Kim and Felicia started the turn but they didn't put any bank into it. The centrifugal force pulled Barry further toward the side. David squeezed his ankle so hard Barry yelped. The baseball bat slid a few inches, still caught in the little groove near the edge of the platform.

The harvesters drew closer, only twenty feet back now. They kept overshooting the carriage's turn, which required them to course-correct. Each one was roughly the same size as the carriage, but more compact, like a knot of metal muscle.

"I'm falling," Barry shouted. His head was right at the edge.

"I got you," David said. "I need you to grab the bat." It was the closest thing they had to a weapon.

Barry shook his head. "I can't."

"You can," David said. "I got you. I won't let go."

Barry flailed over his head with both hands. He slapped the bat, bouncing it.

"Calm down," David said, gritting his teeth. "You can do it."

Barry reached again. His fingers wrapped around the handle.

"Hold it tight." David dragged him forward across the carriage and took the bat. He shoved Barry to the front, between Kim and Felicia.

"We're almost through the one-eighty," Felicia said. "What do we do?"

The gigantic silver shuttle sat on the mountaintop right where they left it, a quarter mile away. It was the only place they could go where they'd be safe.

"You have to fly into the tail."

"It's too small," Kim said.

"You can do it," he said again, forcing his voice to stay calm. "Line up from a distance and fly straight in."

One of the harvesters drew close, only ten feet away. The cluster of metal arms hanging beneath its rounded nose unfolded and reached. The drone was as big as a shark and flew silently, which made it seem even more aquatic.

David crawled on his knees to the center of the carriage.

"Somebody has to call out the movements," he shouted. He couldn't hold off the harvesters and guide them in at the same time.

"I'll do it," Felicia said. "We've got this, Kim." She sounded just as frightened.

The harvester extended its cattle-prod arm toward the carriage.

David braced himself on one knee and looked for the best spot to hit it. If the metal bat made contact with the electrified arm, he'd be fried.

"Turn to the right," Felicia called out.

The carriage swerved out from under the harvester's reaching arms. David teetered and almost fell, but the movement gave him the opening he needed. He swung, smacking the drone in the side.

The harvester only drifted a few degrees from the impact, but it was enough. It bumped the drone behind it and they both fell back.

He grunted with satisfaction.

The other harvesters closed in. A cluster of arms reached forward from each one.

"Level off, now," Felicia said.

David clutched desperately at the surface of the carriage, but there wasn't anything to hold on to. They stopped climbing, which caused him to float for an instant. His stomach clenched, then he came down on his hands and knees, still gripping the bat.

"We're lined up, kinda," Kim said.

David looked forward. They were flying in the general direction of the shuttle's tail, but they were nowhere near lined up.

One of the harvesters burst forward, but it overshot, flying above them. It dropped down, right toward David.

He braced the end of the bat against his palm and shoved upwards against the drone's belly, knocking it higher. At the same time, the carriage dipped slightly and his stomach dropped with it.

"Slow down, shift left," Felicia said.

David grabbed the opposite side of the carriage, bracing himself for the turn.

As they straightened out again, another harvester rose from below, right behind them. He brought the bat up over his head and swung straight down, hitting the top of the drone hard enough to dent it. It dropped, disappearing below the back edge. David's hands vibrated painfully.

"Up a little," Felicia said. "No, not so much. Slow down."

Slowing down would be suicide. The harvesters were only a few seconds behind them. But they had to get into the shuttle.

Somewhere out in front of them, Kona barked incessantly. They were close.

A drone lurched forward. David swung, but the carriage wobbled at the same time and he missed, falling sideways onto his hip.

He scrambled back onto his knees and held the bat out like a lance. The drone's cattle-prod arm slid up next to him, just missing his head. David flinched sideways to avoid it and shoved the end of the bat against the drone's front surface, as hard as he could. It fell back, bumping another drone behind it.

"David, duck," came a new voice. It was Priya. *"Now!"*

He dropped to his elbows, tucking his head.

The tubular walls of the shuttle's tail raced by with a whoosh.

He couldn't believe it. He scrambled forward and jumped down, tumbling as he landed. Behind him, Kim and Felicia continued deeper inside. "Dock it," he shouted without looking back. "You have to dock it." Docking the carriage was the only way they knew to close the hatch at the end of the tail.

Priya lay in the tunnel next to him, clawing her way deeper into the shuttle, dragging her broken leg behind her.

Four drones crowded toward the entrance, bumping each other. One slipped forward, into the opening, blocking out most of the light.

David ran toward it, much more confident now that he was on stable footing. He raised the bat high and brought it down in an overhead ax chop. The bat struck several of the harvester's arms, which sent a jolt of fear through him but no actual electricity. The harvester tilted down. He pressed the end of the bat onto its shiny front face and shoved it out the opening.

The metal door in the tail began to spiral shut. They'd done it. They'd docked. Pride surged through him.

Five harvesters bobbed just outside the entrance as the hole shrunk.

David placed the bat against the closest one and shoved.

A bang went off in his hands, like a gunshot. He flew backwards, rolling down the tunnel. The bat had made contact with the harvester's electrified arm.

His fingers throbbed, like they'd been slammed in a door. Sparks danced in his vision. *Don't pass out. Don't pass out.* He'd been shocked, but he couldn't have gotten a full charge, because he was still conscious. The bat clattered to the floor somewhere, a million miles away.

He could barely breathe. He needed time. He needed to make sure his hand hadn't been blown off. He needed to figure out what to do next. He smelled smoke, and he was pretty sure it was coming from him.

A harvester scraped through the opening as the door spiraled closed. Ten feet long and as thick around as a bull, it filled the top half of the tunnel.

Its electrical arm unfolded as it descended toward Priya. She crawled backwards on her elbows, wailing, "No, no, no, no, no."

The hatch closed completely. David's stomach hiccupped as the artificial gravity turned on, lower than Earth's gravity. He scrambled toward Priya, but it felt like moving in slow motion. His hands tingled all over, cold and numb.

He was too far away. The harvester was already on her. All he could do was watch.

The cattle-prod arm reached for Priya.

She bumped into the control device, which had closed, becoming a solid orange sphere the size of a beach ball. It began to roll, but she grabbed it.

She swung the sphere upward like a kettlebell. The rod on the end of the harvester's arm struck the device right in the center.

Electricity arced from the drone to the orange ball and back again. The sphere exploded with the bang of a transformer blowing on a telephone pole.

Priya tumbled backwards, wailing. Sparks rained down everywhere. The control device blew apart, its two halves flying across the inside of the tube.

The harvester landed in a heap. Blue bolts of electricity coursed up and down its arms, which wriggled in the air. A moment later, the drone settled, silent and still.

David stood, flexing his fingers, trying to get normal feeling to return. He staggered over to Priya. "Are you hurt?"

A pair of shallow scratches lined her cheek. "My leg," she hissed.

He winced. Any bone tissue that had begun to fuse back together had likely been refractured when she tumbled across the floor.

He glanced toward the front of the shuttle, where the tunnel widened, becoming a huge spherical cabin. Kim, Barry, and Felicia stared at him from the carriage, which was docked out in the center. Somewhere below them, Kona barked.

"What happened?" David asked.

Priya winced, clutching her knee. "I don't know. Electrical overload?"

"Well, we're okay now," he said, still breathing hard. "Thank God."

The door was closed and all the other harvesters were outside. They'd done it.

"No," Priya said. "We are absolutely not okay. The control device is destroyed. We can't move the other sled around and we can't bring the pods down from storage. We're in serious trouble."

Chapter Forty-Three

Cameron took off, fleeing while she still could. She climbed the metal ladder back to the metal platform, breathing hard and slick with sweat. Climbing wasn't easy. One arm was still weak from Randall's gunshot wound, and the other from the centipede bite. She looked down into the dim gap between the building and the cavern wall. No one had followed her.

While Sierra, Tyrell, and Reggie had been focusing on the child, Cameron had been looking under the rest of the building. Deep in the dark shadows, she'd spotted big blinking eyes. She'd escaped while she had a chance.

Grunting and hooting echoed through the cavern. Somehow, people were still alive in this godforsaken place. She couldn't believe it.

She should get back to David and the two of them should get the fuck out of here. She reached for the door leading to the surface, knowing full well it would be terrible to abandon the others. *She* would be terrible. It wouldn't be the first time, though.

She stopped. She didn't want to be like that anymore. She couldn't, not if she wanted to stay with David. She had to find a way to rescue the others. At least, she had to try. "Christ, David, you better be worth it," she muttered.

Climbing back down the ladder was out of the question. The ground wasn't safe, not with those freaks running around down there. That left only the rooftop. Maybe she could find some way to help from above.

She lifted her leg over the metal railing. The roof, only four or five feet below, was flat and looked like concrete, undoubtedly reinforced against falling rock. She pushed off and dropped, then landed in a roll to minimize the sound.

The platform she'd jumped from was just within reach, though getting back up might require more upper body strength than she could muster.

She raced along the edge of the roof. Except for the forty-foot deep gutter beside her, it was like running through an empty warehouse. The rocky ceiling above had been carved to exacting specifications. It was nearly as flat as the concrete roof she ran across.

Somewhere below, people grunted and hooted. Every twenty feet or so, she peered down into the three-story gap between the cavern wall and the side of the building, but the only thing down there was an occasional dim bulb strung on a wire.

After running about a hundred feet, she spotted the back edge of the building. Four or five yards beyond, a perpendicular cavern wall boxed in the end of the structure. Rustling came from below. Cameron dropped to her belly and crawled to the edge of the roof.

Forty feet down, a dozen shirtless men carried Sierra, Tyrell, and Reggie up a short flight of metal stairs to a door on the first floor. Their pale skin almost glowed, especially compared to Sierra, Tyrell, and Reggie.

Reggie struggled, twisting and writhing, but he wasn't getting anywhere. There were too many of them. His baseball cap with the orange "I" on the front fell back down the stairs. The other two appeared to be unconscious.

The men slithered as they moved, a mess of wiry arms and legs. Scraggly hair hung from their heads and their pants were little more than rags. At least four of them carried batons, but Cameron didn't spot any firearms.

As the last of the men slipped inside, the door slammed shut with a bang that echoed through the cavern. A dim yellow trapezoid lit the gravel below, presumably shining through a window on the door.

Cameron pushed herself to her feet. The drop was three stories and there wasn't any way down. She looked back across the concrete rooftop. On her right, the wall led to the platform she'd jumped from. To the left, the monolithic building extended farther than she could see.

There was no way to know which way the others had been taken once they got inside.

The only lights came from the gaps between the complex and the cavern walls. She saw none of the crap usually found on roofs, like vents, fans, or communication equipment. The only sound, other than the relentless thumping of her heartbeat, was the distant whine of a generator. The air smelled like an old garage.

Cameron started forward, wondering how long she should search for the others before she said *fuck it* and returned to the surface.

Chapter Forty-Four

A nervous thrill shot up Kim's spine, just like jumping into a lake in early summer, before it was really warm enough. She and Felicia had docked the carriage on their very first try. It had been sloppy. They'd hit the docking arm at a weird angle, but the mechanism had snatched the carriage and snapped it into place. Even Felicia looked proud, which seemed out of the ordinary. Her thick eyebrows usually made her seem angry. Kim gave her a smile, checked to make sure Barry was okay, then looked down from the back of the carriage.

The floor below was eight stories down. The walls around her were eight stories away, in every direction. The carriage jutted out in the middle of the big empty room, kinda like the filament in an old-fashioned light bulb, if it was lying on its side.

Kim glanced back at Felicia. "Do you think we should jump down?" It would probably be safe because of the low gravity, which had turned on the moment they docked.

"No," Dad yelled.

He'd heard her from back in the tail, which narrowed down to a tube, sort of like the part of the light bulb you screwed in, except way skinnier and way, way longer. Kim frowned. It was a crappy comparison, because in a light bulb the filament came from the part you screwed in. Here, the docking arm protruded from the round end.

"Stay where you are," Dad shouted. He said something to Priya, who sat on the floor beside him, then started forward.

Kona, who'd been down in the lowest part of the shuttle, ran up to meet him.

Felicia made a low grumbling noise. Something was definitely wrong.

"I want to get down," Barry said. His whiny tone usually annoyed Kim, but she could tell he was scared. She put her arm around him and he leaned into her.

"I know Bud," Dad called out. "The problem is, once you get down, you can't get back up, so I want you to stay put, in case we need you there."

The tail grew wider and wider where it connected with the main chamber, which meant Dad kept getting lower and lower as he came forward.

"You never said anything about getting chased during training," Felicia said. "I want my money back."

Dad didn't laugh. He walked down the slope until he was almost directly below them, in the middle of the round part. Kona followed, slipping and sliding. Normally, this would have made Kim giggle, but right now she didn't feel like giggling.

Dad studied the front wall. He opened and closed his fists, the way he sometimes did when he was really upset.

"Why can't we just fly down to get you?" Barry asked.

Kim figured it out. "Undocking the carriage causes the door at the end of the tail to open. If we do that, the drones will get in."

"Where's the other carriage?" Felicia asked.

Dad craned his neck to look at them. "It's outside. Priya sent it over to the bunker entrance." His tone sounded angry. He walked halfway back up the slope and turned around so he was only a little lower than them, but still like a hundred feet away.

Felicia nodded toward the back. "Can Priya figure out how to send the drones away?"

"The control device was destroyed," Dad said.

Kim tried to figure out how screwed they were. They couldn't send carriages from place to place, but now that she and Felicia were learning to fly, they had enough pilots for both carriages. They just had to figure out how to retrieve the one that was stuck outside. Her heart skipped as she realized the other issue. "We can't bring down the pods from storage."

"Right," Dad said with a long sigh.

"We can figure that out later," Felicia said. "For now, we have to do something about those drones. How many are there?"

"There were eight," Barry said. "I counted."

"One is busted up back in the tail," Dad said. "One of the others might have been knocked out of commission in the chase."

"That leaves six," Barry said, like he was some kind of math genius.

"Okay, but why did they come after us?" Felicia asked. "How did they find us? I thought the aliens were all dead."

"I checked all the observation bunkers," Priya said. She sounded defensive. "There were only four caretakers. We killed them all." She crawled closer, dragging her broken leg behind her, and now sat right where the tail funneled into the big spherical chamber.

"Maybe you missed one," Dad said. "Maybe one was off flying around the islands."

"It was Randall," Kim said. "It had to be."

"What?" Felicia made an angry noise deep in her throat. "How does he know how to control the harvesters?"

Kim shrugged "He used a harvester to carry away Mr. Vaughn." She wished Sierra had slit Randall's throat when she had the chance. She knew it was an awful thing to think, but she didn't care.

"They can't get in, can they?" Barry asked.

"I don't think so," Dad said. "We're safe here."

"The others should be safe too, as long as they stay inside," Kim said. "That hatch was tiny. The drones wouldn't fit."

"I'm not so sure about that," Priya said. "There may be trouble inside."

Dad turned and looked up the slope at her. "What?"

She held up a thin book. "I found a diary in that woman's purse. It sounds like it got ugly in there. Things went downhill fast. They were eating each other in less than three years."

"Ew," Barry said. "Zombies."

"How do you know about zombies?" Kim asked.

"I know lots of stuff."

"Even so, there can't be anyone alive in there," Felicia said. "They would have run out of food."

"Maybe. Maybe not," Priya said. "They were growing mycoprotein. That would give them a nearly endless supply."

Kim had never heard of mycoprotein, but she knew better than to doubt Priya when it came to science stuff.

"Even after a hundred and fifty years?" Felicia asked. "People couldn't survive cooped up underground that long. They'd go mad."

"It sounds like that's exactly what happened," Priya said.

"We have to warn them," Kim said.

"How?" The hurt on Dad's face showed how much he wanted to help them.

Kim knew he liked Cameron. It made her sad, because she was worried he might forget Mom. She wished Cameron would stay and live inside the bunker, but Sierra and Tyrell had to come back. Kim couldn't bear to lose them. She pulled her knees against her chest, hugging herself. She missed Mom so much it hurt, right in her core, and it didn't seem like it would ever stop hurting.

"We can't do anything until we figure out how to deal with the harvesters," Dad said. "We can't even see outside."

"We've got spears and a few guns in the tail," Felicia said, nodding her chin toward the back.

"That isn't nearly enough against six of those drones," Dad said.

"Maybe they flew away after the door closed," Kim said, hoping as hard as she could.

"Yeah," Felicia said. "What if Kim and I undock real fast? You could take a quick peek and then we'll dock again."

Dad shook his head. "It's too dangerous."

Kim imagined the drones hovering outside the shuttle's tail, just waiting for them to come out. If only this stupid ship had windows. "Wait!" She pushed herself to her feet and pointed at the front wall. "We aren't blind. We have a huge 3D projector right there." It was even better than a window.

Dad's face lit up. The sight gave Kim a warm feeling of pride.

"Tell us how to turn it on." She and Felicia crawled to the console at the front of the carriage while Dad went back up to the beginning of the tail tunnel. He was even farther away up there, but at least he was at roughly the same height, where he could see them.

Dad and Priya talked them through the steps to start up the ship. It took a couple of tries, because they had to use controls Kim and

Felicia hadn't learned yet, but after three or four minutes, the lights came on, shining images into everyone's eyes.

It felt like the front wall completely vanished, showing them a view of Colorado Springs sitting out in front of them, several miles away and several thousand feet below. Beyond that, open plains stretched to the horizon.

"No harvesters," Felicia said.

"They're probably behind us," Kim said. "Waiting at the end of the tail."

"Okay, do a straight rotation," Dad instructed. "Just like when you're flying the carriage."

"Let's turn to the right," Kim whispered to Felicia.

She pressed three fingers into the creepy little holes on the front of the console and nudged the little hockey-puck thing sticking out of the side. Felicia did the same and their view rotated sideways.

The exposed concrete of the bunker's secret entrance appeared, with its little metal hatch on top, still open. The other carriage floated beside it. There was no sign of Sierra or the others.

They stopped rotating when they were facing the same direction the tail had been pointing. There weren't any harvesters there, either. Puffy clouds floated overhead.

"They're gone," Barry said. "They flew away."

"Someone has to go into the bunker and warn Sierra," Kim said. She really hoped there weren't any bad people inside. Her mind jumped to Joe pointing his gun at her.

"Hold on," Dad said. "Keep turning, but go faster."

Kim and Felicia reached for the controls. She nudged the hockey puck more, which made the view swing past in a blur.

The back end of a harvester came into sight, floating sideways, covered with shiny silver and yellow panels, like a big robot wasp. It flew in the same direction they were turning, trying to stay behind them, but the shuttle was faster. The harvester's front end came into view, with all those metal arms hanging under its chin.

They kept turning. A second harvester appeared. Then four more. Then another dozen.

"That's more than six," Barry said.

As the shuttle turned, a wall of harvesters came into view, too thick to see through. There had to be a hundred of them, all jostling one another, trying to position themselves at the shuttle's tail.

Barry leaned into her. Felicia said something in Spanish that was probably a bad word.

They stopped the shuttle from rotating and all of the harvesters slid from view. It somehow felt worse to know they were back there without being able to see them.

"What do we do now?" Kim asked.

Dad looked at her without answering. They were in trouble.

Chapter Forty-Five

Throbbing pain pulled Tyrell from a dark haze. One side of his face pressed against a shag carpet so old and crusty it felt like Velcro. Pain throbbed through his head. He tried to raise his hands, to probe his skull for cracks, but his arms wouldn't move. His wrists were tied behind his back. Bare feet surrounded him, with curling yellow toenails. He craned his neck. Five or six men stood over him. They smelled of waste and rot, and a deep musk that reminded him of oxen at the zoo.

"What do you want?" Tyrell asked, trying to make it sound like a demand. The words oozed out with a whimper. "Why are you doing this?"

"Forget it," came Reggie's voice. "They can't talk."

Tyrell twisted his neck, which sent daggers of pain through his skull. He spotted Reggie's shiny scalp and green shirt a few feet away. "Where's Sierra?" He looked all around, but couldn't see much beyond those nasty feet. It didn't help that the lighting here wasn't any brighter than out in the cavern.

"She's behind you," Reggie said. "Unconscious."

"How bad is she hurt?" Tyrell asked. He'd seen blood on her hands, right before these bastards bludgeoned him.

"It's bad," Reggie groaned. "We're fucked." He looked ten years older without his cap.

"We'll get out of this," Tyrell hissed. "Stay calm. Cameron will save us."

"Bullshit," Reggie said. "She took off and saved her own ass."

"She'll come back," he insisted, though the pain fogging his head made it hard to feel certain.

"She won't," Reggie said. "She never cared about anyone but herself."

Tyrell hadn't known Cameron nearly as long as Reggie, so he had to believe him. "What about David?" He didn't seem like the kind of guy who could abandon anyone.

"Have you lost your goddamn mind? He won't leave his kids and he sure as hell won't bring them here."

Cold fear pressed Tyrell deeper into the crusty carpet.

He had to get through to their captors somehow, to let them know he wasn't their enemy. It was a miracle they'd survived here, for so many generations. He needed to find some sort of common ground, to let them know they could work together.

Moving slowly, he curled his legs under him and rose to a kneeling position. The motion left him dizzy and faint. His throat tightened from the stink of some foul, unhealthy discharge.

One of the men stomped forward and shoved him back to the floor. The throbbing in his head exploded. The man was barely four feet tall. He stood hunched, with spindly arms and legs. Raw, red sores covered skin so thin and pale the veins showed through. Long clumps of hair hung from his head and along his jawline. The tattered remains of old khaki pants were cinched tight around his waist with a length of electrical cord.

"We came to help you," Tyrell said, speaking slowly. "We found a safe place. You can come with us."

The man made a wide circle with his lips and hooted like a gorilla. Scar tissue filled the bottom of his mouth.

"Oh my God. His tongue has been cut out," Tyrell whispered. He felt the urge to vomit.

Four other men crowded next to the first and joined the hooting. They looked similar enough to be brothers, with sunken eyes, pallid skin, and wispy clumps of blonde hair. One of them shoved the first man in the shoulder and he opened his mouth wider, stomping his feet. All of their tongues were gone.

The only light in the room came from two dim bulbs strung along one wall. Sierra lay a few feet away, also bound with her hands behind her back. Blood oozed from the stub where her little finger had been.

Her ring finger ended at the first knuckle, with a white shard of bone in the center. Tyrell's stomach hitched. He looked away.

A grid of light panels checkered the ceiling, but they were all off. Rows of plastic seats faced a podium at the front, with a whiteboard behind it. This had been a meeting room once.

The hooting filled the room. There had to be at least a dozen men in here, all pink and spindly and covered with weeping sores.

"They're animals," Tyrell hissed.

"No, they're people," Reggie said.

"What happened?" Sierra asked, her voice tiny and brittle. She was alive, thank God.

"Are you okay?" Tyrell asked.

"No," she said, her voice high. "It hu-u-urrts."

"We'll get you morphine in the shuttle. Everything is going to be okay." The words felt empty and lame, but he didn't know what else to say.

"How?" Sierra asked.

He didn't answer. Tears moistened the corners of his eyes. He couldn't see any way out of this.

The hooting stopped abruptly and the men all dropped their arms to their sides as a large woman drifted up the aisle, draped in layers of cloth. She walked slowly, holding her hands up before her, like someone wading through muck. Glittering chains hung from her neck. Greasy blonde hair draped her shoulders.

"What a blessing," the woman said, through a mouth so wide it belonged on a fish. She spoke with a lisp. Mascara darkened her eye sockets, creating the appearance of a bloated skull.

"We're from the outside," Sierra said, her voice wobbly. "We can help you."

The woman raised a long finger, adorned with a claw-like nail, and pointed at Reggie.

One of the men stepped forward and kicked him in the ribs.

"Stop," Sierra shouted. "You don't need to do this."

The woman's eyes drew wide with astonishment and her lips pulled down. She pointed at Tyrell with two fingers.

A different man stepped forward and kicked him twice.

"Quiet," he grunted as he took the blows. They weren't allowed to talk. Talking meant beatings. These people were fucking insane. They'd survived all those generations only to go stark raving mad.

A bald naked girl entered the room from a door near the front, taking weird, tentative steps. She held a tiny stick out in front of her, like a sword. "For you, Baybo."

The woman took the stick from her and said, "Well done, Jimmy."

Tyrell turned his head, not wanting to look at a naked child, but the glimpse he caught from the corner of his eyes chilled him with icy nausea. Jimmy wasn't a girl, *he* was a eunuch. His genitals had been cut off, leaving a scarred hole at his crotch. His big toes were gone too, which explained his strange gait.

A tear rolled down the side of Tyrell's face. These monsters mutilated each other.

Baybo raised the stick Jimmy had given to her.

Sierra sucked in a sharp breath.

It was a skewer, holding two small pieces of charred meat. Baybo slid one from the end and popped it in her mouth, smacking loudly as she crunched bone.

Tyrell's stomach convulsed, tightening on itself. The monstrous bitch was eating Sierra's finger.

"Fuck you," Sierra snarled.

The dozen men standing around started hooting.

Baybo's mouth went wide. She cast her claw at Reggie.

"No," Reggie moaned.

Baybo's mouth went even wider. She pointed at Reggie again.

Jimmy shook his head. "These ones learn slow, don't they?"

One of the men stepped forward and kicked Reggie in the side of the head, twice.

Baybo plucked the second finger from the skewer and stuffed it in her mouth.

Jimmy stuck out his lower lip, clearly disappointed he didn't get a bite, and crossed his arms beneath his pale chest, which was pockmarked with half-dollar scars where his nipples had been.

Baybo walked over to Tyrell and Reggie, hands on her hips. One of the men moved close to her, swaying like a cobra. "Butcher these ones," she said, leaning close to him. "Give the blood to the breeders. Do not lose a single drop."

The man nodded, his lips wide.

Tyrell strained at his ropes, but couldn't get any traction. His wrists burned.

"What about her?" Jimmy asked, pointing at Sierra.

The men stood motionless, eager anticipation in their eyes.

"Tell the others to prepare the assembly chamber. We'll stake her down and give everyone a turn."

The men all hooted and shook their fists in the air.

Sierra trembled with sobs as Jimmy ran from the room.

Tyrell's blood roared in his head. How had everything gone so horribly wrong? He couldn't let them hurt her. He wouldn't.

One of the creeps bent to pick up Sierra.

Tyrell pulled his knees under him and brought a foot up until he was kneeling. He launched himself into the man, hitting him with his shoulder and knocking him into the creeps behind him. They went down easily, their bodies thin and malnourished.

Arms still tied behind his back, Tyrell charged at Baybo. The top of his head slammed into her face with a satisfying crunch. She glugged and shrieked like a pig.

Before he could turn around, the creeps were on him, hands and arms everywhere. They swarmed him, grabbing and punching and clawing. He tried to keep his feet, but there were too many. He collapsed to the floor as they piled on.

Chapter Forty-Six

Cameron stood at the edge of the roof, looking down at one of her favorite words. "ARMORY." She'd traversed the complex to the opposite side, some five hundred feet from where the others had been captured. On this end, the cavern extended another thirty or forty feet beyond the building, just wide enough for a paved two-lane road. A golf cart sat out in the middle on four deteriorated tires. The road disappeared into a smaller tunnel to her right and ran alongside the rest of the complex off to her left.

Across the road, a small one-story structure was nestled in its own little hollowed-out nook with that beautiful word stenciled above the door. The armory had almost certainly been pilfered, but Cameron would be thrilled to get her hands on anything, even just a few spare magazines.

The cavern was no brighter at this end. The only light came from a few dim bulbs strung on the walls. Floodlights were mounted on poles along the street, but they were dark. The thrum of the generator, louder here, seemed like it might be coming from the tunnel on the right.

Cameron peered over the edge of the roof, not bothering to crawl on her belly this time. Forty feet down, another short metal staircase led to the first floor, just like on the other end.

She walked right, looking into the tunnel where the road disappeared. It was even darker in there than in the main cavern.

When she reached the corner of the roof, she turned to study the alley between the building and the rock wall. Eight or ten feet back, she finally spotted what she needed. A utility cage full of pipes and conduits protruded from the building just below the roof and ran down to the floor.

Cameron lowered her feet over the edge and used the cage to climb down. Flakes of rust came off in her hands.

She drew her Beretta the moment her boots touched the gravel, then crept along the alley to the front, where she peeked out from the gap between the building and the cavern wall. Nothing moved. The thrum of the generator was definitely coming from the tunnel on her right, but she still couldn't see anything in there.

She ran along the front of the building and up the metal steps to peer through a window in the door. Sierra, Reggie, and Tyrell were in there somewhere.

A hallway extended as far as she could see, vanishing in a dark point. It probably ran the entire length of the building, all the way to the entrance on the other side. Doors lined the hall, some of them open, but she saw no signs of life.

If she went in, she would have to clear each room as she went down the hall in order to make sure she wasn't flanked from behind. It could take hours and if shooting broke out, she only had ammo for a handful of targets. She needed some kind of tactical advantage. She crept back down the stairs and out into the street.

She crossed to the armory, moving quickly and quietly on the asphalt. Much to her surprise, the door was unlocked. She pulled it open and winced as the yeasty stench of fermentation hit her in the face. Gun drawn, she stepped inside.

Plastic bins and vats filled the room, with stringy clumps growing in them that looked like Spanish moss. She frowned. No weapons.

It wasn't an armory any more, it was a science lab gone bad. She found a cart loaded with garden shears, trowels, and stacks of bowls and plates, some with oversized spoons and ladles sitting on them.

Cameron grimaced. They'd found something they could grow underground, which explained how they'd survived so long, but on the other hand, if they'd been forced to eat this shit, it barely counted as surviving.

Stacks of plastic crates sat off to the side. A single bulb hung from the ceiling, putting out a whopping twenty-five lumens or so. She pulled the lid from one of the crates. "Life jackets. Brilliant." Another crate contained little rubber wheels that looked like they were made for shopping carts. Two crates were filled with camouflage netting, still folded in the original packaging.

The last container held a jumbled mess of MRE pouches, all empty. Her shoulders fell. "Terrific." No food, unless you counted the moss, and no weapons.

She would have to infiltrate the main complex building armed only with her Beretta and the hammer, and she still had to locate the others. She eased out through the armory door.

The cavern remained empty, but a knocking sound now came from the left, where the road disappeared into the side tunnel. Other than the whiney thrum of the generator, it was the first noise she'd heard since the attack.

Had the freaks hauled Sierra and the others all the way through the building and back outside again? Cameron preferred the thought of facing them on an open, two-lane road over the close confines of the hallway.

She drew her Beretta and started toward the tunnel.

Chapter Forty-Seven

David tried to squeeze his fingers between two panels on the wrecked harvester in the back of the shuttle, hoping he could open it up and find something useful. Anything. Maybe they had some sort of interface that could deactivate the other drones. Maybe they had control devices inside them. He pulled and pried at every gap in the metal, but nothing budged.

"Shit," he muttered. The secret hatch into the bunker had been left open. If darkness fell before they could figure out a plan, gorgers would crawl in. Cameron, Sierra, and the others would be in serious trouble, assuming they weren't already.

He walked back to the shuttle's bulbous cabin. Kona licked his hand.

"Any luck?" Priya asked.

He shook his head.

Barry, Kim, and Felicia stood up on the carriage, docked in the center of the chamber, but with the projection wall turned on, it looked like they were floating above the peaks of the Rockies. White clouds filled the sky behind them.

"We need ideas," he said.

"What if we fly the shuttle around to the front entrance?" Felicia asked. "Maybe we could find some way to warn them from there."

"How could that possibly work?" Priya asked. "The shuttle is way too big to fly through the entrance, and the moment we undock the carriage, harvesters will be all over us. Never mind the fact that the blast door is closed."

Felicia gave her a glare that could melt steel.

David held up his hand. "Any idea is worth discussing. Don't be so quick to shut it down. It might spark some other idea."

Priya crossed her arms and scowled, which made her look about fourteen.

"What if we make the carriage invisible?" Kim asked. "Maybe that would let us fly past the harvesters."

"They might still detect us," Felicia said.

"Maybe," Kim said. "Maybe not. Their stuff is weird. It's worth a try."

David played it out in his mind. Once they cloaked, Kim and Felicia would undock, which would cause the exit to spiral open. If they hurried, he and Priya might be able to climb aboard before the harvesters got in.

"Even if they couldn't detect us, they'd still block the exit," Felicia said.

"Dad could clear them away with the bat," Kim said. Her eyebrows angled close together, the way they always did when she was scared. "We have to try something."

"Dad could do it," Barry said.

Despite his kids' confidence, David wasn't so sure. He looked down at Priya, who was still pouting. "What do you think?"

"We couldn't do it even if we wanted to," Priya said. "We haven't figured out how to turn on the invisibility field with the carriage controls. We only know how to do it with a control device."

He exhaled. She was right.

"Then we should take the shuttle back to the mothership and get another device," Kim said. "I mean, this shuttle is fast. How long would it take?"

David looked out past her at the mid-afternoon sun. "We've made the trip three times. The duration varied wildly."

Priya cleared her throat.

"Yes?"

"The duration depends upon the position of the mothership. We can get there in a matter of minutes when it's directly overhead."

David dared to hope. "Is it overhead now?"

"That's the problem," Priya said. "Without the control device, we don't have any way to know where it is. We're going to have to fly up and search for it."

His heart sank. "How long will that take?"

She shrugged. "There's no way to know until we try."

"How are we even going to find it?" Felicia asked.

"I've got a pretty good sense of its orbit," Priya said. "It was always easy to find the International Space Station when you knew where to look, and the mothership is exponentially larger."

"Why don't we just fly away?" Barry asked.

"Because the harvesters will follow us wherever we go," Kim said. "Duh."

"That's why we should do it," Barry said. "We can lead them away from here."

No one said anything for several seconds. They all just stared at each other.

"Could it really be that simple?" David whispered. He looked over at Priya. "We fly off and lead them away. Once we're far enough, we turn around and fly back. The shuttle is much faster than those drones."

"How far would we need to go?" Felicia asked.

"I can manage that," Priya said. "If we fly out ahead of them, then wait to see how long it takes them to reach us, I can calculate how long it will take them to get back. Approximately, anyway."

David nodded. "We can pour on the speed for the return trip." He stared off into space, thinking it all through.

"If we get back here ahead of the harvesters, we can use this carriage to fly out and look for the others," Kim said.

He took a deep breath. "Kim, Felicia, back to your seats." They had a plan, and it was about as straightforward as it could get. "Barry, you're a damn genius."

Barry beamed and turned to his sister. He jabbed his thumb at his chest. "I'm a *damn* genius."

"Which way should we go?" Kim asked.

"Head east," Priya said. "The open terrain will make it easier to estimate the harvesters' speed."

As the view swung around, David's heart sank. The clouds had grown thicker and darker. "Hurry," he said. "We don't have much time."

Chapter Forty-Eight

Creeping slowly, Cameron followed the dashed white line down the center of the road. The thrum of the generator echoed around her as she entered the tunnel, punctuated by the mysterious knocking sound every second or two.

She glanced back. The road behind her remained empty. Nothing moved near the three-story building she'd climbed down from.

Inside the tunnel, the road curved to the left. Twenty feet up, a sign hanging from the ceiling indicated "FUEL STORAGE" further ahead and "GENERATOR" on the right. She inched forward, giving her eyes time to adjust. The only light in the tunnel spilled in from the cavern behind her.

Twenty yards in on the right, she found the source of the banging noise.

A skeletal woman face-butted a door over and over again. Above her, "GENERATOR ROOM" was stenciled on a sign in faded white paint, and above that, another one of those miserably dim bulbs stuck from the rock wall.

Reddish-brown streaks ran down the door and blood covered the gravel below, some fresh, some long dried. The door itself was dented, as if it had been used for this purpose over many years.

Cameron lowered her gun, holding it with both hands down toward the ground.

The woman continued to hit the door with her forehead like a human metronome. She wore a jumpsuit smeared with layers of filth. Bony arms and legs showed through tattered holes. A fresh rivulet of blood streamed down the door.

What the hell? She wasn't trying to get in. The door wasn't locked. It wobbled open a quarter inch each time the woman's head came away.

"Hey," Cameron said. "Knock it off."

The woman snapped in her direction. Her bruised purple forehead was split. Dark blood ran down both sides of her nose. She looked Sierra's age, early twenties, but she had the emaciated body of a corpse.

Her eyes grew wide and she opened her mouth in a grimace. She didn't have a single tooth, just empty corn-cob sockets.

Cameron shifted the gun to her left hand and brought her other hand up like a crossing guard. "Stop right there."

The woman lurched toward her, arms reaching.

"Don't come any closer. Last warning." Cameron brought her arm down toward the steel hammer hanging on her belt.

The woman hissed and sped up, closing the gap in seconds. Her eyes blinked with unfocused lunacy.

Cameron snatched the hammer and slammed it into the woman's forehead. She'd meant to hit her with the hammer's face, to try to knock her out, but there hadn't been time to turn it around. The claws sunk into her tenderized skull and she dropped to the roadway without a sound.

Holding her breath, Cameron looked back to make sure no one else was charging toward her, but the main cavern appeared lifeless. She'd taken out her attacker quietly. Hell, the woman's headbanging had made more noise than the hammer.

She knelt beside the body. The woman must have been insane. It was the only explanation. Now that she was dead, her eyes looked peaceful and she actually appeared human. "Shit." Killing this woman had been an act of mercy as much as self-defense, but it still felt awful.

She pried the hammer free and stood. Was everyone here insane? Was this all that was left of humanity on Earth?

"Shit," she repeated.

Her gun at the ready, she pulled open the door to the generator room. It was pitch black inside. She flailed for a light switch. Banks of lights came on overhead, brighter than any part of the compound she'd seen so far. She squinted and put on the aviator sunglasses pilfered from the mummified corpse beneath the hatch.

A thirty-foot console stretched across the room beneath a window that overlooked a much larger chamber. A hulking generator sat right there on the other side. Several generators, from the looks of it. The room smelled of withered onions. Computer monitors ran along the top of the window, all dead or disabled. The console had more switches, dials, and levers than a KC-10 cockpit. A pair of big red buttons sat in the center with hinged plastic boxes over them, cracked and yellowed with age. The label beneath read, "BLAST DOOR."

She found a master switch for the monitors and flicked it on. One monitor powered up, one flickered static, and the rest remained dark. The functioning screen showed an empty conference room with piles of paper stacked on a table. Cameron punched a button to toggle the next feed and got a blank screen. The feed after that showed a naked, rail-thin man pacing back and forth in some sort of command room, with its own set of dead screens lining the wall. He swatted the air around his head as he paced. His hair was white as snow, and every rib was visible against his pale skin.

"What happened to these people?" Cameron whispered, though the answer was obvious. Living their entire lives underground had ruined them. It had *turned* them.

She toggled the view, looking for Sierra and the others, but also hoping to spot someone resembling a civilized human being, maybe barricaded off from the rest.

More than half of the feeds were dead, and most of the ones that still functioned showed empty rooms full of computer monitors. In several feeds, the walls were smeared with something that had to be either blood or feces.

"Come on," Cameron said. "Where are they?"

The next feed didn't have any video, but the audio produced sounds of moaning and wailing. "Jesus. That better not be them." A heavy pit formed in Cameron's stomach.

She looked around. A brittle, yellowed page of lined paper sat on the top of the console, covered with handwritten instructions in faded blue ink. The top line was written in capital letters.

REDUCE FACILITY LIGHTING TO PRESERVE FUEL

"This could be useful." She pulled the sunglasses down to her nose and read through a list of steps outlining the process to dim the lights.

The working monitor now showed a room filled with bones, picked clean and piled high on a desk. The more she saw, the more she worried that if she didn't find Sierra and the others soon, they'd be dead. She toggled to the next feed and saw something she recognized.

The screen showed the vestibule below the hatch they'd entered at the top of the mountain. The mummified woman was gone. Gorgers poured in from the opening and swarmed past the camera, entering the long hall down to the bunker.

The pit in Cameron's stomach doubled in size, then tripled.

It must be dark outside.

Something had happened to David.

She no longer had a way to get out of the complex.

Chapter Forty-Nine

"Stop," Sierra cried. Tears streamed down her cheeks. A dozen brutes piled onto Tyrell. Everything was falling apart and she could barely focus on anything except the need to look at her hand. She couldn't do that one simple thing, though, because her wrists were bound behind her back. Her mind felt clouded, but holy shit, her hand throbbed and pulsed and burned. Parts of her were *gone*.

Baybo moved behind the podium and pulled out a machete. She held it high in the air, the flesh hanging from her upper arm like a bag of gravy.

Sierra flopped herself over onto her chest and pulled her knees up beneath her. Her forehead pressed into the nasty carpet. She wanted to close her eyes and hold them shut, but she couldn't just lie there. She had to do something. She rose, slowly uncurling her body.

The men lifted Tyrell by his arms and legs. He squirmed and wriggled and kicked, but there were too many of them, and his hands were bound behind his back, too. They walked him over to the podium.

Sierra pulled one foot under her and wobbled to her feet. Maybe she could charge into them. Maybe she could hurt them somehow. Maybe she could give Tyrell a chance to break free.

One of the brutes appeared out of nowhere and placed a mop bucket in front of the podium. The men held Tyrell face up, his head right over the bucket.

Despair filled Sierra. She'd hoped to find survivors. People they could help. People who could help them. They'd found monsters.

Someone grabbed her from behind, squeezing the ruined nubs of her fingers.

She screeched. Electric needles shot up her arm as the man touched something sharp and solid. Her finger bone. Darkness crowded the sides of her vision, as if she was falling into a tunnel.

Baybo lowered the blade toward Tyrell's neck, lining up her strike.

"Oh God, oh God, oh God," Reggie chanted.

Tyrell's eyes locked onto Sierra's. His lips pressed together, trembling. Beads of sweat covered his face.

She wanted to close her eyes, but she couldn't. Tyrell needed to hold onto her gaze. It was all he had left and it was all she could give.

The world went white.

Shards of light stabbed Sierra's eyes. She squeezed them shut and blinked. Most of the panels on the ceiling came on. Light shone in from the hallway outside the room.

A klaxon sounded in the distance.

Sierra squinted. Pain stung her eyes, even though she'd only been in the cavern a few hours. The man holding her hands released her, screeching and slapping at his face, crashing into a row of metal chairs. Sierra fell to her knees.

Baybo staggered into the podium, still holding the machete with one hand, covering her eyes with the other. These people had lived their whole lives in the dark.

"Burn," Sierra said through clenched teeth. "Burn your fucking eyes out."

Tyrell twisted and kicked. The men holding him let go, clutching their faces. His head crashed against the bucket, sending it flying. He rolled on his side, trying to pull his hands out in front of him, but he couldn't get them past his butt. One of the brutes toppled onto him. When he landed, his mouth clamped onto Tyrell's shoulder.

"Gaaaah!" Tyrell shouted. "Get off me!"

Sierra crawled toward them on her knees, not sure what she could do with her hands tied behind her back, but desperate to help somehow.

Baybo waddled forward, one hand still covering her face. With her other hand, she raised the machete over her head and brought it down blindly. The blade sunk into the back of the man biting Tyrell. She wrenched the machete from the creep's spine and raised it again.

"Tyrell," Sierra shouted. She stumbled and fell onto her face, unable to catch herself.

The machete slashed down again. Blood spilled from the man's wound, covering Tyrell and peppering Sierra. The gash in the creep's back stretched wide, showing ribs and spine.

Sierra slid closer, pushing herself across the ground with her feet, her leather pants pinching the back of her knees.

Tyrell shook the creep's body off, grunting. His black shirt glistened with blood.

Baybo raised the machete above her head.

"No!" Sierra screamed. There was no longer anything between the blade and Tyrell. The next swing would slice him in two.

Chapter Fifty

The shuttle flew across the plains. From above, it looked like a fat metal tadpole with wings. The cloud of harvesters following behind looked like gnats. "Can't you speed up those drones any?" Randall asked.

Flopsy rumbled. *"No."*

"Well, why don't you send down more to cut 'em off."

Flopsy produced the same sound. *"No."*

The view pulled back until the shuttle was nothing but a silver dot flying over brown plains. "They're gettin' away," Randall said.

"Additional harvesters cannot be spared. Harvesters are needed to collect gravid gorgers."

Randall didn't give a shit about the gorgers or the harvesters. He sighed. "What are my responsibilities going to be, when I become a caretaker?"

Marge answered with a lengthy rumble. *"Caretakers release specimens into the preserve to monitor life-cycles and inter-species interactions."*

"Yeah, yeah, but what am I supposed to look for?"

"Caretakers evaluate reproductive success rates to determine which specimen configurations produce maximum population growth."

"Why?"

"Uninhabited planets are seeded with specimens. When the current generation of gorgers becomes gravid, they will be harvested. The next generation will be deposited on a world that has been prepared with specimens, while Earth repopulates."

Randall replayed everything in his mind, to be sure he got it straight. They collected critters from Earth, dropped 'em off on some other world, let 'em reproduce for a while, and then dropped gorgers on them to eat everything up. "Do you bomb the shit out of those other worlds before you drop gorgers on them?"

"Yes. Extra-orbital strikes minimize the risk of resistance to gorger populations."

"So my job as caretaker is to figure out what sorts of specimen combos you should use on the next planet."

"Yes."

"What does the best combination look like?" he asked. "For the gorgers, I mean."

"Ideal specimens will saturate the planet quickly."

Growing up in rural Oklahoma, Randall had seen enough to know that you couldn't just drop down one type of plant or animal and expect it to take over. Nature didn't work that way. Everything had to eat, and lots of plants and animals depended on each other in all sorts of complicated ways that were too boring to keep track of. Plants needed their seeds spread around and animals needed predators to keep their populations healthy.

One species had overcome all that, though. Humans had proven adept at filling space with all kinds of crops and livestock.

"Got it," Randall said. "I'll be the best damn caretaker you fuckers have ever seen." It was a lie, of course, but a good sycophant always told people what they wanted to hear.

He turned to Flopsy, who seemed to be more of a pushover than Marge. "How 'bout showing me how to fly one of those hovercars?"

Flopsy mumbled a bit. *"Human limbs are not long enough to operate the controls."*

Randall chewed on the answer for a moment. He'd seen Cameron and Dave flying a hovercar together, which supported Flopsy's comment, but he'd also seen Priya flying around in one all by herself. She hadn't even been sitting at the dashboard. She'd been playing with one of those orange devices.

"If I had a control device, I could ride a hovercar around, though, couldn't I? I could send it from place to place, just like when I moved the pods around."

Flopsy and Marge both rumbled for a minute. Finally, the translator spat out a single word. *"Yes."*

He made his voice as syrupy as possible. "Why don't you get me a control device? I'll show you what a good caretaker I can be."

Marge rumbled right away. *"Overseers will discuss further."*

"Take your time," Randall said. Once he got a device, everything was going to change.

Chapter Fifty-One

The most hideous woman Cameron had ever seen raised a machete high overhead. Tyrell lay on the floor in front of her, covered with blood. If he wasn't dead already, he was about to be.

Cameron raised the Beretta and fired twice. The first shot went low, opening a gaping red hole across the bottom half of the woman's face.

Cameron blamed the aviator glasses.

Her second shot hit right on target, between the woman's eyes.

The machete clattered to the floor as the woman toppled backwards. A fan of blood splattered the whiteboard behind her.

Six slimy men wearing rags turned toward Cameron at the sound of the gunfire. They staggered her way, arms out and eyes pinched tight against the glaring light panels in the ceiling. The one in the lead tripped on a chair and went down, along with two behind him.

Cameron snorted. Her plan had worked perfectly. These cave worms couldn't see anything with the lights turned up.

The last three circled wide, coming up the aisle, where Reggie lay with his hands bound. He kicked out with his feet and sent one of them sprawling, bringing the count down to two.

Cameron fired twice, both rounds hitting center mass, right in their sternums. Easy shots, but she hated expending so much ammo.

Reggie struggled, trying to get to his feet.

Cameron ran past him. He was safe for the moment and Tyrell was still in danger.

At the front of the room, another five or six half-naked men clutched their eyes, wailing. One of them crawled across the ground slapping the carpet as he went.

"Help," Tyrell shouted as he rolled away from the man.

She ran over, dropped beside him, and used her knife to slice through the cords around his wrists. "You okay?" she asked.

Two of the closest men staggered toward them.

"I will be." Blood drenched Tyrell's clothes. He snatched the machete and got to his feet.

He swung at the crawling man, burying the blade in his skull, then wrenched it free with a creak. Another man reached for him, grasping blindly. Tyrell sliced him diagonally across his chest.

Cameron turned to Sierra and fumbled at the ropes around her wrists. She sucked air between her teeth when she saw the nubs where Sierra's fingers had been.

"Thank you, thank you, thank you," she cried.

"We have to get out of here, fast," Cameron said, careful not to touch her fingers as she cut through the ropes.

At the front of the room, Tyrell swung and slashed. The men were coming to their senses, but it was too late. Tyrell grunted and swung horizontally, slicing halfway through a creep's neck. Blood spewed in a wide arc. Another man, shielding his eyes, crouched low and fled toward the door. Tyrell ran after him and brought the machete down on the back of his skull with a sound like splitting wood.

Cameron helped Sierra to her feet and scrambled over to Reggie.

Tyrell charged at the other men in the room, still tangled in the overturned chairs. He roared as he took them out, hacking and slashing.

When the last man fell, Tyrell stood, chest heaving and covered with blood. Men lay dead everywhere, in pieces. "I didn't—" Tyrell said. "I shouldn't—" He flung the machete down and stared at his hands.

Sierra crept toward him. "It's okay, it's okay."

He looked around, gasping, his eyes wet. Sierra touched his arm. He flinched.

Cameron finished cutting through Reggie's bindings. "We have to get out of here, now," she said. "I opened the door."

"What door?" Sierra asked.

"The blast door," Cameron said. "The twenty-ton blast door at the front." She ran to the back of the room, where their guns had been laid out on a small desk.

"What? Why?" Sierra asked.

"Gorgers are coming in through our little secret entrance. We can't get out that way."

"But even more of them will come in from the front," Tyrell said. "You just killed everyone in here."

Cameron looked around at all the bloody bodies and snorted. "*You* just killed everyone in here."

Tyrell grimaced.

"Is there anyone who isn't ..." Sierra's lips shook. "Is there anyone we can save?"

"No," Cameron said. "No one here can be saved. Trust me." She offered her a gun.

Sierra held up her ruined right hand.

Cameron scrunched her nose and gave the gun to Tyrell. "Come on, let's go."

"Where?" he asked.

"We need to get to the roof," she said. "Hurry." She led them into the hall that ran the length of the building, and took off toward the back exit, where the three of them had been carried inside.

Her plan was to get to the roof and wait.

The blast door opened into the tunnel where they'd seen all the mating gorgers. If it was dark outside, hopefully most of those gorgers had wandered off to the ruins of Colorado Springs for their nightly feeding. Any that were left behind would have undoubtedly entered the complex when the door opened. Cameron intended to wait on the roof until the exit thinned out enough for the four of them to slip out.

It wasn't much of a plan and she had no idea what to do once they got outside.

As they ran down the hall, they passed countless conference rooms and offices, including one where a dozen people sat slumped against the walls, nestled in piles of old clothes. Most of them were missing limbs. It looked like they'd spent their entire lives slumped against those walls.

Cameron wished she had some way to put them out of their misery before the gorgers found them. Hopefully, their final moments would be quick.

She shouldered open the door at the end of the hall and descended the short flight of stairs to the gravel floor of the cavern. A few spotlights now lit the exterior, but not nearly enough to keep the gorgers at bay. At least half remained dark.

Screams echoed through the cavern. The gorgers had gotten in. They'd found some of the residents.

Cameron checked the corner, then started down the alley. When they reached the ladder leading to the metal platform, she grabbed Tyrell by the shoulder and shoved him to the front. Blood dripped onto her as he climbed.

Sierra went next. She couldn't climb for shit because of her hand. "Hook your elbow around the rungs," Cameron barked.

Sierra tried it and got moving a little faster.

Reggie followed and Cameron started up after him.

Hoots came from the end of the alley. Two men ran toward the ladder, both naked from the waist up, just like all the rest. A gorger emerged from the crawlspace beneath the building, right in front of them. The man in front charged into it, pounding with his fists. The creature's mouth clamped onto his chest and shook him like a dog with a rabbit. He produced a wet, low-pitched wail. The other man squeezed past, which put him only a few steps from the ladder.

Halfway up, Cameron stopped and drew her Beretta. The man started to climb, sneering at her from below. She took aim.

Another gorger crawled out from under the building and sprayed the man's naked back with vomit. His sneer turned to a look of shock, then anguish. The smell of bile and scorched flesh wafted up as he fell back to the ground, gurgling.

Cameron put the gun away and climbed to the platform.

Sierra held her good hand on the door leading to the surface. "Are you sure we can't get out this way?" Her hair clumped at the sides of her face and dark hollows surrounded her eyes.

Something slammed into the door from the other side with a thud.

Sierra shrieked. She normally had her shit together no matter what happened, but this whole experience appeared to be testing her limits.

"If the gorgers came in that way, it must be dark out," Tyrell said. "I thought David was going to close the hatch?"

No one said anything. David and the others were probably dead. Cameron swallowed, trying not to think about it. The way things were going, she'd probably be dead soon too.

The crunch of gorger claws on gravel echoed throughout the cavern, not quite drowning out the slurping sounds directly below.

"Come on," she said, swinging one leg over the metal railing. She jumped to the roof, just like before. Tyrell helped Sierra make the drop, then followed, landing beside her. For a moment, it looked like Reggie might not come with them, but then finally he jumped too.

"What now?" Tyrell asked.

"We cross to the far side and try to find the blast door," Cameron said. "We should be safe up here, at least for a while." She started across the roof in the direction she hoped was correct.

"They can climb, you know," Tyrell said.

"There's plenty to eat below," Cameron said. "They have no reason to come up here."

"And when we reach the blast door?"

"We wait for them to thin out, then we climb down and make a run for it."

Lights blazed up from below along the edges of the compound, but out in the center, the roof was dark. A growing number of screams filled the cavern.

"You shouldn't have let them in," Tyrell said, breathing hard.

Cameron's blood rose. "If I hadn't let them in, the rest of those freaks would be coming after us right now. The ones who were trying to chop off your head, remember? I had no choice."

Tyrell didn't press the issue.

Sierra slowed down, gasping for air. "We can't go through the blast door if it's dark outside."

Cameron didn't offer a response. She didn't have one.

"We're never getting out of here," Sierra said, her chest heaving. "It's over."

Cameron expected Tyrell to correct her, to offer some sort of encouragement, but it seemed his optimism had finally run out. She felt the firestarter round in her shirt pocket. If they were truly out of options, she would lead them back to the generator tunnel and find the fuel stores. She'd rather be vaporized in a fireball than get eaten alive. She glanced in that direction.

Movement caught the corner of her eye. "What was that?" Something had just dropped down out of sight, below the edge of the roof, maybe two hundred feet away.

"What?" Sierra asked. "What did you see?"

Cameron froze, watching. Listening. She pointed. "I saw something over there, just past the end of the building." It didn't make sense. They were three stories up.

Her heart skipped. *David.*

David had flown in through the blast door to look for them. It was the only possible explanation.

Cameron spun on Tyrell, patting him down, slapping at his pockets, searching for the whistle.

"Hey."

She slapped the sides of his thighs. If the whistle was gone, they were truly fucked. She kept patting him down until finally she found it. She jerked open his pocket and her fingers closed on the small plastic object.

Cameron brought the whistle to her mouth and blew. The sound trilled through the cavern, echoing even more loudly than she'd hoped.

The distant crunch of claws on gravel stopped.

"What are you doing?" Tyrell asked.

She sucked in a deep breath and blew again, even longer.

The sound of crawling gorgers resumed, much louder than before.

He snatched the whistle from her hand. "Are you insane? You'll draw them up here."

She ignored him, staring at the far end of the building, hoping. Waiting. Praying.

Movement appeared, right where she'd spotted it before.

A gorger pulled itself onto the roof.

"Goddamn it, Cameron," Tyrell spat. He drew his gun.

"I saw them," Cameron said. "It was David. It had to be."

Another gorger appeared beside the first, then a third. A moment later, the edge of the building was lined with gorgers climbing onto the roof.

"Back to the ladder," Tyrell said. "We can hold them off from that little platform."

They spun around. Gorgers were climbing up behind them as well, even closer than the others. Cameron kept turning. Gorgers crawled up onto the building from every direction.

"What do we do?" Sierra cried.

"Nothing," Tyrell spat. "We're done for."

Reggie snorted.

"It was David," Cameron said. She trusted her eyes. She started forward at a slow march.

The gorgers at the far end of the roof picked up their pace, scrambling toward her.

Maybe David hadn't heard the whistling. Maybe he'd flown out of the cavern by the time she'd found the whistle. Maybe—

A carriage rose at the far edge of the rooftop, right behind the gorgers. It raced forward, flying over the advancing creatures.

"Yes," Cameron shouted, holding up both arms.

The carriage reached her and the others just ahead of the first wave. David and Kim sat at the controls, with Barry between them.

"Get on, hurry," David shouted.

They climbed aboard and lifted from the rooftop as the gorgers converged below them, clacking, hissing, and spewing vomit.

"Let's get the hell out of here," David said.

"No," Sierra growled. "We can't leave yet."

Chapter Fifty-Two

Tyrell hunched down as the flying car floated up to the rocky ceiling and came to a stop. The click-clacking of a hundred gorgers echoed around them, punctuated by muffled screams from inside the building.

David spun around. "What the hell is going on here? That sounds like people."

"They can't be helped," Cameron said. She crawled forward and nudged Kim out of her way.

Tyrell fought the sickening feeling in his gut. She was right. The people here hadn't survived. Not really.

Cameron slid into the co-pilot spot. "Let's go."

"No," Sierra said. "Not till we get what we came for. We can't leave."

"I found the armory," Cameron said. "It was full of mold. No weapons."

The screams below grew louder.

"I still don't understand what's happening here," David said. "Are there people down there? We have to help them."

"Cameron already took care of them," Reggie said. He sounded cold and distant.

"They're monsters," Tyrell said. "They were about to kill us. They cut off Sierra's fingers.

Sierra held up her mangled hand.

David's eyes widened. "Jesus, we need to sterilize that, immediately." He reached into the front corner of the carriage and produced the first aid kit.

"Cameron, how did you turn up the lights?" Sierra asked. "How did you open the blast door?"

"Generator room."

"I want whatever powers that generator," Sierra said. "I want the fuel."

Tyrell squinted, trying to understand. "I thought the alien tech doesn't need fuel."

"If it's fuel, it will burn," Sierra said. "I want to firebomb Fraser."

The image clicked into place. They could dump fuel on the ruins from the air, just like they'd dropped the concrete block on the gorgers at the gas station. If they did it during the day, when the hordes were sheltering from the sun, they could burn them all. Maybe not every single one, but enough. Tyrell nodded. Sierra never gave up. After everything she'd been through, she never stopped.

David dabbed ointment onto the raw, open ends of her fingers. She hissed.

Barry's eyes grew wide. Kim looked green, even in the dim light of the cavern.

Tyrell scooted up close behind Sierra and placed his arms around her, holding her tight. She trembled and shook as David wrapped gauze around her fingers.

"That's the best I can do," he said. "I'm sorry."

Tyrell wasn't sure what that meant, exactly, but it sounded shitty.

David pulled out a morphine syrette. Sierra pulled her arm away and shook free from Tyrell's embrace. "Not until you promise me you'll get the fuel."

"We don't have time," David said. "The harvesters will be back soon."

"Harvesters?" Reggie asked.

Tyrell looked to David. "How long do we have?"

He shrugged. "Less than an hour."

"How do we transport it?" Cameron asked. "Hell, we don't even know if it'll burn."

"I lost fingers for this," Sierra growled. "I'm not leaving without something to show for it."

"A sample," Tyrell said. "Let's get a sample we can test."

David glanced at Cameron. She nodded. "Yeah. Okay."

Tyrell squeezed Sierra's shoulder. "We'll get you a sample. I promise. Let him give you the morphine."

She extended her arm and David slipped the needle into it.

Tyrell helped Sierra lie back. He stroked her hair away from her face as they floated through the cavern, high above the massive complex. "You get some rest, okay?"

"Don't let them leave without the fuel," she said.

"I won't." He flashed her a smile and she closed her eyes. Tears moistened the corners.

The carriage flew past the end of the building, over a two-lane road that ran from left to right, where it disappeared into a small opening in the cavern wall. Below, a cluster of gorgers gnawed on the tires of a golf cart. One crawled up on the seat, chewing on the leather. A stream of gorgers swarmed the front of the complex, up the stairs, and into the entrance, marching like a line of ants.

On the far side of the road, a much smaller building was embedded in its own little alcove, marked with the word "ARMORY."

"Tyrell, get ready," Cameron ordered. "You're getting two things out of that armory. A ladle and a plastic MRE bag. Got it?"

"Roger that." He scooted to the edge of the flying car and jumped down before they came to a stop.

"Hurry," she shouted.

Tyrell leaped up the short flight of stairs and shouldered through the door. A mawkish odor washed over him, like a pile of wet towels left in the hamper for a week.

Tables filled the room, covered with plastic tubs full of stringy moss. He snatched a ladle from one of the tubs, then turned to a stack of storage bins. The MRE bags were all over the place. He grabbed two, just in case, and started to leave.

A crate full of camouflage netting caught his attention on the way out. He dropped the ladle and the bags on top, then picked up the crate, his back twitching from the weight.

Outside, a dozen gorgers had broken off from the line entering the complex. They scampered straight toward the armory.

Tyrell waited at the top of the stairs as David and Cameron slid the flying car closer. Cameron glared. "A ladle and a bag. That's all you were supposed to get."

He hefted the crate onto the back and jumped aboard. The gorgers were still six or eight yards away.

"Camouflage netting," Tyrell said.

"What are we supposed to hide from?" David asked as they floated back up to a safe height.

"We can use it for rope," he said. "We can use it to climb up and down inside the shuttle, and if there's enough, we can use it to climb in and out of the tail."

David glanced back. "Yeah, we could have used that earlier."

Tyrell lifted Sierra's neck and placed a wad of netting under her head, like a pillow. She was out cold.

They flew down the road into the tunnel opening. An emaciated body lay sprawled on the asphalt. Further in, they passed a door on the right with "GENERATOR ROOM" stenciled above it. The sharp tang of oil filled Tyrell's nostrils.

"Get ready," Cameron called out from the front.

Ahead, a metal railing bordered the road. Beyond the railing, a side chamber extended into the dark. A sign overhead read "DIESEL RESERVOIR #1."

Tyrell pulled a light stick from his pocket and snapped it as they flew over the railing. He gave Reggie the light, grabbed the ladle and a plastic bag, then stretched himself prone so that his arms hung over the back. "Lower," he called out.

The carriage descended over the pool, which was eight feet below full capacity. Reggie held the light out, but it barely illuminated anything. The rocky walls of the reservoir muffled all sound. Tyrell could hardly see or hear, though the smell was so strong it felt like his sinuses had been stuffed with axle grease.

He shoved the ladle into the pond's surface, which held firm, like the film on dried-out pudding. Finally, it broke through, and he scooped a portion into the empty MRE bag. "It isn't really liquid any more. Feels like cranberry sauce."

"If it's turned to gel, how is the power still on?" David asked.

"They had barrels of additives in the generator room," Cameron said. "They must have found a solution that worked."

"Can we go now?" Kim asked.

"Yes," Tyrell said. "We got what we came for." It was only a sample, but it would do for now. He folded the mouth of the bag as they began to move again. "If it's flammable, we can come back for more."

"How are we going to carry it up to Canada?" Kim asked.

"Empty pods?" Tyrell suggested.

"Yeah, well, I got some bad news," David said. "Our control device was destroyed. We can't bring down any pods."

Cameron snickered. "It's long past time we paid a visit to the mothership. We've got unfinished business up there."

Tyrell sat next to Sierra and closed his eyes. He tried not to listen to the screams coming from inside the complex. He tried not to remember hacking those people with the machete. He tried to tell himself it had been self-defense.

At least they'd gotten out alive. Cameron had come back for them. David had found them. Tyrell told himself that everything was going to be okay. Hell, Reggie had even stopped talking about how awful people were. He'd barely said a word.

Chapter Fifty-Three

The shuttle rocketed skyward, leaving Colorado Springs behind, hopefully forever. Reggie's face felt stiff, like it had hardened into a mask. He stood on the spare carriage, which they'd retrieved from the mountaintop after flying out the front entrance of the bunker. If he sat down, he'd be tempted to close his eyes, and he didn't dare do that. So he stood and looked out the front of the shuttle as they climbed into a bank of empty gray clouds.

Except for Sierra, the others were all on the carriage that was docked in the center. Most of them were using little clumps of camouflage netting as cushions.

"I don't understand," Tyrell said. "How did they get that way?" His voice trembled, as if he'd only just discovered what people were capable of. "I was trying to get a spot in that bunker back before the pods showed up." He'd wiped off as much blood as possible, but he was still a mess. "Christ, I killed my own people."

Cameron looked over her shoulder at him. "Those weren't your people. Those were monsters."

No difference, Reggie thought. *No god damn difference.*

Sierra lay in a morphine haze next to him, with Kona curled up against her. She still intended to bring everyone out of storage. Reggie wanted to grab her and shake her and hold her mangled hand in front of her face. How could she not understand?

"It doesn't make any sense," Tyrell said. "They were military, for Christ's sake."

"The military lost control in the first three years," Priya said, holding up a journal. "The commanding officer died of an aneurysm while his second was out exploring the surface."

"You mean, getting eaten by gorgers," Kim said.

"Undoubtedly," Priya said. "Anyway, the politicians convinced the third in command that his mission was over, that the military had completed its objective. It was time to cede control back to the people."

"And he just went along with it?" Tyrell asked.

"He wasn't all there," Priya said. "He'd been slowly losing his marbles. He kept it hidden so he could stay in his fancy quarters."

Reggie grimaced. He was keeping his own shit hidden, but he didn't get any fancy quarters.

The shuttle broke through the clouds, revealing the deep black of the night sky, dotted with a billion stars.

"Wait, did you say that place was filled with politicians?" Felicia asked. "That explains everything, doesn't it?"

"Which side was in there?" Kim asked.

Cameron snorted. "The ones who told everyone the comet wasn't real. And then, when everyone could see it in the sky, they claimed it would miss us, that it would just go away, remember?"

"That isn't fair," Kim said. "They shouldn't have been allowed inside that place."

Reggie let out a snort of his own. *They got in because they had all the power.*

Felicia glanced at him, but he avoided her eyes, staring straight ahead.

"I think we've reached the thermosphere," Priya said. "Turn and fly back over the equator."

The view shifted to show the planet's horizon, stretching out in front of the shuttle. No one said anything. They all just stared at Earth.

The thought of bringing people back to something so beautiful made Reggie sick. They should let nature reclaim the planet.

"What if we can't find the mothership?" Barry asked.

Reggie held his breath. Without another control device, they would have no way to bring anyone out of storage. He knew this, but he'd forgotten it. Keeping everything straight in his head was increasingly difficult.

"We'll find it," Priya said. She scooted up between Cameron and David and gave them instructions. "A little higher. More to the right."

Sierra stirred next to Reggie.

He had pinned all his hopes on her. He'd thought things would be different with a woman in charge. His lips pulled away from his teeth and a laugh tried to escape. That monstrous bitch inside the mountain had shown him what a fool he was.

He closed his eyes, but regretted it immediately. He saw Sheriff Dart pointing his pistol at Chase. He flinched, popping his eyes open, but not fast enough. Dart's gun flashed.

"Bingo," Priya said, startling him.

"Where?" David asked.

"Five degrees right and about ten degrees up," Priya said. "I told you I could find it."

The view shifted and a speck in the center of the projection grew larger than the surrounding stars. They were headed straight for the mothership and there wasn't anything Reggie could do.

"I see it," Barry said. "Do you think they'll let us in?" He looked back at the others, his mouth twisted sideways. Chase used to do the same thing when he was concentrating.

Reggie's throat closed up. He couldn't remember what Chase looked like. He could only picture Barry.

"If everything is still automated, we should be fine," Priya said.

As the mothership grew larger, its shape became apparent against the backdrop of space. An enormous dome covered the top and segmented towers hung from the bottom. It looked like a giant metal jellyfish.

"Where's the entrance?" Tyrell asked.

Tyrell had shot the old guy on the golf course. The old guy had hacked up people with a machete. Now Tyrell had hacked up people with a machete. Reggie pinched his lips together to keep from giggling.

Priya pointed to one of the prong-like towers hanging from the bottom of the mothership. "There's an airlock at the base of the longest column there. It should open when we get close."

Reggie prayed it would remain shut. They would be forced to return to Earth, where they would live out whatever time they had left. Not him, though. He was done. He would end it all, just as soon as he got the chance. No more pain. Maybe after he died he would be able to see Chase again, and remember his face.

"What's the plan when we get inside?" David asked.

"We grab a control device first," Cameron said.

"There were several in the bunker closest to the slope chamber," Priya said. "I've already sent us there."

"Once we get a device, we find Randall," Cameron continued.

As they drew closer, the dome rotated out of view. They flew beneath the mothership and faced the entry column dead on.

Please don't open, Reggie prayed. *Please, God, don't let it open.*

The end of the column spiraled open.

He wasn't surprised. His prayers never got answered.

They passed through the entrance and everything grew dark. "We're in the airlock," Priya said. No one spoke for a full minute. The view out the front was pitch black.

Another hatch spiraled open, revealing hundreds of shiny tear-drop shuttles just like the one they were in, all floating high overhead.

"So far, so good," David said.

"Why isn't Randall sending anything after us?" Kim asked.

"We don't have implants," Priya said. "Even if he has one of those devices, he can't spot us."

"Good," came Sierra's voice, right beside Reggie.

He flinched. He'd forgotten she was there. Had she been watching him? Had she seen what he was really thinking?

She rose up on one arm. "It's time to take him out."

"Hey, look who's awake," Tyrell said. He hopped over from the other carriage and helped her sit up.

"We can't be focused on revenge," David said. "That can't be who we are."

Sierra looked at him with steel in her eyes. "This isn't about revenge," she said. "It's about justice. And eliminating a threat that keeps trying to kill us."

David responded with a small nod.

"Revenge is just a bonus," Sierra said.

Cameron chuckled.

Reggie bowed his head. Once, Sierra had reminded him of Chase. Brash, hopeful, full of life, and ready to take on the world.

Now she was filled with hate and anger, just like everyone else. Just like him.

They flew through the dim hangar, beneath all those other shuttles, and passed a wide, dark pit in the floor, nearly as big as the one they'd entered through.

"What's in there?" Barry asked.

"That leads to storage," Priya said.

Barry didn't say anything, but Reggie knew what he was thinking. He was hoping his mom was in there. Reggie knew better. His mom had died of cancer.

He sucked in a breath and held it. *Chase's* mom had died of cancer, not Barry's. What the hell was the matter with him? It was so hard to keep everything straight.

"Just a little farther," Priya said.

Cameron turned around and faced the group. "Listen up. When we land, we gotta be quick. David and I will fly. Reggie, you and Tyrell are going with us. When we get in the pit, jump down, grab a device, and jump back on."

"*Devices*," Priya said. "Get as many as you can."

"Roger that," Tyrell said.

Reggie nodded. He had to play along. He stepped across the gap to the other carriage. Tyrell followed him.

"We'll fly back here and dock immediately," Cameron said. "Once Priya gets a device up and running, we'll track down Randall."

"What do I do?" Barry asked.

"I need you to stay here and hold onto Kona," Cameron said. "Can you do that?"

"Roger that," Barry said.

Reggie's heart shriveled. It should be Chase sitting there, not Barry.

"There's the observation bunker," David said.

The shuttle approached a pit about the size of a backyard swimming pool. A row of orange spheres lined the wall on one side, directly across from an empty carriage.

"There's another sled," Sierra said. "We should grab it."

David looked back, frowning. "We already have two."

"Felicia and I can do it," Kim said. "Please. It's why you trained us."

"She's got a point," Cameron said.

Outside, the hangar was dead. Nothing moved.

"Okay," David said finally.

"I want to go, too," Barry said.

David shook his head. "I need you to stay here, where it's safe."

Reggie pressed his lips together, tight as he could. Nowhere was safe.

Cameron twirled her finger. "Let's spin the shuttle around so the tail is right over the pit."

The view turned away, showing endless empty gloom. When the shuttle settled and the carriage detached, the projectors shut off, leaving only the curved front wall covered with little nubs. A million eyes, all looking right at Reggie.

Barry moved onto the spare carriage and wrapped his arms around Kona's neck. Priya scooted after him, carefully maneuvering her broken leg.

"Let's go," Cameron said.

Reggie squeezed his hands into tight fists and sat down as they pulled away from the docking arm.

At the last second, Sierra jumped across, joining them. She held her injured hand against her chest.

"What are you doing?" Tyrell asked.

"Just riding to the back of the shuttle," she said. "I want to watch."

They floated into the curved tube that ran the length of the tail. At the far end, the door spiraled open. Sierra hopped down, landing next to the crate of camouflage nets.

"You got this," she said as the carriage floated out into the hangar. "Piece of cake."

The pit was a hundred feet below them, vacant, just as they'd expected.

"Everyone keep your eyes peeled," David said. "Call out if you spot anything."

Reggie looked off into the gloom as they descended, praying that something would change their minds or stop them somehow.

For once, his prayer was answered.

A harvester shot toward them, racing silently along the hangar floor.

No one else saw it. They were all facing the other direction.

He took a deep breath and looked away. It would all be over soon. No more pain. No more awful thoughts snaking around in his head.

The harvester hit them from below with a crunch, flipping the carriage into the air. Everyone went flying. Several people shouted. Kim screamed.

Reggie fell with his eyes closed, waiting for the end, waiting to see Chase again.

Chapter Fifty-Four

Tyrell tumbled through the air, five stories above the hangar floor. He fell slowly because of the low gravity, but that didn't stop the awful feeling that the ground was rushing up to smash him.

Stars exploded in his vision as a foot caught him in the temple. Felicia screamed.

"No, no, no," David shouted.

"Help!" Kim yelled.

Tyrell twisted and swung his arms in circles, trying to get his feet under him. The floor kept getting closer.

A series of grinding crunches came from below as the flying car slammed down.

"Oof!" Someone hit the ground.

Tyrell managed to get one leg beneath him just before impact. His foot hit, jarring him up through his hip. He let his knee bend and pushed himself forward, tumbling across the floor. He came to a stop, shuddering and bruised, but he didn't seem seriously hurt.

Smoke billowed from the wreck of the flying car, which lay twenty yards away, in a debris field of metal shards.

He staggered to his feet. Near the observation bunker, Cameron, David, and Felicia were slowly picking themselves up.

"Kim," David shouted. "Where are you? Kim!"

Tyrell spun in a circle. He didn't see Kim, but he did spot Reggie, lying in the opposite direction, motionless. The poor bastard must have landed wrong.

The harvester flew erratically toward Reggie's body, jerking and course-correcting. One of the yellow panels near the front was crumpled inward and sparks fell from its cluster of arms. Two of the arms hung limp, apparently damaged from t-boning them.

"Dad?" Kim's voice came from somewhere beyond the flying car wreck.

Tyrell's heart soared. If she was shouting, she was alive.

David ran in her direction. "Get the other carriage," he yelled over his shoulder. "We need it to get back into the shuttle."

Cameron and Felicia dropped into the alien command pit.

Tyrell spun around. Four arms unfolded from the front of the harvester, telescoping toward Reggie's body.

The drone moved without making a sound. Even its arms were silent. He ran toward it.

A sheet of camouflage netting dropped onto the harvester, snagging on its arms.

"Nice," Tyrell shouted. Sierra had tangled it from above.

The harvester swirled, searching for the source of this new attack. Its arms wriggled through the netting. It banked sideways, back toward Reggie.

Tyrell reached it first. He grabbed a wad of the netting, still caught on the drone's arms and pulled. The harvester swung wide. Its arms scraped along the floor like claws on a chalkboard, just missing Reggie.

Chunks of netting ripped loose in Tyrell's hands as the drone's momentum carried it away.

The harvester rose and turned back toward him. He was its target now. It accelerated straight for him. He slid beneath it as it flew over and grabbed another handful of netting hanging from its arms.

The moment the harvester passed overhead, Tyrell stood and braced his boots. The knobby rubber soles caught on the smooth metal floor. He jerked back on the tangled strands with a grunt.

The drone flipped forward, slamming face-first against the hangar floor in a bone-crunching crash. More sparks fountained from the front, where the arms were attached, and a plume of caustic smoke billowed out of the back. It lay on the hangar floor, jittering.

Tyrell let out a sound that was part cheer, part gasp. He'd just taken out a harvester.

He searched for the others. Kim and David were running toward the pit. *Yes.* They both looked unhurt.

Two new harvesters flew toward them from the opposite side. *Shit.*

Another section of camouflage netting floated down from the shuttle, just missing them. "Nice try," he muttered, not sure Sierra could hear him. He sprinted for the heap of netting. He could still make use of it.

The two harvesters were joined by a third, all converging on the pit.

Tyrell grabbed the netting by one edge and spun in a circle, holding it out at arm's length. The sheet unfolded, expanding twenty feet in front of him. He completed a revolution and let go, sending it sailing.

The net landed on the closest drone where it slid across the shiny top and down the front, tangling immediately in the clump of robotic limbs. One section caught the arms of the drone next to it and they began pulling each other, crashing into the third.

Tyrell grinned. He'd taken the nets from Cheyenne Mountain to use as rope ladders, but this was even better.

A flying car rose from inside the bunker, with Cameron and Felicia at the controls. David and Kim jumped on from the edge of the pit.

"Over here!" Tyrell waved, then ran back to Reggie, praying the man was still alive.

The two drones that were snared to each other pistoned back and forth. The third retreated behind them, out of the way.

He felt Reggie's breath as he hefted him from the floor. "Hang in there. I got you." The grumpy old dude didn't seem to like Tyrell much. Maybe saving his life would help.

The flying car floated close, with the other four on board and several of the orange spheres wedged in between them.

Tyrell plopped Reggie onto the back, marveling at how easy it was to pick up a grown man in low gravity.

"Up," David shouted. "Into the shuttle."

Tyrell jumped aboard and they rose straight toward the shuttle's tail.

The harvester that wasn't tangled swung wide around the two that were.

"More harvesters," Cameron yelled.

Eight or nine drones emerged from the darkness on the right. Another group twice as big dropped down toward them on the left.

"Full stop," David said as they came even with the shuttle's tail.

The flying car stopped ascending abruptly, making Tyrell's ass rise from the surface. Reggie, lying prone, lifted a few inches in the air as well, but they both settled a second later. Kona barked at them from the tube, then pranced out of the way as they shot inside. Sierra was nowhere to be seen.

"Barry?" David shouted as they raced forward. "Barry, where are you?"

The shuttle's tail was empty.

"Are they hiding?" Felicia asked.

They raced down the tube-like tail into the large round chamber and slammed into the docking arm. Behind them, the airlock spiraled shut. They'd made it. All around them, pastel lights powered on.

The other flying car wasn't there. Sierra, Barry, and Priya were gone.

Chapter Fifty-Five

Priya felt completely helpless. The carriage floated upward between rows and rows of shuttles, moving under someone else's control. She couldn't do anything to stop it.

At least Sierra was with her. She would figure out what to do. She always did.

"Where are we going?" Barry asked.

"No idea," Priya said. She lay with her leg stretched out beside her, encased in its wooden brace.

"Who's doing this?" Barry asked.

"It has to be Randall," Sierra said.

The carriage had started moving on its own. Kona jumped off inside the shuttle and Barry might have been able to jump down too, but not Priya. The irony stung. Jumping off a remotely-commandeered carriage was exactly how Priya broke her leg in the first place.

"I'll take care of Randall," Sierra said, squeezing the grip of her big silver revolver. She had jumped aboard right as the carriage floated out the shuttle's tail.

"How many rounds do you have?" Priya asked.

"Two," Sierra said. She held the gun in her left hand because of the missing fingers on her right.

"Make them both count," Priya said, desperately hoping that Sierra was ambidextrous.

"I'm scared," Barry said. He looked like he was about to cry.

"Me too," Priya said. She was terrified. The fact that she felt out of control made it worse.

"David will come," Sierra said. "Kim will use the device to find us."

"How?" Barry asked. "She can't see us without our neck things." He touched the back of his head.

Priya swallowed, her throat dry. He was right.

"What's up here?" Sierra asked.

Priya groaned. "All I ever saw was shuttles and harvesters. I thought that was it. I should have looked more."

She'd intended to study the mothership's schematics from top to bottom once she got another control device. Now, she might never get the chance.

"And carriages." Barry pointed. They rose above the last layer of shuttles and began moving horizontally alongside a layer of carriages. The ceiling, another ten meters up, was gray and nondescript, just like the floor, a kilometer below.

"What are those?" Barry asked. He crawled to the front of the sled and rose up on his knees, holding on to the dashboard.

Clusters of spheres emerged from the gloom, each one three meters in diameter. Metal frames connected them in groups of eight, which made them look like giant grapes.

"I've seen those before," Sierra said.

"When?" Priya asked. "What are they?"

"They were on the recording the caretakers showed me. Harvesters collected pregnant gorgers and put them in those big globe things."

"Do they have gorgers in them now?" Barry asked.

"I don't think so," Sierra said. "The caretaker said the gorgers wouldn't be pregnant for a hundred years."

"Can we use one and fly back to Daddy?"

"We don't know how to fly them," Sierra said.

"Look above them," Priya said. "There's a hole up there." A round maw opened on the ceiling near the spheres, at least two meters across, with curved, irregular sides.

"What's in there?" Barry asked. "I don't want to go in there."

"I don't think the sled will fit," Sierra said.

She was right, it was too big, but uncertainty tugged at Priya's stomach. The carriage floated straight toward the opening. She leaned forward, peering up. The edges of the orifice were smooth, almost organic looking. Shadows hid whatever was inside.

"I feel sick," Barry said, holding his stomach. "Something's wrong."

Priya felt it, too. It was an upward pull, like passing the apogee of a hill on a roller coaster, even though the carriage was slowing to a stop.

"Help," Barry shouted. He floated upward, arms spinning at his sides.

Sierra fumbled the revolver back into her holster and reached for him, pinching the carriage's dashboard with the thumb and forefinger of her bad hand. It was too late. Barry was already out of reach.

Priya's stomach crawled up her throat and she lifted from the surface of the carriage, still prone. She cried out. She thought she'd been helpless and out of control before, but that was nothing. Blood rushed into her head with the sensation of falling upward. This wasn't low gravity, this was reverse gravity.

Above her, Barry's screams were cut off as he disappeared in the shadows of the orifice.

Sierra shouted, "Hold on. I'm coming."

Priya squirmed in the air and managed to roll over.

Below her, Sierra squatted on the carriage, still gripping the front console.

Priya's back hit something soft and squishy. She tensed, waiting for the pain as her broken leg hit.

Instead, she sank into the surface.

A portal. She'd been through this routine before, when she followed Sierra beneath the sea. They'd passed through a similar portal when they exited the islands.

Panic gripped her. If this portal sent her to the bottom of the sea, could she make it to the surface? Could she tread water? She didn't know if the wooden brace around her leg would float or weigh her down.

She took a deep breath as her body was sucked through a gelatinous membrane. Like before, she felt a small electric charge. Pressure squeezed her broken leg, compressing it painfully.

Just a few more seconds.

The pressure around her body lessened and she floated into something warm and wet. She kicked with her good leg and pulled with her arms in a clumsy breast-stroke, squeezing her eyes shut.

This wasn't water.

This hurt. Everywhere.

Pain pricked every inch of her skin, like a first degree burn. She released her breath slowly, desperate to get to the surface before she ran out of oxygen. It felt like swimming in molasses.

Something struck her forehead. She reached up and felt a small shoe.

Barry.

She groped for the boy. He was curled in a ball, shaking. No, he was screaming. She heard the distant roar of his shouting.

Hold your breath. Don't scream. She had no way to tell him that. She did the only thing she could. She grabbed Barry with one arm and kept clawing her way through the muck with the other.

Where was the surface? She was out of air. She let the last bit spill from her lungs and kept pulling and kicking. The stinging crap went on forever. She grimaced. Her chest tightened. She needed air.

Something wrapped around the ankle on her bad leg and pulled. She opened her mouth to scream, releasing Barry. Shards of pain jabbed deep in her calf, and worse, something had hold of her.

Unable to stop herself, she inhaled the viscous goop. It filled her chest, heavy and burning. Panicking, she coughed it out, but then she just sucked in another lungful automatically.

No, no, no.

The thing holding her ankle tightened its grip. She thrashed and kicked, which sent jagged pain through her leg, far worse than the stinging.

Involuntarily, she retched, expelling another gulp of goo. Once again, she sucked more back in.

She froze. She was freaking out and everything hurt, but she was no longer starved for oxygen. The fluid was sustaining her somehow. The stinging had even subsided slightly, down to a steady burn.

The grip on her ankle pulled and she floated downward. Something grasped her brace. Then her hip. It was crawling up her body.

Grimacing, she forced her eyes open. They burned, as if she'd gotten a face full of shampoo in the shower, only here there was no way to rinse them. The pain just went on and on. She looked around, squinting.

Sierra, blurry in the pink light, pulled up beside her.

Barry floated close by, still curled tight in a ball, still shaking.

Sierra's eyes were open and her lips were pulled back from her teeth. She swam to Barry and grabbed his hand.

Priya shook her head. She didn't know what they should do. She didn't even know where they were.

Sierra pointed to a tiny dot glowing overhead, then started kicking toward it, pulling Barry along with her.

Priya swam after them, pulling herself slowly through the sludge. Her heartbeat thumped furiously.

The caretakers had told Sierra about a brood chamber where pregnant gorgers were placed after they were harvested. This had to be it. If the goo somehow nourished the eggs while they gestated, it must also be able to oxygenate her lungs. She wondered what else it was doing to her.

She swam toward the light, following Sierra and Barry. She even managed to kick a little with her bad leg.

She couldn't believe they were breathing this stuff. Her heart ached for Barry. The crap stung like hell.

The glowing dot slowly became a glowing circle. Swimming through molasses should have been exhausting, but she wasn't tired. It must *really* be oxygenating her blood.

Sierra and Barry reached the circle first. Barry still had his eyes closed.

The glowing panel was less than a meter across and embedded in the ceiling. Priya touched it and felt a tiny spark of electricity. Another portal.

She didn't know what was up there, but they had to get out of the stinging goop.

She pointed at herself and raised her eyebrows, hoping Sierra understood. *I'll go first.*

Sierra nodded.

She stuck her hands into the opening and kicked with both legs, pushing herself farther in. The electric spark tingled her wrists, but it was barely noticeable after the constant burn of the goop.

Her fingers touched dry air and she grasped a curved edge. She pulled, rising up through the portal, then fell sideways. Her mind struggled to make sense of the motion as she crashed into the wall. No, it was the floor. The portal had felt like a ceiling from below, but here, it opened sideways through a wall.

Coughing, she spewed goo from her lungs and sucked in air. She'd made it. She cleared her burning eyes with the palms of her hands and blinked, her vision cloudy.

She was in a dome-shaped room, like a planetarium, but much bigger. The floor sloped up to a platform in the center, where two enormous caretakers sat behind a ring of consoles.

"I, I thought there weren't any more aliens," she whispered.

"You thought wrong."

She turned. Randall stood flat against the wall, right next to the portal.

She staggered to her feet, hoping to flee, but she was too slow.

His fist flew straight at her, right between the eyes. For the briefest instant, the room was filled with stars, then everything went black.

Chapter Fifty-Six

Sierra gave Priya twenty seconds, then pushed Barry into the portal. She couldn't keep the kid in this horrible vat of pain slime any longer. The stinging was constant and all-encompassing. It was like floating in a pool of sea jellies. Her missing fingers burned even more than the rest of her, and they'd begun to itch, which was almost worse.

With one last shove, Barry's feet disappeared. At the same time, Sierra drifted backwards, thanks to Mr. Newton.

She swam forward, kicking and pulling awkwardly like a frog. When she got to the portal, she pulled herself in, feeling a spark of electricity as she passed through a thick membrane.

On the other side, she fell sideways, coughing. The slime stung even worse as it drained from her lungs. Her chest convulsed as she spewed it out.

Priya lay sprawled on the floor, motionless. Barry kneeled beside her, tugging on her arms.

Sierra could barely see. The goop clogging her ears made everything sound like she was still submerged and she was wheezing like mad, but she didn't have time to get her shit together. She rose to her feet, careful not to slip in the slime. Her leather pants and jacket felt heavy, soaked through. She reached across her stomach to draw the revolver.

It was gone.

An arm snaked around her neck, pulling tight.

Hot breath hissed against her ear. "Gotcha," Randall said.

The barrel of the gun pressed into her back.

Twenty feet ahead of her, two huge aliens sat atop a conical slope in the center of the room, twice as big as the others.

One of the aliens rumbled and a translation came from the console next to it. *"Human specimens must be eliminated."*

"Don't you worry," Randall said. "I'm going to eliminate the shit out of them, just as soon as you get me a fucking control device."

Sierra tugged at his arm. The fingers on her good hand, still slimy with goo, slid under her chin, wedging just enough space for a whisper of air to make it down her throat. "We have all the devices," she wheezed. She wasn't sure David and Cameron had gotten any devices, much less all of them, but it was the only thing she could think of to stop him from killing her.

Randall swung the pistol out to her right, popping the cylinder open. "Fuck," he shouted, right in her ear. "Only two rounds." His breath smelled like dog shit.

She wedged her fingers deeper, trying to get enough air to keep from passing out. Somewhere behind them, Barry begged Priya to wake up.

A giant dome covered the room, dotted with the same creepy little holes that projected images from the front of the shuttle.

She clawed at Randall's forearm, desperate for air as he marched her away from the portal, keeping to the bottom of the slope. The goop still hurt her skin, though the open air had changed the sensation from a hot sting to a cold burn.

One of the aliens up on the console rumbled again. *"A carriage is approaching with three control devices."*

"Thank you," Randall shouted. "About goddamn time." He leaned close and whispered in Sierra's ear. "This is for lying to me."

Pain exploded in her side as he pounded her ribs with the grip of the gun. Before she could get her arm down, he smashed into her side again. Something snapped. *Oh, fuck, fuck, fuck.* He'd cracked her rib. A wave of dizziness washed over her. Something felt terribly wrong. Had he wrecked her kidney? Her liver? One of those was fatal. Maybe both.

BOOM

A gunshot blast came from the revolver. The sound sent a shockwave of fear through her.

BOOM

Randall had just shot both of the aliens. One of them slithered down the far side of the platform, out of sight. The other one slumped in place, quivering.

"That won't kill them," she said, her words tiny and pathetic.

"You think I don't know that?" Randall snapped. "They're gonna take care of the Hindu and the brat."

A rectangular wall panel slid open on the far side of the room.

"Here's my ride," Randall said.

A sled floated on the other side, but it wasn't empty. David and the others stood on it. Cameron had her gun up, aimed at them.

Randall twisted Sierra in front of him and aimed the revolver right back at Cameron. "Perfect. I've been looking for you fuckers."

"Let her go," David shouted.

Gurgles and hisses came from the raised platform in the middle of the room.

Sierra clawed at Randall's forearm, prying it away from her neck until she got enough air to speak. "His gun's empty. Shoot him."

Randall raised the gun to her face. The sharp tang of gun smoke filled Sierra's nostrils. She couldn't figure out what he was doing. The pain in her side was growing worse. She felt so light headed she didn't think she could stand if he wasn't holding her up.

His thumb came away from the gun's grip and pressed into her eye. She opened her mouth to protest, then felt something pop. Intense pain flooded her face. She screamed, but he tightened his wrist at the same time, cutting off her air. The gun came away from her head and *she couldn't see out of her right eye.*

"Fuck," Cameron shouted.

"Drop that gun or I pluck out the other one." Randall's voice sounded distant. Everything had gone horribly wrong. It felt like someone was holding a burning log against her eye, and she *couldn't fucking see.*

Cameron faltered.

Sierra wanted to scream and scream and scream. She wasn't going to survive this. She was dying. If Randall got Cameron's gun, he would kill them all.

She was in the exact same position Waldmire had been in. As long as Randall had control over her, the others wouldn't do anything. She had to take herself out of the equation, just like Waldmire had.

She mustered every bit of strength she had left and pulled at his wrist until she could speak. "Sycophant." It was the word Waldmire used right before Randall shot him.

"Shut up, bitch." The gun's grip slammed into her side again. Pain billowed, red and hot.

She remembered his girlfriend, back in the village. "Crystal was the bitch. Dead bitch now."

"Fuck you," Randall screamed. He sounded crazed. He shook her and brought the gun out to hit her again. She pulled away, falling slightly.

She didn't fall far, but it was enough.

Cameron fired.

She must have hit him, because Randall toppled backwards, pulling her with him.

Chapter Fifty-Seven

Tyrell jumped off the flying car. Randall fell with his arm around Sierra's neck, taking her with him. She flopped like a rag doll. Goddamn, she looked hurt. Tyrell raced toward them.

Randall landed on his back with Sierra right on top of him. They lay on the slope, their heads at the low end, three feet from the outer wall. This big dome chamber didn't have a proper floor, just a cone that rose to a platform in the middle.

On the platform, a monstrous alien blob gurgled and pulsed. The others had described the caretakers, but Tyrell hadn't realized they were so big. A gash ripped open on the creature's back.

David darted past, running awkwardly along the sloped floor to the other side of the room, toward Barry and Priya.

Tyrell kept his focus on Randall, who lay on his back, one arm still around Sierra's neck. His other arm was stretched out on the floor next to him, gripping her gun. Blood pooled beneath his shoulder where Cameron had shot him. The gun trembled as he tried to lift it from the ground. Sierra had said it was empty, but Tyrell's Momma taught him to treat every gun like it was loaded.

He stomped on Randall's hand. Randall shrieked. Tyrell stomped again, mashing his fingers with the heel of his boot like snuffing out a cigarette.

On the center platform, jagged pink claws ripped through the husk of the big blobby alien. A gorger tore its way out.

Tyrell pried the revolver from Randall's destroyed hand.

Sierra jerked her elbow back into Randall's face. He turned his head, groaning, but she kept going, the point of her elbow smashing him again and again. A tooth pattered to the floor.

"Look out," Kim shouted from the doorway. She was still on the flying car with Felicia, who was holding her back, and Reggie, who had just woken up.

The gorger crawled down from the central platform, straight toward Sierra.

Tyrell dragged her out of the way. He pointed the gun at the gorger and pulled the trigger six times. Sierra was right. It was empty.

Randall tried to speak, but produced only a gurgling hiss. His face was a broken mess. The gorger continued toward him.

Cameron appeared on Sierra's other side and helped pull her to her feet. Sierra's mouth hung open in a hideous grimace. Blood pooled in one eye, which bulged from its socket, unfocused.

"It's going to be okay," Tyrell said, though it was a lie. She'd been terribly hurt. Grievously hurt.

Randall pawed the air, his head rolling back and forth. The gorger stopped at his big black boots. Its neck pulsed and it puked on Randall's legs. A thick glob landed on his belly and sank through his shirt.

Randall wailed.

Cameron aimed her gun at the gorger.

"Wait," Sierra grunted, breathing hard. "Let it feed." Her voice was low and mean.

The gorger bent and slurped one of Randall's knees into its maw. Soupy chunks of flesh fell from the bone. Randall shrieked.

"Don't shoot it until he's dead," Sierra whispered, her face pale. The gorger's mouth clamped on Randall's crotch. The pitch of his screams rose higher, then trailed off to nothing.

Sierra pulled up her shirt on one side. A fist-sized swelling bulged under her skin, covered in dark bruises. Something in her abdomen was terribly broken, far beyond David's ability to repair.

Across the room, David crouched by Barry and Priya. "Come on, let's get out of here."

A second gorger emerged from behind the platform, shuffling toward them along the far wall.

"Fuck," Cameron yelled. "There's another one."

A tiny malformed leg protruded from its head, flopping against the side of its body as it lumbered closer.

"David, look out," Tyrell shouted.

Cameron raced across the slope, firing. Several shots hit the side of the gorger. Several others hit the wall. The creature stopped ten feet from David. Its neck swelled. It planted its claws and arched its head.

David shoved Barry behind him, next to Priya.

"No," Sierra cried.

Vomit blasted from the gorger's mouth, hitting David in the chest. He turned his head and spread his arms wide, shielding Barry and Priya from the spray. Smoke rose from his clothes. His shirt dissolved like tissue.

"*Daddy!*" Barry screamed.

Cameron reloaded on the run, stopped beside the gorger, and blasted it five times in the side of the head. It dropped, lifeless.

Back at the carriage, Kim was screaming. Tyrell's heart ached for her. She shouldn't be watching this.

David slumped against the wall. The skin on half his face was gone. "Bare," he blubbered. "Kimb."

Tyrell dragged Sierra over, more or less carrying her on his hip.

Three shots rang out behind him. He glanced back. Felicia stood by the gorger that had been eating Randall. It slumped dead on his corpse. Smoke wafted from her handgun.

Reggie remained on the flying car, just watching. Kim jumped off and ran toward her father. Felicia caught her by the arm and jerked her to a stop.

"Oh my god, oh my god, oh my god," Cameron chanted. She reached for David, then yelped as acid burned her fingers. Tears ran down her face.

Barry clawed at Priya's arms, screaming, trying to get free, to go to his father.

"Get him away from here," Tyrell said. He pointed back toward Kim. "Her, too. They don't need to see this." The terrible truth was that they already had.

"David, David, David," Sierra said.

A thin hiss escaped between David's burned lips and his eyes rolled back. His jaw went slack. Teeth were visible through his cheek.

Tyrell tried to swallow, but his throat wouldn't work. He had just watched the man die.

Cameron kneeled next to David, shaking her head back and forth.

Priya shuffled Barry over to Kim and Felicia. Both kids were sobbing.

Every few steps, Priya stopped and looked down.

"Help him," Kim cried. "You have to do something, you have to help him. *Please.*"

Tyrell looked back, tears running down his cheeks. "It's too late, honey. I'm so, so sorry."

Sierra brought her hands up to cover the bottom half of her face, sobbing.

Tyrell froze, staring at her. "Your fingers." The bandages had fallen off. Little pink nubs had broken through the scabs. "What the hell?"

"My leg," Priya said.

Tyrell gaped at her. It had been badly broken. Now she was standing. Walking.

"We swam through a chamber that did something to us," Priya said. She pointed at a purple oval on the wall near David's body. She lifted her knee, putting all of her weight on the leg in the brace. "I think it healed us."

Sierra shook free from Tyrell and bent beside David.

"What are you doing?" Tyrell asked.

She reached beneath David's armpits and lifted, holding his corpse against the wall. Smoke rose from her, along with the smell of cooking meat. The acid on his body was burning her skin.

"I have to try," she sputtered. Blood poured from her mouth. She was bleeding internally.

She dragged David along the wall toward the panel, struggling to hold him up, even in the low gravity.

Cameron followed, holding her hands out like she wanted to help, but didn't know what she could do. Tyrell knew exactly how she felt.

Sierra pulled David's corpse tight against her chest and dove headfirst into the portal.

Chapter Fifty-Eight

Kim sat in the dome room, waiting.

Hoping.

Praying.

Tyrell and Reggie were with her, but she felt alone. She'd never felt so alone in her life.

Tyrell paced back and forth in front of the portal on the wall. Reggie lay beside her, his head propped on a pile of netting and his hands clasped on his chest. He closed his eyes.

"Wake up," Kim said, annoyed.

Reggie's eyes remained closed.

She made a fist and punched his shoe. "I said, wake up."

"I'm awake," he mumbled.

"Keep your eyes open."

He'd been knocked unconscious when the carriage got flipped in the hangar. Kim's throat tightened. Cameron said that Reggie had a concussion and wasn't allowed to go to sleep, but Dad had told her once that it was actually okay to let someone sleep when they got a concussion, but Dad wasn't here to clear things up and—

Dad was gone.

Kim squeezed her eyes shut and started sobbing again.

The room stank. Tyrell had dragged away the remains of Randall and the gorgers, but their bodies left nasty messes behind. Felicia had covered what was left with camo nets, but that didn't do anything for the smell, which was only getting worse. It had been hours.

Tyrell walked over and placed a hand on her shoulder. He was waiting for Sierra the way she was waiting for Dad. Kim was pretty sure he liked her. Maybe even loved her.

Sierra might make it out. She'd been alive when she went in. It wasn't fair. Kim's throat tightened. That was such a terrible thing to think. She wanted Sierra to make it out. She loved her, too.

"Maybe I should go in there and look for them," Kim said.

"We need to give it more time," Tyrell said. "You heard Priya."

Kim scowled. Priya believed that when Sierra was in the chamber the first time, she hadn't stayed long enough for her fingers to fully regrow. She said they shouldn't interrupt the healing process.

"We don't have to bring them back out," Kim said. "We can just go in and check on them."

Tyrell stroked her back. "We need to wait out here. They said it really hurts."

"I don't care," Kim said, but that was a lie. Barry had told her that it hurt everywhere, all the time. The thought of going in there terrified her.

"Did you find any more aliens?" Tyrell asked.

"Just that one gorger." She tapped the device in front of her, scrolling through the schematics. "I searched the whole ship three times. I even searched the islands to make sure there isn't one floating around out there, watching the animals."

"What's the gorger doing?" he asked.

"It isn't doing anything," Kim said. "It's just walking around."

"Show me."

She rolled her eyes. He was obviously trying to distract her, to give her something else to think about. She brought up the map and found the little dot moving around at the bottom of the hangar.

"And you think that's the one I kicked?"

"It has to be." Right before Sierra got electrocuted, she had shot a caretaker that had molted and become a gorger. Tyrell had kicked it back into the observation bunker when he rescued her.

Experimenting with the device should have been exciting, but she couldn't make herself care. Not after watching Dad die. She shuddered. Barry said he'd seen Dad's teeth through his cheek. She didn't want to believe him, but Cameron and the others didn't deny it.

Reggie got to his feet, holding his ribs with one hand and his head with the other. He let out a groan.

"If you're hurting so much, maybe you should go in the portal yourself," Kim said.

Priya thought the chamber on the other side of the wall was used to incubate gorger eggs, and that the solution they floated in was some sort of medicine. She thought it nourished them and repaired anything that needed it. Kim didn't know what to think, but it had definitely healed Priya's leg. The bones were fused and strong, even if they were at a slightly weird angle now.

"It won't help me," Reggie said.

"You don't know that," Kim said, her words shrill and harsh. She wanted to believe. She had to.

Reggie stared at her but didn't say anything.

The hatch on the opposite side of the room opened. The others were finally back from the food run. Barry jumped off the carriage, ran over, and hugged Kim, his eyes red and his nose snotty. She hugged him back, afraid to let go.

Cameron marched over. "Anything?"

Kim opened her mouth to say, "No," but she thought her voice would crack and she would start crying again, so she just shook her head.

Kona sniffed at the netting that lay where Randall had died. Priya shooed her away.

Felicia walked over and held out a piece of fruit. "Here. Barry says these are called konapples."

Kim didn't want it, but she took it and set it down beside her so she wouldn't have to argue about it.

"We have a whole carriage loaded with fruit," Felicia said. "Enough to last for days on Earth."

"We can't leave," Kim said, clenching her teeth.

Cameron clapped her on the shoulder, like she was her buddy or something. "Don't worry. We aren't leaving without them." She walked over to the portal and stood in front of it with her fists on her hips.

Felicia sat down next to Kim and patted the control device. "Did you find anything?"

She shook her head. "There aren't any more aliens. I'm sure of it. Just the one gorger down in the hangar."

"We'll take care of him soon enough," Cameron said without looking back.

Felicia nodded. "Priya made progress with the superclusters."

"Superclusters?" Tyrell asked.

"That's Barry's name for those big sphere things."

Priya scowled. "A supercluster is already a word. It's a group of galaxies."

"Lots of words mean more than one thing," Barry said.

Kim wrapped her arms around him. Her heart hitched. He was all she had now.

"What kind of progress?" Reggie asked.

"I can attach the superclusters to the shuttle. They latch on, one on each side, right below the tail. And I figured out how to make them open and close."

"What's the point?" Reggie asked.

"We're going to fill the superclusters with that congealed diesel from Cheyenne Mountain," Felicia said. "Then we haul it up to Fraser and firebomb the ruins." She spread her fingers wide. "Boom. No more gorgers. At least in Fraser, anyway."

Kim wanted to feel excited about the idea, but she couldn't. She didn't care.

"Did you find Mommy?" Barry asked.

She shook her head. There were so many pods and it was hard to tell which ones she'd searched and which ones she hadn't and which ones had people and which ones had other species and—

Kim squeezed her eyes shut. She didn't want to start crying again.

"It's okay," Tyrell said. "You're doing great."

She'd gone through as many of the human pods as she could, skipping past the ones with more than one person, because Mom had been alone.

"I did figure out how to select all the pods at once," she said.

Priya's face lit up. "What? That's fantastic. All the pods, or just all the human pods?" She walked over. "Show me."

Reggie crowded close as well. Kim frowned. He smelled. Not as bad as the rest of the room, but still.

"All the humans," Kim said. "Or whatever species you like."

She touched the controls while they watched. She wanted Mom back so badly, but she couldn't bear the thought of telling her Dad was dead.

"I'm not waiting any longer," Cameron said. "I'm going in." She bent and untied one of her boots.

Kim sprang to her feet, nodding. The control device wobbled on the floor.

"You should give them more time," Priya said.

"No," Kim said. "We waited long enough." She hated being a kid and not being able to make decisions.

"You don't have to," Felicia said. "Look."

A slimy hand reached out from the portal on the wall. Everyone froze. Kim held her breath. *Please, please, please.*

The skin on the hand was brown. The breath she'd been holding gushed out.

"Chase," Reggie whispered.

"Huh?" Cameron asked.

"Nothing," Reggie said. "It's Sierra."

Kim took Barry's hand and led him to the wall. Everyone gathered around.

The arm clutched the bottom rim of the portal and Sierra's face pushed through.

Tyrell grabbed her under the shoulders and pulled her into the room. He hissed and shook his hands, flinging off the goop.

Sierra heaved and coughed, sputtering slime from her mouth and nose. Her skin was shiny-smooth in places, like the skin under a band-aid after a few days. Globs of pink goop dripped down her clothes. Kona got close enough for a sniff, but didn't touch her.

Kim's mouth cinched up tight. She was so happy to see Sierra and furious it wasn't Dad.

Priya kneeled and wiped the slime from Sierra's face, flicking it away with a hiss. "Her eyes look good," she said.

"How's your side?" Tyrell asked.

Sierra made an "okay" shape with her hand. The fingers had grown back. They looked whole, though the skin on them was a shade lighter.

Kim's emotions were tearing her apart. She wanted to be happy and excited. Sierra was alive. She wasn't hurt any more. At the same time, the sadness squeezed her like a giant snake, making it hard to breathe. Making it hard to even think. It wasn't fair.

"That's amazing," Felicia said.

Kim stared at the portal, her lips pulled tight. "Where's Dad?"

"Daddy," Barry whimpered. "Please."

"I lost him," Sierra said, her voice raspy and wet. "I swam all over, but I couldn't find him." She sat back against the wall with pain and sadness in her eyes. "I'm so sorry."

"How do you see in there?" Cameron asked.

"It hurts like hell at first, then it subsides a little."

Cameron bent and untied her other boot. "And breathing?"

"That hurts, too," Sierra said. "You just have to get used to it."

"I'm going in," Cameron said. She kicked off her boots and handed two guns to Tyrell. "I'm not coming out until I find him."

Barry ran to Cameron and wrapped both arms around her, burying his face in her belly. She flinched, like she didn't know what to do, then finally returned his hug.

Tears ran down Kim's face. Her lower lip wouldn't stop trembling. Cameron didn't expect to find Dad. Not alive, anyway. She could see it in her eyes. She was just going in because there wasn't anything else to do. She would retrieve his body and then they'd have to bury him somewhere.

Felicia pulled Barry back to give Cameron room.

She shifted her weight from one foot to the other, like she was steeling herself to dive in.

Pink nubs appeared in the purple membrane. Fingertips.

Kim opened her mouth wide, unable to move. Unable to even breathe.

Cameron reached into the portal and grabbed the hand. Tyrell got up and helped. An arm came through. A man's arm.

Kim clasped her hands together, shaking.

Barry wrapped his arms around her waist and held on like he might never let go. "Please, please, please," he whispered.

Dad's face came through.

She let out a choking cry. It was him. His face looked normal. His mouth was closed and she couldn't see any teeth.

They eased him through the portal. He slumped onto the floor and coughed pink slime all over himself.

Barry pulled free, but Kim held him back, sobbing with joy. She'd never sobbed so hard, happy or sad. "Wait," she whispered into Barry's hair. "It'll hurt you. Wait till he dries off."

Dad sat against the wall and wiped the slime from his face. He broke into a smile when he made eye contact. His skin looked patchy and discolored, but he was alive.

Dad was alive.

Felicia wrapped a camo net over his shoulders. Kim released Barry and they both ran forward to hug him. Some of the slime stung her, and Barry too, based on the little mouse noises he made, but she didn't care.

She had her daddy back.

CONFLAGRATION

Chapter Fifty-Nine

Priya rose up on her knees between Cameron and Felicia as they piloted the carriage through the vast alien hangar. Her leg was strong enough for her to balance without holding onto anything and the wind felt cool on her face. It was delightful to not be sitting on her butt in the back for a change.

They were searching for the one remaining gorger in the ship, the one they'd left behind when Sierra interrogated the caretakers. "It should be close," Priya said. The gorger had been in the back corner of the hangar the last time she checked the control device. "A little more to the right, maybe."

Cameron and Felicia touched the controls and the craft lurched sideways. Priya grabbed the dashboard to keep from tumbling. Cameron and Felicia were definitely not as smooth as Cameron and David.

"Once this gorger is dead, there won't be any aliens on the entire mothership," Felicia said. "It's one more reason we should stay here."

Priya had wanted to remain in the menagerie because it would be safer for her, back when she thought she'd never walk again. Now, her leg felt as strong as ever, despite the little curve in her calf. She was beginning to suspect the alien goo had made other improvements. Her vision seemed better and the appendectomy scar on her belly had vanished. She wondered if she had grown a new appendix.

A featureless gray wall came into view. "We're running out of hangar," Cameron said.

Priya peered into the dark and spotted the gorger. "There." Her eyesight was definitely better.

The gorger crawled against the wall like a distressed tiger in a cage.

"Not too close," Cameron said. She and Felicia brought the carriage to a stop seven meters above the creature.

They weren't cloaked, but the gorger didn't seem to notice them. It just kept pushing against the wall, all ten legs cycling endlessly.

"In the menagerie, there's plenty to eat and the weather is always perfect," Felicia said. "It's paradise."

"You haven't been to the island with the giant centipedes," Cameron said.

Felicia shrugged. "As long as we have the devices, we can stun anything dangerous."

Cameron handed Priya the hunting knife they'd taken from Randall's body. "This was your idea. You do the honors."

"Kill it with fire," Felicia said.

Priya stood and stepped to the back of the carriage, relishing her mobility. She picked up the plastic bag of gelled diesel fuel, careful not to let it spill, and grabbed the long piece of cloth hanging from its mouth. The makeshift wick was soaked through.

"I don't want to spend the rest of my life in a cage," Cameron said. "Even voluntarily."

Priya stretched out the wick. A smaller piece of cloth was tied around the mouth to keep the knot from slipping out.

She unscrewed the end of the hunting knife, keenly aware that Felicia and Cameron were both watching her.

"There's so much to learn here," Felicia said. "I bet you and a bunch of other geniuses from storage could figure out how everything works."

Priya snorted. With the right help, she thought she could figure out quite a bit. She struck the flint with the back edge of the knife blade. Sparks cascaded around the end of the wick. One of them landed right on it and a dark yellow flame appeared, triangular at first, like a shark's fin. It grew quickly, spreading toward the plastic bag.

Below, the claws ceased clicking on the metal floor.

"It knows we're here," Felicia said.

Priya picked up the bag, holding it carefully so the wick wouldn't burn her.

"Any day now," Cameron said.

She lined up the bag with the gorger below and released it. The flames on the wick grew thin as it fell through the air. For a moment, it looked like they'd blown out.

The bag hit the gorger square on the back with a splurt, then bounced onto the floor. In the dim light, it was impossible to tell what had happened to the jellied diesel. Had the bag burst? Had the fuel spilled out or was it all still inside?

A second later, dark yellow flames enveloped the gorger like a grasping hand. The creature jumped around, a sheen of fuel stuck to its body. Globs dripped onto the metal floor.

"Great shot," Cameron said. She nudged Felicia back to the co-pilot spot. "Let's move out of the way so we don't breathe that smoke."

As the carriage scooted laterally, the gorger's abdomen fell to the ground and its legs curled up. A long, drawn-out wail came from its mouth. It continued to burn, clearly dead.

"Almost makes you feel sorry for it," Felicia said.

"They sent a comet that killed eight billion people," Priya said.

Felicia looked over her shoulder with narrowed eyes. "I was being sarcastic."

Cameron sniffed. "Smells like grilled prawns. Do you think it's edible?"

"Good question," Priya said. "We should feed one to an Entelodont or something, as a test."

Felicia glanced back, making a face. "No thanks." Her eyes suddenly went wide. "Incoming. Two harvesters, right behind us."

A pair of silver and yellow drones flew straight toward them.

"Go, go, go," Cameron said.

Priya grabbed her device. "I'll cloak us." She still didn't know if the invisibility shield would hide them from harvesters, but it was worth a try.

The carriage lurched away in a rising arc. "Try to lose them between the shuttles," Cameron said.

"Who sent them?" Felicia asked. "I thought the aliens were all dead. Randall is dead. Why are they after us?"

"I don't know," Priya said, wondering what she'd missed this time.

"Wait," Cameron said, looking back. "They aren't following us."

Priya spun around. "That means they can't detect us when we're cloaked."

"I'm not so sure," Cameron said. "I mean, maybe they can, maybe they can't, but that isn't why they aren't following. Look."

The harvesters sprayed the burning gorger with some sort of foam.

"Go back," Priya said. "I want to observe them."

Cameron gave her a steely glare. "Okay, but keep us cloaked."

As soon as the flames were extinguished, the harvesters ascended, slipping between the lowest layer of shuttles. Priya called up the map on her device and followed the two dots until they parked alongside all the other harvesters.

"Everything really is automated," Cameron said. "Those drones somehow detected the fire and put it right out."

"That's why we should stay," Felicia said. "This place is completely self-sustaining. It's much safer than Earth."

"What if all this automation suddenly sends the ship to the other side of the galaxy?" Cameron asked.

"What difference would that make?" Felicia asked. "We could still live on the islands, whether we're in orbit or flying through space."

"When the ship got to wherever it was going, our descendants would be exterminated," Priya said. "Humanity would come to an end."

She'd been prepared for the end of humanity ever since observing the Ender through her telescope and confirming its trajectory. She'd accepted it. Now they had a chance. They had found the perfect valley to colonize, hundreds of thousands of gorgers notwithstanding.

She'd told herself she wanted to stay in the menagerie because of her broken leg, but if she was honest, she had to admit it was more than that. The device made her feel like she had control in the islands. She was scared to give that up.

If Sierra had taught her anything, it was how to be brave.

"Sierra is right," Priya said. "Earth is our home. It's where we belong. It's the only place humanity can survive, long-term. Our plan will work."

"Are you sure?" Felicia asked.

Priya scowled. She hated that question. Nothing was ever certain, even in science. New data could always come along. But that wasn't what Felicia needed to hear. She took a deep breath. "Yes. We just proved the fuel is flammable, and the gorgers, too. We've got access to plenty more and devices to carry it."

Felicia nodded, though she didn't look entirely convinced.

Priya didn't care. "Earth is ours," she said.

"Well then, enough with the talky-talk-talk," Cameron said. "Let's get back there."

Chapter Sixty

"So, what's it like to die?" Cameron's tone sounded playful, but the look in her eyes was serious. David sat beside her in a carriage docked in the center of the shuttle. The rest of the group was spread out on other carriages, which gave them a modicum of privacy.

David thought for a moment, trying to figure out how to give her an honest answer. "I could tell something was terribly wrong," he said. "A lot of the pain faded away, but something was ... off."

He remembered hoping desperately that someone would take care of Kim and Barry after he was gone.

"Were there angels?" she asked. "Pearly gates?"

He shook his head.

"Well, that's comforting." Her tone dripped with sarcasm.

He raised one eyebrow. "At least there wasn't any fire or brimstone." He'd always viewed the afterlife as a vague state of existence rather than a recognizable place. Now he didn't know what to believe.

"Did you see a bright light? Did your life flash before your eyes?"

"No. The only light was the exit portal, and I didn't see that until I regained consciousness."

"That's an interesting way to phrase it," Cameron said. "You weren't knocked out, you know. You were dead."

The airlock opened and the shuttle burst into space. Earth filled the view. The continents were still far too brown, but splotches of green here and there proved that life could return, and there were still vast stretches of beautiful blue ocean.

What would have happened if Sierra hadn't put him in the chamber right away? Could it have brought him back after an hour? A day? Longer? Repairing damaged tissue was one thing, but what about the synaptic connections that gave him his memories and personality?

He didn't remember anything until the moment he woke, floating somewhere deep in the chamber, every inch of his skin prickling with pain. At first, he'd thought it *was* some sort of afterlife. Then he spotted the distant light and started swimming toward it.

He rubbed his cheek. The skin felt smooth where it had been repaired, without the stubble that covered the rest of his jaw.

"Well, don't get a Jesus complex on me," Cameron said, apparently done with the discussion.

He loved the fact that she could accept what happened and move on so easily.

He looked over at her, sitting next to him in the carriage. He still thought she looked beautiful, but his desire for her went beyond physical attraction. He wanted to build a new life with her. He wanted to teach her everything he knew about medicine, and he wanted to learn from her, too. How to shoot, how to fight. For the first time in many weeks, he was beginning to feel hope.

He reached over and put his hand on hers. "We've got this."

She smiled. The sight lit him up like a floodlight.

They would bring down all the people from storage and start a new civilization. He and Cameron would start a new life together.

The ramifications for the future of medicine were staggering. He wanted to find out if the goop was comprised of nanotechnology, something organic, or something else altogether.

There were so many tests he should try. If they collected a bottle of the goop, could it be applied topically? What would happen if you drank it? What sort of side effects did it have? He would be able to heal any injury, at the cost of just a little pain. David chuckled. As an anesthesiologist, he'd always focused on preventing pain.

"What's so funny?" Cameron asked.

"Nothing," David said. "Everything's good." Everything was better than good. Randall was gone and the aliens on the ship were all dead, this time for real. No one was trying to stop them.

They would burn the ruins in Fraser, and once they made sure the valley was safe, they would bring everyone down from storage. It was a good plan. For the first time since the Ender had appeared in the sky, it seemed like things were going to be okay.

Chapter Sixty-One

Two Days Before Impact

Frank Wharton deserved to live. More than anyone else on Earth, he deserved it. While other people had been killing themselves or drinking themselves to death, Frank had been hard at work. He'd exhausted his contacts, and his contacts' contacts. He'd spent his adult life leveraging one asset to buy another, and now, finally, he'd made the ultimate deal.

Four days earlier, Frank secured a spot in an underground bunker out in the Midwest. The cost of admission had been his very soul, but he was glad to pay it. Souls weren't good for much anyway. The cost of admission, two teenage girls, lay bound, gagged, and drugged in the back of the white panel van Frank was driving from New York to South Dakota.

The bunker was operated by two guys both named Matt who'd bought an abandoned ICBM silo near a tiny municipality with the unfortunate name of Scrotan. The bunker was stocked with a hundred-year supply of food and water. It had its own air purification system. The living space was palatial and included a swimming pool, a cinema, a gym with a half basketball court, and even a one-lane bowling alley.

The Matts only lacked one thing.

Frank shuddered. It was sick, but that's just how some people were.

They'd spoken through an intermediary, who'd told Frank that he could bring a girl of his own if he wanted. Frank had declined. He'd only brought two girls, though he still had a couple of spare syringes in his pocket in case he changed his mind between here and Scrotan.

A means to an end, Frank told himself. *A means to an end.* Unlike the rest of the world, Frank wouldn't die in two days. He would live on. Maybe once the girls were older, one of them would decide she didn't care so much for the Matts and would take a liking to him instead.

Traffic picked up as he approached St. Paul, even worse than it had been while passing through Chicago. People must be panicking now that the end was only two days away. He snorted. They should have taken action before time ran out.

A crowd filled a park on the left side of the freeway, down by the river. He took a second look and decided it was really more of a mob. They were packed in tight down there, probably swarming into the Mississippi, like lemmings.

He turned on the radio.

"... the facts as far as we can tell. Van-sized white pods have appeared across the Midwest, having flown in from some unknown location. Government officials have provided no explanation about the source of the pods, but are urging everyone to leave them alone until we understand where they came from."

A woman's voice cut in. "Good luck with that. No one is leaving those pods alone."

The man chuckled. "The National Guard has been mobilized in those states where the Guard still operates. The President called a cabinet meeting, though the cabinet was down to only eight members at last count."

The woman's voice returned. "Okay, here's some new information. Apparently, the pods only fly away once they have people inside them." The sound of shuffling came over the radio.

"Wait. Where are you going? Come back here."

The air went silent for a moment. "Well, I would ask the booth to hand us off to national, but the booth has been abandoned, so I guess I'm out, too."

The radio went silent for more than a moment.

"What the hell just happened?" Frank looked back at the mob by the river, but couldn't see anything except the lemmings. He leaned over the van's steering wheel and looked up. The Ender hung in the sky like a spiteful eye.

As he continued into St. Paul, he tried to make sense of the radio message. *The pods only fly away once they have people inside them.* He checked his phone, but couldn't get a goddamn signal. The infrastructure had gone to hell in the last two months. Hopefully the Matts did a better job with maintenance than the phone companies. The van hopscotched through a series of tooth-rattling potholes. The goddamn roads were just as bad.

Frank held his breath, listening for any reaction from the girls in the back, but they were silent. The ketamine was doing its job.

Traffic grew increasingly worse, which turned out to be a lucky break, because it slowed him down enough to actually get a look at one of the pods from the radio.

A squashed white sphere lifted above a frontage road on the right, where another crowd had gathered, smaller than the mob by the river.

Frank had attended several rocket launches as the guest of wealthy entrepreneurs. This looked completely different. The pod wasn't rising on a column of fire. It was just … rising. He held his foot on the brake and leaned forward to watch out the windshield until the pod vanished from sight.

Some asshole in a truck behind him laid on the horn. Frank kept his foot on the brake for another twenty seconds just to spite the guy, then rolled forward in the creeping traffic.

A new option had materialized. Frank re-evaluated his plans. He could continue to South Dakota, or he could get in one of those pods. The more he thought about it, the more he liked the idea of taking a pod. He didn't know where they went, but it had to be better than spending the next several decades in an underground bunker with two pedophile preppers named Matt.

Unfortunately, he didn't know how to find one.

After another two hours, Frank broke out of the city and left most of the traffic behind. He continued west, toward South Dakota. The bunker was now his contingency plan. It was better than burning alive, at least, but he was determined to find a pod. He was Frank Fucking Wharton, after all. If anyone deserved one, it was him. Maybe if he woke one of the girls in the back, she could help him search. She would have to be tied up, of course.

"Are you out of your goddamn mind?" he said aloud. Had he seriously considered inviting his kidnapping victim to the front seat of his van? Frank shook his head. He was operating on way too little sleep and way too much cocaine.

As the sun fell in front of him, the route west took him onto smaller roads with even less traffic. By the time it was full dark, he didn't see any other cars, except for the ever-present stalls lining both sides.

He also couldn't see anything except for the road directly ahead of him. There might be a pod thirty feet off the shoulder and he would never know it. He needed a new plan. He'd never find a pod this way. He should have gotten a van with one of those little spotlights mounted above the side mirror.

The road ran straight ahead for as far as Frank could see. He pulled out one of his coke bullets and took another snort, then chased it with a swig of warm Diet Pepsi. The combination had kept him going for a good twenty hours.

He rolled down the windows. The cool air blowing on his face helped some, too. A little after ten o'clock, he finally saw another human being. A woman walked along the side of the road shining a flashlight into the fields on the right.

Frank took a deep breath. "Do you really think you can pull this off?" he asked himself. He was going to pick up a passenger while hauling a pair of kidnapped girls in the back.

"Of course I can," he answered. "I'm Frank Fucking Wharton."

He slowed down and pulled over to the side of the road.

Chapter Sixty-Two

Cameron and David landed the shuttle right outside the main entrance to the Cheyenne Mountain Complex. They both hopped over to one of the spare carriages where Priya was waiting. The shuttle's cabin had gotten crowded. Six carriages floated inside, two of them piled high with fruit they'd collected in the preserve.

"We're taking Reggie along," Cameron said quietly to David. She wanted him where she could keep tabs on him. Things were finally going well and she wasn't about to let him fuck it up. David shrugged, and together they piloted the carriage down to Reggie, who sat alone on a spare carriage below the others. "Hop on," she told him. "You're going with us."

"Why?" he muttered. "Why do you need me?"

"You'll be our lookout," she said. "You can let us know if you spot any signs of trouble."

He grunted. He'd barely spoken since regaining consciousness, which made her nervous. As long as he'd been whining about how terrible people were, she'd been able to gauge his state of mind. The grumbling probably also served as a pressure valve. That's how it worked for her, anyway.

Reggie stepped aboard and sat next to Priya. She adjusted the control device so that some of its lights projected onto his face. "Here, I can show you what I'm doing," she said.

He leaned in, squinting. If he was paying attention, that had to be a good sign.

"Let's get this done," Cameron said. She and David flew down the tail, while behind them, Kim and Felicia undocked the primary carriage.

The hatch spiraled open and they slipped out into a crisp, quiet morning with hazy blue skies above. A monolithic wall of rust-colored rock stood in front of them.

"Close the hatch if there's any sign of trouble," Cameron called out. She glanced over her shoulder at Priya. "Cloak us." Success was so close she could taste it. This was not the time to let down their guard.

Below, the tunnel leading into the main entrance of the complex stared back at them. The bright morning sun ensured there weren't any gorgers about, but there were undoubtedly plenty inside the mountain.

They floated around to the side of the shuttle, where the cluster of ten-foot pink spheres hung alongside the tail. Partially translucent, they reminded her of fish eggs. Gigantic fish eggs.

Priya touched her control device and the cluster of spheres detached from the hull. It floated sideways, still at least fifty feet above the ground. "Okay, this is the part I'm not sure about." She bent over the controls, tapping and swiping.

Reggie watched intently.

The lowest sphere in the cluster broke free and dropped, stopping just above the ground.

Priya let out a puff of air, then looked up. "We can head in now. Just take it slow and steady."

Cameron and David reached for the carriage controls and they flew into the tunnel. "Let's try to keep right out in the center," Cameron said. She didn't want any gorgers jumping aboard from the ground or dropping on them from the walls.

The giant sphere floated behind them, like a ball but not rolling, which felt wrong. It ought to be rolling.

"No gorgers," David said as they passed into shadow.

"They've all gone deep inside, where the food is," Cameron said. She touched the Beretta on her lap, taking comfort from its presence.

They had to drop down to pass through the frame where the massive blast door had swung open. Behind them, the ball squeezed through with a few inches of clearance on each side.

The ruins of a checkpoint gate stood in the chamber beyond the door. Gorgers gnawed on the wooden guard booth where security personnel had once been stationed. Fortunately, the cave's ceiling was sixty feet high. The carriage floated up and over the gate and the giant sphere followed. The air tasted acrid, like bile.

Beyond the checkpoint, the road turned left to wrap around the main building, which filled the cavern. A dozen gorgers clung to the walls, like crabs on shore rocks. Cameron's skin crawled at the sight of them.

"Take the widest path you can find," Priya said. "I need as much clearance as possible."

Several gorgers turned toward the carriage at the sound of her voice.

Cameron glared back at Priya, her finger to her lips.

She tucked her head and whispered, "Sorry."

David touched Cameron's arm. "It's okay. They can't get us," he whispered. "They can't even see us."

She reached over and playfully pinched the smooth skin on his cheek. "That's the kind of thinking that will get you killed again."

He smiled. The sight brought a comforting ache to her core. She had her man back, and she meant to keep him.

They followed the road around to the front of the main complex, where little metal staircases led to doors every fifty feet. The doors had all been torn open, except for one with two working floodlights overhead.

"You sentenced everyone here to die," Priya said.

Cameron clenched her jaw. "Do you think I had a choice?"

"You could have tried to negotiate with them."

Reggie laughed. Several gorgers turned their way.

"You didn't see what these people were like," Cameron said.

"You could have just killed the ones who attacked you. You didn't have to let the gorgers in. You could have found another way out."

"This isn't a goddamn shopping mall," Cameron said. "There isn't another way out."

They flew alongside the massive building. It pissed off Cameron that Reggie, who'd seen it all go down, kept silent, and it pissed her off even more that David wasn't coming to her defense. They'd been in a no-win situation.

"I'm just saying, maybe there was another way," Priya said.

"You're wrong," Cameron said loudly. The gorgers below turned their heads. "I made a shitty choice, but it was the only choice."

"Sometimes you have to do something truly awful," Reggie said quietly. "To prevent something even worse."

"Thanks," Cameron said. It wasn't much of a defense, but she would take it.

Below, clusters of gorgers fed on anything that wasn't rock or metal. Six or eight of them gathered around a stack of wooden pallets. Some unseen number rattled inside a dumpster. Here and there, they crowded together in tight knots along the roadway, slurping up something unidentifiable. Probably the former residents.

"You okay back there, Reggie?" David asked quietly.

"I'm fine," he answered, with a tone that sounded anything but.

"Feeling any fatigue or dizziness? Trouble concentrating?" David had offered to put Reggie into the healing goop, to treat the effects of his concussion, but he'd refused.

"I told you, I'm fine."

"Okay, okay. Just let me know if anything changes. Concussions sometimes have cognitive side effects."

The tension in Cameron's spine uncoiled slightly. The concussion probably explained why Reggie had stopped bitching about how awful people were. Hell, maybe he'd even had a change of heart.

"Slow down a second," Priya whispered.

Cameron and David complied, moving in perfect sync.

Behind them, the sphere floated only a foot or so above a pack of gorgers on the roadway. Priya tapped furiously at her device. A moment later, the sphere rose twenty feet.

The gorgers didn't seem to notice, despite the fact that the sphere wasn't cloaked. Cameron wondered if they recognized it as their own technology, or simply knew it was something they couldn't eat. "How the hell does that thing even fly?"

"The caretakers figured out something about gravity that we never came close to cracking," Priya said. "Hopefully, the people in storage can help reverse engineer it."

In front of them, the golf cart sitting out in the middle of the road had been stripped down to a skeletal frame. On the left, the armory stood nestled in its little side nook. The door was off its hinges and gorgers moved around inside. "That's where they were growing fungus to eat," Cameron said.

"Mycoprotein," Priya said.

She always had a fancy word for everything.

They followed the road to the back wall, where it entered the small tunnel to the generator room and fuel storage.

There was no sign of the headbanging woman Cameron had killed with the hammer, not even bones.

"When we get to the diesel pond, go all the way to the back," Priya instructed.

They passed over a short railing into a hollowed-out chamber that extended at least fifty feet from the road. The surface of the pond was empty blackness and the bitter oily smell made Cameron slightly nauseated.

Behind them, the floating sphere eclipsed the glow from the main cavern. The only light came from the beams shining onto Priya's face from her device. She tapped away at the controls. A three-foot hole spiraled open on the side of the sphere, like the iris on a giant eyeball. The inside was hollow.

"How much will that hold?" Cameron asked.

"Three thousand gallons," Priya said. "Give or take." She touched the device again. "Here we go."

The sphere plunged straight down, breaking through the congealed surface with a heavy wet slurp. Thick gelled diesel glugged into the opening. The sphere continued its descent until it was fully submerged. The surface of the pond gurgled as the air bubbled out.

When the pond grew still, Priya touched the controls again. "That should close it back up. Now let's see if it can carry the weight."

If the sphere couldn't lift out of the pond with a full load of diesel, they were back to square one. Cameron held her breath.

The sphere surfaced with a disgusting slurp. Viscous black oil dripped down its sides. "Nice work," David said. "One down, fifteen to go."

They would drop all sixteen firebombs on the ruins of Fraser while the gorgers sheltered in the rubble. Cameron pictured them crawling out as they burned, dying from both the flames and the sunlight. She smiled. As Priya had pointed out, they'd killed eight billion people.

It was payback time.

Chapter Sixty-Three

Sierra walked up next to Tyrell in the tail of the shuttle, where he gazed down at the dark tunnel leading into Cheyenne Mountain. "How's it going?" she asked.

"They just returned with the fifth sphere and Priya must've figured something out, 'cause they went back inside with two empties instead of just the one."

"Terrific," Sierra said. "At this rate, we can get back up to Fraser before nightfall."

He gave her a grim look instead of the bright smile she'd hoped for.

"What's the matter?" she asked. Everything was going according to plan. With Randall and the last of the aliens dead, there wasn't anything in their way, other than the gorgers, and a whole bunch of those were about to be incinerated.

Tyrell crossed his arms. "Ever since my pod opened, I've been trying to convince people I wasn't who they thought I was." He pointed at Cheyenne Mountain. "But after what I did in there, I'm not so sure."

"You had no choice. You were defending yourself." She touched his arm.

He shook his head. "I killed people who were running away from me."

"They weren't people," Sierra said.

"They were," Tyrell said. "They didn't ask to be born in a cave, to live their whole lives underground."

"Ok, fine. But if they'd gotten away, they would have come back with reinforcements."

Tyrell scowled. "There's no way to know that."

Sierra flexed her hand, unsure what to say. The two fingers that had grown back felt slightly numb, like they weren't really part of her.

"The fact that I killed them isn't the worst thing," he said. "The worst part is that I liked it. After what they did to us, I liked hacking those bastards to pieces." He lowered his face. "My Momma would be so ashamed."

She ran her fingers down his arm and clasped his hand. "It's okay. That's behind us."

He pulled free. "You enjoyed pounding Randall's face into pulp," he said. "You watched that gorger eat him alive, and you liked it."

She felt cold. "Randall had just destroyed my eye. He broke my ribs and I'm pretty sure he wrecked my spleen and my kidney and my liver. I was dying."

"Yeah, I know," Tyrell said. "Randall deserved what he got. That isn't the problem. It's the fact that you liked hurting him."

She couldn't deny it, and she didn't want to. Randall murdered Waldmire. If he was lying here in front of her, she would do it all again.

Tyrell rubbed the back of his neck. "You know, Reggie may be right." His voice was sad and quiet now, which was somehow worse. He waved his hand, pointing upwards. "If we bring all those other people down, we'll just repeat the cycle. We'll kill some of them, they'll kill some of us, and maybe in a hundred years we'll be cutting out tongues and butchering each other."

She put her hands on her hips. "What do you propose, then?"

He shrugged. "I don't know. I don't have any idea." He turned and walked deeper into the shuttle.

Sierra stood staring out the hatch, arms crossed, trying to figure out how to change his mind. Nothing came to her, except the growing possibility that maybe he was right.

Chapter Sixty-Four

One Day Before Impact

Picking up the woman was a risk, but Frank calculated it was a risk worth taking. She could help him stay awake and she could help him search for a pod. He slowed the van to a stop beside her. She wore jeans and a sweater. Her dark hair was knotted in a ponytail. She wasn't ugly, but she was a little on the plain side. A purse was slung over one shoulder and she held a large flashlight.

"You can climb in, if you want," he said, trying to sound casual and hoping like hell she wouldn't recognize him. He'd been interviewed on business programs often enough and he'd even appeared on some magazine covers.

The woman glanced toward the back of the van, a quintessential perv-mobile without any windows. Thankfully, the cab was separated from the cargo area by a wall of storage compartments.

Frank hitched a thumb over his shoulder. "Need any PVC? You're welcome to it." He put a little Brooklyn into his accent, which felt odd after forty years of trying to keep it out.

She offered a smile that didn't look completely genuine, obviously concerned about getting in a car with a stranger in the middle of the night.

"What's your story?" he asked, trying to sound amiable. "Car trouble?"

"I ran out of gas. I was trying to get to my husband. I think maybe he found a pod." She paused.

He decided to play dumb. It might make him less threatening. "What kind of pod?"

"These pods came from the sky. They ... they take people away. It's been all over the news. Haven't you seen it?"

Frank patted the steering wheel. "I've been driving."

She seemed to relax slightly. Bugs chirped in the night.

"Where are they?" he asked.

"They fell in a swath across the Midwest, from Lake Superior down to Death Valley. The biggest concentration was apparently right around here, though. That's what I heard, anyway."

"How do we find one?"

"I've seen three, but other people got to them first." She held up the flashlight. "This should help. They're shiny and the light really picks them up."

"Where did you see them?"

The woman's shoulders dropped. "The last one was two hours back, when I was on the highway and there was more traffic." Her voice rose with frustration. "A car barreled off the road, right past me. They got to it before I could."

"Why don't you hop in? We can look for one together. I'll drive. You shine the light." Picking up a passenger with two teen girls bound and gagged in the back sent a thrill up his spine way beyond what the cocaine gave him.

The woman seemed to think about it.

From the corner of his eye, Frank noticed the tire iron on the floor on the passenger side. He'd pulled it out of the back because he didn't want one of the girls to wake up and use it to pry open the door, or worse, brain him with it. Now he wished he'd thrown it away.

The door opened and the woman got in. She nudged the tire iron aside with her foot as she sat down.

"I'm John," he said, giving her his middle name.

"Lynn." She rummaged through her purse and pulled out a second flashlight. "Here. Point this out your window. Like I said, they're really shiny."

Frank took the flashlight and aimed it out the window as he steered back onto the road. Lynn pointed hers out the passenger side.

"Where are you going?" she asked.

"Rapid City. I'm going to see my sister one last time before the end." Frank stopped breathing. He remembered the ketamine syringes in his chest pocket. Had she seen them? No. She wouldn't have gotten in the van if she had. Or maybe she thought it was insulin. He exhaled, trying to keep his breath quiet. If she noticed, he would tell her it was insulin.

So far, though, she kept her gaze toward the dark fields on the right.

Frank drove on, listening to the thrum of the engine and the air currents coming through the windows. One of his favorite things about coke was how endlessly fascinating it made everything sound.

"Where are you coming from?" she asked after a while.

"New York," he answered automatically, then added, "Upstate." If he gave her too many honest answers, she'd be more likely to recognize him. He was known for his hair, which had turned snow-white by his twenty-fifth birthday. "You say your husband already found one of these pod things?"

"I'm hoping so," she said. "I lost contact with them— *Stop!*"

Frank stepped on the brakes and jerked the van onto the gravel shoulder. Something sparkled in the high grass about forty yards from the road.

"Look at that," Frank said with a chuckle. "I'm lucky I picked you up. I would have driven right past without even seeing it."

Lynn glanced up the road, then checked her side mirror. Frank did the same. There weren't any cars in either direction, just the pitch black South Dakota night.

"What happens now?" he asked. He clicked off his flashlight and placed it on the dashboard.

Lynn fumbled in her purse. "I'm going to try my husband one more time." She pulled out her phone, pressed a button, and held it to her ear.

Frank scratched his chin, then moved his hand down to the needles in his breast pocket. He held it there, like someone standing for the national anthem.

"He isn't answering," Lynn said, her voice thin. "What should I do? I have to assume he found one, right? If we wait around, someone else will come and take that pod." She dropped the phone in her lap and looked up at the van's ceiling with a groan. Her throat was long and lovely in the glow of the dashboard.

Frank wasn't going to get a better opportunity. He shoved the needle into her neck and depressed the plunger.

Lynn's eyes went wide. "Wha—?" she sputtered. "Why?"

"I was never very good at sharing."

She went for the door, but he slammed her back against her seat with his right arm and held her there. She struggled and squirmed, which was perfect. The activity would help the ketamine circulate faster.

Consciousness slowly drained from her face. "Please don't do this. I have kids."

He gave her his prettiest smile, even batting his eyes a little. "Too late. It's already done."

Lynn slumped in the seat.

He pushed open her eye and touched her eyeball to see if she was faking it, but she didn't flinch.

Confident she was out, he gathered his things, including the Ruger and three spare magazines. He thought about checking on the girls in the back, maybe even untying them, but decided to leave them be. Lynn would wake up in four or five hours. She could untie them if she wanted. He left the keys in the ignition and placed a twenty on the dash. She could drive the girls into Aberdeen to get some breakfast. One final meal. He even decided to leave the tire iron, so she could defend herself if some asshole came along and tried something. He wasn't a bad person, after all. He'd just been forced to do some bad things.

He got out, pulled on his blue zipper jacket, and marched through the weeds, shining the flashlight in front of him.

The pod sure was shiny, all right. Frank circled it, looking for a door. "Uh, open up." The nighttime chorus of bugs paused for a moment, but the pod sat motionless. "Hello?" Frank put his hand on the side and leaned close, listening.

The pod split apart. A horizontal seam formed around the middle and the top rose straight up. The inside was empty, but the surface looked soft and comfortable.

Wherever this thing went, there would be lots of other people. Frank would take charge and rise to the top, the way he always had.

He climbed in and the pod began to close.

Chapter Sixty-Five

Tyrell leaned into the turn as the shuttle banked over the ruins of Fraser, even though he didn't actually feel any movement. The view projected into his eyes from the curved front wall was so clear and realistic he couldn't help it.

He stood alone on one of the empty flying cars, troubled by dark thoughts. He could still feel the machete blade sinking through the flesh of those people under the mountain. Each strike had filled him with satisfaction.

His thoughts about Sierra were even more troubling. From the moment he met her, he'd felt an attraction he'd never known before. When he was away from her, he wanted to be with her, and when he was with her, everything felt right. But after what he'd seen aboard the mothership, he wanted to run from her. She'd been a different person. Her malice terrified him.

Off to the west, the sun had passed its zenith and begun descending toward the mountains, where a long bank of clouds capped the peaks.

"The gorgers are out already," Felicia said.

Below, the shadows of the town's buildings stretched to the riverfront. A swarm of gorgers crept down to drink at the shoreline. Dark shapes moved beneath the water.

"Should we bomb them now, before that storm comes in?" Felicia asked.

"That isn't really a storm," David said. "It looks like a small cold front, or maybe just a mountain wave."

"We should give it a day," Sierra said. "Let's wait until tomorrow and make sure it's bright and sunny."

Tyrell nodded, appreciating her heedful approach. They probably wouldn't kill every single gorger with the firebombs, but they might be able to get most of them. They would bring everyone from storage down to the open meadow south of the town, where they could set up a defensive perimeter to deal with any stragglers that remained behind.

David and Kim were piloting the shuttle. Cameron sat behind them, using blank pages in the back of the journal to create a target list. The rest of the group sat on another flying car, floating beside them.

Sierra gestured at the remains of a subdivision on the outskirts of town.

Cameron shook her head. "There isn't enough left of those houses to bother with."

"What about that building?" Barry asked, pointing to a three-story structure by the river.

It looked like it might have been Fraser's predominant hotel.

"Good call," Cameron said. She bent over her pages and scribbled a note. "We've got fourteen targets now. That leaves us with two spare firebombs."

"We can always go back for more if we need to," Sierra said.

There'd been tens of thousands of superclusters in the mothership and hundreds of thousands of gallons of fuel in Cheyenne Mountain.

"Where should we land for the night?" David asked.

"Take us south to the middle of the valley," Sierra said. "Let's get out while there's still daylight. It'll be good to feel the Earth beneath our feet."

This was the Sierra that Tyrell liked. No bloodlust.

"All set," Priya said. She pushed one of the orange devices out of her lap. "We can bring down the pods as soon as we're ready. I've got them all selected, except for Jasmine, Nick, and Kelly."

"Who are they?" Tyrell asked.

"They were in the village before Randall took over," Felicia said. "Good people. They were hurt, so we put them in pods. We told them we would bring them back out when we found a way to treat their injuries."

David chuckled. "At the time, we were hoping to find more doctors."

"Now we can heal them in the mothership," Tyrell said.

"Bingo," Priya said.

"Let's be patient with the pods," Sierra said. "We may want to give it a day or two after we bomb the ruins. I want to be sure this valley is safe."

"Do you think we're missing something?" David asked.

"No," Sierra said. "That's the only town for miles. There's no place for gorgers to shelter out in the valley. The mountains are too barren to provide much shade. Honestly, this place is perfect."

"Then what are you worried about?" Kim asked.

"I want to be cautious, to be sure we get it right," Sierra said.

"You aren't going to just leap without looking?" Priya asked.

"I'm learning," Sierra said with a sly grin.

Tyrell relaxed slightly. The sight of her smile made it awfully hard to harbor concerns about her. He leaned again as the shuttle turned south in a wide arc, almost losing his balance and falling over. What he saw with his eyes didn't line up with what he felt in his feet.

They flew about four miles and landed beside a wide, flat bluff overlooking the river. The meadow continued as far as they could see to the south, where the mountain ranges on either side converged near what had once been the U.S. border. Down there, the ruins of the cities held millions of gorgers, but the barren mountains and open grassland created a natural barrier. The gorgers couldn't come north without enduring a hell of a lot of sun exposure.

Everyone gathered on two of the flying cars. David and Kim piloted one, while Cameron and Felicia flew the other. They shot straight out the tail, which pointed back toward the ruins of Fraser, just visible in the distance.

The bluff below the shuttle was the size of four city blocks and rose twenty feet above the surrounding meadow. Both flying cars circled as they descended so that everyone could survey the area, but no one spotted anything suspicious. They landed directly below the shuttle's tail.

Kona jumped down and squatted to pee. Barry ran over and clipped the leash to her collar.

"Let's check out the river," Sierra said.

The group walked through the knee-high scrub across the bluff. Some lucky combination of geography and climate had allowed more plants to reestablish here than anywhere else they'd seen. They really had found Shangri-La.

David walked beside Priya. "How's that leg?"

She barely limped. "It feels strong, but also kinda unfamiliar."

"I know what you mean," he said, touching the side of his face.

They stopped at the eastern edge of the bluff. A sandy slope led to the sluggish brown river flowing from left to right, probably all the way to Vancouver. Across the water, the meadow extended for several miles before sloping up into the eastern foothills. Red and yellow flowers dotted the soft greens of the grass. The air smelled fresh and clean.

Reggie stood with his hands on his hips. A thin smile formed on his face. For the first time in a long time, he looked content.

Tyrell gave him a friendly pat on the arm. "Things are finally looking up, huh?"

Reggie stared at him.

"Do you think there are gorgers in the river?" Kim asked. The water was too muddy to see below the surface.

"Assume that there are," Cameron said.

Priya bent to examine some berries growing on a two-foot shrub. David and Cameron followed Kim and Barry upstream along the bluff's edge, while Kona sniffed every clump of grass.

"It's nice to feel the sun again," Felicia said, stretching.

Tyrell smiled. He agreed. Things felt almost normal.

Sierra pulled him aside. "Can I talk to you?"

He took in her big brown eyes, so full of determination. "Sure."

They walked downstream along the bluff, passing beneath the shuttle's wing. One of the two superclusters hung from this side of the ship, eight giant orbs full of fuel. They looked like eggs carried by a water bug on the side of its body.

"How are you doing?" Sierra asked.

Tyrell bit his tongue. The guilt of what he'd done in Cheyenne Mountain still weighed on him, but he didn't want to rehash their earlier conversation. "I'm hanging in there." He gestured at her eye. "How are you? All back to normal?"

She tilted her head. "I don't know about normal, but everything seems to be working properly.

"Good."

She stared at him, squinting in the sunlight. "I'm glad you called me out earlier," she said. "I needed that."

He gave her a small nod, happy to know he'd been heard.

"You were right. I wanted Randall to suffer. I wanted to watch him suffer." She shivered. "I'm ashamed I felt that way, but I can't deny it."

"I appreciate you saying that," Tyrell said.

She looked up at him, her eyes bright in the afternoon sun. "Reggie is right. People can be pretty terrible. We've proven it over and over again. Randall. Joe. Thad. The people in Cheyenne Mountain. All the shit that went down before the comet hit."

Tyrell nodded.

"The fact that we can recognize it is our only hope," Sierra said. "We have to change. We can't allow things to get like that again." She shrugged. "I don't ever want to be in a position where I want to watch someone suffer."

"What can we do?" he asked.

"We have a chance to start over here. We can hold each other to a higher standard. We can truly hold people accountable for their actions. And we can also provide more support for the people who need it." She chuffed. "Does that sound idealistic?"

He took her hands. "If there's ever a time to be idealistic, this is it."

She squeezed his fingers. It felt good. It felt right.

"Where do we start?"

She shrugged. "I don't know. I don't have the answers. But I do know what the first step is."

He lifted his eyebrows, eager to hear her plan.

"Rick Preston taught me—"

"Who's Rick Preston?"

She looked down. "My father. The man who raised me, though I think someone else was my biological father. Sheesh, there's so much I want to tell you." She released his grip and waved her hand. "Later. Anyway, Rick Preston taught me that when someone on your team is going up against you, your best response is to put that person in charge."

Tyrell smiled. "You're talking about Reggie."

She nodded. "Exactly. Figuring out how to stop people from being terrible is his number one concern. He's the perfect guy for the job. If we get him on board, it'll be good for him. And he won't be alone. He'll have help."

"Who?" Tyrell asked.

She shrugged. "People from storage. People who care about doing what's right. Historians, sociologists, maybe even a lawyer."

He looked at her sideways.

She held up both hands. "Hey, we'll need all kinds of voices."

"It's a good plan," he said. "It's smart." It was more than just a plan for the future, he realized. She'd found a way to redeem herself. He just needed to find one too.

"Why don't we go talk to him together?" she asked.

He took her hand and they walked back. The sun was still shining and a breeze brought the smell of wildflowers. David, Cameron, and the kids were heading back as well. Priya and Felicia walked with them.

Sierra stopped. "Where is Reggie?"

Tyrell stepped up onto a small boulder. Reggie was nowhere in sight. A sinking feeling grew in his stomach. Something was wrong.

"Everyone get back here," Sierra called out. "We've got a problem."

Chapter Sixty-Six

One of the sleds was missing. Sierra's breathing came faster and faster. She thought Reggie was doing better. He'd stopped complaining, so she'd stopped paying attention to him. She should have done the opposite. She should have known.

"Maybe he just went back inside the shuttle," Felicia said, as she climbed onto the remaining sled with the others.

"I don't think so," Sierra whispered. She should have stayed with him, kept an eye on him.

David and Cameron took the controls and they floated straight up. "He can't have gone far," David said. "We'll find him."

"Did gorgers get him?" Barry asked.

"No, Bud, he's fine."

"There," Cameron pointed.

A tiny dot flew north toward the ruins of Fraser. It was the other sled, with a single figure on board. He'd gone more than a quarter mile already.

"I don't understand," Kim said. "What's he doing?"

"Maybe he just wants to be alone," Tyrell said.

Sierra shook her head. "If he just wanted to be alone, he wouldn't be flying toward the town. He's killing himself. Suicide by gorger."

Tyrell met her eyes. He nodded, almost imperceptibly.

"Wait, how is he flying that carriage?" Felicia asked. "He's by himself."

"He isn't flying it," Priya said. "He's sending it. He took one of the devices."

"He's been watching us use them," Kim said.

Cameron gave Sierra a concerned look.

"Let's go after him," David said. "We can catch him."

A high-pitched whistle pierced the air, faint at first, but growing steadily. Kona whimpered.

"What's that sound?" Barry asked.

A pod fell from the sky and landed right at the edge of the bluff.

"Who sent that?" Kim asked. "What's going on? Are there more aliens?"

Reggie kept flying north.

Another pod fell four hundred yards to the left. A third came down beside the rock Tyrell had been standing on.

"Get us in the shuttle," Sierra said. "Now." They needed the other devices. They had to figure out what was happening.

The sled made a rising hundred-and-eighty-degree turn, slipped into the tail, and landed just inside the long tube-like hallway. David and Cameron remained at the controls while the others stepped off, except for Barry, who huddled against his father's back.

Outside the shuttle, pods fell like rain. In the distance, Reggie continued toward the ruins of Fraser. Above him, the cloud layer crept slowly south.

Priya grabbed a control device and turned it on. "It's the people from storage."

"Shit," Cameron said. "Mother fucker."

"What happened?" Barry asked. "I don't understand."

"He made a mistake, Bud," David said. He grasped the boy's hand, clutching his shoulder.

"He's trying to exterminate humanity," Felicia said. "He brought everyone down before we had a chance to burn the gorgers."

"Why?" Barry asked.

"People are terrible," Sierra whispered. Reggie had personified his mantra. She squatted beside Priya. "You have to stop the pods from opening."

"I don't know how," Priya said.

"It's too late," Felicia said.

Sierra turned toward the exit. Pods continued to drop from the sky, but people were already climbing out from the ones that landed first.

"Is Mommy here?" Barry asked.

"I don't know," David said, glancing at Cameron. "We need a plan. What do we do?"

"We don't have time for a plan," Kim said, pointing north. "Look."

Reggie's sled stopped, then moved left across the meadow, toward the west. Beyond him, a dark line flowed down from the ruins of Fraser. From this distance, it was little more than a smudge, but it had to be gorgers. The smudge kept to the shadow of the cloud layer, which extended from the mountains on the left all the way to the town on the right.

"He's drawing them out of the ruins," Cameron said. "All of them."

Hundreds of pods continued to land on the bluff below, with people climbing out of them as fast as they opened.

"It's going to be a bloodbath," Felicia said.

"No, it isn't," Sierra said. She couldn't let that happen. She turned to David and Cameron. "Fly over the pods. Tell everyone to get back in them. We can send them away. Hurry."

"Daddy, I'm scared," Barry said.

"Stay right here with me, Bud. Hang on to me."

They flew out the tail.

Sierra grabbed Priya's shoulder. "Once everyone gets back in, you've got to get those pods out of here."

She looked up from her device. "Where am I supposed to send them?"

"Back to the mothership," Sierra said. "Or Greenland. I don't care. Just get them out of here."

"What's going on?" shouted someone from below. "Where are we?"

Sierra leaned out and looked down. "Get back in your pod. It isn't safe here."

The man looked up at her. "Who the hell are you?"

"How is that thing floating there?" asked someone else, pointing at the giant shuttle.

Sierra felt helpless. Daylight shone across the bluff, but the sun was moving toward the cloudbank. They didn't have long. She shielded her eyes and searched for Reggie. He was little more than a dot crossing the field.

She turned and dug through their pile of supplies, pulled out the binoculars, then darted back to the opening and brought them to her face. She froze, holding her breath. Her toes were out over the hundred-foot drop.

She stepped back and forced herself to slow down.

In the distance, Reggie kneeled on the sled, waving both hands in the air. The line of gorgers marching south had to be two miles long and nearly a quarter mile deep. He had definitely gotten their attention.

"Fuck," Sierra muttered. She lowered the binoculars.

Below, David and Cameron wove back and forth over pods, which were lined up in a grid, like headstones in a cemetery. "How many are there?" Sierra asked.

"David estimated two hundred thousand," Felicia said.

"No, not gorgers. How many people?"

"More than three thousand pods," Priya said. "Maybe ten thousand people."

David and Cameron were shouting that it wasn't safe and urging everyone back in their pods.

"It isn't working," Felicia said.

Most of the crowd gaped at the flying sled, the alien shuttle, and each other. If anyone got back in the pods, it was impossible to tell, because the top halves hid them from view.

"We should go help," Kim said.

Felicia nodded and followed her deeper into the shuttle where they climbed onto another sled.

"I'll go with them," Tyrell said. He grabbed the side with one hand and leaped up on the deck as it passed. They floated out, leaving Sierra and Priya behind.

"There has to be something we can do," Sierra said.

Outside, pods continued to rain down.

Chapter Sixty-Seven

"Get back in your pods," Tyrell shouted. "It isn't safe here."

A sea of faces stared up at him, blank and uncertain. Most of them weren't listening.

He tried to put himself in their shoes. They'd just left a world that was about to be destroyed. The pods had come along, offering a chance to survive, and they *had* survived. Here they were, in this bucolic valley, with no sign of the Ender.

"Please, listen to us," Kim called from the front.

"You have to return to your pods," Felicia shouted.

The pods were spaced out in a grid covering the bluff, with maybe ten feet between them on every side. A few people climbed back in, though it was difficult to tell how many. Others clumped together in small groups. Some stood staring at the twenty-story alien spaceship. A woman in scrubs performed CPR on an old man. Two dogs barked at a cat on top of a pod. Twenty people stood in a circle with their heads bowed, holding hands. Several men with guns were barking orders, but everyone seemed to ignore them. Most of the people below just wandered aimlessly.

Six or seven pods opened down on the banks of the river. Another three dozen had landed on the opposite side. The gorgers marching south from Fraser were maybe an hour away, depending on how quickly the sun went down, but if there were gorgers in the water, the people at the shoreline were already in danger.

"You need to let me off," Tyrell said.

Kim and Felicia both looked back at him.

"I have to get everyone away from the river. We aren't doing any good up here."

"We should check with Sierra first," Kim said.

"There isn't time," he said. "Drop me off, then go across to the other side. Get those people over there to stay back from the water."

The people whose pods had landed on the opposite bank were making their way straight for the river.

"He's right," Felicia said.

They brought the flying car down alongside the sloping bank. People surged toward them. Tyrell pulled his handgun from the holster and shoved it in his pocket. He wasn't about to let it get snatched a second time.

"There's too many people," Kim said. "We can't get any lower."

"This is close enough," Tyrell said. "Get clear." He jumped off onto the slope.

A million questions flew his way.

"Who are you?"

"Where are we?"

"Where's the Ender?"

"What's going on?"

He ignored them and half-ran, half-slid down the gravelly slope. Ten or twelve people stood by the river.

Tyrell waved his arm and shouted, "Get away from the water." He prayed they wouldn't recognize him. If any of them had seen him shoot the old bastard on the golf course, things could get out of hand fast.

More questions poured from everyone around him.

"Who the hell are you?"

"What's wrong with the water?"

"What is this place?"

"There are dangerous creatures in the water," Tyrell said. He didn't try to explain further, because that would only invite more questions. He took the elbow of a gray-haired woman wearing an orange sweater and tried to steer her into a nearby pod.

A middle-aged guy stepped between them. "Don't you lay hands on her," he snapped. A poor excuse for a goatee sprouted around the guy's mouth.

"Is that a spaceship?" Another man pointed over at the shuttle. "Tell me that's some kind of spaceship."

"Yes," Tyrell said. "The people inside it want to help."

"How do you know we can trust them?" asked the woman in the orange sweater.

The guy with the goatee looked down his nose at Tyrell. "How do we know we can trust you?" A lion tattoo covered his forearm.

That was the crux of it. People had learned not to trust each other.

"I'm not going anywhere near a spaceship," said a bald man in his forties or fifties.

Another seven or eight people wandered down the slope to the river's edge.

Tyrell felt powerless and increasingly angry. He gazed across to the opposite bank and forced himself to breathe slowly.

A dark shape moved through the water toward Goatee Guy. When it reached the shadow of the riverbank, its tail broke the surface. A gorger. No one else saw it.

Perfect. After the gorger attacked that asshole, everyone else would finally listen and this madness would end.

He froze. *God. Was he really standing here thinking like that?* His Momma would have been so ashamed.

He charged at Goatee Guy, wrapped his arms around the man's shoulders, and pulled him away from the river. The guy jerked his head back, smashing Tyrell's nose. They both fell to the mud. Tyrell rolled away and popped up on his feet.

Goatee Guy rose, arms wide and fury in his eyes.

Tyrell pointed behind him.

The gorger emerged from the river right where the man had been standing.

"Holy shit, look," shouted someone in the crowd.

Goatee Guy turned around. "What the fuck?"

The pouch under the gorger's neck swelled.

Tyrell pulled his gun from his pocket and fired three shots. The gorger thrashed and fell back into deeper water. He spun around. Hopefully, people would listen to him now.

The gray-haired woman was already climbing back into a pod.

Tyrell went to her. "It's going to be okay. My friends are going to send you away from here. You'll be safe."

She sat looking back at him. A moment of awkward silence passed. "Okay. When?"

He closed his eyes. "Shit." The fallacy of their plan dawned on him. It was all or nothing. They had to get *everyone* back into the pods. He had no way to let Priya know that this one pod, out of three thousand, was ready to go. And up in the shuttle, they couldn't see which pods had people in them.

"What is it?" the woman asked. "What's wrong?"

"Nothing," he said. "Forget the pods." He helped her climb out and pointed up the bluff. "You need to get up there and stay in the crowd." His throat felt tight. He might be sending this poor lady to her death.

Goatee Guy took the woman's hand. "Come on."

"The rest of you, go with them," Tyrell said. "Get up top and stay together."

"Hey mister." The bald guy grabbed Tyrell's shoulder and shook it. "There's more people over there, by the water."

He spun around. Further upstream, two other pods opened right next to the river. A big bearded man in a plaid shirt peered from one while an extended family climbed out of the other.

All Tyrell could do was get people away from the water. Sierra and the others would have to figure out the rest. He ran upstream.

The bearded man, still in his pod, sounded stoned. "What's going on here? Who are you? Where am I?" He was dressed like some kind of tough-guy lumberjack but he cowered in his pod like a terrified kitten.

"You need to get away from the river," Tyrell said. "Hurry."

In the other pod, a guy who looked eighty stumbled as he climbed down, then turned to help a woman who looked even older. Tyrell ran to them. At least three people were still inside.

"Come on, ma'am," he said. He took her elbow and helped her over the lip.

Her slippers landed in the mud of the riverbank and she teetered forward. Tyrell held onto her until she caught her balance.

"Thank you, thank you," her husband said, in an accent that sounded eastern European.

A curly-haired boy of about ten scooted out of the pod with a baby in his arms.

The lumberjack, who'd finally found enough courage to get out of his pod, wandered over. "What's the story here?" A glaze covered his eyes.

"Everyone needs to get away from the river," Tyrell said.

The man nodded. "Got it." He didn't move.

Tyrell pushed him toward the slope. "Go."

"Got it," the man repeated. He began to climb, following the elderly couple, the boy holding the baby, and the rest of the family.

Tyrell looked upstream and downstream. There weren't any other pods by the river, and no one else had wandered down. He started up after them.

"Help," cried a voice behind him.

Tyrell spun.

A woman with dreadlocks sat in the lumberjack's pod. "Where am I?"

"Ah, shit," the lumberjack muttered, tugging at his beard. He froze on the slope.

Tyrell held up both hands. "Just stay there. I'll get her."

He jogged back to the pod, where the woman was leaning out over the river, looking down.

Tyrell waded in until the water was up to his shins and grabbed her by the arm. "Come on." A cherubic smile spread across her face. She was white, like almost everyone else here, and appeared to be stoned out of her mind, but for a brief moment, her smile made him think of his Momma.

He helped her out of the pod and ushered her onto the bank. He hoped his Momma would have been proud.

A gorger burst from the river behind him, sending water everywhere. It struck him in the ass, knocking him against the woman. She stumbled toward the slope.

Tyrell went down hard, getting a face full of dirt. He scrambled and pulled, trying to get to his feet, but jagged points came down on his back, pressing him into the cold wet mud.

Chapter Sixty-Eight

Sierra brought the binoculars back to her face. Reggie's sled had come to a stop out in the middle of the field, a foot or two above the grass. He stood with his arms at his sides. The shadow beneath the clouds was just beyond him, along with the line of gorgers.

"Get out of there," she whispered. There was still time for him to do the right thing. "Fly over them. Lead them back to the town."

The wall of gorgers converged on the sled. Reggie dropped to his knees and curled into a ball as they swarmed him.

She lowered the binoculars.

He was more than a mile away, too far to hear his screams.

The rest of the line kept creeping south. "Why are they still coming?" Sierra asked. "I thought they were just bugs."

"They're sentient enough to see us as a target," Priya said, her face buried in the control device. "Some insects will do that."

"We have to use the fuel," Sierra said. "We have to bomb them."

Priya looked up. "We don't have nearly enough. The gorgers are way too spread out."

The approaching wave was nearly three miles long now.

"It'll buy time," Sierra said. "We can bring down more shuttles and make a wall around the crowd."

"The shuttles don't land, they hover," Priya said. "The gorgers will run right under them."

"We have to think of something," Sierra said.

"Has *anyone* gotten back in the pods?" Priya asked.

Sierra looked down at the bluff and shrugged. "There's no way to know. There's still a huge crowd down there."

"What if I try to stun everyone?" Priya suggested. "We can get the others to land and gather them up."

"We'd never get them all in time."

"Maybe we need to think about saving just some of them," Priya said.

"No," Sierra said. "There has to be another way."

David and Cameron floated up, positioning their sled right outside the shuttle's tail.

"It isn't working," Cameron said. "Only a handful got back in the pods."

"Which ones?" Priya asked.

"I don't know," Cameron said. "There's too many. It's chaos."

"Wait, where's Kim?" David asked. Barry clung to his back.

"She and Felicia took the other sled," Sierra said. "They're over by the river."

"What?" David craned his neck, looking off to the right. "Get her back here. Now."

"Those gorgers will be here in less than an hour," Cameron said.

"If we drop the fuel on them, can you light it?" Sierra asked.

David continued staring off to the right. He must have spotted the other sled, because he no longer looked like he was about to explode.

"We can light it," Cameron said. "But we don't have nearly enough."

"You got any better ideas?" Sierra snapped. They were wasting too much time.

Cameron scowled. "No. Do it." She turned to David. "Let's head out."

"What about Kim?"

"She'll be fine," Cameron said.

It was clear that Cameron was telling him what he wanted to hear, and equally clear that he knew it.

"You have to go," Sierra said.

Cameron held up a finger. "Wait. Give me the spears."

Sierra ran to the stack of supplies and grabbed the sticks they had collected when they scouted the gas station. She stepped right up to the edge of the tail and handed them to Cameron. "What are you going to do with these?"

"Torches," Cameron said. She placed the sticks on the sled between her and David. "You guys drop the fuel. We'll light it up."

The sled banked away.

Sierra turned to Priya. "Hurry."

Priya tapped her device. "I already got one detached. Help me figure out where to send it."

A moment later, one of the giant bubbles floated over the crowd, drawing a fresh volley of shouts and questions. A gunshot rang out, followed by the zing of a ricochet.

"Hold your fire!" Sierra yelled. If the gunfire punctured the sphere, the people shooting at it would douse themselves in a torrent of napalm.

The giant orb floated north across the plains, then stopped.

Sierra raised the binoculars. "Keep going. Twice that far." The sphere started moving again, drifting along like a giant pink bubble.

When it stopped a second time, it was just past the advancing wave of gorgers. "Bring it back a hundred feet," Sierra said.

Priya tapped again. The bubble reversed course.

"Perfect," Sierra said. "Drop it."

Out in the center of the meadow, the big round hole irised open on the side of the sphere and black sludge poured out as it descended. It landed in sunlight, ahead of the gorgers, but only barely.

"Come on, Cameron," Sierra whispered. "Light it up."

Chapter Sixty-Nine

Cameron fumbled the firestarter round from her shirt pocket and plunged it into the chamber of her Beretta.

The giant sphere landed right in front of the approaching gorgers.

David glanced over. "What are you going to do, shoot it?" Barry pressed against his back, arms wrapped around his chest.

"I'm going to try," Cameron said.

"Bullets don't work that way, do they?"

David wasn't exactly a gun nut. She was impressed he knew enough to ask the question.

"This one does." She'd stuffed a wad of cloth into the cartridge where the bullet normally sat. "This is the one I rigged to start a fire on the island with the sailbacks."

He nodded.

The wall of gorgers was minutes from the sphere.

"Let's land right in front of that thing," Cameron said.

"Land?" David shook his head. "We can't land."

"We have to," she said. "I need to dip these sticks in the fuel. Trust me. We'll be fine."

He frowned but didn't argue. They nosed downward and came to a stop twenty feet from the giant sphere. Thick black goop oozed from the circular opening, like tar.

The wall of gorgers was a dozen yards behind it, keeping right at the edge of the shadow. A few creatures on the front line leapt forward, throwing themselves into the sunlight, which lit them up briefly before they fell back into the shade.

Cameron grabbed the bundle of spears and jumped down. "Stay here."

"Yeah, no problem," David said.

She raced forward. The bitter smell of oil burned her nostrils. Diesel pooled around the massive orb like blood around a corpse. She dropped her sticks on dry grass next to the closest puddle, then grabbed one and snapped it over her knee.

The gorgers rustled and clacked as they inched toward her. More and more of them tested the sunlight, stirred up by her presence. The shadow of the cloudbank inched closer.

"Hurry," Barry shouted from the carriage.

"Yeah, no shit," Cameron muttered. She snapped each stick in two, turning six into twelve. When she was done, she grabbed them all at once and dipped one end of the bundle in the fuel.

"Come on," David said.

The wall of gorgers reached the sphere.

She hefted the bundle under her left arm, trying to keep the diesel from dripping on her.

Gorgers spilled around the sphere, some stabbing their way through the tarry muck. One got shoved and fell over. It picked itself up and continued forward, black and slimy.

Cameron aimed her Beretta at the closest puddle, only a foot away. "This better work." She pulled the trigger.

The shot rang out like a normal round and flames burst forward. "Bitchin'."

Yellow fire covered the pool of diesel. Cameron didn't wait to watch it spread. The gorgers were too close. She turned and ran to the carriage.

"Hurry, hurry, hurry," Barry shouted.

Cameron raced around to the co-pilot's side and dropped the torches on the back of the carriage, with the dry ends close to Barry. "Hold on to these, kid." She jumped aboard. Her hands went immediately to the controls.

David was ready. They lifted off as the first of the gorgers reached them.

Below, flames spread across the fuel puddled around the sphere. At least two dozen gorgers were on fire.

Two dozen wasn't enough. They only had fifteen more spheres. Not nearly enough.

An explosion bellowed from the sphere, sending a bright orange fireball into the air. The blast pummeled the carriage. Pieces of gorgers flew everywhere.

"What happened?" Barry shouted as the carriage bucked from the shockwave. One hand clenched a fist-full of David's shirt and the other was holding onto the sticks behind him. God bless the little bugger.

"The flames reached the sphere and it blew up," Cameron said. Deep black smoke rose from a crater the size of a football field.

"How many did we kill?" David asked.

Cameron shrugged. "A thousand. Maybe more." It was better than a couple of dozen, but it still wasn't enough.

"Another one's coming," Barry said.

A second sphere floated toward them, with a third right behind it.

"Can you see Kim and Felicia?" David asked.

"No," Barry said. "Maybe they found Mommy."

Cameron scowled.

"It's a long shot, Bud," David said. "You know that."

"Kim says Minnesota had more pods than anywhere," Barry said. "She found one. I know she did."

Cameron changed the subject. "I can see Kim. She's still in the air."

Below, the line of gorgers pressed forward, keeping right at the edge of the shadow. She shoved the Beretta in her pocket. She'd only made one firestarter round, and David was right, normal bullets didn't start fires.

"We need to drop back down again," she said.

"Why?" David and Barry asked at the same time.

"We have to use those flames to light a torch."

They descended.

A few stragglers wandered along the edges of the blast zone, but most of the gorgers had passed the crater, continuing their march toward the bluff.

The carriage floated down to the middle, where flames sputtered in the dirt.

"Hand me a torch," Cameron said, reaching back with one hand.

The dry end of a stick smacked her palm. She grabbed it and leaned over the side, holding the fuel-soaked end over the closest flame. It lit right up.

"Straight ascent," David said.

Cameron fumbled for the controls with her free hand and the carriage rose.

The next sphere had already dropped to the ground.

"Get a second torch ready," Cameron shouted over her shoulder. "Just one."

"Roger that," Barry shouted back.

They flew to the second sphere as the third one dropped, splashing fuel all around it.

"Light your torch off mine and hang onto it," she said, reaching back. Barry's stick knocked into hers.

"Got it," Barry said. "It's lit."

"Hang onto that one for me," she said. "Keep it away from the others."

"Nice job, Bud," David said. "You're doing great."

Cameron flung her torch over the side as they passed above the second sphere.

"Did it catch?" David asked.

"Yeah," Barry shouted.

"Hand me the lit torch and get a new one ready," Cameron said, reaching back. "Just like before. We should always have two of them lit, one for me to throw and one that you have ready."

"Roger that," Barry said again.

They arrived at the third sphere right as the second one exploded. The mass of gorgers was even thicker around this one.

Cameron smiled as dead gorgers flew through the air. They didn't have enough fuel to kill them all, but she was damn sure going to kill as many as she could.

Chapter Seventy

Tyrell twisted onto his side, kicking blindly. His boot made contact with the gorger attacking him and he kicked again. He reached for his gun. It was gone.

The gorger's pincers clamped on his boot and all ten legs jabbed into the muck, pulling him toward the river. Gravel scraped his back as his t-shirt rode up to his shoulders.

He looked around for help.

The stoned woman he'd just saved ran up the hill. Her lumberjack buddy snatched her in his arms.

Tyrell clutched at the ground to stop moving, but his fingers furrowed through the mud. The water came up to his crotch. He flexed his foot, trying to slide it from the boot. The laces were tied tight all the way up the ankle, just like they'd taught him in the Air Force. The gorger's pincers gripped the boot like a vice.

He bent forward, reaching, hoping to pound the gorger in the head, or pry its mouth open, or something, anything. It jerked again, pulling him further. Cold water chilled his sides, shocking his breath from him. He flailed, trying to think of anything he could do to get free. Water splashed everywhere as the gorger dragged him deeper.

A stout branch slammed into the back of the creature, just behind its mouth. The pulling stopped.

The stick came down again, even harder, and the gorger released Tyrell's foot.

He scrambled out of the water.

Goatee Guy raised the stick high overhead and brought it down on the gorger again and again until it retreated into the river, gurgling and hissing.

"Come on." Goatee Guy extended his hand.

Tyrell clasped his arm, right on the lion tattoo, and Goatee Guy pulled him to his feet. They ran up the slope together. Several people cheered.

At the top of the bluff, Tyrell doubled over, desperate for air. "Thanks," he gasped.

"Of course," Goatee Guy said. "We gotta look out for each other, right?" He slapped him on the shoulder and took off, leaving Tyrell behind.

To the west, columns of smoke rose above the meadow, some with big round mushroom clouds at the top. They were setting off the firebombs. Throngs of people wandered between the pods, many of them shouting questions at each other. Most were congregating on the far side of the bluff, watching the wall of advancing gorgers.

"Tyrell!" The shout came from Kim. He spun. The flying car floated toward him from the far side of the river.

He waved his arms. "Kim! Felicia!"

They dropped down near the edge of the bluff.

Dozens of people surged toward them, shouting.

"Get us out of here."

"Pick me up."

"Help. Do something."

Tyrell and Felicia locked eyes. If they tried to pick him up, the flying car would be swamped.

He shook his head and waved them away. He had to stay here. He would help as many people as he could. Maybe it would atone for what he'd done in Cheyenne Mountain.

Kim's eyebrows drew tight and her mouth cinched, forming an anguished square.

The flying car lifted off.

"Don't leave us."

"Wait!"

"Come back!"

The mass of people shifted across the bluff as Kim and Felicia rose toward the tail of the shuttle.

A white-haired man in a blue zipper jacket remained behind, staring at Tyrell. "Do you know them? What the hell is going on here?" He looked too young to have hair so white.

"We need to keep people away from the water," Tyrell said.

A syringe sat in the man's breast pocket. He pulled one side of his jacket over the needle. "Don't worry, it's just insulin."

Tyrell swallowed. The poor bastard wasn't going to last long if he needed insulin, and based on the way he was twitching, he was overdue for a dose.

A sliver of hope occurred to him. Maybe the healing slime on the mothership could cure diabetes. Of course, the guy still had to survive the day somehow.

The white-haired man pointed across the meadow. "Those things are coming this way, aren't they?"

Tyrell nodded.

"What are we supposed to do?"

"Tell everyone to stay together. Try to get people with guns to the front lines."

The man scowled. "What are you doing?"

"I'm just trying to keep people away from the river."

Downstream, beneath the shuttle's wing, another group wandered toward the shoreline. Tyrell started after them.

Chapter Seventy-One

Priya looked up from the control device. Out on the meadow, gorgers continued to stream between the blast craters. Their progress was blocked and their numbers were thinning, at least in the middle of the line, but there were still tens of thousands on the sides. Kona lay next to her, resting her muzzle on her paws the way she always did when David was away. Priya had just sent out the first two firebombs from the second cluster, which meant only six remained. The sun shone through columns of smoke and was dropping dangerously close to the cloud bank.

"Send one directly between the last two, but in front of them by the same distance," Sierra said. She stood gazing out with the binoculars.

Priya turned back to her device, where a rough grid appeared. She selected the spot. "Done. What about the next one?"

"Just to the left of that one," Sierra said. "Half the distance forward."

"Got it."

Kona flinched as one of the bombs exploded. "It's okay, girl," Priya said. She tapped her device and sent a firebomb to the position Sierra had indicated.

"Nice work." Sierra lowered the lenses. "If they light those two up, the middle charge will be completely cut off."

"What do we do about the sides?"

"I don't know," Sierra said.

Priya looked up again. The flank on the right, coming down alongside the river, was much closer than the flank coming in from the west.

"I'm going to drop the last four on the eastern flank," Priya said. "If Cameron times it right, we can take out most of them on that side."

"What about the left side?" Sierra asked.

"There's nothing we can do," Priya said. "We don't have enough firebombs. This is the best use of what we've got."

Sierra stared at her, uncertainty on her face.

"I'm sure," Priya said.

"Okay. Do it."

Priya craned her neck to choose the first spot on her own, then looked down at her device. She detached a firebomb and sent it out.

"There has to be something else we can do," Sierra said, not for the first time.

"Sierra! Priya!" The shouts came from Kim. It sounded like she was floating right outside the tail, but Priya didn't look up. She had to keep her eyes on the device or she would lose sight of the correct spot. She detached the second firebomb and sent it next to the first one.

"We convinced everyone on the far side of the river to get back in their pods," Kim said.

"Thirty-seven pods," Felicia added.

"Great," Sierra said. "Priya, send them away."

Priya held up her don't-interrupt-me finger. She sent out firebomb number three.

"Hey, wait," Sierra said. "Where's Tyrell?"

"We dropped him off so he could get people away from the water," Kim said.

"You can't leave him down there," Sierra said. "Go get him."

"We tried," Felicia said. "The crowd was going to swamp us. Everyone wanted to get onboard."

"The sleds," Sierra said. "That's it. Priya, bring down the other sleds from the mothership. We can use them to lift everyone out."

"I've already thought of that," Priya said. "It won't work." She'd done more than just think about it. She'd actually figured out how to adjust the mothership's orbit, sending it to a position directly over Western Canada. It was an astounding accomplishment, but it wasn't anything she should brag about, considering the current situation.

She'd been in the process of remotely moving carriages into shuttles up in the mothership when she realized there weren't nearly enough for ten thousand people. "Each carriage can only hold ten adults, and there are only a few dozen carriages."

"Then bring down the rest of the shuttles," Felicia said. "We can ferry them into the shuttles with the carriages."

"That would take hours," Priya said. "We don't have that long." She tapped the device, sending the fourth and final sphere out to the field. "There. The last firebomb is on its way. It's up to Cameron and David now."

"Did you get the pods on the other side of the river?" Sierra asked.

"I'm working on it," Priya said, annoyed by the barrage of demands. She maneuvered the map to show the far side of the river and selected all thirty-seven pods, then zoomed out to the west. She selected the mountaintop where they had landed a few days earlier to remove Kim and Tyrell's implants. "There. They should be lifting off."

"Yes," Kim said. Based on the shouting below, the crowd had noticed as well.

Thirty-seven out of more than three thousand pods was only one percent. It wasn't much.

"You have to go get Tyrell," Sierra said. "Find a way to pick him up. Get his attention and meet him at a spot away from everyone else."

"Okay, we'll try," Felicia said.

The carriage dropped away to the right, disappearing from view.

"There's still a wall of gorgers coming in from the west," Sierra said. "We have to do something."

"We aren't going to be able to save everyone," Priya said.

"We need another plan," Sierra said. "We need another weapon."

"I'm sorry," Priya said. Dread inched up her spine. When the gorgers reached the crowd below, they wouldn't be able to do anything but watch.

"Wait a minute," Sierra said. "I have an idea. Bring up storage."

Chapter Seventy-Two

Tyrell ran along the edge of the bluff, following the river south. His path took him under one of the shuttle's wings and away from the bulk of the crowd. Some fifteen people had broken off and gathered down by the water. At least half of them were armed.

They stood around the body of a gorger with a dozen holes on its back. Mustard-y fluid leaked onto the mud. Three people lay dead nearby, covered in ghastly wounds.

Tyrell scampered down the slope. "You have to get away from the water."

"That's what I've been telling 'em," said a pudgy man holding a rifle. His cheeks were so red he looked sunburned.

A couple in their early twenties stood shouting at each other. "We never should have gotten in that capsule," the woman yelled. Spittle flew into the man's face.

"We had to get away from the comet," he shouted back at her, jabbing his finger at the sky.

"Let's swim across the river," said an older guy with his pants hitched up to his ribs. "It's a warzone on this side."

Tyrell held up his hands. "You can't." He pointed to the gorger. "These things hide in the water. It isn't safe."

"See, that's what I told you," said the twenty-something woman, still yelling in her partner's face.

Tyrell gestured down at the dead gorger. "That warzone is my friends trying to bomb these bastards."

"How do you know all this?" asked the older man. Curly gray mutton chops framed his face.

"I got here before the rest of you," Tyrell said, trying to think of a way to prove himself.

A gangly teen-aged boy with a face full of pimples squinted at him. "Hey, I know you. I've seen you before."

Tyrell tensed. The kid must have seen the golf course footage. His fingers curled into fists. "It isn't what you—"

The teen cut him off and wagged his finger toward Tyrell's chest. "This guy jumped off one of those flying cars." He looked around at the others. "He's with those people up there. I saw him."

Tyrell's fists unclenched, tension flowing out through his fingertips. "Yes. I'm with them."

The teen nodded. "I saw him helping a bunch of people."

Behind him, a gorger sprang from the water.

The pudgy guy swung his rifle off his arm and opened fire. At least half of the group joined him. The gorger jerked like a marionette and disappeared beneath the surface.

"Got him," exclaimed the guy with the mutton chops.

"That's why everybody has to stay away from the water," Tyrell said.

Several of the others nodded.

"What should we do?" asked the guy with the pink cheeks.

Tyrell forced himself to take a breath before answering. They were looking to him for direction. He could hardly believe it. "We need to defend all those people up there. We need everyone with guns on the front lines. We gotta keep people together and keep them calm." He looked down at the bullet-ridden gorger in the mud. "And you all need to conserve ammo. There's thousands of them."

"Then what?" asked the twenty-something woman.

"My friends are working on a plan to get everyone to safety. We have to buy them time." There was a hell of a lot of wishful thinking in this last part, but it was all he had to offer.

He took another breath, steeling himself for arguments and rebuttals.

The pudgy guy reached up and clapped him on the shoulder. "All right then, let's go."

Tyrell couldn't believe his ears. These people trusted him. They were listening to him.

The group started up the slope, leaving behind the bodies of the people who had been killed.

"What can you tell us about these things?" asked the pimply kid.

"One on one, they aren't too bad," Tyrell said.

"We figured that out, didn't we, boys?" said the old man with the mutton chops.

"Don't let them puke on you," Tyrell added. "It's some kind of stomach acid."

They crested the slope, arriving at the vast field of pods, each one sitting with its top half floating in the air. A dozen columns of smoke rose in the distance.

"Any weaknesses?" asked the man with the pink cheeks.

"They don't like bright light. They keep out of the sun."

Out in the meadow, the line of gorgers was broken in the middle, but large waves still approached from each side. In the sky, the sun was slipping past the cloudbank.

"Looks like we got fifteen minutes of sunlight," said the pimply teen. "Then what?"

Tyrell's chest felt hollow. "We have to hold them off."

Chapter Seventy-Three

Another firebomb exploded with a satisfying boom. A flash of heat licked the back of Cameron's neck. The bombs were perfect. Gallons and gallons of fuel splashed out when they opened, saturating the area, but enough remained inside to trigger a hell of an explosion. Too bad they were almost gone.

"Four more coming," Barry shouted from the back. He held the final torch.

They would light one more bomb and then they'd have to search for something they could use to light the other three.

"It isn't going to be enough," David said.

He was right. They had hit the center of the gorger attack hard, but there were still thousands. Even in the middle, several hundred streamed around the craters, working their way to the front edge of the shadow.

Maybe fifteen minutes of direct sunlight remained. Once the sun passed behind the clouds, the gorgers could run across the rest of the meadow without anything to stop them.

"They're landing in a row," Barry said.

Cameron looked over her shoulder as the carriage circled. Each of the last four firebombs set down adjacent to the previous one, with a hundred feet between them, forming a line in front of the eastern flank, all the way to the river.

She smiled. Sierra and Priya had turned out to be solid battlefield tacticians.

"Let's light up the first one," she said. "They're close to each other. A chain reaction should set off the other three." They wouldn't need any more torches.

"Sounds good," David said. "Down ten degrees."

It would buy them time, but Cameron didn't know what to do with that time. There were still far too many gorgers to drop concrete blocks on.

The crowd had thickened along the front edge of the bluff, watching the action. It might be possible to airlift people away, handful by handful, but there was no way they could get everyone. It would be ugly.

"It's out!" Barry shouted. "No, no, no. It's gone out."

Cameron looked back. Barry held a charred, smoking stick. The last torch had either blown out or burned out. "Fuck."

"What do we do?" Barry asked.

She pulled out Josh's hunting knife. "We land and I light the fuel with a flint."

David's eyes widened. "No. It's too dangerous. The sun will be gone any minute. The gorgers are too close."

"We have to," Cameron said. "Those are the last four bombs. If we don't light them now, the gorgers will get past them and they'll be useless."

He worked his jaw, then reached for the controls to start the descent. Cameron matched his movement.

"You have to make it back," David said as they approached the closest sphere.

"Why? 'Cause you're worried about me, or 'cause you can't fly away without my help." She winked at him.

"Not funny."

She smiled. "Back in a jiffy." She jumped down before they came to a stop, holding the knife out to her side so she wouldn't skewer herself if she tripped.

She ran toward the firebomb and slid to her knees in front of the nearest oily smear.

The end of the knife handle wouldn't move when she tried to unscrew it. She couldn't get a decent grip because her fingers were covered with blisters from one of the torches.

"Open up!" she yelled, banging it against the ground. It loosened. She unscrewed it all the way and the flint spilled out somewhere in the grass. "Fuck."

Gorgers clicked and hissed on the other side of the sphere, an endless row of gaping mouths and teeth.

"Come on, Cameron," David shouted.

"That doesn't fucking help," she muttered, slapping the ground. Her hand closed on the flint.

She brought it up and slid it against the knife blade in one quick motion. Sparks rained onto the fuel. It lit instantly. Yellow flames raced across the field toward the firebomb.

"Oh, shit." She jerked to her feet. She was way too close. It would explode in seconds.

"Hurry," Barry shouted.

"Also not helping." She pumped her arms hard.

"Let's go," David said as she climbed aboard.

She plopped onto her seat, legs folded, and reached for the controls.

The line of gorgers parted around the firebomb, coming right for them.

"Forward climb," David said. "Full speed." They shot ahead, rising, but still only a few feet above the ground. "Hang onto me, bud."

The sound and heat of the explosion hit simultaneously. Cameron slapped at the console, trying to find something to hold onto. Her fingers brushed the surface, the carriage dropped out from under her, and she tumbled through the air.

Chapter Seventy-Four

Frank wandered among the pods. Thousands of pods. Thousands of people, too, and none of them knew what the fuck was going on. Not a single one had recognized him, either. Frank Fucking Wharton. He'd been on magazine covers, for Christ's sake.

He'd followed the Black guy for a while, because he seemed to know the people in the flying cars, but then it seemed like he was just running around helping the rubes.

Frank needed to talk to people in charge.

Nobody here even knew where they were. It sure as hell looked like Earth, but the Ender was gone and there was a huge silver alien thing floating right there beside them. He couldn't decide if it was a building or some kind of giant granddaddy pod.

He pulled out his coke bullet, took another snort, and started across the bluff toward it. Obviously, that giant silver thing was something special.

Each time an explosion went off, Frank felt like he was going to jump out of his skin. The coke made him as jittery as a honkey in Harlem. There was a war going on and Frank had to get off the battlefield.

A cop ran past, her hand over her sidearm.

"Wait," Frank called out. "Officer."

The goddamn cop didn't even stop to look back. She just headed toward the edge of the hill, in the direction of the explosions.

It seemed like nearly a quarter of the people here had guns, but Frank kept his hidden. Except for the ketamine syringe, it was all he had.

What he needed was one of those flying cars. He deserved one. If he could get hold of one, he'd be in charge within a week. He just needed ten minutes with the people aboard them. He'd figure out what they wanted and convince them he could make it happen.

As he got closer, Frank still couldn't make any sense of the giant metallic artifact. A long narrow tube jutted out over the meadow, high above. The tube widened at the far end into a big bulbous ball, a lot like the pods, but shiny silver and as tall as a twenty-story building.

A hundred people had gathered directly below the end of the tube, looking up at it. Frank walked over to them. "What's going on here?" he asked.

"There's an opening up there," someone said. "There are people inside."

Frank lit up. *That's* where he needed to be.

Another ten or twenty people crowded around the lowest part of the artifact, which wasn't even touching the ground. It just floated there. Several people had their hands on it.

Frank turned back to look up at the skinny part. "Who are those people?" he asked. "Have they said anything?"

"Earlier, they were shouting for us to get back in our pods," said the stranger.

"Why didn't you?"

The man pointed to the closest pods. Faces looked out from beneath the top halves, which just floated there. "A bunch of people got in, but nothing happened."

Frank grunted. It sounded like the people in the artifact couldn't be trusted. "How do we get up there?" he asked.

"You can't," said a woman in a long dress. "We're waiting for them to come down and get us. You need to get in line."

Frank glared at her. He was not the sort of person who waited in line.

Out on the battlefield, a flying car zipped back and forth. It seemed to be triggering the explosions somehow. Frank wasn't sure how many flying cars were out there. They raced all around and it was tough to see everything clearly with the tops of those goddamn pods floating in the air.

One of the flying cars swooped down near the front of the bluff. That was his ticket up to the artifact. He sure as hell wasn't going to stand in line. He could barely stand still for ten seconds after all the coke he'd snorted. He started back across the bluff without another word to the sorry bastards waiting behind him.

He wove between pods and quickly lost sight of the flying car. A commotion off to the right distracted him. He detoured in that direction to see if anyone there had any answers.

"Nope," Frank said when he reached the group. Instead of answers, what they had was a poor son of a bitch lying on the ground without any legs.

A man in a bright orange Denver Broncos jersey stood over the body, like he was holding court or something. "And then the pod cut 'em right off," he explained "Right fuckin' off."

Frank looked down at the amputee, who was shirtless and staring up at the sky. "Is he dead?"

"Are you serious?" the Broncos fan asked.

His tone was so fucking condescending, Frank almost drew his gun and put him on the ground, too.

He squeezed his eyes with his thumb and fingers. He needed to keep his cool better than that. He also probably needed to lay off the goddamn nose candy.

"We should put a blanket over him," said a woman in a yellow shirt. "We can't just leave him there."

"We should feed him to those things," said a tall guy who looked like he lived in front of a computer. "That way, maybe they won't eat us."

"That's disgusting," said the Broncos fan.

The woman in the yellow shirt cocked her head. "It might be smart, though."

"What things?" asked a Mexican woman holding an open umbrella. Why in the fuck did she need a goddamn umbrella?

The tall computer guy pointed to the river. "Giant scorpion things. They live in the water here."

"What about the things in the meadow?" asked the woman in the yellow shirt.

"I think they're the same thing," said the Broncos fan.

"What things in the meadow?" the Mexican asked.

Frank hurried away. These rubes were even more clueless than the rest. He passed another handful of pods, wondering if he was still going in the right direction.

"Tyrell!" A shout came from above and behind. He spun around.

One of the flying cars headed toward him with two girls aboard. His luck had finally turned. They were the same girls who'd been talking to the Black guy earlier.

Finally. He had this. Frank Wharton had it in the bag. He skittered around a child crying on the ground and ran toward them.

"Hey," he waved. "I saw Tyrell. I know where he is." The flying car slowed and hovered above him.

The girl on the right was only a kid, with short brown hair, about the same age as the girls he'd abducted in Jersey. The girl on the left was in her twenties or thirties, with brown skin and thick black curls. She looked like another Mexican.

"Where?" the kid asked.

"Young Black guy, right," Frank said. "Cargo pants and a t-shirt."

"Yes." The girl's face lit up. "Where is he?"

Several people crowded around Frank. A larger bunch moved directly beneath the flying car.

"Let me on and I'll show you," Frank said.

"Point to him," demanded the older girl. "Which way?"

Frank hated her instantly. He didn't like anyone making demands of him, especially not a brown-skinned bitch. He ignored her and faced the younger girl. "I'll take you right to him. Just pick me up." His hand trembled. He wondered if he'd overdone it with the coke.

The young girl looked at her friend. "Felicia, I think he can help."

He bit down a smile. He almost had her.

The crowd continued to surge beneath them. Soon, there'd be too many people for them to pick him up without getting mobbed.

"Hurry. I know right where he is," Frank said.

Another explosion came from the big open field. The crowd turned to look that way. Fucking sheep.

"Let's pick him up," the girl said.

He reached for her, curling his fingers in a come-closer gesture.

The older bitch, who was looking off toward the explosion, grabbed the younger one on the shoulder. "Shit. David just went down."

The little girl's eyebrows angled up toward each other. "Go, go, go," she said.

The flying car banked and rocketed away.

"Goddamn it," Frank said, lowering his arm. He'd been so close.

A second explosion boomed over on the meadow, followed by a third, and a fourth. They really were lighting shit up over there.

He took another snort of blow, just to keep his wits about him, and wandered in that direction to see what was going on. He had to find that Tyrell fucker again. When he found him, he'd finally have a bargaining chip.

Chapter Seventy-Five

David crawled through the tall grass, his ears ringing so much he could barely think. The ground seemed to teeter beneath him. His wrist throbbed and his ankle screamed if he tried to flex it too far. How did he get here? He squeezed his eyes shut. The carriage. He'd tumbled across the ground after being blown off the carriage. Burning gorgers lay dying all around him.

"Daddy!"

Barry. Oh, God, Barry had been on the carriage with him. He popped up his head and saw three things at once.

His son staggered across the meadow, spattered with blood.

The carriage floated twenty feet off the ground. It looked undamaged, but there wasn't any way they could get to it.

The sun had finally passed beyond the clouds, leaving only flat, late-day light.

He lurched to his feet. "Barry!" The ankle was definitely sprained. Maybe even fractured.

Barry turned at the sound of his name and ran over. Cuts covered one side of his face, along with his arms and legs, but they looked superficial.

David dropped to his knees as they collided, wrapping his arms around his son, trying to squeeze him tight and be gentle at the same time. He inhaled the boy's smell, a mixture of sweat and dirt and something else that was simply "Barry."

"I'm scared," Barry said.

"I know, Bud. Me too."

Fresh columns of smoke rose where the last four firebombs had exploded. The meadow stank of burning diesel. They'd done everything they could. They'd pulverized two thirds of the gorger line, from the river all the way out past the middle of the meadow. It wasn't enough. Plenty of stragglers remained in the area and a massive swarm continued to surge in from the west. They'd bought time for the people on the bluff, but it simply wasn't enough.

"I want Mommy."

"I know, Bud. Me too," David repeated.

Two hundred yards away, gorgers wove between the craters and flames, scrambling closer. There was no longer a wall of them in this part of the meadow, but there were far more than an unarmed man and a six-year-old boy could handle.

The bluff was at least a quarter mile away. It would take ten minutes to walk that far with his injured ankle. The gorgers would reach him and Barry in half that time.

Unless ...

If Barry ran the whole way, he might make it. Especially if David served as a diversion.

He cupped his son's face. "I need you to run to those other people."

Barry shook his head. "I can't leave you."

"You have to. Go look for Mommy. Go find her for me." David didn't believe Lindsey was actually there. He couldn't allow himself to get his hopes up, but it was the one thing that might get Barry moving.

Barry looked at him, his face a desperate mixture of hope and despair. "I can't. I'm too scared."

Gunshots came from behind. David spun, sending aches into his neck and back. Cameron stood over a gorger that had gotten ahead of the others. It slumped to the ground.

He raised his hand and she staggered over.

"Are you okay?" she asked. Blood dripped from her nose.

"Not really. How many rounds do you have?"

"Two," she said, her lower lip quivering.

"What about your other gun? You always have another gun."

She scowled. "Not this time."

The closest gorgers scampered toward them through the burned grassland, now a hundred yards away. They would be here in minutes.

Cameron held up the gun. "I could ... you know."

All of the air spilled from David's lungs. The thought horrified him, more than anything he could imagine.

No. The thought of acidic bile dissolving his son's flesh while he was eaten alive was even worse.

"Barry, you have to run." If he didn't go now, he wouldn't make it.

"*Da-a-ddy,*" Barry sobbed.

He grabbed his son's hands, hissing as pain jolted his wrist, and pushed him out to arm's length. "You have to."

Somewhere above, another whistling sound began.

Barry looked up. "Do you hear that?"

A tiny object twinkled against the blue sky, high enough to catch the sun's rays.

"That's a pod," Cameron said.

"I thought Reggie brought down all the pods," Barry said.

The bright shape grew larger. It was coming straight toward them and growing larger. Much larger.

One of the gorgers broke into a run, galloping in their direction. Several others followed behind it.

The sound shifted to a pulsing hum, creating the impression of deceleration.

David grabbed Barry and pulled him back into his arms.

A round white object as big as a two-story house slammed into the ground with an Earth-shattering boom, crushing the charging gorger.

The shockwave from the impact knocked David off his knees. He fell sideways into the coarse grass, still clutching Barry. Cameron raised her gun.

A horizontal line appeared halfway up the enormous pod. The top lifted, revealing a monstrous shadow inside.

Three gorgers circled around it, still heading for David, Cameron, and Barry. Eight or ten more followed behind them.

The shadow moved inside the pod.

Cameron pulled David to his feet. "We need to get some distance."

The gorgers passed the pod, on a beeline straight for them.

A forty-foot-long *Tyrannosaurus rex* jumped down, crunching two gorgers between its teeth in a single bite. The third one kept going, but the dinosaur snapped again, grabbing it as well.

"Holy fuck," Barry said.

The three of them continued to retreat, looking back as they ran. The Tyrannosaurus jabbed at the other gorgers passing by, snatching them, one after another.

Whistling noises came from every direction. Pods descended all across the meadow. Several others had already landed and opened.

"Sierra and Priya?" Cameron asked, breathing hard.

"Yeah," David nodded. He limped toward the bluff as fast as he could.

A carriage descended right in front of them, with Kim and Felicia at the controls.

"Get in, get in," Kim yelled, before they'd even come to a stop. "Hurry, hurry, hurry."

David staggered over, hefted Barry onboard, and then fell onto the back of the carriage. Cameron gripped his arm and they lifted away.

All around them, pods continued to fall.

Chapter Seventy-Six

Sierra stood at the tail end of the shuttle with the binoculars to her face. Hundreds of pods landed throughout the valley. Priya had done it. She'd gotten them down in time. The whistling trill of their descent was deafening.

Near the last four firebomb craters, a gorger puked onto the foot of a chonky Tyrannosaurus with brindle feathers along its back. The dinosaur roared and grabbed the alien, shaking it. Pieces flew everywhere. A dozen other Tyrannosauruses crunched on gorgers like candy.

Across the meadow, all sorts of dinosaurs clambered out from pods of every size. Off to the left, where the largest wave of gorgers remained, forty or fifty Triceratops charged into the creatures, trampling scores beneath their feet. The gorger surge broke, scattering in every direction.

Sierra chortled and offered the binoculars to Priya.

She waved them away, focusing on her device. "I still have things to do."

To the north, thirty or forty pods as big as the shuttle landed near the river. A snake-like neck emerged from the first one, followed by a four-legged dinosaur bigger than a bus.

"That's Brontosaurus," Sierra said, smiling wide.

"Dreadnoughtus," Priya corrected without glancing up.

Their necks towered a hundred feet in the air. They unfolded themselves from the pods and marched across the river. Sierra couldn't tell if they even noticed the gorgers, but they had to be stomping any that were in their paths, and maybe they were drawing some of them away.

Back to the west, twenty or thirty Mastodons stumbled from a row of pods not too far from the Triceratops herd. They charged into gorgers, swinging their tusks. "It isn't just dinosaurs," Sierra said.

"I know." Priya still didn't look up, but a devilish grin spread across her face.

As they'd discussed, Priya hadn't brought down any pods right next to the bluff. Most landed along the front lines of the gorger wave, including a bunch carrying dinosaurs that looked similar to Tyrannosaurus, but with different colors and proportions.

Every time a dinosaur took down a gorger nearby, cheers erupted from the crowd below. Sierra scanned the mass of people, searching for Tyrell, but she still couldn't find him.

The dinosaurs were keeping the gorgers from reaching the bluff, but it was up to Priya to keep the dinosaurs away as well. They would tear through the crowd as indiscriminately as they tore through the gorgers.

Fortunately, the aliens implanted all their specimens with an off switch.

"We need to get down there," Sierra said.

"I know," Priya said. "Almost done."

A two-legged dinosaur strutted from left to right, approaching the people lined up directly below the shuttle's tail. It looked like a small red Tyrannosaurus with much longer arms.

"There's a nasty-looking red guy getting close," Sierra said.

"Okay," Priya said, tapping her console. "Here comes our ride."

One of the spare sleds emerged from deeper inside the shuttle and stopped right next to them. Priya hefted the control device aboard and climbed on.

Sierra followed. Kona jumped up next to her, but Sierra pushed her back down. "Off. You have to stay here, girl."

Kona tilted her head with a whimper.

Priya tapped her device and they floated out of the shuttle. Behind them, Kona barked once and sat down, watching.

As the sled floated out, Sierra got a better look at the crowd, which extended much farther than she'd realized from up inside the shuttle's tail. There were a bunch of people back to the right, under the wing, and another group directly beneath the hull. She'd never find Tyrell. He could be anywhere.

Priya's flight path took them straight down.

The red two-legged dinosaur darted closer. Beneath the shuttle's tail, everyone scattered onto the bluff, disappearing in the forest of human-sized pods.

The sled jerked to a stop about twenty feet above the ground. Priya touched the control device and the zipping sound seemed to come from everywhere at once.

Below them, the dinosaur collapsed in a heap. Cheers came from the crowd.

Sierra turned back to the west and raised the binoculars. There were still thousands of gorgers out there, but they were no longer approaching in an organized front.

Several herds of Stegosauruses stood clustered in circles with their heads together. Any time a gorger came close, a spiked tail smashed it. Mutilated gorgers lay all around them.

One Stegosaurus wandered off by itself, where a swarm of gorgers overwhelmed it. Three of the creatures climbed between the diamond-shaped plates, puking on its back. The dinosaur bleated like a sheep and fell on its side. Several other gorgers ran over and began feeding.

Sierra nodded. Dead dinosaurs were just as helpful as living ones. Gorgers had no reason to advance on the bluff if they had plenty to eat right in front of them.

"We've got a problem," Priya said.

Sierra lowered the binoculars and looked around. "What? Where?"

"North, by the river. Hold on." Priya sent their sled in that direction.

A row of new pods sat along the riverbank, less than a half mile past the bluff. Sierra brought the binoculars back up. Eight giant cats crept south, straight toward the crowd. Long, curved teeth hung from the sides of their jaws. Their shoulder blades cycled up and down as they walked.

"You brought saber-tooth tigers?"

"Saber-tooth cats," Priya said. "They don't call them tigers anymore."

"Whatever," Sierra said. "I don't see any gorgers up there."

"Yeah, I know," Priya said. "That's the problem."

"Stun them," Sierra said. "Hurry." She lowered her binoculars.

The sled was closing fast.

"I'm on it," Priya said. She tapped the console and the zipping sound blasted around them. "Sweet dreams."

The cats didn't fall. They weren't quite close enough.

"Hit 'em again," Sierra said as they passed over.

Priya triggered the device a second time, but it was already too late. One saber-tooth, the one in the rear, dropped in a heap. The other seven kept going.

"They were practically right below us," Sierra said. "What happened?"

"We're twenty feet up," Priya said. "That adds to the distance." We need to be lower."

On the bluff, people had started backing up, but the crowd bunched and knotted where they tried to squeeze between the pods.

"Turn us around," Sierra said. "Those cats are almost to the bluff."

"I can't turn us around. I can only send us to a new spot when we arrive at the last one. You know that."

Screams came from behind.

"How much longer?" Sierra asked. Even if they started back now, they wouldn't reach the bluff in time.

David, Cameron, and Barry flew in from the west, straight toward the saber-toothed cats. They dipped low in front of the bluff. A moment later, the zipping sound buzzed from their sled.

All seven cats dropped where they stood, along with the closest ten or twenty people on the bluff.

"Yes!" Sierra shouted. "Wait, where are Kim and Felicia?"

"Over by the shuttle," Priya said.

Sierra raised her binoculars. A forty-foot crocodile waddled toward the bottom of the shuttle, where dozens of people still congregated. Kim and Felicia approached the giant reptile in the other sled. They zapped it from behind, far enough away to avoid taking out anyone in the crowd.

The crocodile plopped onto its stomach.

"We did it," Sierra said quietly.

Priya smiled. "We did."

"Move us right in front of the bluff," Sierra said. "We need to do something about those people who just got stunned."

"Sure thing." They started moving again.

"Listen up, everyone," Sierra shouted as they drew close.

To her amazement, the crowd quieted. Hundreds of people stopped moving and looked up. She studied as many faces as she could, hunting for Tyrell. He wasn't there.

She pointed to the bodies lying near the edge of the slope. "Those people aren't dead. They're just knocked out. We need your help."

"Who the hell are you?" shouted a burly man in a leather jacket. "You can't tell us what to do."

"My name is Sierra and I'm trying to save your ass," she shouted back. "We'll explain everything once it's safe. Right now, we need you to put those people in pods. We'll get them out of here."

"Bullshit," shouted the guy in the jacket.

Sierra leaned close to Priya and lowered her voice. "Can you take care of him?" When they triggered torpor using sleds, it zapped everything within range, but with the device, Priya could select specific individuals.

"You got it," she said.

Arguments bubbled up in the crowd below. It sounded like most of them were against the guy, but not all.

"We don't have time for debates," Sierra shouted.

The control device produced the zipping sound. The guy's knees buckled and he toppled onto his face.

"Anyone else?"

Silence hung in the air, at least over this part of the crowd. Off to the left, it sounded like David and Cameron were zapping another animal that wandered too close.

"Okay then. Gather up those people and put them in pods." Sierra swung her arm along the edge of the bluff. "Use the front row." That way, Priya would know which pods to send away.

A chubby, round-faced man holding a rifle shoved to the front of the crowd. "You heard her. Let's get to it." He shouldered the rifle, picked up a stunned woman by her armpits and dragged her toward a pod.

Others started moving. They grabbed arms and legs, lifting people into the pods, positioning them side-by-side.

Sierra pointed at the man in the leather jacket. "Don't forget that guy."

Three people moved to pick him up.

"See if you can get more people into pods," Priya said quietly. "Use the front two rows,"

Sierra nodded, though she didn't want to lose anyone helpful. "Listen. If you're armed, we need you to stay and fight. But if not, we can send you somewhere safe. Just get in the pods in the first two rows."

The chubby man with the rifle gave her a salute.

A few people started climbing into pods, but not nearly enough.

"There's a constrictor getting kind of close," Priya said.

Sierra spun around. A twenty-foot snake slithered toward the slope.

"Holy crap, Priya, is there anything you didn't bring down?"

"I left most of the ungulates behind."

She shook her head, not sure what that meant and not caring. "Move us farther out. We need to make sure nothing else wanders over. Put us in the center. David and Kim can take care of the sides."

She turned around as they started moving again. Priya zapped the snake and it stopped right at the base of the slope.

Out in the meadow, hundreds of dinosaurs and other creatures wandered around between pods of all sizes. Most of the animals roared, stomped, and chomped as if whipped up in a frenzy. Maybe they were disoriented from waking up in an unfamiliar location. Maybe they were overwhelmed by all the foreign species around. More than a few were probably pissed at the nasty little bug things that kept trying to vomit acid on them.

Gorgers no longer marched toward the bluff. Many were fleeing. Some were feeding on carcasses of animals that had been killed. Tens of thousands were dead.

Direct sunlight had long since vanished, but there was still enough light to see, at least for now. The sky had turned the pale blue color of daytime in the menagerie. They might have an hour before full dark, maybe more, thanks to their latitude.

"Now we need to figure out how to get through the night," Sierra muttered. "We can't leave everyone down there. After dark, the gorgers could wander in from any direction. We won't be able to keep them safe." She took a deep breath. That included Tyrell, assuming he was even still alive.

"I'm two steps ahead of you," Priya said.

Chapter Seventy-Seven

David kept his head on a swivel.

On the bluff, the crowd had broken into multiple groups, at least along the front edge. Some were loading stunned people into pods and several were climbing into pods on their own. A large group was watching him and Cameron and Barry. Several had guns out and ready, including a uniformed police officer.

A family that looked a lot like his own stood along the northern edge of the bluff. A boy between Kim and Barry's ages held the leash of a black lab, who barked furiously at the chaos. When this was over, if they survived, Kona would have a playmate.

Straight out from the center of the bluff, Sierra and Priya hovered fifteen feet above the ground. The lights from Priya's device lit her face in a pastel glow. Sierra stood lookout. Every time she spotted an animal venturing their way, Priya maneuvered their carriage over to stun it. Three big brontosaurus-like behemoths lay in a triangle below them. A few gorgers fed on the torpored creatures.

Beyond Sierra and Priya, the top of the shuttle reflected the last rays of the setting sun. Kim and Felicia zig-zagged back and forth in a wide area near the huge ship. The abattoir below them was much more spread out than the one beneath Sierra and Priya.

Further west, where they'd dropped the firebombs, three enormous apes squatted along the edge of a smoldering crater. They looked like the offspring of an orangutan crossed with a sasquatch. Every time a gorger ventured close, one of the apes would dart over, grab it, and tear off every single limb. They moved surprisingly fast for their size.

Legless gorgers writhed on the ground all around them. Without any limbs, they looked quite a bit like their caretaker forms.

David had seen giant bears too, but they seemed to have wandered away.

A quarter mile north of the bluff, a group of seven or eight gorgers startled a massive herd of duck-billed dinosaurs. Hooting and honking, the dinosaurs reared up on their hind legs and came crashing down, stomping the gorgers into the mud.

"Hold up," Cameron said. "There's a stray below."

They stopped circling and David leaned over the front console. A small gorger crept through tall grass toward the bluff.

Cameron took careful aim and then pulled the trigger a single time. The gorger collapsed.

"Nice shot."

"Who do you think killed the most gorgers?" Barry asked. "I bet it's a *T. rex*."

"My money's on the giant crocodiles," David said. Most of the Tyrannosaurs had wandered off to the northwest, but all of the giant crocodiles had remained in the area. "Those guys are totally gorging themselves."

Barry laughed. The idea that his son could laugh at a stupid dad joke felt absurd. Minutes earlier, he'd considered shooting him so he wouldn't be eaten alive.

"I'm pretty sure the correct answer to your question is Warrant Officer Alice Cameron," Cameron said. "I lit all those firebombs."

David laughed.

"Hey, we helped," Barry said.

"Terror bird," Cameron said. "Ten o'clock."

A ten-foot-tall terror bird strutted toward the bluff. The Labrador at the front of the crowd barked even more furiously.

"I hate those things," Barry said.

"Me too," Cameron said. The bird squawked as they swooped over it, then fell onto its back when they hit the stun controls.

"Got him," Barry said.

"Yeah, we got him," Cameron said. "But we can't do this forever."

"There's pods going up," Barry said.

David swiveled his head. A row of pods lifted from the front of the bluff. They glowed orange when they were high enough to catch the late-day rays of the sun. The second row of pods began to close, though half of them looked empty. Moments later, they flew away as well.

"At least some people are safe," he muttered. He wasn't sure what would happen to the thousands remaining on the bluff.

"Is Mommy in one of them?"

"I really don't think so, Bud."

"How do you know?"

He wasn't sure how to answer that one. Because it was such a long shot? Because he didn't want to raise his hopes, only to reset the cycle of pain and grief? Because he'd had sex with Cameron?

He settled for, "I didn't see her."

"Duke, no," yelled a boy's voice. "Come back!"

At the edge of the bluff, the black lab broke free from the kid holding his leash. The dog took off down the slope, barking madly. He ran in the general direction of Fraser, his leash flopping in the grass. The boy started after him.

"Carlos, stop!" yelled his mother. She held a toddler against her hip.

"Carlos!" shouted the boy's father. He glanced at his wife and took off down the hill, chasing their son.

Duke was already at the bottom of the slope, racing toward the herd of duck-billed dinosaurs. They were several hundred yards away, but Duke was closing fast.

"Let's get over there," David said. He and Cameron turned the carriage north.

"Trouble's coming," she said. She swung her arm, pointing.

A red two-legged dinosaur as tall as a man strutted toward the dog, coming in from the left at an intercept angle. Its head bobbed forward and back like a bird. Shiny blue and green feathers covered its arms and its floppy, bird-like tail.

"Carlos, get back here!" shouted the father.

Carlos either didn't hear or didn't care. He kept running. The little bugger had some wheels on him.

Duke slowed down about a hundred yards from the herd of duck-billed dinosaurs, who had turned at the sound of his barking. It seemed as if the dog suddenly realized they were a lot bigger than they'd looked from the bluff.

"Carlos, goddamn it, stop!" The father stumbled as he ran, but managed to catch himself.

"Faster," Cameron said.

"Hurry," Barry cried, squeezing David from behind.

The dinosaur's trajectory shifted away from the dog and toward the boy.

"Zap it," Cameron said, reaching for the torpor controls.

"Wait," David said. "We aren't close enough." They would zap the boy and the dad, but not the dinosaur.

Off in the distance, one of the duck-billed dinosaurs hooted and charged at Duke. The dog turned and ran straight back, yelping.

The carriage shot forward, fifteen feet above the ground, passing over the father.

Ahead, Carlos stopped and held his arms wide, waiting for Duke to return.

The bird-dinosaur launched into a sprint, closing the gap. It leaped, flying through the air straight toward the kid.

"Now," David said. He touched the controls and the zipping sound burst from the carriage.

Carlos slumped forward in the weeds as the dinosaur sailed over him, its talons just missing his head. It tumbled and flopped through the shrubs where it landed, also stunned.

"The dad's down, too," Cameron said, looking back.

Shouts came from the bluff behind them.

"We gotta land," David said. "Hurry. We have to grab them."

"Can't you wake them up?" Barry asked.

"That would wake the dinosaur, too."

Duke must have been out of range, because he was still moving. He ran back to Carlos and stood beside him, barking.

The carriage touched down halfway between the boy and the father.

"I got the kid," Cameron yelled, already jumping off.

"Stay right here," David shouted at Barry. He didn't see any more dinosaurs, but the light wasn't great and the last one had come out of nowhere. He climbed from the back of the carriage and limped toward the father.

"Hurry," Barry shouted.

Duke barked, letting out a series of angry staccato bursts. The duck-billed dinosaurs responded with deep hooting noises.

David grabbed Carlos' father under his armpits and dragged him backwards, ignoring the sharp pain in his wrist and the even sharper pain in his ankle. He looked over his shoulder to gauge the distance.

Cameron had Carlos in her arms. Behind her, the duck-bill herd was stampeding toward the carriage. The ground rumbled as they approached.

The black lab ran around Cameron, bouncing and jumping.

"Duke, come," Barry shouted.

David and Cameron reached the carriage at the same time. She laid Carlos next to Barry and came around to help David lift the father, who had a hell of a beer belly. They hefted him up, leaving his shins and feet hanging off the rear.

"Good enough," David said. He and Cameron raced around to the front.

The thundering rumble grew louder. The duck-billed dinosaurs were directly ahead of them, only seconds away.

"Come on, Duke," Barry said, slapping the surface of the carriage. "Up!"

The dog jumped aboard and stood over Carlos.

They lifted off just as the herd barreled by below. Dust kicked up all around them.

"We gotta stun them," Cameron shouted. "They're headed for the crowd." The carriage was still flying up and backwards.

David reached for the little knob, then paused. Below, the dinosaur herd curved away from the bluff, heading back out toward the west. "Let them go. They'll trample any gorgers in their path.

He glanced back. Duke was still standing, keeping his balance over Carlos. Barry had one hand on the father's shoulder. David exhaled. It had been close, but they'd made it.

They turned toward the crowd, moving slowly for Duke's sake and to keep Carlos and his dad from rolling off. Sierra and Priya were still straight out from the middle of the bluff, and Kim and Felicia continued to patrol the far side, near the shuttle.

"Look for the mother," he said, searching for the woman holding the toddler. He didn't want to fly around with a pair of unconscious bodies on the back.

"She's right up front," Cameron said, pointing. The edge of the bluff had grown more crowded.

"David, Cameron!" This shout came from Tyrell, who was waving his hands in the back of the group, trying to push closer.

"Let's pull up to the edge of the slope," David said.

As they drifted lower, various shouts rose from the crowd.

"Are they okay?"

"Who are you people?"

"What's going on here?"

David ignored the questions.

"Should we revive them now?" Cameron asked.

David shook his head. "There's a giant snake down on the slope. We might wake it up. We have to get Priya to select them individually."

She nodded.

Hands reached for them as the shuttle came close. "Just hold on," David said. "We'll pass them down to you."

"I'll find Mommy," Barry shouted.

"Sit tight, Barry," David said.

The carriage was six feet above the ground, then five.

The hands weren't reaching for Carlos and his father. They were reaching for the carriage. They grabbed the edge and pulled.

"Stop," Cameron yelled.

Everything happened at once.

The carriage listed twenty degrees. Duke jumped off and disappeared. A man pulled up next to Carlos' father, his elbows on the edge of the carriage. Barry shifted away from him, toward the back. Cameron spun around and shoved the man off. He fell onto three people below, knocking them down.

Carlos rolled into his father, then slid off the edge. His mother screamed.

A second later, another man stepped back, cradling the unconscious boy in his arms. "I got him."

"Up," David shouted. He and Cameron hit the controls to rise away from the mob, but they didn't move.

The crowd roared, pulling harder on one side. Dozens of hands grabbed the edge. David hooked his arm over the front console to keep from sliding as they tilted farther.

Carlos' father slid off. He hit the ground, now less than two feet below. Someone screamed.

Barry slid down the side of the carriage and jumped off.

"Wait," David shouted. "Barry, get back here."

BAAMM! Cameron fired her gun into the air.

Everyone let go at once. The carriage righted itself, wobbled past level, then tipped in the other direction.

David tumbled over the side. He dropped four or five feet, landing on the slope that ran along the front of the bluff. He tucked his head and pulled his arms and legs in close, hoping to keep from breaking anything as he rolled down the hill, unable to see and barely able to think. He slammed into something solid.

Stars swirled in his vision. He blinked, trying to clear his mind. He lay against a scaly wall. It was the giant snake Priya had stunned earlier.

Staggering to his knees, he looked up the slope. The carriage floated above the crowd, out of reach. Cameron kneeled on it, alone. Half the crowd was yelling for her to fly back down, but without a second pilot, she couldn't go anywhere.

"Where's Barry?" he shouted.

She shook her head. "He took off. I can't see him."

Chapter Seventy-Eight

The goddamn flying car was up near the front of the crowd, and there was no way Frank could get to it. Hundreds of people blocked him. That Black guy Tyrell had gotten close, shoving through them, but now he'd lost sight of him again.

Everywhere Frank turned, shouts surrounded him, just like they had ever since he got out of his pod. He was struggling to focus. Too much blow. Or maybe not enough.

"Has anyone learned where we are?"

"I saw Triceratops. How many kinds did you see?"

"Keep to the middle. It's safer. People are getting killed on the sides."

"They're just big bugs. Three people shot one and killed it dead."

"Yeah, but what are they?"

"Fuck this place. I want to go home."

"Where did they come from?"

"Someone said we should get in the pods."

"I'm not getting in a pod."

The noise was more than Frank could handle.

A boy ran past, calling for his mommy.

"Good luck with that, kid," he muttered.

He stopped and leaned against the closest pod, patting his pants pocket to make sure the coke was still there. He decided to take one more hit, just to be safe.

Tyrell appeared out of nowhere, his eyes wide. He put his hands on Frank's shoulders. "Did a little boy just run by?"

Frank's first instinct was to tell the motherfucker to take his paws off him, but he held his tongue. If the kid had value to the people on the flying cars, that was information he could use. He gestured between two pods, where the kid had run off. "He went through there a few seconds ago."

"Thanks." Tyrell slipped away, darting through the crowd.

Frank hurried after him. He heard the boy shouting for his Mommy over the din.

He wove around a pod, shoved past a circle of idiots holding hands, then pushed through a cloud of marijuana smoke.

Tyrell was gone. Frank spun. The boy's shouts had ceased. People streamed past him on all sides. Most of the mob was headed in the other direction, toward the front of the bluff, where all the action was.

He walked around another pod, heading toward the river, leaving the crowd behind.

There.

Tyrell knelt by the boy right where the plateau ended, holding the kid's arm. The little shit was pulling away from him, still whining for his mommy.

Frank's eye twitched. He wasn't about to let that guy rescue the kid. It would be him. Frank Fucking Wharton. As he marched toward them, he pulled the last ketamine syringe from his shirt pocket and yanked off the cap with his teeth.

He wouldn't get a better chance. The kid was looking off in the other direction and no one else was around. Frank walked up, plunged the needle into Tyrell's throat, then flicked it aside.

Tyrell slapped his neck and turned on him, his eyes full of fury. "What the fuck?" He shoved Frank in the chest.

Frank staggered, but managed to keep his feet.

The boy took off and raced along the slope without looking back. He disappeared around a pod.

Tyrell shook his head, blinking, over and over again. "What did you do to me?"

Frank put on his best innocent expression. "You look exhausted. Let me help. I'll take care of the kid." He held Tyrell's elbow as the guy plopped on his ass.

"Shhtay away from him," Tyrell said, slurring. He shook his arm free.

Frank placed his foot on his back and pushed. Tyrell rolled right down the slope, coming to a stop on the muddy riverbank below.

He turned and jogged along the ridge in the same direction the boy had gone. "Hey kid," he shouted. "I found your mom."

Several yards ahead, the boy stopped and turned back.

"Where is she?" The boy's tone was red and snotty, just like his face.

Frank walked over and took his wrist. "This way. I'll show you."

"Where's Tyrell?"

Frank pulled him around a pod, away from the river, back toward the crowd. "He asked me to help you."

"Why?"

"Because I found your mother."

"Where?" the boy demanded.

"She's up ahead." Frank gestured beyond the first few people he saw. "She's mad at you for running away."

"You liar." The little brat jerked his arm, trying to break free.

"What's going on?" asked an Asian guy wearing a green polo.

"I'm taking this kid to his mom," Frank said.

"No," the boy shrieked. "Somebody help me."

The Asian started forward. Frank pulled his gun from his jacket pocket.

"Hey man, no need for that." The Asian backed away, but more and more people were looking at Frank.

"Help me," the boy shrieked again.

Frank pulled him up against his chest, trying to cover his mouth in the crook of his elbow.

Searing pain tore into his forearm as the boy clamped down, his teeth sinking deep. He kicked with his heels, nailing Frank in the shin.

Frank released him and squeezed the trigger at the same time. The gunshot terrified him. His arm shook all the way up to his shoulder and his foot throbbed with pain. Why the fuck did his foot hurt?

The little shit took off like a subway rat, weaving between the pods.

Frank looked down and gasped. Blood oozed from his loafer. His fourth toe was gone. That cocksucking little motherfucker made him shoot off his goddamn toe.

Grinding his teeth, he limped after him. His foot screamed with every step.

He rounded a pod in time to see the boy pushing through a wall of people. Frank fired, but the shot went high.

Staggering, he crashed into the closest pod, breathing hard. He felt dizzy and feverish.

The crowd spread wide and the boy broke through. Frank raised his gun and fired again.

Blam!

The kid tumbled forward onto his face.

Frank laughed and lurched after him.

Chapter Seventy-Nine

David ignored the gunshots and kept running, searching. He'd heard sporadic gunfire all afternoon. Most of it came from the front lines, where people were shooting gorgers that made it to the bluff. He raced through the crowd, freezing every time he saw anyone less than three feet tall. There were dozens of children here, but none of them were Barry.

A shout came from the same direction as the shots. *"He's shooting at a boy!"*

David's heart stopped. He turned and pushed through the crowd, shoving people aside.

He spotted Barry, picking himself up from the ground. Blood streamed from his arm.

"Barry!"

"Daddy!" Barry ran straight at him, one arm hanging at his side.

David slid to the ground in front of him. "Barry," he panted. "What happened?"

"Get out of the way!" bellowed a man with stark white hair. He limped forward, holding a pistol out in front of him.

Gasps came from the crowd.

David wrapped his arms around Barry, shielding him with his body. He craned his neck to look at the man. "Get away from us," he yelled. His mouth felt chalky.

The gun trembled in the man's hand. A crazed sneer spread across his face. "Give me a goddamn flying car."

Whispered voices came from the crowd.

"Stop this," someone cried.

"Drop the gun."

The man snorted. "Shut up." He swung the gun around, pointing from person to person, trembling. "All of you. I'll kill every last one of you."

The lunatic was high as a kite.

Everyone shifted back.

David pulled his hand away from Barry, sticky with blood. A furrow ran across the boy's bicep. Red rage clouded his vision. "You shot him."

"Get me one of those flying cars and take me up to that silver thing, or I'll shoot you, too."

"Never," David roared. "You're never going anywhere." Somewhere in the back of his mind, he knew he should keep his mouth shut, but he couldn't. This madman shot his son.

"Fuck it." The man brought up his other hand, steadying the gun.

A shadow moved behind him. Someone familiar. Someone feminine. *Cameron?* It couldn't be. She was stuck twenty feet off the ground in the carriage.

The black hole at the end of the barrel pointed right at David's face.

As the man steadied his feet, the woman behind him reared back and swung a metal rod like she was swinging for the fences. The end connected squarely with the side of the man's head.

The gun went off, but the bullet went high over the crowd. Blood spurted from the man's ear, soaking his bright white hair. His left hand went up, reaching.

Thonk!

The metal rod hit the side of his head again with the unmistakable sound of breaking bone. He slumped to the ground.

David's wife stood behind the man. She held a bloody tire iron, and was taking long, heaving breaths.

"Lindsey?" he whispered.

It was impossible. Everyone shouted and screamed, but David could barely hear it. He was in a dream. His wife was here.

Barry burst out from beneath him. "Mommm-eeeee."

David stood in slow motion, joy and relief filling him. Lindsey was alive. He took a step forward.

Barry jumped into his mother's arms. She dropped the tire iron.

Two people crouched next to the asshole who had attacked them. One snatched his gun and held it between finger and thumb like a dead mouse. The other man touched the attacker's neck. "He's dead."

David ran the last few feet and wrapped his arms around his wife. It really was her. He breathed in the smell of her hair. His cheeks pulled into a grin so tight it hurt. "Oh God, Lindsey, it's you." Tears fell from his eyes.

She wrapped her arms around him and kissed him. "Is Barry okay?"

David pulled back and inspected the wound on the boy's arm. It needed a bandage, but he'd only been grazed.

"I'm good," Barry sobbed, still clinging to her. "I'm so good."

"Kim's okay, too," David said. "She's safe."

"I know. I saw her flying one of those things."

David opened his mouth to speak, but all that came out was a sputter.

"What's going on, David? Where are we? What's happening?"

"I— I'll explain everything." He remembered Cameron and the smile fell from his face. Christ, he had a lot of explaining to do.

"Look," someone shouted. "They're coming."

A carriage floated over, fifteen feet up. Was it Cameron? If so, what the hell was he supposed to say?

Sierra leaned over the side, ignoring shouts from the crowd. She cupped her mouth with her hands. "Are you okay?"

Next to her, Priya offered a small wave.

David gave them a thumbs up.

Sierra nodded, then stood and addressed the crowd. "I know you all want answers."

Dozens of people responded with shouts of agreement.

"You'll get them, once everyone is safe."

This was met with uncertain murmurs.

She pointed at the massive silver shuttle. "We need to get everyone inside one of those. Forty or fifty people will fit."

Questions rose from the crowd.

"What is that thing?"

"How do we get in?"

"Where did it come from?"

Sierra patted the side of her carriage. "We're going to ferry you into them with more of these. Ten people will fit at a time."

The murmur started to grow louder.

"Ten people at a time," Sierra repeated. "Once everyone is safe, we'll explain everything and talk about what's next."

"Let's get to it, then," shouted a man nearby.

A couple of others shouted in agreement.

"Who is she?" Lindsey asked. "How do you know her?"

"She's Sierra," Barry said. "She's cool. She got her fingers cut off and they grew back."

Lindsey tilted her head and narrowed her eyes.

"There's a lot to tell you," David said. It was quite the understatement.

Up on the carriage, Sierra raised her hand. The crowd grew silent. She pointed down toward David. "I need help from this guy."

Lindsey looked astonished. David wanted to wrap his arms around her and never let go.

"We're going to pick him up," Sierra continued. "If anyone else tries to get on, you'll all be zapped."

She pointed toward the west, where Cameron floated their way, her carriage apparently under Priya's control.

David's mind raced. As soon as the carriage dropped low enough, the crowd would swamp them, just like earlier. He was opening his mouth to say as much when a series of gasps rose all around them.

Hundreds of sparkling silver shuttles descended through the evening sky. Some dropped in the middle of the battlefield, where dinosaurs were still killing gorgers. Others landed on the far side of the river, or further south. They were everywhere.

"Hey Ace, are you okay?" Cameron called out as she drew close.

David looked up, but couldn't form words. *Please don't say anything. Not now. We can explain later. Somehow.* He nodded.

Priya and Sierra couldn't have timed things any better. The crowd watched in stunned silence as the giant ships landed. David, Barry, and Lindsey climbed aboard the carriage with Cameron. David sat at the controls and they lifted away without a single person trying to interfere.

"Where's Kim?" David asked.

Cameron pointed out across the meadow, where the third carriage was still on patrol. "You and I need to take over for them," she said.

"Priya needs Kim to help with the airlift."

"Wait," Lindsey said. "I came here with two teenage girls. They're still down there."

"They'll be okay," Cameron said. "We're going to get everyone out of here."

David glanced back, barely able to believe it was really her.

Lindsey sat with her arms wrapped around Barry. "How do you know how to fly this thing?"

"Dad's the best pilot," Barry said. "He can fly the shuttle too."

"I really don't understand."

Cameron gave David a look that held a mix of bemusement and sadness.

Barry must have noticed the injury on his arm, because he blurted out, "Hey, I'm bleeding."

"We'll patch you up, Bud," David said.

Empty carriages floated out from the closest shuttles.

"I'm Alice Cameron, by the way," Cameron said.

"Uh, sorry," David said. "This is my wife, Lindsey."

"I sorta figured that out," Cameron said.

Heat rose up the sides of David's neck. Lindsey had to suspect something. She was too smart, too observant.

"*MOM!*" Kim shouted. She and Felicia brought their carriage close.

Lindsey's face cinched tight, tears glistening at the corners of her eyes.

David swallowed, barely able to breathe. His family was whole again.

"You guys have all been here a while, haven't you?" Lindsey said. Too smart, too observant.

"Priya needs your help, Kim," Cameron said, strictly business.

Kim opened her mouth, but nothing came out. She was bawling.

Felicia gave a small wave. "There's some dinos with spikes on their backs circling around to the south. Out here, it's mostly quiet now, but there's an Allosaurus who keeps looking this way.

David nodded. "We'll watch for them." He reached for the controls, then stopped himself. "Wait. If we stun the dinosaurs, it will stun Lindsey, too."

"What are you talking about?" Lindsey asked, shaking her head.

He turned to face her. "You need to go with Kim. It's safer."

She gave him a dubious look, then nodded.

Kim and Felicia brought their carriage to a stop beside them.

"I'm going too," Barry said.

David tried to keep any emotion off his face. Especially guilt. He could spend the next few hours trying to figure out how to explain what happened between him and Cameron, how to beg for forgiveness. He also had to figure out what he was going to say to Cameron.

Lindsey hopped over to the other carriage. David helped Barry across while Kim smothered her mother in a sobbing hug.

"You okay there, Ace?" Cameron asked quietly.

He swallowed and looked at her. "I don't know what to say." This had to be painful for her.

She gave him a dry look. "Sometimes it's best not to say anything. Come on. Let's get to work."

On the other carriage, Kim finally returned to the pilot's seat.

"Be safe, Daddy," Barry shouted as they began to fly away.

David's heart fluttered as he watched them all. He had his family back.

Barry cupped his hands beside his mouth. "And no more kissing Cameron!"

Chapter Eighty

Sierra turned the binoculars back to the bluff, searching for Tyrell. With more than half the crowd airlifted to the shuttles, it was increasingly difficult to have faith. She'd counted thirty-eight dead bodies so far, but the endless rows of pods probably hid twice that many.

Please don't let Tyrell be one of them.

David's wife Lindsey sat in the back of the sled with Barry. She looked like an adult version of Kim, but with stronger cheekbones and longer hair. She had the same hazel eyes and confident smirk.

A steady train of sleds conveyed people from the bluff below to the shuttles parked around the valley.

Priya and Kim had synched up with each other so that they always had a new sled ready to pick up the next load of survivors as soon as the previous one lifted away. Priya had even set up a third control device to monitor the number of people in each shuttle so that none became overcrowded.

On the ground below, several men and women coordinated the loading, grouping people to make sure every sled had exactly ten people onboard, while keeping loved ones together.

"So, how did you get out of the mothership?" Lindsey asked. She had apparently found a pod after rescuing two teen girls from the back of a kidnapper's van. Earlier, she'd spotted the girls below and had insisted that they got onto one of the first sleds.

"The whole ship is automatic," Barry said. "You can come and go whenever you want. They made it that way 'cause they're lazy."

Lindsey must have looked dubious, because Felicia said, "That's actually pretty much true."

Sierra swung the binoculars back to the west. The sun had dropped behind the mountains now and it was too dark to see very far across the valley. "Another one of those big sloths is getting close," she said.

"That one isn't a sloth," Priya said. "That's Amphicyon."

"What?"

"It's a bear dog." Priya kept her face buried in the device.

"You're making that up," Sierra said.

David and Cameron must have spotted it, because they peeled off from the front lines and headed toward the creature.

A series of cries came from behind. Two gorgers were creeping between the pods, making their way to the crowd. The pudgy guy with the pink face sent a small posse after them. Moments later, shots rang out and both gorgers dropped.

People would need to collect wood for spears in the days ahead, before the ammo ran out. The local gorger population was manageable now, but it would still need managing. They also needed to figure out a way to store water. And sterilize it. She sighed. There were too many things to think about, and she couldn't give them any attention until she found Tyrell.

"I think I can manage four carriages at a time," Priya said.

"If you can, I can," Kim said.

"You guys are doing great," Sierra said. "I just wish you could figure out how to broadcast a recording. We're going to have to spend hours going from shuttle to shuttle to explain everything."

"I've got an idea about that," Priya said, without looking up from her device. "I think I can get five shuttles parked in a circle with their tail hatches close to each other. We can float in the middle and talk to all five at once. That way, we'll have to explain everything thirty six-times instead of a hundred and eighty."

Sierra glanced over at her. "I thought you could only make this stuff land in a grid pattern?"

Priya still didn't look up, but she grinned. "I'm learning."

Sierra raised the binoculars and began another scan of the area. She spotted something that looked like an oversized Komodo Dragon creeping toward the bluff from the north. Twenty or thirty people were still clustered over that way for some reason.

She whistled in David and Cameron's direction, but produced only a tiny trill. She wished she'd inherited Waldmire's piercing whistle. She wished Tyrell was here with his emergency whistle. *He's okay,* she told herself. *He has to be.*

"I'll get him," Barry said. *"Daadddy!"*

Within seconds, David and Cameron flew over.

"Giant lizard," Sierra said, pointing as they passed.

Thirty seconds later, she heard the zipping sound, but from this distance, it was more of a buzz. The giant Komodo Dragon slumped over.

Sierra raised the binoculars. Four people were also down. They'd been too close, and had gotten stunned along with the lizard. "We need a sled over there," she said.

Kim held up a finger. "I'm on it."

Sierra lowered the binoculars. "Wait, bring it here first. I'll go down to supervise."

Priya and Kim exchanged a glance. "You're going to look for Tyrell, aren't you?" Kim asked.

"Yes."

Kim nodded, her face solemn. "Good. Find him."

An empty sled arrived and floated alongside theirs. Sierra jumped across, then turned back to face the others. "Once I get those people loaded, put this carriage back in rotation." She handed the binoculars to Felicia. "Keep an eye on things."

Felicia extended a gun toward her, handle first. "Yours is empty, remember?"

She pulled Joe's revolver from her holster and put Felicia's gun in its place. "Don't stop the evacuation to look for me," Sierra said. "I'll be fine."

Kim and Priya both stared.

"Promise," Sierra demanded.

They nodded.

Kim tapped the controls and Sierra's sled floated off over the crowd.

She tried to figure out the right priorities for what to do next. The wounded had to be triaged. They needed teams to make supply runs up to the menagerie for food. They would need candidates to learn how to fly the sleds and the shuttles. Eventually, they had to figure out how to plant crops and start raising goats or pigs or sheep or something.

The sled touched down between four pods at the north end of the bluff. People crowded around before Sierra had a chance to climb off.

"Everyone just hold on." She pointed at the stunned bodies. "We need to load those people aboard first."

"They're dead," shouted a pasty man with spiked hair.

"No they aren't," Sierra said. "They're stunned."

The man frowned. "How do you know?" He wore a t-shirt with "Big Jeff's" written across the top in looping cursive. Below, a cartoon guy held two oversized burgers, one on each hand.

"They got stunned when we stunned that lizard." Sierra gestured toward the giant Komodo Dragon lying several yards away.

"Why'd you do that?"

She rolled her eyes. "So it wouldn't eat you, Jeff."

He looked confused, then glanced down at his shirt. Obviously, it wasn't his name, but she didn't care.

Three people lifted the first body onto the carriage. They positioned it carefully, then went back for the next.

"Who else gets to go?" Jeff asked.

The volunteers returned with another body.

"Well, for starters, those three," Sierra said. "Since they jumped in to help."

An older man in a cowboy hat and bolo tie stepped forward. His mustache and wrinkles reminded her of Waldmire. He pointed back toward one of the pods sitting nearby. "There's a child over there who's pretty scared, and an elderly couple. Can you take them?"

"Yeah," Sierra said. "Get 'em over here."

Jeff glowered.

Sierra looked around. At least a dozen people remained. She pointed to the sleds holding Kim and Priya, floating above a much larger crowd. "The rest of you need to head over there with the others. We'll get you out of here as soon as possible."

The man in the cowboy hat returned with the elderly couple and a girl about Barry's age. He helped them onto the sled.

There was room for one more. Sierra extended a hand to the old guy in the hat. "Thanks for your help. Climb aboard."

"What about you?" the man asked.

"I'm staying here for now," Sierra said.

The man tipped his hat at her, then gestured at Jeff. "I think he's in a bigger hurry than me. Let him go."

Jeff climbed up without even thanking him.

Sierra memorized the older man's face so she could find him later. He was the kind of person they would need if they were going to make this work.

She raised her arm and waved. Felicia must have been watching through the binoculars because the sled lifted off a moment later.

Sierra returned to the guy in the cowboy hat. "Can you get everyone to move toward that larger group over there?"

"Will do." He touched the brim of his hat again and began to herd people away.

"Thank you." She took a deep breath and turned to search for Tyrell.

Someone tapped her shoulder and she turned back.

"Where are you going?" asked a woman in a pink t-shirt.

"I'm looking for someone." Sierra didn't have time for this. It was almost full dark. The moon had risen to the east, which helped, but only a little. "It isn't safe here. Please. Go with the others."

On the woman's shirt, a dolphin jumped over sprawling letters that said "*FLORIDA KEYS.*" She looked worried. "Are you sure it's safe to go off all alone?"

No, not really, Sierra thought, but she couldn't put anyone else in danger. "Yes. I'll be fine. Please, help get everyone over to the main group."

The woman gave her an unconvincing nod.

Sierra started off. She wove between the pods, their top halves still floating magically in the air. In less than a minute, she encountered her first dead body, a guy with his fingers clenching the front of his shirt. His skin was ghastly pale, even in the dim light. He appeared to have suffered a heart attack.

She pushed on, working her way toward the river. She passed three more bodies before she reached the eastern edge of the bluff, none of them Tyrell.

Below, the river's surface sparkled in the moonlight. Several bodies lay on the bank. It was too dark to make them out from this distance. She had to go down and inspect them up close.

Please don't be him. Sand spilled into the tops of her boots as she shuffled down the slope.

Deep, foul holes covered the first two bodies, clearly the victims of gorger attacks.

Sierra froze. The third body was Tyrell, lying in the mud with frothy foam on his lips.

"No, no, no."

She dropped to her knees beside him. His eyes were rolled back in his head. Sierra's breath spilled out in a low wail. She'd done everything to save all those strangers, only to lose the one person she had feelings for.

The river churned past, masking the sound of her cry.

She patted him down, probing for signs of injury, but couldn't find any. His skin was warm and he had a faint pulse. She bent close and thought maybe she felt his breath on her cheek. "What happened?" she whispered. "What's wrong?"

She started to call for help, but stopped, afraid she might attract gorgers.

"Gotta get you out of here." Standing, she grabbed his wrists and pulled. He only shifted an inch.

"Shit."

A gorger emerged from the dark, less than thirty feet away, creeping up the riverbank.

Sierra released Tyrell's hands and drew her gun. The gorger crept toward them. She forced herself to wait until it got closer. She couldn't afford to miss.

"Tyrell, wake up." She patted his cheek, but he didn't move.

The pincers on the sides of the gorger's hideous mouth opened wide.

She took a slow, steady breath and pulled the trigger, just like Wayne had taught her. The gun roared. The gorger flinched but kept coming. She fired twice more and it fell in a heap.

She gasped. The light from the gunshots had illuminated two more coming up behind the first. She walked on her knees beside Tyrell's body, squinting into the dark, barely able to see anything past the afterglow on her retinas.

The closest gorger ran toward her. She fired again, shooting it twice in the face. It slumped over.

The third one sidestepped, then lurched closer. She had to fire three times before it went down. Her hand throbbed from the recoil.

She glanced up the slope, but saw only the tops of the nearest pods, floating against the dark sky. The others wouldn't come to her rescue. She'd made them promise. She was on her own.

"Tyrell, wake the fuck up." He didn't move. If the gunfire hadn't roused him, nothing would.

She didn't know what to do. If she left him, they would eat him alive. But if she stayed, she would die as well.

Two more gorgers came from upstream. She blasted one, taking it down with a single shot, then aimed at the other and pulled the trigger.

Click.

The gun was empty.

The remaining gorger was less than twenty feet from them.

Sierra scrambled to her feet and waved her arms. She ran sideways, luring the monster away from Tyrell. It stalked toward her. Something moved behind her, downstream. More gorgers. The closest one bent to feed on one of the corpses.

The gorger she'd lured to the side reared back and puked. She jumped away. The vomit splash just missed her.

She ran back to Tyrell, putting herself between him and the gorgers coming up from downstream.

"Wake up. I really need some help here." He still didn't move.

The closest gorger hissed. Stomach acids dripped from its mouth. Two behind it sidestepped, surrounding her.

A jab of pain tore her heart. She had to leave him. She was out of options. She had to run up the hill to escape and leave Tyrell behind. She bent and kissed him, shaking with anguish.

BLAMM!

She flinched.

BLAM! BLAMM! BLAMM!

Gunshots rang out around her. All of the gorgers dropped dead.

Six people walked down the hill, their faces in shadow.

"You look like you could use a hand," said the woman in the dolphin t-shirt.

The people around her fired additional shots. Two more gorgers, which had been feeding on the corpses, fell over dead.

"Yes," Sierra cried. "This guy is alive. We have to take him back." She trembled, overwhelmed by emotion and exhaustion.

Two men went to Tyrell's feet and a third kneeled at his shoulder, across from Sierra. "You came for me," she said, filled with gratitude. These were the people Reggie had condemned.

"Hell yeah, we did," the dolphin woman said. "You needed help."

They carried Tyrell up the slope, flanked by armed guards.

Three carriages met them at the top of the bluff. Priya sat on one with Barry and Lindsey. Kim and Felicia piloted the second one down to the ground. David and Cameron swooped around on the third.

"We did it," Kim said.

Behind her, the field of pods was silent. Everyone had been airlifted to the shuttles, which sat all throughout the valley, sparkling in the moonlight.

They loaded Tyrell onto the back of the sled.

"He's unconscious," Sierra said. "I don't know what's wrong with him."

"We think he was drugged by the guy Lindsey killed," David said.

"It was him," Barry insisted. "I saw him."

Sierra shook her head, confused.

"He'll be okay," David said. "He should wake up in a few hours. He'll be woozy, but he's going to be fine."

That was all she needed to hear. Relief washed away all the fear and anguish. Exhausted, she climbed on next to Tyrell and they lifted off.

It would be hours before they could sleep. They had to go around and explain to everyone what had happened, and what still needed to happen. The amount of work in the days ahead was staggering.

But they would do it, and they would do it together.

As they floated up, the distant roars of dinosaurs echoed in the dark, along with the trumpets of mammoths and the occasional snarl of a cat.

AFTER

The Days Following
The Reintroduction of Species

Chapter Eighty-One

One Day After

Sierra shivered in the early morning sun while she waited for the last sled to land. Three dozen strangers stood in a circle on the bluff, one representative for each cluster of shuttles, all eager to discuss the next steps.

Priya and Kim sat on a sled of their own behind Sierra, where they were using the devices to assemble a thirty-foot high wall around the bluff, using empty pods as building blocks. All of the prehistoric animals had wandered away. The wall was being built in case any decided to wander back.

Tyrell put his arm around Sierra. The gesture warmed her, literally and figuratively. She wondered if he felt the same way she felt about him, or if he was just a hugging sort. Using pods to build the wall had been his idea. He told the group about trying to pick one up with an eight-ton backhoe. It hadn't budged.

David, Lindsey, and Felicia stood beside them, though Lindsey was keeping her distance from David. Cameron had remained behind in the shuttle, claiming she had no interest in administrative bullshit.

True to her word, Priya had positioned the shuttles in groups of five, with their tails pointing together. One hundred and eighty shuttles were organized into thirty-six groups spread out around the meadow. Each shuttle held between forty and sixty people, bringing the total population to roughly nine thousand.

The last carriage descended to the bluff and a middle-aged man with a goatee stepped down.

"I know that guy," Tyrell whispered. "He's ... abrasive."

"Is he trouble?"

"No. He saved my life."

She nodded and stepped forward. "Welcome. I hope you all got some rest. We have a lot of work to do." She'd only slept for an hour herself.

Everyone began speaking at once. Some asked about the gorgers and the dinosaurs. Some wanted to know if this was really Earth. Many expressed doubts about the aliens. At least a third complained about the lack of toilets in the shuttles. All of them said their people were hungry and thirsty.

Sierra held up a hand until the questions petered out. She and the others had explained as much as possible the night before, thirty-six times, but she wasn't surprised to hear all the doubts and questions. "As soon as we're done here, each of you will go back to your shuttles. We're going to reposition them so they're lying on the ground, like that one over there." She pointed across the river, where Priya's practice shuttle sat with its tail sloping down to the meadow. Priya had figured out how to disable the ship entirely, so that it no longer hovered above the ground. "You'll be able to walk right out. Everyone can come and go as they please."

"Is that safe?" asked the guy with the goatee. A tattooed lion sat proudly on his right arm. "If we can walk out, can't those creatures walk right in?"

"Or the dinosaurs?" asked someone else.

As far as Sierra was concerned, it wasn't safe to leave people in shuttles where the only exit led to a hundred-foot drop. It was a wonder no one died from falling out.

"The gorgers won't come out in direct sunlight, so we don't have to worry about them until night. Fortunately, there shouldn't be many left in the area." She pointed to the growing wall, where pods continued to float into place. "The shuttles will all be positioned so that their exits will slope down inside this wall. The wall will keep the bigger dinosaurs out, but we'll need volunteer patrols to raise the alarm if anything small comes close."

Kim was using the human-sized pods to fill in the gaps, but there would still be lots of small openings.

"What about toilets?" someone shouted.

"Last night, we asked you to take inventory of the people in your shuttle groups. How many of you found someone with construction experience?"

Most of the representatives raised their hands.

"Perfect. Put them in charge of figuring out the toilet situation. There's wood along the riverbank you can use to build outhouses. It should be safe by the river once the sun is high overhead, but be on the lookout. Gorgers like to hide beneath the surface."

"What about food and water?" asked a gray-haired woman in her fifties.

Sierra nodded. "How many of you have people in your shuttles with hunting experience?"

Again, most raised their hands.

"We need to butcher the animal carcasses that are still salvageable after last night." Several people nodded, probably having reached the same conclusion. "We need to get the meat cooked before it spoils."

Priya looked up from her device. "Tell them about the water."

Sierra nodded. "As soon as the wall is completed, we're going to bring in fresh water from a nearby lake. Just be patient."

Priya intended to haul water using a supercluster orb, just like they'd hauled fuel from Cheyenne Mountain.

The representatives from each shuttle looked at one another. Some actually seemed impressed.

"Next, we need people who know how to farm. We need to start growing food as quickly as possible. Try to get teams lined up for that."

The middle-aged man with the lion tattoo raised his hand. "Why should we do what you say? We don't know who you are. We don't know why you're doing any of this. Who put you in charge?"

Tyrell gave Sierra a wink. *Abrasive.*

She shrugged. "You know, those are great questions, buddy." She was too tired to argue with him.

"Neil," the man corrected. "Neil Hemingway."

Felicia stepped up next to her. "Actually, those are stupid questions. Sierra busted her ass to save you people. We all have. You don't have to listen to us. You're welcome to do whatever you want."

The gray-haired woman, who looked like she might have been a librarian, leaned into the circle to face Neil. "They haven't given us any reason not to trust them. Why don't we all try to help out?" Definitely a librarian.

Neil pressed his lips tight. It wasn't quite a frown, but it was close.

"Tell you what," Sierra said. "Why don't you talk to the people in your shuttles and see if anyone has ideas about how to run a settlement like this. Come up with a plan to hold elections or something."

She didn't want to lose what little authority she had. She didn't trust anyone else to make the right choices. But Neil had a point. No one had put her in charge.

Chapter Eighty-Two

Two Days After

David walked Jasmine across the sloped floor of the alien dome room, helping her keep her balance in the low gravity. They stopped at the portal leading to the brood chamber. She held her injured arm out in front of her and he carefully removed the bandages he'd applied after she was attacked by a gorger in Washington, D.C.

The slices looked brand new, though Jasmine had been sealed in a pod for more than a week. She grimaced and drew air through her nostrils.

"This is the worst part," he said. "You can do it."

Jasmine nodded and looked around, her eyes glossy. They'd opened her pod in the mothership's hangar, loaded her onto a carriage, and flown her up here. He tried to imagine how overwhelmed she must feel.

He helped her plunge her arm through the portal. Her lower lip began to tremble immediately. The stinging gel was doing its work.

Tending to Jasmine's injuries helped distract him from the fact that neither Lindsey nor Cameron wanted anything to do with him. He'd told Cameron they had to end things and she'd avoided him ever since. Lindsey had been giving him the cold shoulder, too. He'd said he was sorry, but she hadn't given him the chance to say anything more.

"Talk to me," Jasmine said. "Distract me. Tell me what I missed. Is everyone okay?"

David started to tell her about the settlement in British Columbia, but she asked another question before he could begin.

"How's Reggie?"

He exhaled. "Reggie ..."

"What? Is he okay?"

"No. He's dead. He tried to kill everyone."

The tears in Jasmine's eyes broke free and rolled down her cheeks.

David clenched his jaw. Reggie had gotten people killed. He'd almost gotten *everyone* killed. He didn't deserve her tears.

"It wasn't his fault," Jasmine said.

"It was," David said. "You weren't there."

"No, Shug. I'm not saying he didn't do whatever he did." The skin on her chin cinched tight. "When Reggie found a pod, there was a policeman who tried to take it. He shot Reggie's son in the face. Right there in front of him."

"Jesus." David's throat tightened. "Why?"

"He didn't want to share a pod with us because we're Black."

David's mouth had been open, ready to say something else. He chomped it shut.

She nodded, barely moving.

"We need to find that guy," he said. "The cop. He can't be allowed to stay in the colony."

"Reggie killed him. Crushed his throat with his bare hands." Her expression somehow grew sadder. "It tore him apart, doing that. Almost as much as Chase getting shot. It broke him."

Neither of them spoke for a long time. David tried to put himself in Reggie's place. He wasn't sure he could have kept his sanity for even half as long as Reggie had.

"When you get back to the colony, tell Sierra and the others," David said. "They need to know."

Jasmine nodded. "Tell me about the rest."

He talked for a half hour, going over everything that happened. When he finished, he asked her to flex her fingers inside the gel. "How does that feel?"

"It stings, but the deep pain is gone."

"Let's have a look. Try not to let it drip on you. Or me."

She withdrew her arm. Tan scars ran from her elbow to her wrist, but they looked like they'd healed years ago.

"Oh my God," she said.

He smiled and gave her a hug, careful not to touch the goop on her arm.

"The others can't wait to see you." He would send Jasmine to Earth on the next shuttle and get started with Nick and Kelly. Their injuries were much more serious, and David expected to be up here all day. Nick would need to be fully submerged.

He wondered if he should try to get Carol into the chamber, too. She was suffering from early-stage Alzheimer's. Could the goop restore her mind? Could she handle the pain that came from floating in it?

He walked Jasmine over to the room's exit, feeling very much alone. If only the alien goop could heal his marriage as easily as it mended flesh and bone.

Chapter Eighty-Three

Three Days After

Sierra held a zebra-print tank top against her chest. "What do you think?" She'd taken off her jacket, which was seriously in need of a wash, leaving only a light camisole.

"I would need to see it on you before I could judge," Tyrell said, tapping his lips thoughtfully.

They were back in the village, collecting spare clothes and supplies from the storage sheds.

Tyrell held a tiny skirt in front of his hips. "You think I could squeeze into this?"

She smiled. "I'd like to see you try."

They'd brought two sleds and a control device, with a page of notes from Kim explaining how to move the sleds from point to point and how to operate the stun controls. Before landing, they'd stunned two nearby Allosauruses. They needed to ask Priya to put them back in storage, because Kim's instructions didn't cover that detail.

They loaded the spare sled with all the clothes, tools, baskets, and other supplies that had been left behind, bantering as they worked. It was nice to be away from the valley and the non-stop barrage of questions and debates.

When they'd gathered the last of it, Tyrell stopped and stood with his hands at his side, looking somehow casual and serious at the same time. "What do you want?" he asked.

She gave him a smile that she hoped was coy and alluring. "Is that a trick question?"

"No. A real one," he said. "We saved everyone. We made it back to Earth. Now what?"

She thought about it for a moment. "I want things to be better than they were before. I don't want it to all be for nothing. What about you?" she asked. "What do you want?"

He stared at her for a long time, then finally said, "You."

A shiver of heat climbed through her chest.

"Ever since I saw you lying in that alien hangar, I haven't stopped thinking about you. The more I get to know you, the stronger it gets."

She stood straight, forcing herself to breathe slowly. "You told me I scared you."

He nodded. "You did."

"And now?"

He smiled. "I'm trying to be brave."

"Here's what I want." She stepped closer, until they stood only a foot apart. "I want to make sure we're never in a situation where we scare each other, or ourselves."

He nodded. "That's a lofty goal."

"Those are the best kind," she said. "And one other thing." She leaned up and kissed him. The heat rushed to her ears and down her back. The warm glow of lust filled her hips.

He was feeling it, too, judging from the bulge pressing against her belly.

Tyrell slipped his hand beneath her shirt in the back. His fingertips were warm, soft, firm.

She stiffened. "Wait."

He withdrew his hand.

"Not here." She glanced around. "Too many bad memories."

He looked like he was trying not to let his disappointment show, but he wasn't doing a very good job.

"I have an idea," she said.

"I'm listening."

"Two words. Low gravity."

His smile returned, bigger and brighter than ever.

They made love in one of the side tunnels that branched off from the giant slope room beneath the sea, in front of a window overlooking Earth. The low gravity allowed her to ride him with effortless control, at least for the first several minutes. When it seemed as if he couldn't take it any longer, he lifted her away and held her up against the window, her bare ass mooning the planet. She surrendered all control as he filled her completely, moving faster and faster. Within seconds, they both climaxed, trembling with pleasure and grasping each other tightly.

Afterwards, she lay beside him, enjoying the feel of his naked body against hers, and they talked for an hour. She told him about growing up with Rick Preston, how Waldmire was always there across the street, and how she now saw both of them as fathers. He told her about his childhood in rural Alabama and how he'd rescued a hundred dogs before the Ender hit.

When they heard Priya calling their names, they scrambled to get dressed. They'd parked the sleds out in the middle of the slope, away from the tunnel, but it had to be obvious where they were.

They walked into the cavernous chamber, giggling.

"Do you want the good news or the bad news?" Priya asked, looking down at them from another sled.

"Always start with the good," Tyrell said.

"I figured out how to activate the projection system in the command dome. It's even better than the projectors in the shuttles. The view comes from every direction. It's like you're actually there."

"And the bad news?" Sierra asked. Her mind raced. Had the colony walls been breached? Had someone like Joe seized control?

"David and his team of doctors were in the dome room at the time, discussing the brood chamber. They all got quite the show when the camera activated inside that little hallway behind you."

Chapter Eighty-Four

Four Days After

"I need to talk to you," Lindsey said.

Those six words terrified David almost as much as alien bug monsters, man-eating dinosaurs, and homicidal madmen.

She led him onto the bluff over the river. A pair of long-necked dinosaurs lumbered beyond the wall, nearly two miles away.

"I've learned a lot about what happened," she began. "When I first heard about you and Cameron, I didn't have the full picture. From my perspective, you left me behind on Earth and hooked up with the first tall blonde chick you came across."

In another time, David would have gotten defensive. He would have argued that their vows hadn't specified what was permitted after a comet ended life on Earth.

Now, he kept his mouth shut and let her talk. He listened.

"In the last few days, I've learned it wasn't that simple. You crashed your plane. You were shot. You got strung up for an entire day, and you were sentenced to be executed. From a cliff, no less." She looked back toward the center of the bluff, where a few simple structures were being constructed. "Through it all, no matter what happened, you kept our kids safe. You must have felt pretty alone."

David took a deep breath. "That doesn't excuse what I did. I should have waited until I knew for sure."

Lindsey nodded. "It hurt. I survived the Ender, barely, and the first thing I learned is that you moved on."

"I'm so sorry, Lindsey. I really am."

She looked directly at him. "I understand you actually died."

He made a small motion that was almost a shrug.

"Do you love her?"

"No. I cared for her. And we made a good team. But I didn't … She wasn't *us*."

She kept looking at him. Those eyes made his knees weak.

He took a deep breath. "I was an asshole during those last few weeks on Earth. It killed me that I didn't have any way to save you and the kids. That isn't an excuse though."

Her face softened slightly.

"I want to start over," David said.

"Okay," Lindsey said. "I— I'll give you a pardon. We can move forward. For the sake of our kids."

The words relieved him, but they also carried some bite. It wasn't for the two of them, it was for the kids.

"I was hoping you could forgive me," he said.

She took in a deep breath. "I'm not ready to do that. It still hurts too much."

It wasn't what he wanted to hear, but it wasn't his choice to make. "Okay."

They walked along the bluff for a few minutes before he spoke again.

"I'm sorry for a lot of the things I said before, back when the Ender showed up."

"I'm sorry, too," Lindsey said. She gave him a grim smile. "I was in denial. About Mom. About the Ender." She chuckled. "You were right about that, obviously." She took his hand. "The problem wasn't always what you said, by the way. It was how you said it."

"I know. I got tied to a wooden post for mouthing off. I'm starting to learn."

This time she smiled for real.

He squeezed her hand. He'd gotten a second chance, in more ways than one. Maybe someday, she would forgive him. For now, all he could do was give her time. Fortunately, dying had done wonders for his patience.

Chapter Eighty-Five

Five Days After

"I'm so sick of meetings," Priya whispered to Felicia while they waited for everyone to gather on the bluff. She wanted to get back to the command dome. Other than turning on the projectors, she hadn't learned much. She needed help. She was no closer to understanding how the aliens manipulated gravity, what powered their technology, how torpor worked, or a myriad of other things. "Do we really need another discussion about irrigation?"

She'd hoped to find people who could help reverse engineer the alien technology, but instead they'd gotten motormouths who were determined to debate every little detail and ask the same questions over and over again.

"We're lucky to have so many farmers," Felicia said. Hundreds of colonists had backgrounds in agriculture, some from small family farms and others from big corporate outfits. "We have to eat, you know."

Priya rolled her eyes. "We handed them everything they need on a silver platter."

She had discovered that dozens of spheres floating in the slope room in the mothership contained seed vaults, with botanical samples that had been collected over the millennia.

"Would you like to be out there digging and planting all day?" Felicia asked.

Priya frowned. Of course not. She'd busted her butt to earn a PhD in astronomy so she wouldn't have to do that sort of thing. Fortunately, she'd also developed enough social skills to recognize that saying that out loud would make her sound like a jackass. "I just wish we had one theoretical physicist. That's all."

"Hey, we got Bill Alvin," Felicia said. "That counts for something."

The most famous person in the settlement turned out to be a hunky movie star who'd been driving from Los Angeles to his hometown of Winnipeg when the pods showed up.

"Seriously?" Priya snorted. "His movies were mindless drivel."

Felicia grinned. "I didn't watch them for the plot."

The last few people arrived and the meeting began. Sierra stood before everyone and asked if there were any emergencies that needed the whole group's attention. Seven hands went up.

"Are they truly emergencies?" she asked. "Or could they be addressed later by a smaller group."

All seven hands went down.

Sierra looked pleased. "Dr. Christopher asked if he could say a few words."

"About what?" Priya called out.

Sierra shrugged. "Couldn't tell you." She turned to a tall lanky man with perfectly combed hair and a salt-and-pepper beard. "Priya doesn't like meetings, so please be brief." She sat down next to Tyrell, who put his arm around her. Lucky girl.

"Hello everyone, I'm Dr. Ray Christopher," the man began. "I taught Political Science at the University of Illinois, and I've already spoken with many of you." He polished his glasses on the hem of his button-down shirt.

He looked like the sort of man who insisted on being referred to as "*Doctor* Christopher."

"Four days ago, several of you asked me to come up with a plan for how we might organize ourselves governmentally. I interviewed more than a hundred people." He walked around the circle, keeping just on the inside. "I heard about Thad and Joe and Randall and everything that happened in Cheyenne Mountain. Many of you also talked about how poorly our leaders handled things when the Ender was discovered, and even some crises before that."

Several people snorted.

"Almost everyone told me the same three things," Dr. Christopher continued. "The first is that they just want a good person to be in charge. However, the second is that you tend to believe most people don't really care about anyone but themselves."

"Yeah, we're fucked," said one of the representatives.

Dr. Christopher held up his hand. "Based on everything I heard, I propose that we install a chancellor to oversee the colony, operating under a five-year term. The chancellor will coordinate with the thirty-six representatives, but will ultimately have the final authority on decisions."

"Sounds like a dictator," shouted Neil, the representative with the goat goatee and the lion tattoo. So far, he'd been full of questions and complaints, but few actual solutions.

"A dictator generally doesn't follow term limits," Dr. Christopher said. "This would be more like a constitutional monarchy. If you need a more detailed explanation, I have office hours at noon." This brought several laughs.

Priya found his schtick horribly tedious, despite the fact that he was kinda cute.

"Does that mean we need to hold an election?" Neil asked.

"I don't think so," Dr. Christopher said, tilting his head. "The third thing that almost every single person told me was that they want Sierra Preston to be our leader."

Sierra appeared speechless for once.

Dr. Christopher turned to her. "The people here trust you. For the past few days, you've worked tirelessly to get this colony started."

"I second the motion," Felicia said.

Several people shouted in agreement.

Sierra held a modest expression on her face. When everyone finally quieted, she stepped forward. "I appreciate your confidence, and I'll accept the nomination on one condition." She turned as she spoke, looking at everyone. "Instead of a single chancellor, we should have three, working together."

"A triumvirate," Dr. Christopher said, stroking his beard.

Priya rolled her eyes. He looked so proud of his big words. She was convinced she could take him. Her vocabulary was far more exorbitant.

"So we'll hold elections to pick the other two?" Neil said. He stood with his arms crossed, probably hoping to show how serious he was, despite the silly lion tattoo.

"No," Sierra said. "I'm prepared to make nominations."

Dr. Christopher encouraged her with a flourishing wave.

Priya was pretty sure Sierra was going to say her name, at which point she would promptly decline. She had no patience for bureaucratic nonsense and she had more important work to do.

"My first suggestion is Dr. Christopher," Sierra said.

He looked genuinely shocked. "Why me? I just got here. I haven't done anything."

"You've shown an interest in coming up with a better system, and you've studied this stuff for years."

He looked down at his hands. "It's a lot of responsibility. I'm not sure I want the job."

"That makes you a perfect candidate," said one of the representatives.

Dr. Christopher's eyes went wide, but he didn't have an argument for that one.

"My other nomination is Neil Hemingway," Sierra said.

The crowd grew completely silent. Priya smiled. Sierra never ceased to amaze her. Neil was an ingenious choice.

"Why me?" Neil asked.

Sierra held her hands wide. "Conflict breeds innovation. You've asked good questions. You've challenged us. You also seem to care about what happens here."

"Should we give everyone time to discuss the nominations?" Dr. Christopher asked.

"No," Priya shouted. "We've got too much to do. You three are the triumvirate." She looked around. "There. Done."

Lots of people were smiling.

"I second the motion," David said. "All in favor?"

Everyone shouted, *"Aye!"*

Chapter Eighty-Six

Eight Days After

David found Cameron sitting in a carriage with Bill Alvin, showing him how to operate the controls, much the way he had taught her. He stuck out his hand. "David Williams."

Bill flashed him the million-dollar smile that had once lit up movie screens. "I know." He stood and shook. "Bill Alvin."

"I know," David said.

"I can't thank you enough," Bill said. "You saved us all from the Senders."

"Senders" was the name the colonists had come up with for the alien race based on the fact that they sent the Ender. The term covered both the caretakers and the gorgers.

David nodded politely. "How's the flight training?"

"I'm getting there." Bill gave him a bashful tilt of his head, oozing charisma.

"Yeah, he's getting there," Cameron said.

David stood looking at her.

"Oh, hey," Bill said, taking the hint. "I need to get some water and a snack. Mind if I take twenty minutes?"

Cameron nodded. "Bring me back something."

Bill's million-dollar smile returned. David even saw a twinkle in the man's eyes.

Cameron stared as he walked away. "Would you look at that ass," she whispered.

The comment didn't trigger David's jealousy as much as watching him operate the carriage had.

"I understand you're leaving."

"That's right. "I'm not the sort of girl to settle down. I want to explore. There are a lot more bunkers out there, especially small ones. Hopefully stocked with all kinds of supplies."

He nodded.

"How are things with Lindsey?" she asked, using a tone with a razor-sharp edge.

"We're talking now. We're better. She hasn't exactly forgiven me, though."

"She will. You've got a pretty good ass yourself."

"Cameron ..." He didn't know what to say. He'd felt guilty for hurting her. "Will you be okay?"

"Are you kidding? I'll be great. I'm banging Bill Alvin."

He couldn't tell if she was serious or hiding her pain. Pressing the issue might make her feel worse. He raised his eyebrow. "How did you convince him to go with you?"

She gave him an exaggerated double-take. "I'm pretty and I'm good with a gun."

David smiled. "You are."

"Bill doesn't really have a role in this world." She winked as she made the pun. "See, I'm also hilarious."

He chuckled politely. "Are you worried about the gorgers?"

She gave a dismissive wave. "We'll float right over them. We'll be fine. Bill is actually pretty good with a gun, too. He had lots of training for those silly *Agents of Danger* movies."

David rubbed the back of his neck, searching for something else to say. He felt like it was his fault she was leaving. "I just want to know that you'll be okay."

Cameron held up her hand. "Don't worry about it, Ace. It was fun while it lasted."

He wanted to tell her that it had been more than just fun, that he had cared about her, but this was another one of those times when the best thing to do was just keep his mouth shut.

Chapter Eighty-Seven

Eleven Days After

Sierra, Neil, and Dr. Christopher walked along the inside of the perimeter wall, discussing the business of the day, which meant setting priorities for various teams to focus on. Things like sanitation, composting, crop maintenance, and sleeping arrangements. Priya kept asking for research assistants. Sadly, there weren't any astrophysicists in the colony, and they couldn't spare anyone, anyway.

"What are we going to do about Stuart?" Dr. Christopher asked after they'd covered the more mundane topics.

A man named Stuart had assaulted another man, leaving him with a broken nose, a black eye, and two missing teeth. According to witnesses, Stuart had been ranting about the fact that his shuttle representative was gay. The guy he assaulted had simply asked him to shut up.

"Lock him away," Neil said, without a moment's hesitation.

"We don't exactly have a prison," Dr. Christopher said.

"Build some stocks, right out in the middle of the colony." Neil grinned from ear to ear. "Make an example of him for everyone else to see."

Joe's words echoed in Sierra's mind. *People must be punished.*

She stopped walking and waited until the other two stopped as well. "No."

"So Stuart just gets away with it?" Neil asked.

"Of course not." She scowled. "He should be forced to make things right somehow, to make up for the pain and suffering he caused."

Dr. Christopher stroked his chin whiskers. "Restitution. You want a system that's compensatory, not punitive."

"Exactly," Sierra said. "And not just for his victim, but also for the people around him."

"For society," Dr. Christopher said. "That could be effective. It would certainly highlight the ramifications of the crime, which could be helpful with deterrence."

Neil huffed. "How does he make it right? A system like that is just asking for abuse."

Dr. Christopher nodded. "Corruption is definitely a concern. Who determines what makes things right? What if Stuart refuses to make things right? What if someone does something so horrible they can't make it right?"

"In that case, there's only three options," Neil said. "Exile, prison, or execution."

"Exile is probably the same as execution," Sierra said.

Dr. Christopher tilted his head. "Historically, capital punishment and incarceration have both been used unfairly against minorities."

"Historically, *everything* has been used unfairly against minorities," Sierra said. "We have to do better."

"This all feels very idealistic," Neil said.

"Yes," Sierra said. "That's exactly right. That's the whole point. If there was ever a time to be idealistic, this is it."

"She's right about that," Dr. Christopher said. "But, what about my questions?"

"I don't have the answers," Sierra said. "That's why I nominated you to be a chancellor."

He looked down his nose at her through narrowed eyes. "I see."

"Can you come up with a proposal? Some sort of judicial system for us to follow?"

A strange expression filled his face. He looked like he was trying to hide his excitement. He was a political science professor, after all. Nothing could be more thrilling than developing a new system of law and order. "I can work on it. Any other stipulations? Is capital punishment allowed?"

"Yes," Neil said immediately.

Sierra thought about Kevin, who'd killed Wanda and Harmony. There wasn't any way Kevin could have made things right, and she'd executed him for it. She took a deep breath. "If you do something so horrible that you can't make it right, you forfeit the opportunity to participate in society." She thought about what had happened to Reggie's son, and what Reggie had gone on to do as a result. "We can't allow people to be terrible. The impact goes way beyond the initial crime. It propagates."

"Amen," Neil said.

"What about past crimes?" Dr. Christopher asked. "What about the fact that some of the colonists here may have killed people to get to the pods?"

The same thought had troubled Sierra.

"Without evidence, there isn't anything we can do about it," Neil said. "If anyone here did something like that, they gotta live with it. Either their guilt will steer them straight, or maybe they'll do something else and we'll nab them."

Dr. Christopher nodded.

"One more requirement," Sierra said. "Corruption and abuse of power need to be treated at the same level as violent crime. No, higher. The people with authority must be always held to a higher standard. They have to be more accountable than everyone else."

Dr. Christopher and Neil exchanged a glance. She was putting their necks on the line, and they knew it.

"What do you think?" Neil asked.

Dr. Christopher nodded. "No system is perfect, but we can give this a try."

"Gotta do as we can," Sierra said, remembering how Reggie used the phrase. His memory haunted her.

"In the meantime, what about Stuart?" Dr. Christopher asked. "We can't just let him run around free, after what he did."

"Get him on a carriage," Neil said. "Send him two hundred feet straight up and let him sit there until we figure out how he can make things right."

Dr. Christopher smiled. "Absolutely."

Chapter Eighty-Eight

Fourteen Days After

Tyrell took a break from chopping wood and admired the progress they'd made. A dozen structures stood on the bluff. Five were smokehouses, six were storerooms that were basically just sheds with shelves, but the most impressive one, which was almost complete, was a large roof that covered three rows of worktables. The colonists would be able to work in the shade and stay dry during the frequent afternoon rainstorms.

Cooper barked.

He ruffled the dog's head. "What do you think, boy?"

Three days after their first tryst in the mothership, Sierra had surprised him by bringing down a pod with a beautiful tri-color shepherd mix inside. The dog had been timid at first, but warmed up quickly, and they'd been inseparable ever since.

Cooper nudged his hand and barked again.

"Tyrell!" Kim shouted at him from the meadow below, where she'd been holding a training session. Every morning, Kim spent a few hours showing six or eight people how to use the control devices. They met on a flat patch of grass in the shade of one of the shuttles, away from the distractions of the colony.

Tyrell scanned the area for signs of trouble. He saw no dinosaurs, and it was too bright out for gorgers. He patted the gun on his hip, making sure it was there, and started toward Kim, with Cooper close behind, still barking.

Kim met him at the bottom of the slope.

"What is it?" he asked. "Is everything okay?"

She took his hand and pulled him back the way she'd come. "You've got to see this," she said, breathing so hard she could barely get the words out. "Or hear it, actually."

Cooper ran out ahead, his tail wagging, but Tyrell's hackles were up.

They jogged to the little circle where six people sat in pairs, each of them facing a control device. The students ranged in age from ten to seventy. Kona jumped up and charged at Cooper, her tail flapping back and forth.

All of Kim's students were grinning.

Tyrell took his hand off the gun. "What's going on?"

Nobody answered, but they all laughed as Kona and Cooper ran around them. Kim looked like she was about to burst.

Kona stopped on the far side of the circle and emitted a playful growl.

A robotic voice came from one of the control devices. *"Run. Chase. Run."*

Tyrell tilted his head.

Kim pressed her lips together. Delight shone from her eyes like a beacon.

Kona growled again and barked twice.

"Run, chase," said the device. *"Please, please, please."*

Cooper took off after Kona, chasing her around the circle and barking furiously.

"Run run run run run."

Tyrell smiled wide. "It's translating the dogs."

Kim jumped up and down. One of her students broke into applause.

"What else can she say?" Tyrell asked.

"Her vocabulary is pretty limited," said one of the women in the class. "She knows 'food,' 'play,' 'bored,' and 'pet me.'"

"Cooper, come here, boy," Tyrell called, unable to stop grinning. "Say something."

Cooper walked over and sat in front of him.

The woman laughed.

"We're going to try to get it to work with the other animals, too," said a boy about Kim's age. "The goats and pigs and sheep."

Tyrell glanced across the meadow at the pens holding livestock. The smile fell from his face. "Yikes. What if they beg us to stop eating them?"

Kim shrugged. "There's always the gorgers. I had my first taste yesterday. It wasn't bad."

A few days earlier, after realizing that the dinosaurs were still alive after eating gorgers, a group of young men had caught one of the alien creatures, cooked it, and eaten the meat in its legs. None of them had gotten sick, and now more and more people were trying it, though gorgers were increasingly difficult to find in the area. The meat reportedly tasted like crab. Tyrell hadn't quite mustered the courage to try it.

"Can you show me how to do the translation?" He couldn't wait to hear what Cooper might say, as well as the rest of the dogs in the colony.

"Come back after class," Kim said. She sat down in front of her control device.

Tyrell nodded. "Come on, Coop. Let's go tell Sierra."

Cooper barked as they started off.

Behind them, one of the devices said, *"Hungry!"*

Chapter Eighty-Nine

Seventeen Days After

Sierra sat in a shuttle, flying back to Earth with Dr. Christopher and Neil. The other two were silent, awed by the view, but Sierra wasn't paying attention. Her thoughts were weighed down by a sensitive and ponderous subject. She was trying to figure out how to bring up her concerns about religious fundamentalism.

Three carriages floated around them, loaded high with fruits and vegetables harvested on the islands by a team Felicia had put together.

In front of them, the night side of Earth filled their view, an empty black circle with wisps of gray starlight reflected off the clouds.

Sierra drew in a deep breath, ready to broach the delicate topic.

Before she could begin, Dr. Christopher started talking. Apparently, he'd been harboring his own subject. "Let's discuss jurisprudence," he said. "I propose that we elect a panel of judges."

"Is that necessary?" Neil asked. "We handled the business with Stuart well enough."

After questioning the witnesses, they'd learned that in addition to assault and battery, Stuart was guilty of making death threats against the man representing his shuttle group.

Sierra, Dr. Christopher, and Neil had come up with a twenty-two-step plan for Stuart to make things right.

He'd listened to the first three items, then told them all to fuck right off. They threatened to exile him and he begged them to do it. Soon after, he was flown to a region in central Wyoming that was chosen for its comparatively low gorger count.

"The triumvirate shouldn't be in a position to decide the fates of individuals," Dr. Christopher said. "It's a crucial separation of powers. Having a panel of judges will help stave off corruption."

"Why not a jury of our peers?" Neil asked.

Sierra answered before Dr. Christopher could. "Because a jury of our peers would include people like Stuart."

"Point taken."

Neil liked to be adversarial, but when he heard a good argument, he was quick to concede.

"Judges should be full-time," Dr. Christopher said.

Sierra winced. "We can't really spare anyone."

"It's critical, if we want to make this work. We need to convey that this is a sacred duty. This isn't something to spend a few spare hours on after a day of pulling weeds."

"How many people are you talking about?" Neil asked.

"I propose at least eleven. We need enough so that some of them can recuse themselves if they are close to the litigants, and if it ever comes to it, we need enough so that a group of them can stand judgment over one of their own."

"Sold," Sierra said.

"Term limited?" Neil asked.

"Absolutely."

Out ahead, an arc of light appeared on the horizon. Sunrise. Sierra decided it was her turn. "I want to talk about fundamentalism."

"What about it?" Dr. Christopher asked.

"It's dangerous," Sierra said.

"Oh, now you want to control what people believe," Neil said. "That's a great way to get people to turn on us."

Sierra steeled herself. She knew this conversation wouldn't be easy. "When the first group showed up in the menagerie, a guy named Thad told everyone they were in Purgatory."

"So what?" Neil said. "Obviously he was wrong. What's the harm?"

"He drowned ten people so they could go on to heaven. Four of them were children."

"I understand your concerns," Dr. Christopher said. "But you have to remember, religion can also be beneficial. And I say that as a resolute atheist. Our colony has eighty members of the clergy. They've been helping people. Providing comfort and support." He pointed at the silhouettes of mountains ahead of them. "Remember, everyone here just lost friends and family. The grief is overwhelming."

"I'm not talking about religion," Sierra said. "I'm talking about fundamentalism."

"Yeah, but how do you tell the difference?" Neil asked.

Dr. Christopher stroked his beard. "That's a problem humanity has grappled with for, well, forever."

"I don't care," Sierra said. "We have to make sure what happened with Thad won't happen again. Or anything like it."

Dr. Christopher held up his hand. "The problem may have solved itself, at least to a degree. Many people in the colony are questioning some long-held beliefs. Recent events on our planet have had quite an impact." He paused. "Pun intended."

She humored him with a polite chuckle.

"Life on Earth was all but wiped out by an alien race. That alone has shaken many beliefs. A lot of people believed that the pods were sent by God. Now we know that isn't true."

"Isn't there something we can do?" Sierra asked. The shuttle swooped through a bank of clouds.

"There's always social pressure," Dr. Christopher said. "For a very long time, religion and politics were off limits. People looked the other way out of politeness. Terrible ideologies were allowed to fester and flourish."

She let her shoulders drop. She'd known there wouldn't be an easy solution.

"One more thing," Dr. Christopher said. "Sierra, you and the other seven have an advantage that rarely comes along in history."

She tilted her head. "How so?"

"You're heroes. You saved humanity. People will listen to you. They will believe what you say and follow the example you set. As long as you keep doing right by people, you've got an enormous amount of political capital to spend."

She nodded, feeling the weight of his words. "Will our efforts be enough?" she asked. "Can we prevent people from being terrible?" It was a rhetorical question, but Dr. Christopher didn't let that stop him.

"Of course not. But we have a good shot at making things better."

Sierra nodded. It would have to do.

Chapter Ninety

Twenty-One Days After

"Priya, there's a monster coming," one of the colonists shouted, a kid from the sound of his voice.

Priya had already been tracking the monster for the last half hour. It was actually an Entelodont that had wandered up from the south and was approaching the settlement in a zig-zag pattern, probably drawn to the bleating of the goats.

Today, Priya was assigned to cover perimeter security, which meant that she was supposed to walk down to the wall and stun the "monster" with her control device as soon as it came within range.

She didn't budge from her seat under the newly-constructed awning. The shade felt nice, and she had more important things to do than wander all the way down there.

The spotter ran up to her, exasperated and breathing hard. "Did you hear me? There's a monster." He pointed to the south. "It's a giant warthog thing. It's as big as a horse."

"Can you go get Sierra for me?" Priya asked.

The spotter, a plain-looking teenage boy wearing a Batman t-shirt, frowned. "She's in a meeting."

"That's okay," Priya said. "She's always in a meeting."

The boy looked uncertain.

"You better hurry," Priya said. "Or the monster will get in."

He took off.

The Entelodont sniffed the skeleton of a stegosaur that had been stripped clean by gorgers in the great battle, then turned back toward the perimeter wall, still a good five hundred meters away.

The boy returned with Sierra, Neil, and Dr. Christopher. Tyrell tagged along behind them. He followed Sierra like a puppy everywhere she went.

"What seems to be the problem?" Neil asked.

Priya turned to look at him. "Good morning to you, too. The problem is that I need assistance. I've spent the past week working in the dome room, and I haven't been able to do a single thing except turn on the projector lights." This was an oversimplification, but only a slight one.

Sierra shrugged. "If you figure everything out too quickly, you'll get bored. You might turn into a criminal mastermind or something."

Tyrell chuckled.

"That isn't funny," Priya said. "I'm getting nowhere. I need help."

"It's coming closer," said the boy in the Batman shirt, his voice cracking.

"Let me know when it's within a hundred meters," Priya said, reasonably confident he didn't know the difference between a meter and a hexagon.

"You're doing pretty well, as far as I can tell," Dr. Christopher said. "Everyone appreciates the extra quarters, by the way."

The night before, Priya had brought down another two hundred shuttles, which allowed the colonists to spread out more.

"That was easy," Priya said. "I'm talking about figuring out how the aliens control gravity." She refused to call them "Senders." The term was both banal and bromidic.

"It's almost here," the kid said. Gauging from his tone, the Entelodont was probably near the hundred-meter mark.

Priya stood. "This is what I wanted you to see." She held her hands up by her shoulders, as if surrendering at gunpoint.

The Entelodont had been loping toward the wall at an angle. It turned inward and charged.

A harvester swooped down from the sky, bright yellow and silver glinting in the sunlight.

A few seconds later, they heard the familiar zipping sound and the Entelodont fell over sideways.

"You stunned it," Neil said. "What's the big deal?"

"Look at my hands," Priya said. They were still in the air.

"She didn't stun it," Tyrell said. "The harvester did. All by itself."

Sierra smiled. "Nice job."

Priya lowered her hands, also smiling. Configuring the harvesters to automatically patrol the perimeter was an awesome accomplishment, she had to admit.

"Is it programmed to handle relocation?" Dr. Christopher asked.

"Not yet," Priya said. "I need a team. I need a group that's dedicated to researching the alien technology full-time. We need to spend most of our days in the mothership."

"We double-checked," Sierra said. "We don't have any experts on interplanetary engineering."

"Fine," Priya said. "I still need a team. Find me people who are annoyingly picky. I want detail-oriented perfectionists."

"I can help with that," Tyrell said. "There's a couple of people on the construction crew who drive everyone nuts with that kind of thing."

"Perfect," Priya said.

Dr. Christopher wagged his finger in the air. "One woman in my shuttle is constantly challenging everyone else. She's always got a better way to do things."

"Are her solutions actually better?"

He gave her a humble grin. "Honestly, yes."

"I want her," Priya said. "I'll also take anyone who likes to take notes."

"What if we found someone who was always correcting other people's terminology?" Sierra asked.

"You're mocking me, aren't you?" Priya said.

Sierra grinned. "How many people do you need?"

"Six," Priya said. Any more would be too many. "No, wait. Find me five, and give me Kim."

The girl was a genius. She'd figured out how to access the language interpretation system on the control devices.

Priya wanted to broadcast a message to any other gorgers out there, announcing that the mothership had been destroyed and that Earth was no longer a viable food source.

Sierra glanced at Dr. Christopher and Neil.

Neil shrugged. "Kim is almost finished with her first round of training classes. We've got plenty of people who can send carriages from point to point now."

"It will be up to her parents, of course," Sierra said.

Priya wasn't worried about that. Kim wanted to be on her team and the girl knew how to get what she wanted.

"When do you need them to start?" Dr. Christopher asked.

"Yesterday," Priya said. She was also learning how to get what she wanted.

Dr. Christopher held her gaze. Normally, Priya would have looked away. Direct eye contact made her uncomfortable. Something in his eyes made her keep looking, though.

"I say we give her everything she wants," he said. "It's an investment in the future."

A strange wash of heat rose up the sides of Priya's face. She was blushing. "Thank you, Ray. Why don't you come check on our progress in a week?"

He broke eye contact, looking off in every possible direction, then finally met her eyes again. "I might just do that."

Chapter Ninety-One

Twenty-Five Days After

David, Barry, and Kim flew over the Coast Mountains and dipped down into the valley, heading back to the colony. The shuttle reeked of fish. He and the kids probably did too. Maybe they would fly up to the mothership where they could rinse off in the menagerie's freshwater seas. There were perks to being members of the team that saved humanity, after all.

"That was fun," Barry said.

David smiled at his son. It was nice to have a small semblance of normalcy again.

They'd caught forty-two fish using homemade gear one of the farmers had helped them assemble. David's mouth watered at the thought of fire-roasted steelhead.

They'd parked the shuttle on the beach and then floated out over a deepwater channel in a carriage. They had caught fish almost as fast as they could get hooks in the water.

"We should take people on excursions," Kim said. "You know, to break up the routine." They'd even seen a pod of dolphins.

"Definitely," David said. "How do you like working with Priya?"

He spotted the settlement ahead, across two hundred miles of rolling green terrain. From this distance, the shuttles were just a ring of shiny dots, but at three hundred miles an hour, they'd be there soon. The thought saddened him. He didn't want the outing to end.

"It's good. I'm not sure we'll ever figure out the gravity stuff, no matter how much she wants to. It isn't like studying a car would teach you how thermodynamics work, you know?"

"What have you learned?"

"We spend a lot of time monitoring Earth. She's looking for the best places to send more specimens from storage. We found a prehistoric wolverine the size of a jaguar that kills gorgers like nobody's business. Priya thinks it's a territorial instinct."

"Is anyone worried all these animals will become bigger threats than the gorgers themselves?"

"Once the gorgers are mostly gone, we intend to let a bunch of the carnivores die off before we bring down too many herbivores. That will also give plants time to recover."

"Is that going to work?" David asked. "I mean, you're talking about bioengineering an entire planet."

Kim shrugged. "I don't know. We'll find out, won't we?"

David grinned. Kim gave him a smile that lit up the whole shuttle.

"Dinosaur!" Barry shouted, pointing to the right.

"Let's check him out," David said. No one had seen any dinosaurs around the colony for several days. Spotting one in the wild was kind of exciting now, at least from the safety of the shuttle.

They banked south. Kim had become quite the pilot, better even than Cameron had been.

"*T. rex,*" she whispered as they drew close.

David sucked air between his teeth, remembering the Tyrannosaurus that had pursued Kim and Barry over a cliff.

This Tyrannosaurus wandered across the open meadow to a massive log that looked like it might have been lying there since the Ender hit. The dinosaur bent low, sniffing, then placed one foot on the log and rolled it. The log had to weigh at least two thousand pounds.

A half dozen gorgers were clustered in a tight crevice beneath. They writhed in the bright sunlight as the Tyrannosaurus plucked them up, two or three at a time.

"Get 'em," Barry said.

The Tyrannosaurus looked up at the shuttle as if it had heard him, then turned and stomped off toward the mountains in the west.

Chapter Ninety-Two

Thirty Days After

Sierra, Neil, and Dr. Christopher invited the whole colony for an update at the one-month mark. Several thousand attended, including all of the "storytellers," people who filled the role held by town criers in the eighteenth century. They collected news and shared it throughout the colony. They also told stories from before the Ender, both true and fictional, to help keep the past from dying off.

The colonists all sat along the front slope of the bluff, with the chancellors and representatives lined up at the bottom.

Sierra waited while others gave updates on their areas of expertise. David announced the colony's first pregnancy. He also shared that Priya had figured out how to adjust the settings in the neck implants, so that the animals they'd released could breed, but could also still be stunned if they got too close. She was working on getting harvesters to place implants in the necks of their offspring.

The colonists were divided on the neck implants. Many people wanted them removed, and David's team of doctors and nurses was obliging as quickly as possible. But half opted to keep them. Some didn't want their necks sliced open. Some simply wanted reliable birth control. A few forward-thinking individuals wanted the ability to be stunned if they ever needed treatment in the brood chamber. For many women in the colony, not having to deal with monthly cycles made the decision easy.

Tyrell had already been reimplanted for the birth-control benefit. He'd also maintained a running list of new sex positions to try in low-gravity whenever he and Sierra returned to the mothership. Her favorite so far was an inverted arrangement he referred to as the Bavarian Mallard, for reasons she couldn't quite understand.

David finished his update. Though he wasn't ready to share the news publicly, he and his team suspected they could use the alien goop to prolong life expectancy.

Felicia spoke next. She announced that she was forming a second colony in the mothership. The island habitats were too perfect to leave empty. She invited the other colonists to apply for positions there, while acknowledging the risks. The mothership could fly away at any time, or simply stop functioning.

When Felicia first raised the idea, she claimed she wanted to develop a breeding program for animals in storage. She wanted to breed enough predators to eradicate the gorgers worldwide. Sierra believed her, but also thought it was something more. When prodded, Felicia admitted that she felt overwhelmed in the colony. She missed being part of a small team that looked out for each other.

Neil spoke after Felicia. He told everyone that scouts had flown carriages as far east as Edmonton and as far south as Vancouver. They confirmed dense gorger populations in both areas, but along the way, they also spotted a fair number of dinosaurs and other animals that had been released in the great battle.

Scouts along the coast reported gorgers on every island they'd visited. The creatures didn't seem to be able to swim, but they apparently crawled along the seabed like crabs. The good news was that the oceans were full of fish.

Sierra spoke last, announcing that a group was going to search for other sites on Earth where additional colonies could be established. If they found any strong prospects, they intended to collect fuel from Cheyenne Mountain and firebomb any gorger concentrations nearby.

When she finished, she opened the floor for questions.

Someone asked if anybody had heard from Cameron and Bill Alvin. The answer was "no."

Someone else asked about Stuart, the man who had been exiled. Sierra explained that he had been killed by gorgers in less than a day.

One of the storytellers asked how many cases had been heard by the judges so far. The answer was "forty-eight."

"And the outcomes?"

"Most people have embraced the opportunity to make things right," Sierra said. The majority of the crimes had been petty theft, and the perpetrators had been forced to give up property or perform extra chores to compensate their victims. At least a dozen cases had been dismissed due to lack of evidence.

"What about Voight?" someone asked. A man named Ricky Voight had been caught sexually assaulting a fourteen-year-old girl. He'd offered several ideas about how he could make it right, from marrying the girl to buying her off with half his food rations.

Sierra glanced at Dr. Christopher and Neil. They had agreed to be honest. "He's been stunned and placed in a pod."

"For how long?"

"Indefinitely." The pod had been sent to the bottom of the Mariana Trench.

"That's capital punishment," said one of the colonists. "That's horrible."

"It is horrible," Sierra said. "It's also necessary. If you don't like it, you're free to leave." Of course, after what had happened to Stuart, she didn't think many people would choose that option.

A bearded man in a plaid shirt held up his hand. "Do you really think we're going to make it?" A hush fell over the crowd.

"I won't lie to you," Sierra said, looking around. "We have plenty of challenges ahead. Earth is not a friendly place. But we will survive."

The bearded man scowled. "What if gorgers find their way to this valley? What if the Senders return? What happens if the dinosaurs start breeding and we can't stun them?"

The crowd murmured.

These things worried Sierra too, though not as much as threats from within. She waited for everyone to grow quiet. "Whatever happens, we'll deal with it, together. We are going to make it."

The man held out his hands. "How do you know?"

She smiled. The air grew still. "I don't know. I believe."

He looked disappointed, like he wanted a concrete answer. "What difference does that make?"

"I believe because believing helps me."

Off to the side, Waldmire smiled at her. She blinked, her eyes watery. He placed a cowboy hat on his head and touched the brim. It wasn't Waldmire, of course. It was the old guy who had helped her wrangle people onto the sled during the airlift.

Sierra smiled back at him. She really did believe.

Chapter Ninety-Three

Thirty-One Days After

David and Lindsey flew a carriage along the rugged coast, where fjords cut between craggy shorelines and the lush ocean smell permeated the air. He gave her instructions patiently, allowing her to absorb everything.

"You're doing great," he said.

"Thanks. It's a lot to keep track of."

"I'm not just talking about the flying, your honor."

She produced a cute little snort. "Please."

Lindsey had accepted the role of judge, along with ten other men and women. She was perfect for the job. She'd always been great at finding ways for the kids to make things right when they got into trouble, which was apparently the foundation of the new justice system.

"I heard Mitchell Vaughn met with the court yesterday to plead his case," David said.

Kim had told him about Mitchell's attempts to ingratiate himself with Randall, only to end up getting stunned.

Lindsey laughed, a sound that made David feel weightless. "There wasn't any case to plead. He was just scared." Her tone became serious. "We don't want that. We don't want people to be afraid of us."

"What did he say?"

"He was worried we would find him guilty by association. You know, with Randall. We told him to get back to work. From what I've heard, he's actually been busting his ass."

David nodded. "Good. I'm glad to hear it."

She looked over at him. "I think he was also worried that I would punish him for taking the pod that landed on our street. You know, because I'm a judge, and you're one of the heroes who saved us all."

He laughed. "Actually, Mitchell invited us to get in with him."

That morning seemed like a long ago nightmare, but he could still taste the overwhelming fear and confusion as if it was yesterday.

"Why didn't you?"

He looked at her and waited until she looked back. "You weren't there."

She reached over and touched his hand. "Thank you."

He smiled.

"You know, for the first time in a long time, I'm starting to feel hopeful about the future."

David nodded. Every few days, Kim reported some new discovery on the mothership. Barry still woke occasionally with night terrors, but those had become fewer, and he was making friends. He was getting a chance to be a child. Even Kona was happy. Most of the time, when they turned on the translator, her little belly moans were interpreted as *"Love my pack. Love my pack."*

Lindsey squeezed his hand. "I need to tell you something else."

David raised his eyebrow.

"I forgive you."

PREHISTORIC SPECIES

Razanandrongobe sakalavae (Dog-Croc carcass)

Allosaurus fragilis (Allosaurus)

Coelodonta antiquaitatis (Woolly Rhinoceros)

Dimetrodon angelensis (Sailback)

Tyrannosaurus rex (Tyrannosaurus)

Triceratops horridus (Triceratops)

Dreadnoughtus schrani (Dreadnoughtus)

Mammut americanum (Mastodon)

Utahraptor ostrommaysi (Red Two-Legged Dinosaur)

Stegosaurus ungulatus (Stegosaurus)

Smilodon populator (Saber-Toothed Cat)

Purassaurus brasillensis (Giant Crocodile)

Laophis crotaloides (Giant Snake)

Gigantopithecus blacki (Giant Ape)

Magnapaulia laticaudus (Duck-billed Dinosaur)

Phorusrhacos longissimus (Terror Bird)

Gastonia burgei (Spiky Dinosaur)

Varanus priscus (Giant Komodo Dragon)

Entelodont daedon (Entelodont)

Megalictis ferox (Prehistoric Wolverine)

THE PRESERVATION OF SPECIES

PART I

RULE OF EXTINCTION

PART II

STRUGGLE FOR EXISTENCE

PART III

BEASTS OF PREY

ACKNOWLEDGEMENTS

I couldn't have written this book without my family. Thank you Erin, Shannon, and Sydney for your patience, encouragement, and support. And also to River, who often lay curled at my feet.

My editor, Jacquelyn Ben-Zekry, helped me fine-tune this trilogy. She taught me the value of a dependable editor.

Jim Stigall's excellent cover design sets the mood and entices the reader, all while balancing a tremendous load of words.

If you ever want to revisit this story, I recommend the audiobook. Stacy Carolan's narration truly brings these characters to life.

Special thanks go to Andrew Caldwell and Michael Smith for providing astronomical information. Their knowledge made the book stronger, though any inaccuracies should be attributed to the author.

Additional thanks go to my critique partners for their feedback along the way. Dani Coleman, Heidi Farmer, C. R. Hodges, Steven Johnson, Beth McCabe, Margot Romary, and Jason Rush. Look them up and read their work!

I'm also indebted to beta readers who gave valuable feedback: Greg Chiarella, Mike Giese, Jordan Itkowitz, Christopher Jones, David Jones, Erin Jones, Shannon Jones, Sydney Jones, and Danny Talavera.

Thank you all so much for your time and your insights.

Finally, thank you, the reader, for coming along on this adventure. Losing myself in a story is one of my favorite things to do and I hope I have been able to create that experience for you.

If you enjoyed *Beasts of Prey*, please take a moment to leave a review and share your thoughts on social media.

Every single review helps a book find its audience.

Geoff Jones
Broomfield, Colorado

THE PRESERVATION OF SPECIES

Dedicated in loving memory to
Bill Jones

Also By Geoff Jones

THE DINOSAUR FOUR

Ten strangers trapped in time ...

A ticking sound fills the air as Tim MacGregor enters The Daily Edition Café, hoping to meet his new girlfriend for coffee. Moments later, the café is transported 67 million years into the past, along with everyone inside.

Time is running out as ten unlikely companions search for a way home, while one member of the group plots to keep them all trapped in the past.

Who will survive?

Available now at Amazon and Audible